Beyond Confusion

[Doretta Wildes]

Poor Pearl Press

This is a work of fiction.
Names, characters, places and incidents either are the
product of the author's imagination or are used fictitiously.
Any resemblance to actual persons (living or dead),
events or locales is entirely coincidental.

Poor Pearl Press
ISBN-13: 978-0692102848
ISBN-10: 0692102841

For Steve with all my love and gratitude

for your constant faith and support

"When we look back, the only things we cherish are those which in some way met our original want; the desire which formed in us in early youth, undirected, and of its own accord."
-Willa Cather, *The Song of the Lark*

"And I gave my heart to know wisdom, and to know madness and folly: I perceived that this also is vexation of spirit. For in much wisdom is much grief: and he that increaseth knowledge increaseth sorrow."
- Ecclesiastes 1:17-18

"Here are your waters and your watering place.
Drink and be whole again beyond confusion."
-Robert Frost, "Directive"

Author's Note

Throughout my home state of Connecticut are many towns and villages from which I have drawn geographical details to create the fictional settings of this story. It should be understood, however, that no actual location has been singled out as a likely site for a crime or an injustice. Such incidents happen in real places, and fiction has to begin somewhere. In this story, like the quilt pieced together within it, that place is imaginary.

May 1971

1 / Taffeta

The girl on the ledge was thin. Her features – the hook nose, the black, shag-cut hair, the panda bear eyes and horse teeth – fought for room on her face. Even the kitten held close to her chest seemed aware of her scantiness. It pricked her windbreaker, nuzzling the zipper, searching for a foothold of flesh. But the only refuge was the girl's long, chapped hands. She cupped one beneath the kitten's flanks and another around a ribcage as frail as a bird. She had wanted a kitten all her life.

This one, her first, had been a rescue. She had plucked it from its coffin the night before. A pack of boys had taken it into the woods above the quarry and forced it underneath an empty Schlitz carton. They were falling-down drunk, but this had been easy. The hard part had been punching holes in the box with a corkscrew. After a lot of pounding and cursing, they had lit their joints and blown smoke through the holes, taking deep hits and crouching to exhale. It was homegrown mixed with hashish oil sold by a newsboy who delivered drugs rolled up in the morning edition. The idea had been to get themselves and the kitten high, then chuck it, box and all, into the quarry lake below. It would have been their second execution.

But they made up for in noise what they lacked in everything else. It jolted the girl as she slept in the trailer she shared with her mother. Dressed in an old black slip, a windbreaker and a pair of plaid Keds, she had stood behind one of the larger, empty trailers and beamed her flashlight on the boys. It had been as satisfying as winning a bet. The light made them swear, collide and scatter. Narcs, they'd assumed, or one of the tramps rumored to live on the ledge, scouting for easy targets.

Once she was sure they were gone, she'd made her way through the damp, compacted leaves, squishing along on tiptoes, her Keds snapping against her heels. The miniature keening had made her eyes water, pulling her like a string. She lifted a corner of the box. *Kitty, kitty,* she whispered, reaching in blindly, expecting to be slashed. It would have been worth it.

But the kitten was limp as the mink collars old ladies wore. It let thin hands scoop it up and carry it into the trailer. Its fur stank of pot smoke and urine; the pure, unhinged cry seemed to ache in the girl's throat.

The girl stayed rigid in her cot throughout the night, afraid she might crush the kitten if she turned in her sleep. When she awoke at dawn, the kitten was a tight gray bun curled in the crook of her neck. It uncurled, stretching its legs in unison. The girl stifled her joy.

The girl's mother slept on, her ratted blonde hair all that was visible on the sleeping bag of the other cot. Keeping the kitten fed and out of her mother's way would require subterfuge at first, then an old towel, a cheap supply of food, a paper route. No need for a litter box. It would have the woods.

She squinted at the close space around her. It was swept and "picked up," her mother's term, but oppressively yellow. The furniture was meager and raddled, some of it covered with tacky paper in a yellow check pattern. A card table doubled as a desk and vanity. On its yellow check top a grubby adding machine and file folders competed with a makeup mirror with small onion-shaped light bulbs, cosmetic jars and aerosol hairspray cans. Two chrome chairs, upholstered in gold vinyl and strips of yellowing tape, were pushed against a smaller card table. This held an amber glass ashtray spilling over with butts, a package of Larks, a TV topped with a plastic daffodil in a Mateus wine bottle. A drift of mostly black lingerie in a laundry basket was shoved beneath her mother's cot with an orgy of shoes. Also, a vodka bottle. The girl checked to see how much was left. Her mother drank what she called nightcaps. In the past few weeks, the nightcaps had accompanied scenes. These involved wailing, a lot of phone calling with ominous, hissed words that gave the girl a stab in her chest.

The windows were grimy enough for her to draw hearts on. Her mother had found yellow curtains fringed with brown pom-poms at a yard sale, and hung them. But no pictures. Nothing to read either, apart from movie magazines stacked on an ironing board. Instead, there were rosy-brown stones, some marked by vague tracks, others as flat as tablets, ranked on a metal shelf. Airlessness intensified the odors. The girl was used to it. Tobacco smoke, musty bedding, pan drippings in an old coffee can, hairspray were the smells of home.

Her name was Taffeta. A stupid name, she thought, too fussy for someone who climbed trees and fished with her hands. Yet it suited her. This year she had turned twelve, and her body still resisted the inevitable, hanging onto its mayfly proportions. While other girls her age grew obsessed with their bodies, Taffeta clung to the shelf of land around the stone quarry. It was as good as a body to explore.

The land skirted a meadow that backed up to a jumble of vacant buildings, a bar and a motorcycle shop. Fossil Circus, the migrant carnival that Taffeta's mother held a share of in a tense arrangement with several quarrelsome relatives, owned the ledge and meadowland. Sunless and stony, the ledge was flat enough to support a caravan of rusting carnival trailers and mobile homes. It begrudged enough topsoil for tall but spindly evergreens and maples. A few of the trees' roots formed caves above the ground that Taffeta filled with her treasures. Cans, coins, discarded *National Geographics*, a can opener, anything the tramps, carnies, bar hoppers and grocery shoppers had left behind. She had grown too tall to crouch inside all but the cave nearest her lookout. Toward this she headed with the kitten after pulling on jeans and the windbreaker.

She fumbled through her stash until she found a can of evaporated milk and a rusty can opener. The milk had rolled out of someone's grocery bag into the parking lot, along with a pack of Chiclets she'd chewed through the winter. Squatting with the kitten inside her jacket, she punctured the can, releasing a little milk into her palm. This was heaven, Taffeta thought, a live kitten drinking out of her hand, pricking her wrist and quivering its tail. It was savagely hungry. She hadn't picked a name; she couldn't even tell what sex the kitten was. None of it mattered.

She sat cross-legged on the chilly lookout rock. A good way to get hemorrhoids, her mother had told her. Sitting gave you hemorrhoids, cats gave you fleas. Men gave you unpleasant things, too, Taffeta knew, but her mother never said anything about those. A few feet from her knees, the rock ended and plummeted, as if it were trying to escape the town. She fed the kitten, watching early sunlight perform alchemy on the quarry lake, then recklessly cast diamonds all over it.

The view was the town's only jewel. Beyond the lake was a tangled forest with treetops coming into bud, touching blush brushes to the horizon. Between the lake and forest an oil company squatted, with storage drums like giant marshmallows that boys climbed on summer nights. An eyesore, but a necessary one.

Taffeta watched two men lower a rowboat off a promontory into the lake. Her promontory, she had come to think of it, a long stone finger that pointed directly to the base of quarry cliffs. Carved into its stone knuckle was a narrow opening with stone stairs. Only a thin, wiry child could go down them all and get into the cave beyond.

Taffeta thought of it now as she watched the men cast their lines, dimpling the water. It was her secret place. In it she had stored her prize finds and, so far, none of them had been disturbed. There were plenty of children willing to trespass, to break a window or scale a fence, in the cheaper neighborhoods surrounding the quarry, but none had figured out how to squeeze between boulders and cross safely over rock snot to a cave the size of a refrigerator box, a cave pooled with bathwater. Most were too large, others too stupid, she guessed, looking down. The kitten had begun to purr.

At first she thought the body in the lake was a float. The carnival sold beach floats shaped like women that people could win if they were good enough shots. But this float was grotesque, bloated. She blurted out a laugh like air from a balloon. She had never seen a pregnant woman naked. This is what the maternity clothes must hide, she thought, a big old balloon. Taffeta squinted an eye and made a visor with her hand. Even from this distance, she could see the float's head was perfectly bald. Her knowledge of male anatomy was limited to carnival posters, *National Geographic* and the hysterical whispering of her peers. Her mother sent her to the relatives on nights when she had a guest. But she recognized the protuberance. If it hadn't been swollen to ten times its normal size, she would never have known the body was a man's.

One of the men in the boat turned around and began gesturing to his fishing partner, pointing toward the body, which was turning slowly.

Taffeta couldn't decipher all they were saying, but their jagged exchange rebounded off the cliffs. She recognized the emotions. Fear, a coarse elation, the pride of owning dangerous knowledge. She had been a frequent witness to them all in the adults she knew. As the men began to row toward the body, she stood up, caressing the kitten, who pricked her windbreaker, its purrs throbbing against her chest. She had been the first to see the body, but was glad to leave the telling to the fishermen.

January 2003

2 / Rose

It was the second winter after nine-one-one, and all Rose can think about is money. When she goes out to buy a gallon of milk or fill a prescription, she keeps her head down and sometimes leaves without a receipt, which causes them to run after her, shouting, "Miss!" Then the pellet of fear explodes and she hurries to her car, pretending to be deaf. People are still wearing little metal American flags on their lapels. They're sold at the supermarket, at the library and at the school her daughter, Eve, attends. Rose keeps wondering who's getting rich this time.

The gray bomb she's driving to her meeting is an '83 AMC Spirit with rust pocks, as if someone had been putting his cigarettes out all along the door trim. The tail pipe has begun to drag and makes a menacing sound where the snow hasn't yet been packed down by traffic. It reminds her of her estranged husband, Randall, who had once put out a butt on their dining room table.

She parks as close to the bald storefront as the snowdrifts permit. Across the street, the boarded-up gas station still has twin gas pumps, each shouldering humps of snow, which makes her feel nostalgic despite her dislike of the cold. Seeing her breath, she covers her mouth with her scarf.

It has snowed all day, then stopped, then snowed all the way to the storefront. Rose's boots punch craters into a lunar surface. The parking lot looks celestial from the storefront window. Afterwards, she knows, it will look as terrestrial as everything else in Swannboro. But for now, before everyone arrives, she enjoys the clean-cut planes that wind is carving out of the drifts.

Going to the meeting, for an acknowledged good cause, isn't her idea. She had been coerced by Natalie, who has given her steady housework since her arrival in town. She regards causes and earnest people with suspicion.

But here she is, about to sit in a roomful of middle-aged do-gooders, people who would as soon snub her. They're here to preserve a rundown area of town, an old quarry that had long passed its productive years and become, everyone said, an eyesore. They're here to give history its due and geography a facelift. Her estranged husband, Randall, would have said, *Bull.* They were here for the power. They were here for the money tourism could bring in.

With the power part, she would have had to agree, but not the tourist part. Swannboro, she knew, would never attract the kind of people that it wanted.

She enters the empty store, expecting warmth, but the air is chill, smelling of grease from the pizza palace next door. The Stone Circle members are misers, not that she blames them. Her own oil bill is bleeding her. She opens a metal folding chair, cringing at the sound, and sits on it, waiting, shivering. Just to stay warm, she gets up to look at the gallery on the wall.

It exhibits yellowed photos of the quarry and the sepia postcards the Circle had been selling. The quarry was a Mecca for local historians, planners and well-to-do people like Natalie. It was Swannboro's little acropolis mirrored in a silent quarry lake. Rose scuffs along, looking. Like anything unusual in a place whose center is mostly cramped yards and asphalt, the quarry seems out of place.

The sudden, rose-brown cliffs look like a cake someone had carved up then abandoned, leaving the heavy remains in the kitchen sink.

Floods had done the rest, turning a bustling, dangerous stone business into a lazy fishing hole. Water out of stone. Commerce had quickly jumped in. In the more recent photos, Rose sees small industrial shops and rust-scabbed oil drums rimming the water. And progress sitting on top of the cliffs where a seventies developer had shaved off a place for a chain gang — a fast food restaurant, a big-box pharmacy, the usual suspects displacing a down-and-out trailer park.

A woman scrapes her boots on the mat outside, then trudges in with a rocking, sideways limp. She has a large face, made larger by a hat with a pompom, and a puffy coat with matching puffy mittens. In winter, Rose thinks, they all dress like children. Her face is plain and intransigent, her body large, and between them a scarf cinches her neck. Rose knows her only by face.

The woman nods at Rose, seats herself in a metal chair and pulls a magazine out of her bag. They're all like that, ignoring outsiders is the rule, Rose thinks, for the townies who had lived here all their lives, as if it were an accomplishment to stay in one place, like a rock. Swannboro is not Rose's hometown; she spent most of her growing-up years some fifty miles from here near the seashore, in Rockton, and lived in Millsap, Virginia more recently. And once, for two weeks, she had lived in Richmond with Eve to get away from one of Randall's drinking binges.

She had decided on Swannboro because of its name. It was part of a game she had played with Eve, to find the town with the prettiest name in Connecticut, which quickly ruled out Rockton.

"This one has a swan in it," Eve had said. She had been tracing the map with colored pencils and markers.

"But it also has a burro," said Rose, and they had both laughed as Eve drew a swan's head and neck on top of a donkey's squat body. They had taped it to the refrigerator. When Randall had asked her what it was, Rose told him it was Eve's school assignment. "They're studying Greek myths." And Randall had laughed along with them, but his eyes hadn't laughed. These were of the kind certain men possess, deep blue and thickly fringed, that would look as much at home on a girl. And had attracted them, pretty young ones, old ones, thin ones, fat ones. Once she had found a couple of young, thin ones in her closet, who had taken Randall home from a bar and crashed while he slept it off, and the next day, Randall had accused *her* of infidelity.

But he hadn't suspected her real intentions, and one night, after wrecking the place, punching a kitchen cabinet and destroying her college typewriter, he had left with a bag of his clothes. So she had packed for two, taken Eve and fled, before he could change his mind, leaving behind most of her quilts and furniture. Swannboro, Connecticut was as good a place as any. Out of Randall's range, which was limited to the hot, damp, slow-moving margins of the country, Mississippi, Louisiana, Alabama, as well as Virginia. Still, she is afraid. Afraid he'll come looking for them, charging her with kidnapping or some other absurdity. For months, an unexpected move, a sharp cry, the sudden acceleration of an engine have made her jump, her heart skitter. Randall, like many insecure men, wore a costume, a cowboy hat and boots, a big suede jacket with fringe. Since leaving Randall, Rose had seen only one man dressed like this, a fat man in the back-to-school section of a Walmart, larger than Randall by fifty pounds at least. Rose hadn't lost any time leaving her cart in the aisle, rushing home, paying twice as much for Eve's school supplies in a local store.

Rose removes her gloves, an old pair of Eve's with the fingertips cut out, then pulls them back on. Other people begin to arrive in brusque, stamping groups, mostly gray-haired, mostly women, although it's hard to tell. They chatter and chuckle, rustling in their puffy coats and one of them asks if anyone has a cough drop. Rose recognizes the asker as a man, one she had seen at the school, a teacher, one of Eve's actually. He was one of those who still wear bowties and vests, whose skin erupts from a disorder, the name of which she knows. *Rosacea.* It had once been her nickname. She still has a few of the acne scars that had inspired it, and the nervous habit of touching her face.

"Come to the meeting, it wouldn't hurt to make a few friends," Natalie had said a few days before. Natalie had founded the Stone Circle out of the love of local history and of being in charge of things. Rose visited her house twice a week to clean, which meant dusting and vacuuming mostly, but sometimes scrubbing and waxing and polishing silver. It was about four weeks past Christmas, and the depressing holiday greens, still stuck to Natalie's window sills with scotch tape, were beginning to shed their frail needles, which Rose swept into a dustbin.

"I already have friends," Rose had said, thinking of her brother, Arthur, who was subletting her basement. Arm, he is called, because of his violin arm.

"What I mean are nice people. People it would do you some good to know."

A look around the room confirms that these are the dominant species present. Business people and teachers and people who work for the town. People likely to own nice homes that need cleaning and nice things, like oriental rugs, which Rose can repair by hand. Women who might like a handmade quilt, although not the kind that Rose is hoping to create. They would want something to match the couch or a baby gift or a comforter. Cold people always want comforters.

The man with the sore throat and bow tie calls the meeting to order and except for a few women, knitters who draw elaborate sweaters and scarves out of tote bags, everyone gives him their attention. The quarry is now officially an historic landmark, he says, and everyone applauds. Usually this would draw tourists in, he says, but not here.

"Swannboro's planners were thinking about taxes, not the eye of the beholder." Several laugh politely, then Natalie comes in and no one pays attention to the man anymore. A few women stand up and hug her and all but the knitters stand up and clap. Rose knows it's because Natalie had used her influence to gain the quarry an official place in history. "Oh, dear," says Natalie. "Oh, my." Someone offers her a chair, but she sits next to Rose instead.

Rose feels her arm being squeezed while Natalie whispers in the ear of the person sitting to her right. Then the meeting is called to order again and they discuss the paths they're cutting through brambles to the quarry lake.

A glowering woman with a lisp, the treasurer, stands up and begins a dull monologue. Rose attempts to concentrate, but as usual the numbers fall through cracks in her mind that she is sure are there to keep her poor. Resistance to boredom is required for success, she had concluded many years before.

The quarry and the river had been the whole point of Swannboro once, the man in the bow tie says. Then unaffordable houses began going up in the middle of shocked-looking fields. The discussion meanders and digresses, with some people wanting a water park and others wanting motels, restaurants. Behind it all lies the impenetrable money talk.

Her stomach begins to growl, and she presses down on her ribs. She had fed Eve leftover soup and had fed herself crackers before the meeting.

Money always leads to arguing, as it does now, a rambling parry between the puffy woman and the man in the bowtie, which fatigues Rose even more. She doesn't like to argue; she seldom wins. She would always begin with a deep breath, a sting in her chest, sensible rhetoric she rehearses silently, but which sounds aimless when spoken. Caving in and sorting things out afterward seems saner, although it seldom works out well in practice. With Randall, it had led to misery, penury. Against her judgment, Randall had hired an unemployed friend to fix a leak in their rented house and the friend had botched the job. For a year, she had managed with buckets and bleach to keep the mildew from spreading, but the water bugs were clever, an army of black helmets with eggs that were time bombs. The walls had bubbled and cratered and the ceiling in Eve's bedroom had caved in. A sickening odor began with a taste that remained in her mouth wherever she went.

She feels her eyelids grow heavy as the voices in the room fade, then seem to bark as she jolts awake. But the room is quiet and she realizes that her name must have been spoken because a few of the knitters have put down their work and are staring at her. She brings her hand up to her face.

" … a degree in fine art. Several years in a museum in Millsap, Virginia. Then she worked alongside her husband in his oriental rug and tapestry repair business, Flying Carpets. Some gorgeous original quilts of hers are now on display in galleries. Well, one is in New Haven. I know that because I'm on the board." Natalie pats herself on the shoulder and some of the women laugh. "So without further ado, I'd like to introduce Rose Strang."

Rose sits there impassively. Then she puts her gloved hands

together and makes a little bow like an Asian. When no one says a word, she blushes hard and studies the pattern that is beginning to emerge in one of the women's knitted scarves. It looks like the peel of an apple, a corkscrew of red on white.

"Rose would love to create a patriotic quilt to display in our storefront. A quarry quilt." Natalie's laugh is a tinkle. "We have a little left over from the state grant we received, so we can afford her. I think. Can we afford you, Rose?"

Rose begins to sweat. "I don't know," Rose says. "Sure. I guess." She blushes and touches her face. Her voice has involuntarily reverted to a Southern accent that makes her feel out of place.

"Spoken like a true *artiste.*" Natalie clears her throat and changes the subject to the brambly mess around the quarry. The Circle has made long, secret-garden paths that keep on going. Nowhere, it appears. It doesn't seem to matter that its end is a field in someone's backyard, with a sagging clothesline and a swing set. There are lookouts worth climbing toward with a view of the river. The river had once been the whole point of Swannboro, the man in the bowtie says.

The Circle members talk about picnic grounds and playing fields. Rose says nothing, relieved to have escaped scrutiny. It would be rude to leave, yet it would be boring to stay. She decides in favor of boredom.

A patriotic quilt. Randall would have laughed bitterly, but then he would have agreed. *We need the money.* If patriotism would put food on the table, he would have been all for it.

3 / Eve

Before their move to Swannboro, it was easier to take things. They were just dumb, lost things no one wanted, unless you like keeping things in jars and looking at them. A jar makes junk look like something.

Eve takes an empty jar out of the back of her closet. She used to have a jar of buttons, one of glass bits and one of marbles, one of pencils, bird feathers and a rock and seashell collection. All of these she had to leave behind. Now she has a jarful of Halloween candy saved from last year. She has a jar with three grubby combs and half a jar of scratched lottery tickets, and lately has been keeping playing cards in a jar, in case a kid ever comes over.

The prize is the jar of carpet and tapestry scraps from her father's shop. She had smuggled it into Momma's car before they left the South for good, together with the jar of broken typewriter keys. These she hadn't gotten in the usual way. Usually, she would wait for something to drop off someone, out of a pocket and onto a floor. In stores it happens all the time.

The empty jar would be for feathers. She found a blue jay's in the woods out back, gray-blue it had looked on the dirt. But in the jar, it looks eye-blue. Eve pushes her hair out of her face and uses the tapestry clip her father had made to hold it up in a thick whorl. Her hair is Daddy's and so are her eyes. What she has of her mother's, olive skin, frail, narrow shoulders and sturdy legs, are things of no account. Girls her age admire hair and eyes and breasts. She has no breasts so far.

She turned twelve last August and has begun to care what her peers think, despite what she thinks of them. Only one had ever been here, and Eve hadn't shown her the jars.

The hot soup her mother left was inedible. She had thrown it down the sink and eaten a few bars of old Halloween candy instead. Before Uncle Arm left for his job, he asked if she liked the soup, and she had lied. Her uncle made soup from greens, carrots, and strange, coiled grains that looked like worms. *Panty-waist.* The epithet, one her father had used, meant nothing to her, yet it had stuck in her brain. "Momma should be home in fifteen minutes," Arm had said in his crisp voice.

From her room, she hears Momma's car scrape, then Momma's voice, cheerful but false. It irritates her, although she isn't sure why, since it's preferable to other maternal voices, the nervous, huffing one, or the stern command or the screech. She calls out "Yes!" when Momma asks if she's doing her homework, which is inside her pack. She would do it in her own time. She would do it and get an A for it as always, and no one would be the wiser.

She spills out her money jar on the bed and counts her cash tensely, standing up. Ninety-eight dollars and eighty-five cents, some of it found, some of it gifts, most of it earned. She had swept her father's shop floor, had polished his shoes, washed coffee mugs, emptied ashtrays. The truth is that she likes earning money. The truth is that she *misses* him. He had been her pal, which is what he called himself, and she had liked that, too, despite other things he did and said. She had liked doing chores in the shop and outside of it, and the musty way things smelled, the rugs rolled or piled on top of each other like continental shelves, the sloppy counter. There had been a battered cash register on top of it with piles of receipts and greasy binders and a lava lamp that was ugly, almost nasty, but fascinating with its oily orange globs coming together then pinching off in a long, lazy ballet. Momma had said they reminded her of Daddy.

The money may be enough to get back to him if necessary. She slides the jar with the carpet scraps out, motley threads to distant times, to other people's history as well as to her own. But she doesn't open the jar. Like certain feelings, like a fire extinguisher, it's meant to be looked at, respected, known, but opened only in an emergency.

She counts the money again, then returns it to the jar. Ninety-eight dollars might be enough to pay for a train ticket home, meals included. They had taken the train to Richmond once, and Momma had complained about how much everything cost. They had eaten breakfast bars for most of their meals, but Eve had been happy and Momma had been cheerful, feeding some geese that lingered near a park lake. There had been an animal refuge where you could see bison from a distance and falcons close-up. Momma had taken her to the art museum, but it was too cold and quiet, and the exhibit of Fabergé eggs they had come to see was long gone. Instead there were porcelain bowls, the kind Arm would have liked, but which had made Eve yawn. "Cover your mouth," Momma had said sharply.

She sits on her bed and opens the jar of typewriter keys. She arranges them on her bedspread, the numbers on top, then the serious-looking letters in the order in which they had once appeared, Q W E R T Y U I O P.

She had come by the keys secretly but honestly the day before she and Momma had left. Daddy hadn't been home much that week, going out with a buddy after supper and you never knew when he'd return. On such occasions, Eve would sleep with Momma in the big bed, according to an agreement they never discussed. Sometimes she'd wake up and there Daddy would be getting into bed with his clothes on. He would smell like burnt cooking. There would be smoke in his clothes and an adult smell like grapes and glue mixed up with sweat. She would hang onto Momma's side of the bed.

But that night, she had awakened to loud male noises in the living room. Daddy had been laughing on top of other men's laughs and strange metallic clattering and kicks, then Momma had woke up and told her to stay in bed. Eve could see her crawl to the door and open it a crack and look out. She made a sound like a toy before shutting the door and turning the lock and crawling back to the big bed. She had grabbed Eve who sensed that she wasn't being held, but being held onto. It had made her feel sick to her stomach.

Eve yawns wide open. She lies on her stomach and composes words with the typewriter keys, an easy game.

B I S O N. Each word could have only one of each letter. F A L C O N. She had wanted a falcon, had pestered her mother for one after the Richmond trip, but it had been no use. Home had remained pet-free because Daddy wouldn't allow animals in the house, protecting his rugs and tapestries. But a falcon could be kept outdoors in an aviary. Neither parent could be persuaded.

"Raptor" wouldn't work; it had two Rs. C A P T O R.

Momma had held her too tight, she remembers. Then she had turned away and begun to cry, and Eve could hear Daddy and the other men laughing and whooping. Something metal was being kicked and pulled apart with nails or tacks flying against the wall and furniture. Eve had rolled off the side of the bed and taken her pillow to the closet where she made herself a bed on the floor. Something hanging from a hook was soft and sour. She had pulled it down and it was Daddy's bathrobe. She had heard Momma crawl to the door a couple of times, then back to the bed where she sat with something in her arms. It was one of the boards that lay in a pile under the window. After a while the laughing and banging stopped, or Eve fell asleep, which one came first she could no longer remember.

Then Momma was standing over her with light all around. "Poor thing, you slept on my shoes," she had said. Eve could see from the puffs around her eyes that Momma hadn't slept, and she had felt badly about leaving her mother alone in the big bed.

Daddy had left that morning with his clothes, some beach towels and Eve's Girl Scout knapsack. Eve could hear Momma crying and cleaning, sweeping things out the door and carrying something outside. The floor had been scoured, but Eve could still smell cigarette odor in the Pine Sol. One of the kitchen cabinets had a punch in it revealing fake wood. Momma had made breakfast and Eve could hear her sniffing as the eggs spat in the pan. They had stiff lace edges.

Later when Momma was sleeping on the couch, Eve had taken a good look around the place in her socks. There wasn't anything new except for the punch in the cabinet, so she had put on her shoes and gone outside. Some starlings yacked and perched on the roof. She had poked around the woods for a while, looking for glass bits and nails. But there were only plastic bags holding onto leaves and beer cans full of mud and other yuck. There was a sodden half-donut on the curb she had poked with a stick and thrown in the woods. And there had been a flat dirty white balloon she stayed away from because she knew what it was.

A D U L T, she spells out now. She often wonders if adults share a real secret, savage and potent, because the ones she has discovered so far seem no better than what a child might invent. Clownish ways of touching body parts, tongues and hips and peters and holes. Habits that unleash mad dogs.

After seeing the balloon, she had headed toward a wet pile of lumber that had been left in the yard. The broken machine was sitting underneath a piece of the gambrel roof that had been ripped off the house months before by a workman. The machine was a funny beige color like chicken gravy. No one would have known it was a typewriter because all the keys had been torn off. It could have been any broken machine.

But she had known: It was Momma's college typewriter, which Eve had been allowed to play with since she was a baby. She could see its name, Smith Corona, on the top. She had sat down on top of the broken roof and hugged her knees, looking at the typewriter's remains. It didn't have much of a shape anymore, a face with all of its teeth gone.

She had hunted for typewriter keys in the grass. Z 1 R O E. "Zero," she had said aloud. Some of them still had long metal roots attached to them; others were just the teeth. All of the letters and the numbers with the symbols over them and the punctuation marks chattering away in her pocket. She had gone inside and washed them.

Now Eve scoops the keys off of her bedspread and clinks them back into the jar. She shakes the jar and sniffs. The jar still smells like pickles.

4 / Arm

Whenever he looks at the sky, he can tease out the artificial clouds from the real. One of the legacies Mark had left him. As he shovels snow around his sister Rose's car, he looks up and sees it, a thick white line scripted by a jet. It holds its own in a way he now has to admit is not the nature of ice crystals, and gradually begins to spread, like paint on cheap paper. The one he witnesses crosses over another, and to the west, in plain view, are several parallel lines, spreading and, he knows, coalescing. Conspiring.

Chemtrails. Aerosol plumes made by the military industrial complex to change weather, conduct war games and mind-control the population. He would burn with shame whenever Mark discussed them in front of friends, musicians and professionals, most of them gay, falsely genial and genuinely satirical, people with real lives and work, not the quixotic missions Mark supported with a series of menial jobs. Shit work. But now Arm seeks the terse, tense reports about manmade weather on the Internet. Some are merely factual, others illiterate, full of misspellings and extraneous apostrophes, but it no longer matters to him. It was what Mark had preferred, truth in its raw form.

And yet Arm knows that Mark Castleman had seldom revealed the truth about himself. Coworkers had never been invited for dinner, to meet his lover, Arm. "They're all Mossad," Mark had joked, yet his eyes remained serious. But they had turned out to lack rudimentary spy craft. When Mark died, they hadn't known whom to call. Neither had Arm.

There was a much older brother, he knew, but no phone number, no address. And no one else. Mark's death was lonelier than most.

The shovel makes a terse, tense sound. Arm cuts through glaze, then powder, then something underneath, something that had once been alive, a mole or a mouse. The rust stain in the snow makes him jump. He buries it quickly with a scoop of fresh snow, but the damage is done. He thinks he may as well go in, but then he would have to face Rose and the beginnings of her quilt on the kitchen table.

He makes another tentative cut into snow, hitting bottom. He scores and scrapes neatly. Too neatly, Mark would have said, yet this compulsion for an orderly life is what had kept the two of them housed and clean, fed and out of debt. Most of Mark's earnings had gone into the projects. The chemtrail project, various videos and interviews, an intractable blog to which only Mark's few friends had subscribed. Other blogs, too, on UFOs, nine-one-one, and what he called the Nazification of America. Post-mortem they are out there still, orbiting, dark stars of warning and political reproach. For this Mark had gotten out of bed before dawn and made his stocky body perform the work for which it was made: heavy lifting.

After failing as a reporter, he had become simply a porter, then a cab driver, then a waiter during his brief career. He had ended it as a furniture mover. Poor Mark, the entire world tilted against him, it seemed, as his large, splendid, self-built body was forced into smaller and meaner labor camps; no wonder he was paranoid. At least, Arm thinks now, his last job had been the work to which Mark's personality was best suited. Moving furniture in cities like New York requires a strategic mind, staunch pessimism. Anything could go wrong. Nearly everything had.

Ironic, he thinks, that Mark should have been the one to die when he, Arm, was the natural target, a second-generation Lebanese-American, an Arab of sorts, likely to be lumped in with the presumed guilty, post nine-one-one. But Mark's death was an accident, he assures himself, not sabotage, not revenge, nothing to do with his conspiracy theories, his blogs. No one had been after either of them; such ideas are false and self-aggrandizing. He takes comfort in his calm reasoning, his probity. But he still wishes it had been him instead of Mark.

It had been easy to leave their cramped studio after Mark's death. Mark's employer had paid for the move, so the ordeal had cost him nothing but time. Arm had never liked the city, had never understood its hold on his peers, the gifted and the gay. Mark had made the city's insomnia and insatiability bearable. Without him, Arm felt he would eventually be eaten alive, so he had left the city to its glittering devices. He'd returned to Connecticut, avoiding his hometown of Rockton, found a cheap cabin rental in Windham and indulged himself in ten months of nearly perfect isolation. When Rose moved to Swannboro and offered him her basement, he had jumped on it, not because he relished the idea of living with his sister, not even because the rent was a pittance. Swannboro had been one of those coincidences he could not explain to himself, much less his sister. It was where the needle of Mark's compass had been pointing.

A plough drives by, spitting red dirt all along the edge of the road and onto the drive that Arm had worked to the pavement. "Shit." He punches the frail shovel into a mountain. But he picks it up again and keeps going, feeling the resistance of his muscles, not made for heavy lifting, but for bowing a string. He had played the violin in several good small orchestras, taught as much as he could bear, recorded when he could control his nerves, but had given it up after Mark died. He can no longer stand the sound of his instrument. Too much like the human voice.

He hears his good violin now, involuntarily keening and spinning in his mind. The Sibelius in D, the treacherous passages he had never mastered, the Vivaldi clichés, endless celestial prattle, Bach, Mozart, Haydn. It amazes him that he had wasted so much time on a talent that had demanded suffering and abstinence for rare bursts of redemption. Not the flood he desired. Long ago, a scholarship to Julliard had made him feel obligated to take the hard, classical music path. Kids would kill for a music scholarship nowadays. He shovels around the dainty tracks of a squirrel, too pretty to destroy, he thinks.

The school bus steams to a halt, and Eve steps down wearing, he notes, no jacket, no gloves. "Hello," he shouts, waving, but she snubs him with a listless motion of her hand and marches up the walk he'd shoveled earlier. The cheap aluminum door clangs and bangs. He's alone again with, it appears, the maker of the tracks, its thin gray plume curled around its head. "Hello," Arm whispers, and the squirrel bounds up a tree.

What is he doing here? For now, he has a driveway to clear, a guitar gig to show up for later in a local bar, not a gay bar, but tasteful, nothing to be ashamed of. The ugly, poky ranch house is a different story, shingled in something cheap from the 1950s in an aqua color time had done nothing to improve. Well, you can paint shit even if you can't polish it, but no one had ever bothered, it seems.

He has its basement to himself, with olive-green sixties paneling and a damp odor. He has a broken career, memories of a dead lover. Tragedy. If he were still in his twenties it might be a point in his favor, but he has already rounded the corner of his fourth decade. He will be forty-four this year. Gay men are unforgiving about failure, the soft sags of the body. Men, as a rule, are unforgiving, unrepentant. This is everyone's tragedy.

He digs out through the sanded hulk at the driveway's end. There is no way around it. He needs Rose's car this evening, and what remains of its tailpipe would surely snap off if it lodged in a hard crust of snow. Besides, the exercise is doing him good, whipping his lungs and heart. Mark had failed to shame him into lifting weights. He had needed his violin arm then, a weakness out of which Mark had ferreted a new name for him: Arm. And it had stuck. His given name had been Arthur, a name he had struggled to fit himself inside and carry. He had been glad to cast off its iron mail for flesh and bone.

Once he's cleared about half the driveway, the shovel spade splits off from the handle, as he had known it would. This kind of snow is death to cheap equipment, cheap old cars. It gives him the excuse to knock off, make the coffee he craves. Better that, he thinks, than the wine he craves, which had made him put on weight. He hunches his way in through the cellar bulkhead to avoid his sister upstairs, being careful not to breathe too deeply at first. The mildew smell abates once he squats down the stairs and enters the room, paneled in an olive green color that depresses him. It's only then that he can stand up straight, feeling constrained to bow his head a little. The floating ceiling is yellow and warped, with one missing tile replaced by a paper plate.

He makes coffee, filling the room with the smell of French roast, sitting with his mug on a kilim he'd draped over the tattered couch. Otherwise, the furnishings in the room gleam incongruently, comforting him with the cabriole legs and barley twists he had sought in antiques shops over the years and bought with his tax refunds. He can hear the scrape of Rose's chair above him, her slippered steps on the crackling floor, but not the whir of the sewing machine yet. By now he knows the sequence. First the pencil drawings, then the selection of fabrics and dyes, the painting and cutting, the hand-stitching and machine work. He can hear her rustle and pace indecisively. It seems too much trouble for what will amount to a lie.

When she had told him about the commissioned quilt last week, he had tried to appear happy for her, but she had detected his ambivalence, misinterpreted as scorn. She'd hectored him, trying to force an admission, and he had danced around the subject until she cornered him, which cued him to leave the room. "Think what you like." It hadn't been fair. She deserved to know what he knew.

He stands up tentatively to get dressed for his gig. The reflexive glance in the mirror assures him that he is still himself, the dark circles under his eyes accentuating the Mediterranean good looks he still possesses, framed by dark hair he still possesses, worn long, in a ponytail.

He selects a white, collarless shirt, a pressed pair of jeans, the inevitable boots, his only untidy possessions, gritty and scarred. He looks through a drawer for shoe polish, a cloth, then thinks better of it. No one is likely to notice his boots.

He meets the cool eyes of Mark in a portrait on his dresser, which had stalked anything corrupt while he was alive. Is Arm now the quarry? Dressed in his bar minstrel uniform, anxious for the approval of strangers, flirting with them after drinks, past a certain hour. Mark would have snorted and left the room. He, who had loved battle fatigues, had never worn them. He had known soldiers, he said, it wouldn't be right. Mark had known too much.

What does Arm know? That his lover had been crushed to death by an armoire his team had been guiding down through an eleventh story window. The piece had been antique, mahogany, with medieval griffins carved into its crown, its burled trunk coming down on Mark like the belly of Godzilla. It had happened after Mark began posting his and others' theories about nine-one-one on the blog, based on firsthand witness. Mark had been near Building Seven when it came down, snapping pictures as usual. Imploded, he had written. The building had been imploded, falling neatly, to the extent that pulverized glass and concrete could, into its own footprint. Arm has to admit this is odd, given the fact that it hadn't been hit by the planes.

Mark had said something similar about the Murrah Federal Building in Oklahoma City, humiliating Arm, during one of the rare times they had attended church together. It had been a saint's birthday, Arm could no longer remember whose, and there had been a community prayer to which all were invited to contribute a few words.

Mark had said his piece about the Murrah Building, which "blew up from the inside out, not from a car bomb." God forgive us all, Mark had prayed. And, of course, everyone in the prayer circle nodded and mumbled, too polite to dispute him. Episcopalians freezing their frozen butts off in the drafty nave. But Arm knows what they were thinking. He knows, because he cares what people think. He knows because, apart from being gay, he follows the standard line. Most classical musicians do, trained to play music as it's written.

Arm needs to visit the bathroom, but this would mean crouching upstairs, entering the chilly kitchen, passing Rose in her bedroom slippers and the quilted robe she wears indoors for warmth. It would mean ignoring the mess on the table, the quilt that is to become the Lie. It would mean creaking through the living room to the nook they share for cleansing themselves, and peeing into a toilet separated from his niece's bedroom by a wall he knows is a boundary to sight but not to sound.

He grabs his parka and, stooping, leaves the house through the bulkhead.

5 / Rose

She should have begun with the research. She had known all along, had put off the dredging until after a design had emerged and she had selected the cloth, the dyes. Knowing better, she had made a drawing to scale, dithering over colors, driven by impatience and the prospect of money. Arm's displeasure had advanced her timetable.

But she knows the work will win, slowing her down, consuming every minute that isn't spent on other people's houses or her daughter. No time to weep, although the silver polish she's using is making her sneeze. She rubs her way through Natalie's spoons, forks, serving spoons, butter knives, steak knives. As she works, she hums in a mellow, untrained alto. She possesses a fine singing voice, everyone has said so, which she has never put to any use. Growing up, there had been money only for her brother's talents. Yet she had wanted to be a singer once, more than anything.

She toils over a pie server tarnished to char and a brassy crackle, seeing the flash of her eyes, her capricious hair, her skin, which appears smooth in the silver spade. She shares Arm's striking Arab features, but not the treasure of his looks. Yet Natalie's house, which is nearly always dark beneath a canopy of beeches, makes her appear either better-looking or uglier than she is in its baroque, distorted mirrors. A perverse vanity makes her spy on herself in them as she vacuums, dusts, polishes, imagining the pleasure and pain of owning Natalie's things. She would have dinner parties, she would celebrate the birthdays of artists. She would celebrate wind blowing her quilts into sails on the clothesline, a solitary hour, a day without rain, the return of hummingbirds. But she hates to cook and, anyway, knows only a handful of people in Swannboro, the women whose houses she cleans.

Rose saves the depressing collection of silver children's spoons and forks for last. No harm could come out of taking, say, a spoon. Natalie, who is childless, never displays them. They're buried in a drawer fitted with special, velvety slots, inanimate little mouths. Rose had slipped a baby spoon in her pocket the first time, months ago, but had dutifully replaced it before leaving the house, knowing it would burn into her skin and leave another scar. She doesn't covet it; it was only by a strange impulse that she'd taken it.

She polishes an oval with a curled handle, worn thin at the tip by the teeth of babies who are grown now and likely dead. The simplest of spoons. Does Natalie count her silverware? Rose thinks not, but who knew? Hidden splendor, hidden rituals. People with money remain that way by good fortune, work, theft, vigilance or greed. Natalie doesn't work and isn't greedy.

She had, in fact, insisted on paying Rose more than her regular pay rate, the only customer who had in Swannboro. The remainder tacked on little jobs, then quibbled over surcharges. Scrabbling, squabbling, Rose thinks, slipping the last baby spoon into its velvet mouth. Natalie's elderly clocks cluck and tick mild reproof. Rose senses that the clocks, the antique furnishings, the Persian rugs, the vases are looking her over, expressing condemnation. In her marriage to Randall, it had been the same, although for different reasons. And in that case, there had only been rugs, other people's, amid the rabble of their furniture, passing judgment on her.

"Leave early," Natalie had urged when Rose told her she had to get to the library to do her "quarry research."

"You don't mind?" Rose had known she wouldn't mind.

"Leave early," Natalie had repeated. "And help yourself to the quiche." Natalie still baked quiches, or had them baked, between appointments and management meetings. She liked running things, managing people. *Manage,* her word. How will we manage? Natalie knew perfectly well.

Rose wolfs down a wedge of broccoli and cheese while standing up, before pulling on her jacket and boots. As her car coughs its way to the library, she sneezes. It might not be the silver polish. She might be coming down with something. Or perhaps she's succumbed to the enemy of her occupation, a dust allergy.

"A Quarry's Quarry by Annette Gallo." Rose's voice is scratchy when she asks for it, and the librarian looks confused.

"It's in circulation, just not in the regular collection," Rose explains. "It's an academic paper." The librarian says, "Ah," and heads into a back room. Natalie had told Rose about the book weeks ago. "Written in 1979 as part of her master's thesis in anthropology and geology. No one ever got around to publishing it." The librarian returns with a thick binder, which she hands to Rose, leaving her fingerprints on the dusty spine.

Obscurity is good, thinks Rose. Most serious people are obscure. She finds an empty carrel near some whispering teenage girls, all of them dressed in black, and begins to examine Annette Gallo's work. It had been printed on one-hundred-seventy-two sheets of middle-aged photocopy paper. Rose thumbs through them, prepared to be bored, but instead she finds an acute, orderly mind. She admires this because, although her physical habits are orderly, her mental habits are not.

One of the teenagers begins to hiccup, which her companions accompany with snorts and giggles. Rose touches her face and looks up. Each of them is riddled with metal piercings, the most developed of them, a redhead with sooty eyes and inflamed skin, with a large discoloration, a tattoo, on her back, visible where her leather jacket has ridden up. Rose has seen her around town before, smoking with boys. A troublemaker. Seeing Rose's interest, the teenagers quiet down, hands over their mouths. The hiccuper flees to the bathroom.

Rose begins to read. She hunches forward, close to the page. She should have brought the glasses she is beginning to need, but is content to mole her way through. Bent over like this, reading, she has spent some of the happiest hours of her life. She begins as the author intended, with prehistory, and is suddenly aware that the entire library is hung with slabs of Swannboro stone stamped with the footprints of dinosaurs. She wonders how she had missed it before.

Across from her table is an oblong stone that hangs by a meeting room, a purple-brown frieze-frame of prehistoric time. Across it run the tracks of small prehistoric creatures. They had made three-toed tracks, wavy, ending in witchy toenails. At the level of Rose's eyes are two typewritten labels on the stone.

Swannboro was, of course, the point of origin. The tracks were made in seconds caught somewhere between the Triassic and Jurassic. One of the creatures (An_____uripus danasus in the worn, torn type) was probably Anchisauripus danasus. Rose flips through Gallo's index to learn this. Then she flips to page 33.

"The bony fragments of an anchisaurid, found in 1818, were first mistaken for human remains. It would take until 1855 to correct that assumption." The creatures who left tracks in Swannboro stone were more likely the pursued than the pursuer, wrote Gallo.

Rose decides to focus on Gallo's chapter on geology ("Stone Ages") and leave it at that. She reads the names of Swannboro's ancient residents. Grallator. Batrachopus. Otozoum moodii. Eubrontes giganteus. "The names are a distant cry from the smooth, whispery names of Swannboro's old families, its Swanns, Hills, Russes, Reids, Marches, Sneaths and Heaths, names that embodied civility — but who knew?" wrote Gallo. " Perhaps there was a little Eubrontes giganteus in the Dutch and English descendants who first obtained deeds to the quarries. Aggression is rooted in the pit of the brain where biologists say we're most like our scaly predecessors."

Rose stretches, gets out of her seat as quietly as possible. The teenagers, who had been giggling over something one of them had drawn, are suddenly silent, looking down, as if Rose has authority over them. She makes her way to a slab on a wall near the fiction section, which bears the tracks of Otozoum moodii. According to the label, Otozoum was a giant biped who probably hunted for salad rather than blood, but who would want to be under those feet, wide and heavily nailed.

She stretches again and turns to go back to her carrel when she sees him in the fiction section like a book character manifesting right there in the stacks. She can't see much of him: the rawhide brim of his cowboy hat, the drape of his fringed jacket. The wrinkled inseam of his jeans over the toe-box of a cowboy boot. Crouched, as if he had been there all along, waiting to spring on her. It could be her imagination or some other cowboy, searching the bottom shelf for novels about the Wild West. But it's Randall, she knows. It can be no other.

Along the wall, past the dinosaur slab, are coat hooks, and past these the refuge of the ladies room. She heads for the restroom door, facing the wall, and lets herself in. The long hall of mirrors has no patrons but herself. She enters a stall, locks the door, seats herself on the rim of the commode. The moments tick by and she thinks, if he saw her go in, maybe he'll just station himself by the door and wait. Stupid. Stupid to let him trap her once again.

Hadn't she fallen into all of his traps? His smile most of all, his eyes, clear blue even when he was drunk. His ideas about sexual equality, which meant he cooked while she cleaned and each of them was entitled to decorate the house. To him, this meant dragging in anything off the street. She had lived with orange highway cones, splattered with tar, in the living room for months. And, for one ugly week, a gigantic girdle sprouting long frayed garters that he had suspended above their bed. And people had been dragged in, too, smelling of vomit and fried food, allowed to sleep on the floor because they were his "friends," what he called his drinking buddies. And there were the grocery bags full of women's underwear and the shoeboxes full of pornographic Polaroids. She had learned the hard way to ignore his peccadilloes, which had seemed charming when she was younger, more liberal in her definition of "art" and "household," and "normal." But later, after Eve had been born, they had just seemed bizarre. Sick. For saying it aloud, she had paid.

The biggest trap, she admits only to herself, is the child they had produced together. She had suffered the guilt of the damned for thinking this, two abortions later. She had made up her mind; she had her reasons. And Randall had pronounced the final judgment on her typewriter.

And here she is now, hiding in a stall. She hears the restroom door swing open and someone walk in, the footsteps of a boot wearer. Rose knows the sound. *Clock-click, clock-click* across the restroom tiles.

Then it stops. Someone is rustling around, then running a faucet and there is the miniature sound of a toothbrush. Rose stops breathing and tries to get a glimpse through a crack. From the look of the long graying braid down the person's back, it appears to be a woman. Or maybe not. All that matters is that the person isn't Randall.

Rose flushes and carefully makes her way to a sink. It's obvious that the person is using the library restroom for her daily ablutions. Around the perimeter of the sink are toiletry items, a brush with a snarl of hair, a yellow cake of soap, a rolled facecloth, a tube of toothpaste with a dent. The person ignores Rose and continues her solemn task. She is easily the most peculiar-looking woman Rose has ever seen, so she is hard put not to stare, which she manages through her mirror as she washes her hands vigorously.

Two fierce black eyes, a mouth too small for teeth that protrude grotesquely, and between them a mountain of a nose. But the woman is small and her rough hands are thin and long and finely made. Above her plaid shirt peeks a white tee shirt. Both are tucked neatly into blue jeans with cuffs.

"Hi," says Rose. The woman nods. "Sorry to disturb you," Rose says.

The woman spits out her gob of toothpaste, rinses out the brush and wipes her mouth with her facecloth. "You aren't disturbing no one."

"I was wondering," says Rose. "Did you happen to see a man standing outside the door?"

The woman stares at her. The faucet releases a cold drop that echoes. "There's nothing out there but a bunch of rotten kids," the woman says. She packs her toilet articles into a cloth pucker bag with a string.

"Thanks," says Rose.

The woman nods and leaves the ladies room with her bag. Rose stands there a minute, then walks to the door, taking care to peek outside of it before setting her feet on the worn carpet of the library. Rose sees the woman taking her cowboy hat and fringed suede jacket from two coat hooks, and it isn't until this moment that she blows out the breath she had been holding. No Randall. Just this odd-looking woman.

Rose turns and walks back to her seat and Gallo's open book. As she approaches, she can see the red-haired teenager standing over it, her head cocked, papers in her hand, furtively reading while she pretends to be on her way to the copier. She spots Rose and mock-flees on tiptoes to the island of the copy machine. Her friends snort and gasp. Rose ignores them and continues to read.

Reptiles were always in a hurry, Rose reads. Not so with sandstone. Gallo wrote that millions of years went into the making of Swannboro's quarries.

"Flecks of sand, including feldspar and mica, are all part of the mix, churned and strewn by water. Feldspar's palette ranges from pinks as delicate as a fingernail's to muddy purples and brick reds. The same element that causes sandstone to redden with age, becoming hematite, runs in our veins — iron."

Hematite means bloodstone, *haima* from Greek, meaning blood, wrote Gallo.

Rose wonders if the quarry's history is as full of blood as it must have been of sweat. The quarrying men were hard as granite and probably not too nice. It must have taken guts, brawn, something not too far from the grasp and slash of mailed forepaws.

She closes her eyes and sees them, the reptile's paws, the color of an Army tank, the olive drab of dust, transforming into coarse human hands with broken knuckles and crooked bones.

She flips back to the table of contents and finds a chapter that stands out from the rest. "Suicides in Stone." Of course, the quarry would be the perfect place to jump. She flips to the page, which includes an old photo of the quarry from decades ago, with police milling around and a few locals with shaggy nineteen-sixties hair.

She reads Gallo's description of the suicides, which isn't imaginative, but accurate enough. A teenage couple, a homeless man, a lonely divorcée on the verge of bankruptcy, a drunk entertaining his friends in the woods, exactly what you'd expect, she thinks, skimming Gallo's terse accounts. There had been carny trailers and mobile homes in the woods behind some of the cliffs during the sixties and seventies, "a breeding ground for crime."

She arrives at a double-dashed line that Gallo apparently made to separate the suicides from the rest. The next section, a scant three paragraphs, is titled "Stones Unturned." She doesn't read it so much as fish through until she catches something hard and inexorable. It is about the shooting murder of a man named Taft Said, whose body had been dumped in the quarry.

Rose feels the urge to sneeze and reacts too late to stifle herself. The teenage girls erupt, one of them falling off her chair, which rousts the librarian. She marches over, beet-faced, but the girls are already shouldering their backpacks and scuffing out, looking down. Bless you, says the librarian to Rose, rolling her eyes.

Rose reads the name again. *Taft Said.* A foreign-sounding name, not easily forgotten. And Rose, in all this time, has never forgotten it.

6 / Eve

She normally sits in the back of the classroom, but had learned it was dangerous to do this on the school bus. It was where Connie sat, Connie Dukas of the Golden Drones, a gang of three. Connie was pierced, and did other colorful things to her body like tattoos and dyed hair, which looks like dried red seaweed. She was more dangerous than a boy and taller than all of them and she took a knife to school, secreted in her shoe. Eve knows, because Connie had let it be known last week when Eve made the mistake of sitting in the back of the bus.

In some ways it's worse to sit in front, where you risk being labeled "Drac's pussy." Drac is the bus driver, a retarded man, so-called, but Eve is sure that even a bus driver has to be of normal intelligence. Drac has a long, sharp face overhung by caveman eyebrows, with prominent, yellow eyeteeth, suggesting fangs. Children who have long since moved on to the high school gave him his name, but Eve knows his real name is Mr. Drake. Mr. Drake's speech is indecipherable, punctuated by "sheesh" and something that sounds like "succotash" to Eve, translated as "suck my ass" by several boys. The nicest of the boys imitate Mr. Drake while the meanest get in his face with swears or nasty noises, and last week, on his way out of the bus, one had popped a condom, filled with his own urine, on Mr. Drake's lap.

Connie had been strangely mute during and after this incident, which had resulted in the boy's suspension. A rumor that Mr. Drake was Connie's real father sticks in Eve's mind as she picks her way around book bags to reach a seat in the middle of the bus next to a girl slouched over, pecking at a game boy. Game boys aren't allowed in the school, but in the bus, no one cares. They're better than drugs or fistfights, better than noise. The girl ignores her, focused on the minutiae within her screen, for which Eve is grateful, concentrating her gaze on her lap and on the large head in front of her. It's kinky-haired and precisely braided, a black American head that bobs above a brown puffy jacket. Eve wishes to touch it, to glide her hands along the gleaming, orderly rows, but, of course, this is not what she does. She sticks her hands in her jacket pockets and fishes for a box of mints.

She hates her quilted, baby-blue winter jacket with its silly, peaked hood (she had removed the pom-pom), which her mother had bought on sale at a department store. It has a silver snowflake embroidered on the collar and makes fussy, whispering noises whenever she moves. Ordinarily, she balls it into her pack, but it's well below freezing today. She hates winter, which drags along with school, filling her with a feeling that hardens and clings like dirty snow. In the South, winters were kind, days when it snowed meant a day off from school. Here the bus is undaunted by snow, and since she lives on a rural road, her front yard is her bus stop. The first face she sees each school day belongs to Mr. Drake, wolfish yet hangdog. Not the kind of face to frighten her. In the South, such faces had been common. "Hash," Mr. Drake says each morning. "Hash, hash, hash." Eve has stopped guessing what he means. Back home, certain people slopped words together the way Mr. Drake does, but she had been able to understand them. It was the way they spoke. Mr. Drake's sloppiness is because of rotten and missing teeth.

Since the balloon incident, a raw-faced teacher with a bowtie, Mr. Warner, has been riding the bus, so the usual bus noise is subdued.

Eve can hear a tiny rhythmic beat coming from the earphones the black girl is wearing. Girls behind her whisper, and someone cracks his knuckles. The bus air is cold despite the closeness of bodies, the large number of them. Damp, rife with smells, the atmosphere has artificially stiffened, the way it does in church. It feels like church, except for the absence of boredom. Eve sneaks a look at the faces on the other side of the aisle. Everyone looks embarrassed, guilty, but not bored.

As the bus rumbles forward, she can hear the victim, Mr. Drake, muttering, keeping his voice uncharacteristically low as if he were the subject that the teacher is there to monitor. Perhaps he is. Everyone is being monitored. Eve takes a mint out of her pocket and pops it in her mouth. Her good Southern manners instruct her to offer one to her neighbor, but when she looks at the girl next to her, sucked deep into her digital game, she decides now is not the time.

None of the usual horsing around, the obscenities and spittle, elbowing, kicking, punching and thumping of backpacks, as students exit the bus. At each stop, the outgoing riders look where they're going, trudging slowly, the taller boys leaning, tentatively reaching for the ceiling, the smaller ones allowed to step over boots, some of the girls giggling at first, then catching themselves and assuming red, poker-faces. Eve likes them even less for pretending.

The bus route begins and ends at Eve's house. This means Eve witnesses the circumstances of her bus mates, without being similarly observed. She knows who lives close to the curb and who lives up the prettiest, velveteen hills and in the best houses, which to her are the newest and largest ones. She's glad none of them can see where she lives.

After the girl with the game boy leaves, Eve scoots toward her window, taking care to place her backpack on the seat to discourage anyone from sitting next to her. Not that anyone would. She doesn't dare look behind her, but can feel the luxury of emptiness. Connie's stop would be next, and then she would be free of the fear, the tension of being watched. Connie has been looking at her in a mean, predatory way for weeks. In the North, girls fight with each other, not like boys, but like animals, with pieces of glass, combs and pens for claws and teeth. In Connie's case, there would also be the knife. Eve has no desire to fight with anyone. The fights she'd witnessed at home convinced her.

Momma would needle Daddy about money or housekeeping while he was drinking. Usually about both. Dishes left in the sink, overflowing garbage sacks, or a leak or dry rot or spongy bathroom tiles would get them started while Eve lay in bed listening, wishing she could stop them with a distraction, something funny. She had been convinced that she could once, clicking into the kitchen and performing a dance for them in a pair of old tap shoes. It had caused Momma to cry and Daddy to crumple a beer can and leave the room, but the shouting and swearing had stopped. The same tactic had not worked that other, more recent time, however, when the argument had not been about money. It had been about something else, something Momma had done. "What about *my* choice?" Daddy had yelled, slapping his hand on the table. And for her trouble in trying to make them both laugh, Eve had received a slap on the butt from Momma, who had then sat on the floor and wailed, her thin nightgown hiked up around her thighs. Eve could see the little bluish bundles of veins beginning to form on Momma's white legs, which sprouted black hairs around the ankles, and the coarse, hairy lobes of Momma's privates through the nylon gown, and she realized Momma had taken off her underpants. It had made her feel slightly sick. She'd looked around the room, on countertops and under the table, to see where they might be. Daddy had called Momma Yankee Bitch and Slope-head Cunt, then left in a roar on his motorcycle. There was a sour, potent, female smell coming from Momma. Eve flushes remembering it now. How stupid she, Eve, had been. There was a better word, a vocabulary word for it. *Presumptuous.* The body is disgusting, she thinks, drooling and swelling up. She prefers objects. Stones, feathers, shells, coins, little squares of cloth, typewriter keys.

The bus comes to a stop with sounds that remind Eve of the zoo, although it has been a long time since she's been to one. An elephant's blare, a hyena's scream. A small boy at the front with moon boots struggles with his backpack and one of the taller mothering girls, a Drac's pussy, gets up to help him, but he brushes her off before pitching down the stairs and trudging toward one of the squatty little houses fanged with icicles, or perhaps he lives in the projects across the street, where Connie lives. Eve waits for her to scuff out, dragging the tattered hems of her jeans and groping in her pocket for an after-school cigarette, her weedy, scarlet hair over her eyes.

But Connie misses her stop and the bus jolts forward. Has she fallen asleep? Has Eve mistaken her for someone else at an earlier stop? Eve knows she hasn't; she can feel Connie in back of her, can smell her smoky, fried odor, and realizes that Connie is within stabbing distance of her back, of her neck, which stiffens. At any moment, Connie could reach into her shoe. Keeping her neck stiff, Eve side-glances Mr. Warner, who appears to be reading a newspaper. She had heard once that if you stared at someone's back long enough, he would eventually feel your gaze and turn around. But Mr. Warner's head remains still and bowed.

She wants to crouch down, dart into the aisle and squat her way toward Mr. Warner, but all she can manage is to bend slightly, pretending to be busy with a game boy, which is actually just the tin of mints from her pocket. When the crumpled ball of paper falls into her lap, she freezes. When nothing happens, she brushes it off her lap, letting it fall into the grime and snowmelt beneath her.

As the bus slows and screams, she feels something being shoved into the empty hood of her jacket and knows that, whatever it is, a loaded condom or a firecracker, she will not be able to remove it on the bus. To reach behind her head would be as dumb as dipping her hand into a pot of boiling water.

But it's only another crumpled ball, she discovers, opening it with shaking hands once she's on her doorstep. Inside, in sloppy capitals: I SEEN WHAT YOU DID. It isn't signed; she knows it came from Connie, as she knows the face in the bus window, shrouded by a hood, is Connie's face, with its artillery of screws, barbs, hooks and rods. Running from the bus, she imagines a crude, comic-strip face sticking out its tongue, as she has seen girls do throughout her life. Connie did it to show off a mad row of studs, and Eve knows she's doing it now.

The worst of it is that Connie now knows where she lives.

7 / Arm

"I wanted to tell you," he says. "But I thought it might upset you."

He's standing in the kitchen in his socks, still wearing his leather jacket, smelling of other people's tobacco smoke. It would be a few years before smoking is banned in bars, too late for his lungs and sensibilities. Rose had waited up for him with a glass of wine. *Her* wine, of course. Remarkable, since she hardly ever drinks. More remarkable is the tight-lipped inquisition that begins before his boots are off. He regrets having come in through the front door, instead of the bulkhead. If the set of stingily made, diamond-shaped windows in the door had been normal glass, he might have seen her at the table, but as it is, they're opaque. Ugly, in any case. He doubts the material is real glass.

She's angry, he can see that, but not for the right reasons. She should be angry because she's being played by a group of silly know-it-alls to push a patriotic message that has nothing to do with the quarry's violent history. Instead, she's angry at him for knowing more than she does about Taft. That is the surface of the scab, which he knows is really a tumor.

He shrugs. "I honestly didn't think you'd want to know."

"Not want to know that Taffy's body was dumped two minutes from this house."

You were obsessed with him when we were children, he says, knowing the depth of her feelings. Why get you started all over again? He speaks softly, but means his words to sting. Since his birth, it seems, she has been envious of what is his, talents and looks achieved by genetics, tyrannical little twists beyond his power. He can't understand her envy of the kind of attention it had brought him, the lessons from Taft in that little room of their childhood home where the raincoats hung and boots stood, crookedly, on a mat. The "breezeway." The old couch had built-in ashtrays in its arms, and these were usually full of cigarette stubs, their parents'. His job was to empty them, making him gag, so he would let them fill up and spill over until his mother threatened him.

The room had been the only one in their house where his mother had put up with human sloth for long. It had been freezing in winter, blazing in summer, making his strings go sharp or flat, but it was something Rose had envied, despite the lack of any recital, or anything to show for it beyond the technique drummed, literally, into his fingers by Taft. "Taffy," everyone called him. A clown's name, but the sort of clown for an opera, not a circus. Pagliacci, Arm thinks. Or, more to character, Peter Grimes. Taffy had been a taskmaster, cruel at times, demanding perfection. He would bring a drumstick with him to the lessons and brandish it, occasionally rapping Arm's knuckles and, once, the top of his head. He was the son of someone his mother knew, a Lebanese, from long ago and far away.

Taffy had never made much of his keen talents once he established a heroin addiction and trade. The lessons had been pitifully cheap even then. God knew how much Taffy had stolen to make up for his losses. Arm takes a deep, cleansing breath. He should have put an end to the sibling competition while he was young. He should have refused the lessons, as most boys his age would have done.

Rose sits there, drinking, spilling a little on her bathrobe, touching her face. "I suppose Ma told you everything," she says with sarcasm.

No, not at all, he had been in the dark about Taffy's death, as she had been, before he had done his own research, he tells her. He had known because he had looked into it. Actually, Mark had looked into it, but he, Arm, doesn't tell her that. Why complicate matters? He isn't as sentimental about the facts as Mark was, as she is. And now she's asking him the next question, the one he had known was coming.

"It's why you came here, isn't it. To be near his grave."

"Ridiculous," he says. She really should stop and think about what he had recently been through. Hadn't he had his fill of tragedy? He had come all the way out here to help, to add an income, but here they are. It was already beginning to feel like a suffocating suburban marriage. He lowers his voice. And he wouldn't mind, he says, he wouldn't mind for the sake of Eve, but he isn't going to be questioned this way. He watches her face go from the rash of anger to pale acquiescence, feeling ashamed of himself, though not enough to tell the truth. He has given her nearly all of his earnings at the bar. That is sufficient. He watches her swirl the remains of wine in her glass and is glad he has given up drinking for the sake of his good looks. This would be an excuse to get drunk, guilt having been his reason more often than not.

The kitchen has been tidied since he had left earlier. She had been at it, washing the dinner dishes and neatly setting them in the dish rack. Nearly all of the plates are from a different set, picked up at yard sales, but each is china with dainty rims. His coffee cup and hers, set upside-down to drain, are the only matching items, in a cheery, majolica pattern that suits neither of them.

Like him, she is a slave to the ghostly domestic tyrant who still possesses them. The table has been polished, the floor swept, she has placed a candle in a glazed candlestick he recognizes from childhood, stenciled with a rooster bearing one incredulous-looking eye. The matching salt and pepper shakers had been the rooster's brood hens, he remembers, now missing in action. His sister's homely touches, the quilted oven mitts she had stitched and hung from hooks, make the room appear sadder than it already was, its wallpaper, patterned with faded cherry blossoms, curling at the seams. Surfaces are beginning to peel back, the countertop formica, the linoleum, the ceiling paint. The room looks, he searches for the word, *piecemealed.* Is it an actual word? He feels sorry for his sister, always salvaging people's castoffs and bringing them together like the scraps in her quilts. The kitchen chairs come from different sets, one of them their mother's Windsor chair, with a worn saddle and scarred, pitted stretchers, another a veneered atrocity that had been left by previous renters, the rest barrel-chested maple clunkers from Goodwill. The kitchen table is a card table. "Antiques," she calls them, but they both know better. He would never express such opinions to her, of course, but the truth is that he has never liked quilts, which seem to him more like jigsaw puzzles than art.

Without a word he goes downstairs, rummages in a drawer until he finds the tin that holds the old clippings Mark had collected for him, then marches back up staunchly. He doesn't have to say anything. The newspaper headlines he spreads out in front of her are two inches high. She stares, then says she'll have to get her glasses, and goes to her bedroom, but they turn up in her bathrobe pocket. He paces as she reads and at one point stands over her. Then he sits down and mines her face for reactions, finding nothing but a pursed mouth and a reddish crease between her eyebrows.

He gets up and pours himself a coffee cup of wine. One wouldn't hurt, and this is a cup, not a glass. As he sips, he reviews the facts mentally. The body was found May 21, 1971 by Swannboro fishermen. How strange that their lines and hooks should have become tangled up with Taft. The death had been ruled a homicide from multiple gunshot wounds in his chest and arm.

The police suspected that Taft's testimony in a drug case against someone, a dealer named Manny Manciani, might have been the motive. Manny Manciani, a name you just couldn't make up, thinks Arm, picturing a greasy man with a swagger and the likely insecurity behind it.

They sent scuba divers into the murk to search for Taft's car, and pulled it out of a sixty-foot depth. A 1963 Cadillac sedan, a whale of a car with giant fins. Arm could feel its weight on the prongs, could hear the hemorrhage of water when it reached the surface, losing its last inhabitants, very likely some giant bass that still inhabit the lake. The car windows must have been open for Taft to have floated out, already shot and dead.

Arm gets up to pour Rose another glass of wine, but she puts her hand over her glass. Reluctantly he re-corks the bottle. If she won't drink with him, he won't drink. Simple. Yet not easy. He wants another cup of wine, but knows where it will lead.

"Well," says Rose hoarsely. "Now I have something for you to read." She hands him a January issue of the *Swannboro Ledger,* folded in half with the cover story on top and he looks at the smudgy front page. The usual brassy headlines with their fishhook words and numbers. Nine-one-one. Anthrax. Funds. Corruption. Mark would have read them all, but this last one is what Rose means. It leads with a photograph of a wattle-jawed man in glasses pointing his finger in a castigating manner.

He skips down granite paragraphs, looking for whatever Rose

wants him to see. What would Mark look for? Arm seldom reads a newspaper anymore and this article confirms why he shouldn't. A series of brutal murders and racketeering in the '70s and '80s committed by Mafia stereotypes with flaring sideburns, bulldog profiles and mouths set in perpetual leers. They have weapon titles after their names like "The Rifleman" and "The Cleaver." The murderers are all FBI informants, "assets" they're called, so they were never indicted or convicted. In their place went honest men, or as honest as men can be, four of them framed for murder, one of them spending most of his productive years in prison before his name was cleared. The others died "behind bars." Sad, he thinks. He, Arm, will likely die in a bar.

The FBI agents who let this happen are now on trial, he sums up aloud. "They'll never be convicted." Mark would have said as much, but Mark would have tried to do something about it. He refolds the newspaper and tosses it on the kitchen counter.

"But don't you see," says Rose. "They let mobster informants pick off their enemies. People who could testify against them. And the FBI looked the other way."

"So?" says Arm. Rose punches the table and flings out her hands. "I mean, so what else is new, Rose? Do you expect me to go after the Mob and the FBI? Look at me. I don't see how this relates to our lives."

"You don't see how this relates to Taffy."

"Yes, well. Of course I do."

"You're just saying that. You don't understand. Taffy was an informant. He was supposed to testify in a drug trial before he was murdered and thrown in a lake. " She pauses affectedly. "It has a Mob signature."

"What, you mean dying with the fishes? He was already dead.

Someone was trying to dispose of the body. Simple. They put him back in his car. They push his car over a ledge." He knocks the coffee cup back for the last drop of wine. "He wasn't what you thought, Rose," he says softly. "He was into things you wouldn't know."

"And you would?"

"Rose, listen. Music does not redeem people. It did not redeem Taft. People are complicated. A life isn't the sum of one fact."

"I know what he did. I'm not saying he was a saint."

"You, for instance. You can't tell me your life is simply what you do for a living. Scrubbing people's floors." Arm knows he should stop there. "Or being married to that Southern belle." Arm's face is uncharacteristically expressionless. *Couch fungus.* That had been his name for Randall, her lazy husband, whom he despises. The one time he had visited them in that pothole they lived in, Randall had been recovering from a hangover on the only decent furniture in the living room and he, Arm, had been forced to sit on the floor.

"This isn't about my life," Rose is saying now.

"Maybe it is, Rose," says Arm. "Maybe it is." He is suddenly hungry and offers to make both of them an omelet. Rose shrugs, so he gets out a pan and spatula, cracks their six remaining eggs and hunts for seasonings. Thyme, a little oregano, sea salt. He grinds the white pepper he bought yesterday and whisks everything vigorously. As he works, he hums to fill in the silence his sister is creating to make him feel guilty. Humming is a family trait. Everyone had hummed, his mother, father, Rose, himself, his grandparents. He hadn't thought of it before. Carefully, he rotates the pan, allowing the mixture to slide around the edges, then he carefully eases the edges of the omelet upward to test. There is no decent hard cheese, so he uses what they have, packaged Parmesan, and thinks he really will have to get out of Swannboro soon to buy gourmet essentials. He folds the omelet like fine linen, and it obeys him, as food always does. He scores it in half and serves each of them on mismatched china.

They eat in silence, except for polite silverware noises. At one point, Arm can't stand it anymore.

"Because Taft was a poor idiot," he says, "he informed for them." He clears his throat.

"Who?"

"For the FBI. For the state police. Anyone who'd pay him." A muscle in Arm's jaw tightens.

"So you think --"

"I don't know what I think, Rose. It doesn't matter what I think. The only thing that matters is facts beyond our reach. The FBI won't release them because Taft was an informant. And anyway the Justice Department has everything locked up. Freedom of information is dead." He spears his last bite of omelet, chews it thoroughly, and swallows.

"That much we do know," he says.

8 / Rose

A thaw shrank the snow and now the yard looks like the man in the TV show who grew into a muscle-monster whenever he was enraged, his clothes hanging off him in shreds. What was it? *The Incredible Hulk,* she remembers. Early in her marriage, Randall had watched the reruns, which meant Rose had watched them, too, and during commercials when Randall would flip around and land on sports, she had watched her fill of football and boxing.

The snow is in ragged patches that Rose steps over as she scrapes her car windshield. All around she hears gurgles and trickles of water as snow melts on the roof, slipping down gutters and spouts, to a brook still locked in ice behind the house. It's Saturday, the sun steaming through clouds by late morning, and a little bird — sparrow or house finch? — observes her from the top of a broom that got buried in snow and is still partly frozen in a corner where she had propped it last month. On ordinary Saturdays, she sprinkles birdseed on the top of her car. Not this morning. An adamant crust of snow remains on the top and hood, which she leaves for the sun to burn off.

This morning she's going to the quarry to snap pictures and sketch. She's taking Eve along, dragging, more like, because it's been a while since they've spent time together and it will be good for Eve to see her mother doing something besides housework and grocery shopping. They have already argued about what Eve should wear, and Rose has agreed to a heavy blue sweatshirt with a hood and jeans, but this is not her first choice. She would prefer the winter jacket and sweat pants, but is learning to pick her battles. A thin live wire pulses between herself and Eve.

Eve has surrendered to a pair of winter gumboots she declares "dorky," whatever that means. Rose does not know. Typical Saturdays of her own childhood had been spent up and down the aisles of a crowded grocery helping her mother and grandmother find items to match up with their coupons. Afterwards, she had dusted her mother's furniture and when that was done had sat at a metal folding table and pasted green stamps into books that took hours to fatten and fill, hours she would have preferred to spend reading or outdoors. Her mother would use the stamp books to purchase more furniture for Rose to dust: lamps, end tables, a rocking chair with a formidable array of spindles.

Rose thinks that Eve is lucky to have a mother who puts homework ahead of housework, who lavishes her with the freedom of fresh air. But all Eve seems to want to do is sit in her room and count coins and curios she keeps in jars, which Rose thinks is obsessive, an activity for an old man, but she holds her tongue. Ever since the move, she has had to be careful.

Eve doesn't sit in the passenger seat next to Rose, but in the back, huddled in a corner, cupping her chin. Her face in profile, observed by Rose in the rear view mirror, is a cameo of contradiction, vulnerable yet impassive, soft and sullen. To Rose's light chatter about the quarry, Eve responds with grunts or nothing at all. Momma is making a quilt about the quarry, Rose says, does Eve know the quarry is famous? It's where brownstone came from, carved out like cheese and used for important buildings. Only a few months ago, facts like these would have been geysers, with questions from Eve gushing out of them, and Rose becoming irritable. But now Rose yearns for a question. The single fact that might prompt one, about the murder of Taft, she does not share. Is it a fact you should share with a young girl? Rose is tentative, used to deferring to Randall on issues about which he knew even less than she. No, she decides. The story has heavy chains she does not want around Eve's neck.

The neighborhood she must drive through to reach the quarry is scrambled with houses and gas stations, a weathered strip mall and random blighted storefronts, a halfway house. Then the town hall and other government buildings, all the same, ubiquitous quarry brown. Rose remembers something from her research, a quotation by the writer Edith Wharton, about brownstone being the most hideous stone ever quarried, and thinks she might agree. Drab, porous, incapable of reflecting light like a bad complexion. She touches her face. She has already decided to experiment with dyes to capture the brownstone color in her quilt, which is not chocolate-colored as Wharton wrote, but a melancholy rust with mauve undertones. Feldspar was the culprit, making it unpleasantly muddy. Bloody, actually, the color of an old bloodstain.

"Did you know," she begins, then decides not to tell Eve what Edith Wharton wrote about brownstone. Eve broods, saying nothing until after they make their way down the hill, hemmed by crusts of dirty snow, which borders the quarry on one side. Rose parks in a small, sanded lot near the promontory. Beyond is the lake, still taut with ice, and above it the high-browed cliffs, scored and stained. A sculpture museum. But in today's light they look pastel, almost pretty, topped with a white glaze. They don't belong here, thinks Rose, any more than I do. Men are working near the fuel tanks across the street, shouting over the noise of engines and pumps. Unfortunate, but she doesn't need silence to sketch or work a camera. The problem is the wind, which badgers her, lashing at her hair and jacket hood. Without a sheltered area for setting up an easel, she'll have to settle for snapshots.

"This place is ugly," says Eve, who gets out of the car, then returns to the backseat to sit hunched over with the door open. Rose says it's a matter of perspective. "Look up there." She points to the cliffs and Eve scowls until something catches her eye and she stares. Rose hangs her camera, which is actually Arm's, around her neck and plods through snow already pocked with the boot prints of Circle members and, she suspects, tramps, vagrants, kids playing hooky. She zeroes in on a rosy cliff, snapping pictures from several angles. Etched surfaces pull her in, baiting her eyes with what looks like a painted page, a face, ancient calligraphy. But it's only the illusion created by quarrying saws and time.

The lake is what she's been dreading, even though it won't require as much from her as the cliffs. *He* was found in it, and now that she knows, he'll be the secret subject of her quilt. She trudges out to an area that might be where his car plunged, where the ice is no longer opaque. The water came in the late 1930s, she knows from Gallo, rushing out of the river during the great hurricane. No one could drain it after that. The water won the quarry away from whoever owned it then, the town or a company. And it became a reservoir later during a drought, before it became a burial ground for Taffy. Click, click. She adds shots of an area where the ice is thick and ponderous, almost marble.

After a while she turns around to see what Eve is doing, but the car is empty, its doors shut. Her heart kicks her. She whirls around and nearly slips, craning for Eve in the mess of oil drums across the street, scanning the cliffs, the lake of ice. Then she spots her crouched by the promontory. Rose marches over with the fury that follows relief, her camera swinging, worried that Eve might slip and fall into ice water. "Careful," she shouts and, before she can stop herself, "What d'you think you're doing?" But Eve is on her feet, sour-faced, wiping her hands off on her jeans before Rose reaches her. "Nothing," she says. She picks up a long twig, a stick that she has obviously been using as a writing instrument. Something has been written and crossed out in the remnant snow.

Eve stands there with her head hanging. "This is boring," she says. "I want to go home." Rose says only boring people are bored and examines the end of the promontory, which is a brownstone finger pointing to the cliffs, with a sheer drop beneath its tip. She stands on its knuckle, lets the wind blow at her, snapping pictures of the cliffs as giant, ancient witnesses. Then she walks around, discovering a manmade hole in the finger, a keyhole that opens to a rough brownstone staircase leading down, it appears, to the quarry lake. Afraid of falling, she squats at the top of the well and counts ten, eleven stairs; the rest, if there are any, buried in snow. There's a green slime, encased in ice, on the walls and a smell she recognizes when she sees a yellow trail of pits in the snow that ends in a partially frozen puddle of urine. Boys, she thinks. Eve has approached her and together they look down. "Gross," says Rose, using the adolescent catchall word, but Eve simply shrugs. "It's right nasty," she says.

Rose says there are granola bars in the car but Eve makes a face and says she isn't hungry. Rose wants to explore the cliff nearest the car, knowing she must bring Eve along if she does, so she bargains with her. You can take Uncle Arm's camera, she says, you can be the photographer. A cloudy, half smile appears on Eve's face. She aims the camera at Rose, who mugs and stretches out her arms, which makes Eve snort and giggle. She hesitates, then clicks. I'll need you to get some good shots of the lake from up there, Rose says, as they hike up the road toward the lowest cliff.

The noise from the men around the oil drums is harsh and hectic; Rose must turn around to make herself heard. Eve pauses along the way, snapping pictures of the sky and a small house in ruins across the street. Don't waste film, Rose says, then shouts, but Eve dawdles and disobeys, pulling on a pine tree branch and shaking off snow, taking pictures of her boots and strange outcroppings. She reaches down and pockets something, Rose can't tell what, likely a piece of stone. Rose huffs up the road. Let her waste film if it makes her happy. She hasn't seen Eve absorbed in a real activity for so long, it's worth several rolls of film; besides, she, Rose, has had her fill of the camera.

There used to be a brownstone cemetery on the little strip of land she's crossing, she knows from Gallo. Holding onto tree branches, she makes for a saddle-shaped rock carved with a date: 1871. She brushes off a snowcap and sits on the rock, hoping it isn't a headstone they'd forgotten to relocate to a local church back when quarry business trumped burial grounds. Out of the corner of her eye, she sees Eve stumble, then recover. "Careful." She restrains herself from shouting the word, whispering it instead, then forces herself to look away from Eve, down toward the lake below, perfected by distance, pearl on crystal. Closer to the edge of the cliff, there is a rock shaped like breasts, with a cleavage down the middle that people, kids probably, have stuffed crushed candy wrappers and other debris inside. She wants to stand behind it and peer through the cleavage at the lake, but her insides collide and drop and pull her back. She's forced to look at the lake from the saddle rock.

Taffy, she thinks, wouldn't have been daunted. He'd have taken a dive off this cliff and survived if he hadn't been shot first. "Where do you live?" Arm had asked him once. He must have been nine years old, she remembers, because she had just turned thirteen. Taffy, of course, was somewhere in his mid-twenties, although he looked and acted younger. Her periods had begun that year, arriving unpredictably and lasting too long. The three of them, Taffy, Arm and Rose, had been sitting in the breezeway after Arm's lesson. Rose had crept in toward the end of it and sat on a chair covered with a white chenille bedspread of her mother's, cheerfully sprigged with rosebuds. She had listened while pretending to read a woman's magazine, *McCall's* it must have been, full of makeup and detergent ads, and continued to flip the pages as quietly as she could with sweaty hands. At some point she felt a warm trickle, which she tried to control by squeezing foreign parts of herself, not wanting to leave the room.

She had looked at Taffy furtively, seeing Arm's profile elongated and honed in his. Taffy's hands cradled the back of his head and his elbows were pale olive and poignantly sharp, the fine black hair on his arms gleaming. This must have been after he had moved on to methadone from heroin. The anger in his eyes had been replaced by friendly mockery.

"I live in a tree," said Taffy. Then he had looked directly at Rose and smiled at her and winked. They had looked steadily at one another, and all through it, until Rose broke their gaze, she had been convinced that Taffy knew how it was with her, that she was in the middle of having a female accident, staining her mother's white bedspread. Then Taffy had laughed, reached out and grabbed Arm, and began tickling him, giving Rose a chance to escape. But she could not move. Arm and Taffy had gamboled for a while, poking, throwing fake punches, while Rose looked on in misery. She had touched her face and let the magazine slip off her lap before fleeing from the room, menstrual blood trickling down one of her legs.

In between some pines are patches of snow shaped like little continents. Eve stands on Antarctica, taking pictures of something that isn't the lake. Rose cranes. She sees Eve aiming the camera toward the parking area or the oil drums. Whatever it is, Rose thinks it's time they left. She clambers down through clots of snow, sand and mud to where Eve is shifting her position, readying herself for the next shot. Eve is startled when her mother puts her hand on her shoulder and she nearly slips, but Rose pulls her back and they crash on a pine branch. They thrash together, trying to loosen themselves from the branch, which has spared them from muck and unforgiving surfaces, stone and crushed beer bottles, but something is wrong.

Eve struggles to pull something, a jagged stone, out of her hip pocket. "No broken bones?" Rose asks. It's her fault, she thinks, it is always her fault. She laughs nervously, while Eve makes a childish, truculent sound. When her mother tries to tickle her, she slaps her away and runs down toward the car, leaving the camera where it lies. It stutters out a tired, mechanical noise. Broken, thinks Rose, then remembers it makes that noise when a roll is finished.

She is tired herself, with blades of afternoon sun suddenly slashing her eyes, making her feel emotionally overexposed. It is like this with her always, she thinks, running to enfold and embrace what turns out to be a shut door. She knows what adolescent girls are; she had been one herself, with all of the feelings, none of the rights. She snags the camera and trudges down to the car, picking her way carefully around brown streams full of twisted debris, Styrofoam cups and plastic bags that persistent sun is freeing from weeks of snow.

Eve is sitting in the car with the door open, knees up with her arms around them. Get your dirty boots off the seat, Rose is about to say, before she sees that Eve has taken her socks and the hated gumboots off and laid them on the floor of the car. Her feet are pale and lissome, smooth as soap, delicately carved by genetics Rose doesn't share. They're the slender feet of Randall's side, Strang feet.

"You ruined my jeans," accuses Eve. She still has her accent from the slow, sloppy South, thinks Rose, which melts her diction. Rose can see she's been crying, sulking, but isn't sure whether sympathy will extinguish or fire up her temper. She sees the muddy mess along the thigh of Eve's jeans, which they'd purchased weeks ago at Sears on sale, relieved, both of them, to find an affordable pair they could agree on. Practical but tight. Too tight, Rose had thought then, but she had compromised. As she has always compromised. "I'm sorry," she says simply. The quarry lake, brittle with sunlight, bites into her eyes. Suddenly the engine and pump noises stop, and silence thuds around her until she hears the miniature sound of coughing and talking from the workmen across the street.

The stick Eve had been using is on the hood of the car. When Rose pushes it off, she notices. Words, half-melted, have been incised in the snow crust. "WE SEEN YOU."

The warning amuses Rose at first. Surely, she thinks, these aren't her daughter's words. Despite the slang Eve has begun to use, her grammar, at least, is impregnable. Some kids, low life, must have been here. *Low life.* No, she corrects her thoughts, disadvantaged kids. Children, who, unlike my child, don't know any better. "Did you see any kids?" she asks. She tries to keep her voice cool and sunny, nonchalant, revealing none of the middle-aged fluster she feels, but Eve turns away as Rose starts up the car. I only manage to provoke, to inspire mutiny, she thinks. The car splits the silence between them, crunching down on ice-slivered puddles. She argues with herself: I should sit her down and make her talk to me. When *I* was her age. But she wouldn't wish that on her daughter.

She wishes she were better at play, at aimless, genial, easy talk. Perhaps if she could loosen up a little, lighten up, the way Randall had urged, her daughter would come back to her. Randall had always been at her to lower her standards and join the human race. "Relax!" Relaxation was held up by him as some kind of triumph, a virtue, when she knew it was likely the opposite. Even if it weren't, she can't relax, not in this world.

As she pulls out, guiding the car carefully around the vivid wreckage of thawed ice and sawn rock, she tells Eve to buckle her seatbelt.

9 / Eve

A pair of keys is all it was. One is gold, but not real gold, how could it be? Still, a pretty key, the old-fashioned kind, with a handle shaped like a heart and a slender pin. And attached to it by a ring is a smaller key, steel and squat, with a tube at the end. She likes the way they look together, fat and skinny.

She had lifted them off the cold floor of the locker room. Afternoon sun through the high, wired windows had made them sparkle. She had been on the floor with the rest of them, grubbing around for her gym clothes. Man-sized navy tee shirts, baggy white shorts, so ugly they left them balled up in their lockers, growing ripe with their smells and their grime. All winter, nearly everyone had forgotten to bring them home to be laundered, until Ms. Camp, the gym teacher, dumped the contents of their lockers on the floor, saying they should all be ashamed. Gym clothes were supposed to be laundered every week. Their clothes smelled like feet and armpits "and I won't say what else," scolded Ms. Camp, who is shorter than most of them, with a large, naked, frowning face, and who wears a silver whistle on a chain. So they had sat on their bottoms sorting out their laundry, every last one of them, avoiding each other's eyes. While hunting for hers, Eve had found the keys near a child-sized wooden desk that Ms. Camp uses. Lucky charms, she had thought, scooping them up.

She has taken other things from school. A pale pink comb specked with glitter she found on the floor of the cafeteria (and soaped and scrubbed later); a colored pencil, unused, but with tooth marks;

someone's abandoned action figure, a Hercules, ugly and contorted (she had later discarded it). Lost money, pocket change. They all took that when they could. Nice girls like Jill Rathbone, mean ones like Connie Dukas and boys. Eve had found nickels, dimes lying in the slot of the snack machine just outside the gymnasium doors. But these keys are different, she knows. Different from typewriter keys and her other junk. She has only one other key and it unlocks her diary.

She should never have taken them. And Connie must have seen, or one of the other two. What else would they want with her? They had been there at the quarry, she had spotted them and tried taking their picture, and they have been staring her down whenever they get a chance, in the bus, and lately in the school corridors. Which means, she guesses, that she is being stalked. They have a masculine presence, large and abrupt, bursting into laughs that are either hoots or long wheezes. The last time she'd passed them in the hall, Connie had poked a finger down her throat and gagged. The other two had banged a locker with their fists, which made Eve jump. A teacher had stuck her head out of a door and demanded names, writing them down. "You, too," she had said to Eve sternly. That was how Eve had learned who the other two were. Sisters, with flirty names like after-dinner drinks: Brandy and Bailey Halen.

She would put an end to it all by returning the keys. Leave her dirty gym clothes in her locker and go back for them with a special pass from her art teacher, who could be lenient, even lax, if not pushed too far. Then she would put the keys back where she'd found them.

In the bus, things are back to normal, with Mr. Drake rumbling up hills and down narrow, twisty lanes amid chaos. At one stop a boy puts his foot out and a bigger boy trips. He swears and gives the smaller boy a shove, which leads to missile attacks of pencils and spitballs, until Mr.

Drake stands up unsteadily and yells something unintelligible. "Suck my ass!" the boys blast, some of them standing and rocking in place the way Mr. Drake does.

Eve shuts it all out by pulling up her hood and closing her eyes. There is a dark closet inside of her, and it is full of shoes. She tries them on with one half of her mind while the other half thinks about the keys. It dawns on her that she doesn't have to return them after all. She could bury them in the woods in back of her house. Or just throw them in someone's trash receptacle. But she realizes she can't do this. The keys are as precious as money, dead serious, not to be thrown away.

When they reach Connie's stop, Connie is missing, but Brandy and Bailey stump up the bus steps, taking their sweet time finding seats, pausing to raise their fists and pound the palms of other pierced friends. Like celebrities, they have an audience in the boys, who hoot and make obscene noises.

Eve can't remember which of the sisters is which. Both have dead-black hair and pasty skins, and they're short and squat with broad, low foreheads, Goth eyes and snub noses that make them look like babydolls whose faces have been pushed in. The rest of them is the usual black jeans and black man-sized leather jackets with logos. One has Red Door Roadhouse and the other has Coors Beer. Whatever Connie has done to her body, Brandy and Bailey have done to theirs, hickeys on their necks, gauges in their ears, rows of studs packed tightly into their auricles, in their tongues and hidden places Eve is glad not to see. One of them rolls up her pants to show off a new tattoo of ants marching up her leg. "Ooh, that must have stung," says a girl with a nose ring. "Nah," says Brandy or Bailey. "It only took two hours." A boy says, "The ones on her ass must have took all day." Jeering, snorting. Brandy or Bailey stands over him, grabs his lank, silky hair hard and yanks out enough to nauseate Eve. "That's for being a dickhead," she says.

By the time the bus unloads them at school, Eve has a full-blown sour stomach. No breakfast on top of all that commotion and the sickening, torn-out clump of hair. At the pit of it all are the keys. She sits in homeroom with her head down, hugging her midriff to purge herself of stomach pangs. When the girl in back of her taps her on the shoulder and hands her a note, she thinks it must be from Connie and opens it. "Pass it to Brian, moron," the girl hisses, and Eve realizes that she has once again trespassed, skidding past the invisible lines her peers can see. No wonder she's friendless here. Connie wasn't even on the bus, and she isn't in Eve's homeroom. Eve passes the note to a freckled, indifferent boy with braces.

She feels hot and cold and mad at herself during her morning classes. Most people would just keep the keys and forget all about it. Toss them in the quarry if they liked. In her history class, her empty stomach has passed the point of pain and feels like a negligible part of her, an ear lobe or a toe. She thinks, one more class until gym, then lunch, then art class. The teacher is talking about Pompeii, which she has already read about in last year's history class, when she lived in the South. How was nine-one-one-oh-one like the volcano of 79 AD? What, if any, were the warning signs of both disasters? The teacher is Mr. Warner, wearing a purple bow toe with tiny yellow ducks. Jill Rathbone, a nervous girl with a plague of acne across her forehead, is scribbling away in her notebook instead of raising her hand, the way she normally does.

People died in buildings they expected to be safe in," blurts Eve. She hasn't raised her hand, yet Mr. Warner looks at her and nods. This causes Eve to have misgivings; because of her accent, loosening up her tongue is risky. A comedian near her, Blaine Kendall, mimes the way she sits with her knees pressed together and hands clasped tight.

"So," says Mr. Warner, "what made the buildings in Pompeii safe? What made the twin towers safe?" Lost, blank faces all around. The classroom is silent, yet these are mostly smart kids, the studious, obedient ones and therefore, Eve thinks, maybe not so smart. Her face feels swollen with embarrassment, the hot, reckless desire to relieve tension, knowing she is responsible. There is no answer to such a question, she thinks, because no building, no home is safe. Water seeps through cracks and causes bubbles, then bulges and holes. Fire eats up everything and ash fills lungs. People make mistakes and cover them up. She knows.

But she can't drum up the words to express her thoughts. "Because," she murmurs, knowing Mr. Warner has lost interest in her. He is looking over her head and pointing to someone else, a terse, skinny Asian boy, Ko Phuong, who talks about Pompeii's serial misfortunes, the earthquakes it survived before being buried in twelve layers of volcanic ash. "People did not die of suffocation," he says precisely. "They were baked to death. Even in the buildings." No one laughs at Ko, Eve thinks, the way they would have laughed if she had recited these facts. They sense, in him, a deadpan taste for disaster. But he doesn't talk about the towers, the people who jumped out of them to escape, the ash that got carted away, the melting point of steel. Or stranger facts that she's overheard Uncle Arm tell Momma. *Explosions. Implosions. Transactions.* She doesn't understand much of it.

Gym class is a disaster of its own because Connie shows up for it, along with the other two. She hadn't been on the bus, but here she is, in the only class she has in common with Eve. Everyone goes to the gym, you simply have to show up in what they make you wear. Eve looks for cracks of opportunity to return the keys, but someone is always hanging around, watching. After she changes out of her sweater and jeans into her gym shirt and shorts, she stuffs the locker with her school clothes, with the keys beneath her balled-up sweater.

And then comes an opportunity. After the usual sit-ups and running in place and a long, punishing volleyball game that the sportier girls dominate, one of them, Brooke Moore, comes out with a copious nosebleed. This isn't discovered in the gym, but later, in the locker room, while they're removing their shoes and shooting their mouths. Girls gather around her to stare and give unwanted advice to Ms. Camp. "Stand back," she warns. "Unless you want to scrub out every commode in this room." She calls the toilets "commodes," which Eve likes, because where she comes from, that is what polite people call them.

Ms. Camp pages the school nurse, then sits Brooke down on a stool, bending her head back while Brooke holds a towel to her nose. Brooke is a leggy, suntanned girl with breasts and that kind of pure, straight, beach hair that falls in place without a comb. Everyone covets her hair, dyed and striped purple along the ends, plus a new color every week. Eve covets her breasts and the tan Brooke gets in a salon owned by her aunt. And now they all want to bleed from the nose the way she does, to be tipped back and held tight by someone, even if it's just Ms. Camp.

Girls crowd around looking, despite Ms. Camp's blustered orders, standing there in sweaty, dorky gym clothes, when they should be undressing and showering. The air is heavy with body heat and Ms. Camp says to move away and give Brooke some breathing space. "Whoa, whoa!" she keeps shouting, as if they're horses. Jill Rathbone is holding Brooke's hand and two maternal, brown-nosing girls Eve doesn't like are offering big wads of brown paper toweling from the dispenser in the locker room, hanging over Brooke until she practically falls off her stool. "Whoa!"

shouts Ms. Camp, then plugs the whistle in her mouth and blows, which causes several girls to shriek, their voices careening and bouncing off the high ceiling. This provokes a lot of shushing and more chatter, with girls clapping their hands over other girls' mouths.

Another group of girls hangs around like a cloud of gnats, whispering. One of them, Molly Flume, looks as if she's on the verge of tears or rage, her hands clenched, eyes rolling and lids fluttering, though making a big production out of things is, Eve knows, normal for her. *Drama queens* is what Ms. Camp calls them, girls giving themselves over to crying and gossip, to endless rounds of back-stabbing, break-ups and reunions. Eve is glad she isn't one of them, but fears she could be lured in. Molly had been at her house once and told her secrets about other girls that Eve had found strangely satisfying.

Through all of this, Connie, Brandy and Bailey are leaning against a shower stall door watching, silent but snotty. Mean. You could see it in their eyes, they're enjoying the blood, which is the only reason why they're hanging around with the others. Now and again, one of them, Brandy or Bailey, leans over and utters something that sends them both into dry heaves of laughter. Connie just stands there, rangy and pale with that screaming red hair, cracking her knuckles, but mostly just looking around with her own kind of superiority, of knowing more than the rest of them about blood and bloodshed. Brooke's nostrils are plugged with blood, which keeps chugging out all over the towel and Ms. Camp whenever she tries to sit up. But a nosebleed must be nothing, Eve thinks, to someone who'd been under a needle as often as Connie. To someone with a knife.

Eve watches them from the edge of the crowd, waiting for her moment, then ducks around toward her locker, thinking she could slip the keys out and put them back under Ms. Camp's desk without anyone seeing. She eases the locker handle up carefully, but her own careless habits rat her out, the door catching on something. She jerks the metal door open with a clash, and a gumboot drops out. The whisperers turn around and look. And Connie's eyes are on her, she knows at once. Eve's heart hammers her throat; she is sweating, seeking refuge near the whisperers, unsure of what to do.

There would have been too little time anyway, it turns out, because the school nurse marches in and takes over with Brooke, stridently ordering everyone to get dressed, there would be no showers, just get dressed and move on to the cafeteria. Eve stuffs her gym clothes in her locker with the keys.

During lunch, which is pizza, they're all monitored and head counts are taken. Afterwards, it turns out the lenient art teacher is home with a cold. A substitute sprawls in her chair, a pit-faced youngish man who is wise to everyone, making them all watch a video on Vincent Van Gogh while he stares into his cell phone. So Eve doesn't ask to be excused to fetch her dirty clothes.

In language arts, there is a test, then a kind of game. Whoever quotes a line correctly from the poem *Ozymandias* wins two points toward the grade. Jill Rathbone raises her hand; *The lone and level sands stretch far away,* she quotes correctly. A few others raise their hands and win. Eve knows the poem, has memorized it, but offers nothing, resentful of the bribe and the snare of competition. Ashamed of her accent. In math, all she can think about is Ms. Camp opening lockers, hunting for left-behind clothes and hurling them on the floor. The key would fall out and Ms. Camp would know. Eve wheedles a pass for the girl's lavatory in the middle of a math quiz, her bladder burning, but there are eyes everywhere, teachers, a hall monitor. She stumbles in her gumboots.

It isn't until everyone is lining up for buses that Eve decides. She waits until the noise of engines grinds out voices and the crowd is thick with dodging, pushing bodies and bobbing heads. Then she rushes to the gym locker room, looking sideways but not looking back.

If someone is there, she'll peel down the hall and hide in the custodian's closet or a classroom. She opens the heavy locker room door gradually. Grayness, emptiness, a sudden layer of chilly air. The walls are bleak as the end of the world, echoing the drip of a faucet and the squelch of her gumboots. She smells cigarette smoke (stale or recent?), which alarms her at first. Smoking is against the rules except in a teacher's lounge in the basement, but Ms. Camp sneaks her smokes in the locker room, everyone knows, cracking open the high windows.

The custodian's cart is pushed against one wall, and on another, a long, smudged mirror over a bench reflects a girl too short for her jacket and the backpack she's carrying, with hair that levitates around her head, clinging to her hood from static electricity. Eve ignores her reflection, heads straight for her locker, and with shaking, cold hands clears out her clothes, groping in the back of her locker for the keys and groping again. Her lungs ache where her heart pounds, which starts a brilliant tingle in her ears. She shakes out her gym shirt, her shorts, turning out the pockets, then works her hands deep into her sneakers, thinking *oh God, oh please.*

But the keys aren't there. It takes a minute to understand what this means. Someone has removed them. Someone, she thinks, could be Ms. Camp—but her thoughts are snuffed out by footsteps and a shock of fluorescent light.

At first, she thinks the man in the doorway is a tramp, dressed like a lumberjack in a red plaid vest. But it's the custodian; Mr. Keith is what he's called. She isn't sure whether Keith is his first or last name.

Mr. Keith squints and looks at her hard. He has a long, sour face, purplish like a sponge dipped in grape juice, framed by gray hair with wet-looking grooves made by a pocket comb. He's gaunt, with a sagging stomach, and wears jewelry—a pierced hoop earring and a gold chain with a medallion around his neck—that does not match the rest of him. His mouth is screwed up in a permanent look of disgust. Eve assesses him in the mirror. He's holding something in his left mirror hand, which is his right real hand. The keys, she thinks, but it isn't the keys. It's a cigarette lighter, and in the pocket of his vest is a package of cigarettes, *sthgiL oroblraM.*

"I must be seeing things," he says. Eve feels safer where she is, hunched down on the floor.

"Must be a ghost or a kid. If it's a kid, you better tell me what you're doing."

Eve is aware that her face is red, guilty. "Nothing," she says. She stifles two urges, to laugh and to pee, aware that her body, her face are her enemies.

"You better run fast if you don't want to miss the bus."

Mr. Keith has a canine voice, blunt and booming, but his eyes fidget like a rabbit, dodging Eve, looking to her left and right. For someplace to hide, Eve thinks. He reminds her of one of Daddy's friends. She knows that she isn't supposed to encounter, alone, an unrelated adult male about to light up a cigarette in a locker room. It's, in a way, worse than what she has already done, entering the locker room after school hours.

She pushes her gym clothes into her pack, and she runs. She runs in the dumb gumboots that Momma has made her wear, which are not made for running, which stub on the floor like big toes. When she turns around to look, her charged hair crackles across her face and into her mouth, and although she can't see Mr. Keith, she thinks she can hear him laughing. *You better run fast.* Down the long hall, past a display of sports trophies, past a muddy entrance hall, through swinging doors to the bleach-smelling cafeteria where chairs are upside down on long tables. She nicks one of the chairs, which catches her in its metal legs like horns.

She misses the bus anyway. Barely audible now, the distant caravan has broken up, toy cars between toy buses. She will either have to take the late bus home, which means sitting in a roomful of jokers and slackers serving their detentions, or walk. She decides to walk home, a half-hour away by foot.

Frail flakes and sequins of snow whirl around her. More mud than snow underfoot now, cracked and cratered, with underlying tatters of frozen leaves from last fall, and over it all is the coarse red sand that the snow trucks have spread. *The lone and level sands stretch far away.*

The temperature has plunged again, hardening the mud. She finds a stick and pokes the mud savagely, then tosses her stick in the road and sets out. For the time being, she thinks, she'll wear her hood.

The middle of February is raw, harsher than snowy January, harder than the rain he knows will come. It sinks a cold knife in his back while the sky disarms him with guileless, pale blue enamel. Easter egg blue, he thinks, and wonders if he should buy one of those kits for dyeing eggs. It would be something to do with Eve, if she'd give him a chance. This, of course, seems unlikely. When she had finally arrived home from school the other day, it was dark and she was damp, up to her knees, shivering, angry. Angry because, it seemed, he had been there waiting for her.

He had tried to be cool, offhand about it, although he'd been on pins and needles all that afternoon, privately pacing, entering her tiny bedroom and standing there, looking for he knew not what. He'd called the school, the bus company. He wasn't sure whom else to call. She had no friends he knew of, and Rose was out cleaning. "Did you fall in the river?" he had joked when she finally stumbled in, out of breath, and she had shot him a look of poison before slamming her bedroom door. Everything too large in scale for ordinary talk, he thinks, requiring cartoon noises, Booms, Whacks and Bangs. The curse of youth, of rawness. He had brought her his own comforter, standing there, tapping her door lightly, but she had remained shut in. He had left the comforter near her door with a dinner tray. Broccoli quiche, his own, buttered slices of homemade wheat bread, salad, a glass of chocolate milk. Plain food. She had eaten the bread, except for the crusts, and the milk was gone, but she'd left the rest for him to carry away.

Today, he's in the local dime store buying space heaters for each of them. Of course it isn't a *dime* store, it's called a dollar store. Despite the salvaged appearance of the merchandise under bright lights, nothing is a dollar anymore. The heaters alone cost him over one-hundred dollars, but he throws in the Easter egg kit anyway, conned by the happy memory of decorating eggs as a child. The whisper and tap of eggs in the pan, the lovely pink, aqua, lavender and yellow blurs on the eggshells, except where he'd painted them with wax. Stripes or polka-dots or crosses. His sister's patterns had rivaled his, which he had taken as much delight in as his own artlessness. It was fun, simple and dispensable, never to be experienced on a playing field or in a concert hall.

He plugs the heaters in at home, tests them a while, then unplugs them, stowing them in his basement room. He'll present them tonight when both of them are home. He has planned a night off and a day shopping for ingredients that seem to have been banned from local grocery shelves. For this expedition, Rose has loaned her car. "How will you get around?" he had asked, and she'd said, don't worry, if they wanted their houses cleaned, they could damn well give her a lift. Apparently, someone had, before breakfast.

The woods out back look arthritic. Now that a more vindictive cold has set in, he can almost feel sorry for the trees, an elderly confusion of mousy, barbed wire claws. He feeds the birds and is repaid in grateful squawks, pecks and silvery three-toned bursts. Mir-a-cle, mir-a-cle, mir-a-cle. He and Rose had been leaving bread crusts, suet and sunflower seeds on the roof of her car, but now that the snow has melted, he relocated the lost feeder, pried it out of ice and hung it from a dogwood branch. Even with his boots on he can feel the ground, like corrugated steel.

The cold takes shape differently on the highway, the rock ledge on both sides shouldering heavy cascades of bottle-green ice as if winter had snapped its fingers, he thinks, and the waterfalls had frozen in place. And how appropriate. Everything about where he is going has frozen, it seems, in time. To his mind, at least. *Rockton.* Home of the giant sub. Well, actually, nuclear submarines. It seems impossible that he could ever have survived adolescence in that town. And yet, here he is.

Mrs. Cauliflower, whose tightly packed, cement-floored grocery is his destination, had been one of the reasons. She had funded his housing at Julliard, making his narrow escape from Rockton possible. Childless, she had been a benefactor to other kids, mostly of Arab descent, with musical talent. In another way, however, she had helped seal his fate as a teenage misfit, embarrassing him, swooping down, kissing his cheeks, gushing Arabic in front of his peers. She had supplied half of the Middle Eastern community in Rockton and surrounding towns with their spices, bulghur, tinned grape leaves, halva and olives in his growing-up years. She adored him. "Habibi," she still calls him. "I could eat you up!" she would shriek when he was young, offering the nut-filled, honey-drenched delicacies that were set apart in a refrigerator with a sliding door. Ignoring Rose at first. But eventually begrudging her a sugar-haired lump molded from dates or a shell-shaped cookie dipped in confectionary sugar that flew up in tiny squalls whenever you took a bite. Rose would devour hers quickly, suspicious that she was the one Mrs. Cauliflower really intended to eat up, like Hansel in the fairy tale.

Arni adjusts his CD player, which spins on the passenger seat. Rose's car radio had been dying off and on long before she bought the car. Before setting out today, he had loaded up on music. He doesn't believe in patching together homemade CDs. He believes in buying CDs and fishing for tunes, arias, movements. This isn't easy while driving, but Arm manages. He selects "Embryonic Journey" by Jefferson Airplane, then several piano selections by Samuel Barber and Erik Satie. Diaphanous quartets by Germaine Tailleferre. He labors through portions of *Peer Gynt,* but gives it up once he approaches I-95. For this stretch of the journey, he snaps in Beethoven's *Ode to Joy,* then a CD by Simon Shaheen playing the oud. A labyrinth of Middle Eastern sound, dissonant to the western ear, but not to Arm's, which was attuned by Taffy to the quarter-tone scale as well as the diatonic.

He checks the speedometer, slowing from sixty-five mph to sixty, because one never knew. He has never received a speeding ticket, never experienced a run-in with the police, a record he credits to caution. He's an easy target with his long hair, swart good looks, and all that lies beneath. He dodges the arrow by slowing down. But, of course, this is not the same as blending in. Cars roar past him.

Crossing the bridge to Rockton, he is stuck behind a car that pokes along at 50 mph and, at first, he wonders if the ancient, slump-shouldered driver is Mrs. Cauliflower. But as he passes cautiously, using his blinkers, he sees it is only an old man wearing a hair net. Odd, he thinks. But no odder than Mrs. Cauliflower.

Her real name is Zillah Khouri. Sallow, lumpy skin and a dumpy shape conspired to suggest the secret other name to Rose when she was young, and she'd passed it along to Arm. For decades, Mrs. Cauliflower has worn a hairnet and a man's shirt with a bleached butcher's apron over it, settling into a witchy ugliness that was at the same time masculine. It had been good for business. Women of his mother's generation felt intimidated by yet physically superior to her, which kept them loyal. And now Arm. Hartford is closer to Swannboro by miles and out of it has sprung two trendy Arab groceries run by a group of svelte, somber-faced Egyptians and Syrians. Yet Arm makes the trip to Rockton, to ill-favored Mrs. Cauliflower. It's a sacrifice more of his sanity than his time. But he owes her.

Rockton emerges like a crocodile lying in wait beneath the bridge. Rather, its industries do, a submarine manufacturer and a chemical plant hunkering down, bristling and snapping with cranes, pulleys, barges and rusting, scrambled structures that appear abandoned. Arm avoids looking. The river has been encroached upon and filled up over many years, its shores supporting a complex sprawl.

He drives through the main part of town to avoid the chemical plant, which he associates with a foul smell. Long gone now, the smell used to hang over his school bus route and fill his nostrils, until it became a metaphor for all he hated about his childhood. The smell was Rockton itself, the power to subvert beauty to venal ends, the construction of death machines and lucrative chemicals. The power to dominate and snuff out sensibilities. He smells and tastes it now, despite the detour, and rummages around in his coat pocket for a lozenge.

Mrs. Cauliflower's shop is squeezed in between a beauty parlor and package store. The neighbors have changed many times over, but the grocery remains the same, crowded and redolent, with the same cash register up front and old album covers, tacked on the walls, displaying fez-capped oud players and a belly-dancer with a mole above her cleavage. The store sign is hand-painted, bearing a single flourish in Arabic with the English translation beneath it, *Season*. Of course, the Arabic word has countless other meanings in different contexts. *Decouple. Disembody.* He figures that Mrs. Cauliflower knows this far better than he, as she makes a little money on the side as a translator. Mushy love poems, letters between distant relatives, he imagines.

When he enters the store, she is arguing in Arabic with a large-nosed, pop-eyed man who is gesticulating wildly, wielding an arrogant intensity. He reminds Arm of Picasso. Arm's Arabic is vestigial, so he can't make out the gist of their disagreement. Is it about politics or the price of eggs? Only the gutter language is decipherable, mostly *Whore* and *Motherfucker,* terms that Mrs. Cauliflower enjoys hurling. Arm makes himself inconspicuous, examining foreign-made cans of tahini, letting the lively, piquant fragrances of the grocery supplant the remembered odor of Rockton.

When Mrs. Cauliflower sees him, she explodes into English hyperbole. *Darling, Most Beloved, My Brilliant Boy. You have come, I knew you would come! Darling Habibi!* The man throws his hands up in the air and shuffles over to one of the aisles while Arm is engulfed by fragrances, effusions and Mrs. Cauliflower. The top of her head comes up to his chest.

Mrs. Cauliflower has shrunk over the years and her brown eyes are diluted, like olives in oil, but otherwise her appearance is the same. The hairnet pulled tight over white hair with shiny, shell-pink scalp showing through. The immaculate apron over khaki workmen's clothes. A face that is the mask of tragedy, destroyed not by time but by genetics and bad luck. Ill-favored. Arm hugs her with genuine affection, wishing she would curtail the flattery, which embarrasses him. It doesn't help that the old man, whom he doesn't know, smirks, and coughs into his hand to draw attention to his smirking. As if he knows something he shouldn't about Arm.

Now Mrs. Cauliflower wants to know where he is playing. And what is he studying? She still asks about his studies despite the almost two decades since he left Julliard. "And when will I receive my front row ticket to Carnegie Hall?" He does what he has always done, dodging her questions with jokes and false modesty. He can't bear to break her heart, and although he won't lie to her outright, he will glissando over facts. He tells her he has regular performance engagements, but doesn't say they are in a bar or that his instrument is an acoustic guitar. She would never understand. She adores what she calls "culture," opera, Shakespearean plays, concerts, and wants tickets, invitations, which he once sent her by post from New York. He says she's too discerning, too demanding a critic now. "I'm afraid I'm several squeaks beneath your standard, dearest."

He begins to shop, Mrs. Cauliflower chattering happily beside him. First the papery, glazed pastries, which she says arrived yesterday. She makes him bend down so she can pop a glistering sweet in his mouth, and he experiences an infusion of joy. "Food of the gods!" she exclaims. He gathers together several cans of tahini, containers of olives, cous-cous, pita bread, baba-ganoush, dried mint, apricots and dates, and a large plastic zip-lock bag filled with zatar, a sage-colored, tart seasoning made of oregano, sesame seeds and crushed sumac. Mrs. Cauliflower always labeled these bags in her lithe Arabic calligraphy, like 2D wrought iron. Her handwriting, her one beauty. In old age she hasn't lost it as her peers have lost theirs. It must be, he thinks, a mild form of revenge. On top of this, of course, she's still alive well into her eighties.

She insists on charging him nothing and they argue back and forth. It's their ritual, which always ends with his giving in, then slipping cash under a crackled paperweight on her countertop. "Age cannot wither you, darling," he quotes pompously on his way out the door after hugs, kisses, promises to visit, and, at least for the moment, he means what he says. She hasn't changed. Any withering happened long before he was born. He wishes he could see her more often, without also having to see Rockton. Because he, too, hasn't changed. He is what he has always been, a bit of a deceiver, a bit of a snob, without wholeheartedly embracing either. Which makes him, he thinks, a bit of a coward.

He drives home with the Shaheen CD on full blast, floating at 55 mph down I-95, despite the temptation to avoid his usual itinerary. Pulling off the ramp to Route 7, however, he spots trouble, flashing police lights and full brakes in the car ahead. He slows to a crawl, poised for the next exit sign, then veers to the right and the road less taken. Lovely, he thinks at first, admiring the postcard views on either side of him, elderly homes with chimneys pluming, red barns, stone fences, frozen topiaries, a clapboard church whose sign invites him to *Awaken.*

He comes to a full stop at the bottom of a hill and observes the strip of road ahead, a corridor walled by pines. Something catches his eye, a figure hunched down in the road. And then he sees that it isn't human, but avian. A wild turkey; actually, a Tom. Nearby a herd of his kind is nervously pacing in the frozen woods. Delightful, Arm thinks, braking to a stop before inching ahead. This seems the only sensible approach. The turkey has taken his stand in the middle of the road for no apparent reason. Americana, Arm thinks, here right in front of him.

Arm admires the enormous fantail, the irate head with its red, swinging sack of wattles. The turkey observes him sideways at first, then struts over, his feathers erect and iridescent. Arm rummages in the glove box for his camera, but apparently Rose still has it from the other weekend. *Drat.* Arm thinks, isn't it always the way, when you most need technology, it either fails you or is in someone else's pocket. He watches the turkey approach slowly as if strained by his burden of plumage, cocking his head and giving Arm a long, malevolent stare. Accusing almost. It's unnerving, but Arm forces himself to note the beauty of his accuser. What he would do for a camera. Then the turkey struts over and pecks hard on the door of the car.

Arm panics. He has read about this happening, but can't remember what the human victim is supposed to do. He looks around for hens or young turkeys, then backs up. But the Tom advances and bullies him, lunging and pecking. Arm begins to sound his horn in short, peevish honks. This provokes the turkey to flap and make a strange, beating sound. Arm edges ahead slowly, but the turkey won't retreat, stretching its neck, ugly really, rippling with ruddy, pimpled flesh, and pecking at the door. Arm is afraid that the other turkeys will charge, but they are passive, hanging back, pacing and flapping in the woods. A few have begun to gobble. The Tom persists, pecking at the door, and Arm bucks the car forward, only to find that he can't free himself from the turkey without destroying him, trampling the exquisite headdress beneath his wheels. And this he refuses to do.

This goes on for several minutes, with Arm honking and edging forward and the turkey assailing the door with his beak, until a truck rumbles up from a side road and idles in back of Arm. As if a bigger toy has been offered, the turkey stalks toward the truck. Arm charges forward and speeds up the road, feeling relieved but ashamed. The whole horrible ordeal could have been avoided if he hadn't been tempted by impatience, by the prospect of a scenic road, a ramble. He should have stuck with the main route. He races to the next highway exit and swerves onward, bringing his speed to 73 mph before he feels safe enough to slow down.

But it's too late. As if it had been waiting for him all along, a state police car flashes him down. Arm is so rattled by the prospect of a speeding ticket that he has trouble rolling down his window. His throat dries up and he has difficulty swallowing. The policeman, D. Mooney, is heavy and poker-faced, speaking into a crackling receiver while taking notes. Or is that a ticket he's writing? He leans over and squints at the front seat. The CD player is still spinning out one of Shaheen's Middle Eastern enigmas. Arm reaches to switch it off, but Mooney isn't listening. He's looking. He looks at Arm's raven pony tail, his old but expensive wool coat, the melancholy black coffee eyes, the sharp, shadowed features. He looks at the exotic groceries on the passenger seat, at Mrs. Cauliflower's Arabic calligraphy. To Mooney, Arm thinks, it must look like the Koran.

"License and registration, please." As Arm hands them over, he knows. "Arthur Guest," the name on his license, has a ring of falsehood, all things considered. And who is "Rose Strang," the name on the registration? My sister, says Arm, but he knows this will not be believed. Mooney assiduously calls him "Sir."

"Sir," he says, "Do you realize you were driving ten miles over the speed limit?"

Yes, says Arm. Yes, I know, Officer, I know. Mooney listens and Arm is encouraged. "There was this aggressive turkey," he says. "It attacked my car. I can honestly say I've never encountered anything like it."

"Please step out of the car, Sir, and place your hands on the hood."

Mooney carefully pats him down. Like many sloppy men, he is meticulous about his job. Then he calls for help, describing Arm as "a suspicious Middle-Eastern-looking male in his forties." He uses code words and numbers for the rest of it. Drugs, car theft and, no doubt, terrorism.

Arm stands there with his legs spread and his hands on the hood. Since Mark's death, he thinks with bitter irony, this is the first time a man has touched him.

11 / Rose

The furnace had stopped working overnight, but, after a few kicks, had started up feebly this morning. She has a call in to the landlord. In the meantime, she and Eve have their space heaters. She's set hers up in the kitchen, so she can work on the quilt, but the heat is too dry and has made her eyes smart. Ice, she thinks, and limps over to the fridge in an Indian-print skirt that drags on the floor, but of course, there are no ice cubes in the yellowing trays. She fills them with tap water, sloshing half of it on the floor en route to the freezer.

She settles for a cold, wet dishrag to soothe her eyes. For warmth, she rubs her hands together like a miser, turning the heater off and on again. Her day had begun at four in the morning, the silent dead cold waking her like a ghost, dragging her downstairs to check the furnace. She had known, even in her half-asleep state, and went about her business quietly in the basement, shaking with cold while checking the boiler and furnace with a flashlight, trying not to awaken Arm. But Arm wasn't in his bed. After that discovery, she had kicked the furnace a few times, and it had cut on. Then, like clockwork, Arm had arrived, sneaking in through the bulkhead. "Where in hell were you when I needed you?" was her first question. They had argued, waking up Eve and after that, no one had gone back to bed. He had offered them the space heaters. It had been good timing, and thoughtful of him, she had to admit.

And yet, he had made her out to sound selfish and small-minded earlier. As if she had no rights at all. As if it were petty of her to worry about *her* car, *her* reputation mixed up in his trouble with the police. It was *her* car, bought and paid for by *her*. All she expected from him was that he treat her property with a modicum of respect. "Bourgeois" he had called her, articulating the word in that way of his, reminding her of all the times he had pumped fuel into *her* car, which was a gas guzzler and a menace to the environment. She had steered him in another direction, calling him a "squatter," going off on tangents about all the other appliances of hers he used, the washing machine, the dryer, the fucking furnace, until they got back to the car, then they had chased around in circles, with her asking questions and him giving her little bites that didn't sound credible. A wild turkey in the road. Something about Al Qaeda and police harassment. It had all seemed paranoid or maybe even a cover-up for driving under the influence. The police had granted him one call, he said, which he'd lavished on Mrs. Cauliflower.

"You should've called *me*. I would've found you a lawyer." That had started it all over again. She had touched her face while picking at him as if he were a blemish. "You needed a lawyer, not that hag. They had *my* car, *my* registration papers. You should have called *me*."

"Mrs. Cauliflower bailed me out," he'd repeated shrilly. "She confirmed who I am and they let me go." Do you mean that you're a famous violinist, she'd asked nastily. *That I'm not a drug dealer or a terrorist.* He had stamped upstairs and she had followed him. He had coughed a few times with his mouth shut, *heck, heck,* then sulkily fussed with his packages, stuffing seasonings, coffee and sweets in the fridge and on the hobbled lazy Susan.

"She knows her way around the cops," said Arm. "She translates for them, since nine-one-one, I mean. Documents, emails. Who'd have thought?" He had shrugged as if it were no concern of his. She had tried jabbing him for more information, and he had begun shouting. He was catching cold, couldn't she hear him coughing for fuck's sake? He needed rest, not another inquisition. That was when Eve had come into the kitchen, sullen and bleary-eyed, wrapped in her comforter. Arm had changed his tune then, offering the heaters. And Rose had accepted them, thanking him, for Eve's sake. Had it been just herself, she would have told him where to shove them.

From Arm's basement comes music that makes no sense to her. Dissonance, chaos, nothing as simple as sadness or love. Music of the mind, like a hoard of educated locusts. Whatever happened to musicals? Gay men were supposed to like them, and he had once, they'd sung duets from *Showboat, Carousel, Oklahoma* when they were kids. *West Side Story,* with her singing the tenor's part because she couldn't strain her voice past a high G, and he wouldn't let her. "You sound like a boy in your lower register," he'd say. "And a cow on top. Don't strain. Never strain."

What did he know about strain? He had never strained. She had strained her whole life; it had been her ticket along with a certain kind of dexterity, she thinks, while mopping the spill on the floor. It had gotten her through community college, waiting on tables, modeling for art classes, swabbing hospital linoleum at night, or living off boyfriends, bartenders mostly, in drafty dumps that were tacky in both senses of the word. One of the boyfriends had painted neon murals, gigantic bananas and grapes, on their bedroom walls. At night the cockroaches would rustle across them as if they were real fruit.

Wanting the apricots and dates Arm brought, she eats instead the last of the breakfast oatmeal congealing in a saucepan. She eats standing up, over the sink, spooning gray lumps in her mouth while staring out of the window. Something in the house is drip-drip-dripping. It seems that in all the places she has lived, there has been the same leak running down different drains.

Maybe she shouldn't have been so hard on him. She had been freezing and her foot hurt from kicking the furnace, which lit her up. She *is* grateful for the space heater. It means not having to wear a bathrobe or outerwear over her indoor clothes. She had dressed herself in a droopy Indian print skirt over fleece sweats and long johns, with two thermal shirts and a bunchy brown cardigan sweater topped by a plum shawl she'd knitted, the clean underside out. Randall had liked her this way, loose and sloppy, menial-looking, but she doesn't like herself.

She scrapes back her chair noisily and limps to the stove where she boils water in a pan, pours some in a mug and adds sugar. They've run out of teabags and she doesn't want to brew a pot of Arm's gourmet coffee. Hot sweet water is enough; the mug warms her hands. She catches a glimpse of her foreshortened image in Arm's fancy chrome coffee maker, troll-faced in her fat cardigan and baggy skirt. She looks like a refugee.

Had things gone her way, she would have dressed in narrow suits and returned to work half-time in the museum, instead of wasting her eyes and hands on Randall's filthy flying carpets. But her qualifications were always radically under or marginally over. She lacked the year abroad that her betters took for granted. She lacked confidence and whatever makes people want to keep someone around. "You try too hard," Randall had put it.

She can hear her brother down there, coughing to himself, the complaint of old box springs as he gets up to change the music. This time it's a scratchy vintage recording of a virtuoso cellist. Better, she thinks. At least there's a heart behind it.

She had seen Eve off to school, boiling oatmeal, adding the honey Arm had brought. There was no milk. For once, Eve had eaten her breakfast, but Rose had to keep her mouth shut over the way Eve was dressed. A plaid flannel shirt that was actually a pajama top. The same jeans again with chalky rings around the knees, as if she'd been wading in a salt marsh. Not that Rose is setting much of an example. She had kept silent even when Eve didn't zip up her jacket and her mittens fell out on the icy porch. By the time Eve returns, they'll be frozen stiff, which will teach her a lesson. Rose had washed the breakfast dishes roughly, clapping bowls on the drain board and chipping one of them. It didn't matter. Everything was already chipped.

The quilt demands precise, tiny decisions. She had laid it out in sections, using the lap quilt method, which allows her to pick away at little blocks of her design, enclosed in hoops. Each block has been pieced, sewn, batted and backed, ready to be worked with stitching and appliquéd figures. She has hooped several blocks already and works them a little at a time, hopping around, restless yet punctilious. Pick, pick, pick. She needles the cloth like an addict on a vein.

Tiny is her preferred scale. As a schoolgirl, she had sewn clothes only for dolls, never herself. The same sewing machine she had used then, her deceased mother's jet 1945 Singer Featherweight, is on the kitchen table, ready to add its high alto hum to the house music. She had left most of her quilts behind when she moved north, so it's her only real valuable, gleaming jet animated with gold lettering, like a beloved black cat perched there, its eyes shining.

A seam is off and a corner puckered in one of the blocks. She pulls out thread, re-pins, lowers the Singer's foot and races out pure, satin lines, then takes her sweet time raising the foot and clipping the thread, knotting it by hand. She had always wondered why Randall had chosen her Smith Corona typewriter for destruction instead of the Singer. It had been a rare piece of luck, one of his few drunken sacrificial rites that had put her on top. The chattering body had died; the singing soul had risen. It had given her the kick she needed to leave.

Humming to herself, she clamps the repaired block in a hoop and rummages in a basket for her thimble. She's always forgetting it, paying the price in blood. The needles for her art are called 'betweens,' small but sharp on both ends, and she has come to think of quilting as her *between* occupation, between cleaning jobs, between death and life. Her finger capped in its little helmet, she needles a wavering line across the quarry lake.

She had discovered quilting late, during her fourth part-time year at the university. Going there had meant giving up meat, movies, dental appointments, sex. Through a supermarket bulletin board, she had found a small, dry room in a parsonage, rent-free in exchange for cleaning, some cooking and endless dog walking. The room offered what she craved: Warmth, hissed out of the freshly painted white coils of an old-fashioned steam radiator. And privacy, though not enough for the kind of sex partners she tended to attract. Fornicating in a parsonage would have been squalid, even for Rose. The minister's wife, a sweet-natured, Corgi-loving matron, quilted tapestries, formal and florid, on sacred themes. The wife had offered her lessons. It had been a kind of religious conversion, leading Rose to switch her major from journalism to art. The needle liked her hard, calloused hands and she liked the tiny, fairylike instrument, the power of creating counterpane landscapes. It was like having a yard of her own, or a new skin.

Rose sets down her hoop and picks up another, which displays the cliffs in intricate tangrams. She's stitching an undulating line, but loses her rhythm. She teases out thread and begins over, not minding the extra work. It's easier for her to justify time wasted on an art like quilting because so much of it is tedium, a chore. It had taken her seven years to finish her fine arts degree.

She breaks to sip her cup of lukewarm sugar water and survey her work, pacing and fretting, rubbing her hands together. The quilt's color theme is flesh and bone: mauve, beige, olive, umber, rust, a dirty cauliflower cream. Fingernail-pink. All vintage fabric, or remnants she has hand-dyed. Time-consuming, but cheaper than music. Many of the fabrics had come out of her closet. A once seductive peasant blouse, mauve damask, is now one with the quilt. She touches the cloth, touches her face and shivers. The small radius of warmth from the space heater brings her back to the chair.

She can hear Arm moving around in the basement again. Then the unhappy metal creak of the bulkhead. He has gone out to pee in the backyard, she thinks, his way of avoiding her. The plastic pail he set out there for this purpose disgusts her, but it's better than turning her flower beds into a urinal, as Randall had. Peeing in the backyard had been part of his daily routine, standing there where no one could see him but her, a cigarette in one hand and his ding-dong in the other. Fire and rain. And now, here is Arm, doing the same thing, without the fire.

Restless and cold, she rearranges the quilt blocks in a neat pile, shuts the lid on the chaos in her sewing basket, and rifles through her notes, the quarry photos she took with Eve, a library book with the cloth stripped off its spine (*The Complete Poems of Gerard Manley Hopkins*) and several photocopied newspaper articles on Taft Said. Her life-size drawing of the quilt is lying under this, folded. The tracing paper crackles as she pins it to the wall. It seems so small; it *is* small, a bit over one square yard, minus the border. Too small to contain Taffy. Yet not too small for a love song. She leaves a *Gray's Anatomy* illustration of the brain where it is, propped against the candlestick with the one-eyed rooster.

Getting the whorls of a brain into the cliffs had been the easy part, a natural stitching pattern. The idea came from a line in a Hopkins poem she remembered from college English. *O the mind, mind has mountains; cliffs of fall.* On it went, all downhill, plummeting to a tragic end. It had made her think of Taft.

The hard part had been convincing the Stone Circle women to approve her design. At first they had nodded and kept up an edgy, pretentious silence. Then one of them had nudged the woman next to her. "Why is there a violin at the bottom of the quarry?" she had asked. No one had made eye contact with Rose. "Why is the American flag floating in the lake?" asked another, addressing Natalie. Rose had touched her face. "What are those bones doing in the quarry cliffs?" "Whose headstone is that at the top?" One of them had let it be known that her sister-in-law was a quilter.

Rose had opened her mouth and stammered, but in the end didn't have to say very much. Natalie had supplied convincing rhetoric; Rose had simply agreed. *Anyone* can see that these are dinosaur bones, said Natalie. Anyone can see that the headstone is the famous headstone, the one that hadn't been moved to the cemetery. And obviously, the flag in the water suggests Connecticut's maritime history. Rose had nodded, yes. As for the violin, does there have to be a reason for everything? It's lyrical; it's *poetic*; there's real *pathos* in Swannboro's history. Men had died hauling brownstone out of those cliffs! The women had settled back into their chairs. I'm glad we all agree, Natalie had said finally, even though not all of us are qualified art critics. Rose had thanked them solemnly and insincerely. They had given her a small advance, which she cashed the same day. Money, not music, soothes her savage heart.

Flipping around in the library book, Rose finds the Hopkins poem. She admires its broken surface, like a patchwork, gaudy bits threaded with starched swathes and satiny loops. "Frightful, sheer, no man-fathomed," she reads aloud. She sets the book in front of her, reading the poem and rubbing her hands together.

Capping her finger, she begins again, appliquéing red-striped muslin, folded into an origami shape, at one end of the quarry lake. It's an American flag, or a little striped man floating on the lake, it all depends on the eye of the beholder. At one end, where his neck would be, is the field of stars she'd lovingly cross-stitched herself, arranged like a neckerchief.

Her eyes are now bone-dry; she can actually hear herself blink. The sound of snoring comes from downstairs in soft, tidy beats beneath the heavy breathing of the space heater. It's snowing again, slow-dancing flakes twisting down in the dim afternoon light. The cheap kitchen replacement windows rattle and one has begun to go sour, a spidery mist forming. Snowplows are already sanding the road, making her glad Eve will be home before it ices.

Reaching for her mug of cold sugar water, she upends it on the table. It could have been a disaster, but isn't. Only one of the articles on Taft is soaked. A sentence dissolves as she blots it with her rag, but the dry paragraph above makes her put her glasses back on.

"Said had recently been living in the Swannboro trailer park abutting the quarry," she reads. She had missed that somehow. And up further there's something about his clothes. She blots carefully. " … found in Succour Brook, several miles from the quarry. The jacket, shirt, pants, briefs and shoes were all identified as belonging to Said."

Still reading, she cuts, pins, threads her needle clumsily, forgetting her thimble and stabbing herself. She's about to wipe the drop of blood off her finger when she has a covert impulse. Pressing her finger to a corner of the flag/man, she lets her blood seep in.

She goes to work on the headstone, obsessively stitching as she's read books all of her life, hunched over with her nose to the subject, straining. She's cold, her eyes ache and her foot is swollen, but she keeps on. She keeps on, as she must.

12 / Eve

She keeps trying to place her feet in the footprints ahead of her. But the footprints belong to Connie, whose stride is longer. So she settles for getting her feet in just where she can, until it's too hard with the other two in back of her, bumping along, stepping on her heels so that she has to stop and yank up her gumboots. It's a silly game anyway. A child's game.

"Ass wipe," says one of them behind her, although she isn't sure whether the insult is directed at her. Bailey and Brandy have toilet mouths, which they use on each other. Connie says nothing at all, plunging across snow with crooked, forlorn twigs sticking out everywhere. They're in the woods a mile or more from the school, but Eve doesn't know where and doesn't think it's a good idea to ask. She can hear the other two sputtering behind her, laughing at something or, more likely, someone. A hard, glazed patch ahead, smashed where Connie had stepped, makes Eve slip, then it abruptly buckles and caves beneath one of her boots, and she wonders if she might sink, suddenly, down into a hole beneath the path, into a drowned fairyland. But her foot comes loose and she continues to struggle, trying to keep up, using the wake Connie has trampled. Exhaustion and the cauterizing effect of shock prevent her from crying.

Money had been stolen. Everyone had known about it that morning, whispering behind Eve, but only Jill Rathbone had looked at Eve with secret pity when she'd been called down to the Office. Eve had watched her gumboots carry her out of the classroom and over the stampede of muddy footprints in the hall, her bladder burning. Someone ahead of her, a teacher, had on the kind of shoes that clicked in that satisfying adult way. It had made Eve feel left on the wrong side of something.

The place they are going is the quarry, where Connie says they have "business," and if Eve cooperates everything will turn out "good," and if she doesn't, her life won't be worth much, they'll tie her up and leave her there for the boys or the tramps. Eve is relieved there is no mention of the knife. She knows about deals, transactions from Daddy's business: there were things you had to do. There were certain people with whom, when they did you a favor, you had to reciprocate. And Connie had done her a favor.

In the room where they'd waited that morning, there had been a large, raggedy flake of paint hanging down from a crack in the ceiling. Eve had kept her eyes on it, waiting for it to drop and crumble. Now she's keeping her eyes on the treetops, which hold clods of snow that the afternoon sun teases out and drops in bursts of sparkling dust. The sky is spread with those clouds again, the kind that looks like scrambled eggs, and the stiff pallor all around foretells more snow. She's come to read the signs here in the North, the same way she could tell whenever the sky was going to belt out a good hard rain in her old life down South. Of course, it has snowed nearly every day for a week.

They come to an incline where ledge pokes out of the snow and she has to use her numb, bare hands to balance herself. Her mittens are gone, fallen out of her pockets somewhere. At one point she slips and lands hard on her duff, which gets her sworn at and cuffed and shoved around by one of them, until Connie tells them to stop dicking around, there isn't going to be much light left and they don't want to damage the merchandise. She grabs hold of Eve, drags her up and tells her to move.

For a while, Eve gets pushed along in front of them. Seeing a flash of red, she thinks one of her hands is either bleeding or frostbitten. She doesn't want to look because she doesn't want to cry.

When they reach the top of the ledge, they veer toward a blackened area where someone had recently built a fire with charcoal briquettes, leaving beer cans, cigarette butts and the dead remains of a meal in a tarnished pie plate that had been stomped on a few times. Connie pushes at it with her boot and says it isn't burnt-up food. "That's a dead rat," and the other two agree, messing around in the ashes. Brandy pulls out what they think is a carcass, but it falls apart in her hands, no bones, no teeth, just greasy, wet ashes. "It must have stank when they burned it."

"We seen a boy sacrifice a rat last year. Up there." Brandy points to a vague ruin of browning snow with scraggly vines growing over logs that have been rotting there a while, stacked up by someone who never got around to dragging them away. Eve thinks she sees something else, a cross made of sticks, but it could be an optical illusion. There are so many sticks, thorns, roots and vines snapping and twisting up out of the snow like broken springs.

"A bunch of fags come up here, too." Connie makes a gesture that Eve recognizes, of a finger poking at a fist. She says something Eve can't hear to the other two, who snort, then she turns around so that Eve gets a good look at a tattoo of barbed wire that winds around Connie's neck. "Rumpy pumpy!" Brandy is shouting, provoking hoots from Bailey. Their voices climb and clash until Connie snarls at both of them to stop acting like retards.

She had called them retards that morning, too, getting herself on the wrong side of an old person who was writing their names in a book.

"We don't use words like that in this school," the woman had scolded. They'd been sitting in a room outside the Office until they were brought in, one by one, to be questioned, Connie first, then the other two, then Eve. Then Connie and Eve. It hadn't seemed fair to be left sitting there longer than the others, being watched and, she was sure, being lumped in with them. She'd never been in the Office before. She stared down at a rug that was tan with the seams splitting apart and thought about Daddy's shop where the carpets were dirty but complicated and unreal, like paintings.

The principal was Ms. Coatsworth, a woman with good posture whom Eve had previously seen only from a distance, and in a chair too small for him sat a man with bad posture, who was Mr. Keith. Ms. Coatsworth looked different up close, bonier yet bustier, Eve thought. Many teachers in the school as old as Ms. Coatsworth still had that hippie look, but Ms. Coatsworth's short thick hair was white, sitting upright on her head like the fur of an angry dog, over a pair of formal, pessimistic gray eyes. She was the kind of woman who wore pins. A pearl oval gleamed in the folds of her scarf. She smiled briefly when Eve entered the room, which was comforting, until Eve figured out that she smiled when she was angry. Mr. Keith scowled, slouching in his chair with his legs crossed and his stuck-out foot busy, occasionally pulling on an earring or his hangdog face.

Ms. Coatsworth wanted to know why Eve had been in the girl's locker room after hours on Friday. "Why," she had asked, not "If." Eve's excuse about dirty gym clothes didn't seem to satisfy her. Money for varsity sports had been taken from Ms. Camp's strongbox. Did Eve know anything about that? The keys were missing, too.

No, said Eve, she didn't know. Her voice went dry. She shot a look at Mr. Keith, who said nothing. After a while, he took a foil wrapper out of his pocket and folded a stick of gum into his mouth, chewing slowly and glumly with his mouth closed. Eve sat up straight with her hands folded tightly in her lap, but soon they were sweating and there was nothing to wipe them off on but her jeans. The room reeked of peppermint and the school smell.

After a lot of silence, Ms. Coatsworth got up and fetched Connie. They looked bizarre together, Eve thought, Connie with her collection of piercings and tattooed spider webs and barbed wire, with hair like Medusa's from the Greek myth, and Ms. Coatsworth with her upright hair and the ladylike pin. Harsh early afternoon light was beginning to streak through the high windows, making everything appear dusty. Connie squinted and yawned, sitting on a chair with her legs splayed out. Ms. Coatsworth smiled angrily. "I want you to tell me one more time, Miss Dukas," she said. " Are you sure this is the girl you saw take the keys?"

Connie didn't bother looking at Eve. She picked up a Rubik's cube off Ms. Coatsworth's desk and began playing with it. She had long, thin hands, large for a girl her age, with screws tattooed across a few of her knuckles, which you couldn't help noticing as she twisted the cube around and around. Ms. Coatsworth said Connie could sit in silence all day if she liked, but it would have to be in the detention room. Connie gave Eve a snake-eyed look that lasted a few seconds, and Eve sensed that nothing good would come of it. So she was surprised, at first, to hear Connie say she'd made a mistake, it was easy to do that around here, she said, since all the white trash looks the same. "But that chick I saw was fatter than this one."

They've reached a pass where the frozen lake can be seen down below through the trees. And rising up like the faces of Indian chiefs are the cliffs, some of them bearded with ice, unmoved by what's going on beyond or underneath. The English and Dutch had stolen Swannboro from the Indians who were here first, Eve had learned in school. She spots another cross of sticks bound up with what looks like a red rubber band, and knows it's real this time. She wants to stop and look, but Connie pushes her along the path, which veers close enough to the edge that she feels her stomach in her throat. Whatever comes to hand, she grasps, barbed branches and tree trunks, sticks coated with slicks of ice. Connie grabs her hood and steers her forward. Brandy and Bailey had been told to shut their yaps ever since the two of them had screamed about a bear, which had turned out to be some rotten stumps, so there's silence for Eve to brace her thoughts against, punctured by a woodpecker and the murmur of faraway cars. To calm herself, she focuses on the horizon of woods, a whiskery brown sameness.

After Ms. Coatsworth dismissed her, she'd thought she was in the clear. She'd been allowed into her classes, where she sat shivering and reticent. Afraid they were waiting to jump her in the lavatory, she'd fought off the urge to pee until she could hold it no longer, racing to the nearest stall and gushing over the commode, straining to keep her feet up and out of sight. Afterwards, she'd huddled behind her locker door, piling up books, pulling on her jacket and dawdling until the bell rang and kids poured into the corridor. Anxious to get lost in the shuffle, she forgot her backpack and began marching with her head down toward the bus line. But it ended near an exit door. She was yanked by her hood and led backwards, practically choking, until there was nothing to do but go along.

Fear and exertion are making her sweat, warming her up, then leaving her clammy and cold. They're walking into what's left of the sun, burning a hole through an unruly mass of clouds, when it begins to snow lightly. Pitiless little diamonds pinprick their faces. They pass a ridge where the snow has melted away and the earth has become a dark sponge with trees gripping it, their roots exposed like the wires of the world.

She hurries along, pushed by Connie, getting past the point where Momma had taken her that day, past the headstone and the boulder that looks like breasts and the rocks where they'd fallen. She's forced to head down the hill with Connie on top of her like the wrong shadow. Her heart skips when she realizes they're nearing the area with the oil tanks and pumps, but there are no workmen on the ladders. No one she could scream at and beg for help. Where are all the adults when you need them?

Snow fingers, frozen mists blown about by wind, are sneaking across the asphalt where it's been cleared. Eve's jaw clamps and her teeth chatter. She wishes *she* had a knife. And then she's where she knew they were headed all along, the underground place with the stairs. Snow had piled up since she'd been there, but in the hole it's been scrabbled and scraped to one side in a snow wall, with footprints all over and last autumn's remnant leaves. The stone stairs are naked and muddy, with a rusted shovel, the kind used for ditches, down there, vertical. Why would anyone bother to shovel? The place is nasty, a toilet, with yellow stains where the mounded snow had been scorched by urine, and what looks like dog turds, shiny and showcased in ice.

"I'm not going down there," says Eve.

Brandy thinks this is funny. "Ah'm not goin' down they-ah," she mimics, and Bailey huddles over laughing. "Say it again!" she shrieks.

"Ya'll are nuts," murmurs Eve.

"Yowl are nuts!" mimics Brandy. Bailey says that's Eve's name, from now on they're calling her "Yowl."

"I need a smoke," says Connie. Still holding Eve by the hood, she pulls a lighter and a grubby package of Salem Menthols from her jacket, which she holds out to Brandy and Bailey, then Eve. Eve shakes her head at first, then takes one and slips it in her pocket. Connie has Brandy pull out a cigarette and stick it in her mouth, which she lights while gripping Eve, with a little snap of fire and a hiss. The sisters light up on Connie's flame and inhale, blowing smoke out of their noses. They're experienced smokers, Eve thinks, exposing her as the lonely outsider and making her miss Daddy, who had smoked most of the time, in between slivers of quitting. Smoke had been an everyday part of her life until recently, until moving up north. Yet, looking at all three of them now in the glum snow light, dressed in their burly leather jackets, she understands the difference between herself and them. Daddy's smoke had crept into her clothes and hair and lungs, but hadn't been able to get hold of her.

Connie inhales as if her whole life depends on it. "After what I did for you, you should be licking my hand," she says to Eve. "I could've sold you out. You could've ended up in juvy with that janitor." She jerks on Eve's hood. "He's going to jail, not juvy," corrects Bailey. "Oh, shut your yap," says Connie. Bailey and Brandy drag on their cigarettes and blow smoke at each other lazily, which makes their pushed-in, stray cat faces look almost pretty. Bailey says she's hungry, does anyone have a cheeseburger? That janitor smelled like feet, says Brandy, and they argue aimlessly about whether he likes girls better or boys, as they wander down to the quarry. The wind infringes on everything, beating up their hair, whipping the snow around in miniature tornadoes. Connie stamps out her cigarette and pulls Eve. "Come on."

Out of earshot of Brandy and Bailey, she becomes almost kind, telling Eve to watch her step as she leads her down the stairs, strewn with ice shards, to the surface. They walk on gritty, dark prisms, icicle fingers that splinter and crunch beneath them. Eve holds her breath against the stink of beer and grime and ammonia from the pee.

You can keep your clothes and boots on, Connie says, just hand me your jacket. Eve does as she's told mutely, eyeing the dog turds as if they're alive, grateful that there is this other Connie, looking out for her. Her nipples harden under her flimsy plaid flannel pajama top. Connie pulls Eve's hood over her own head so it covers her brow, letting the sleeves dangle. "Look, I'm a nun," she says. "Sister Mary Immaculate Jacket." She clowns around in Eve's pale blue quilted jacket, her sour Goth face peering out with a grin before it goes back to being dark and moody. The black rings she has painted around her eyes have smeared. Eve can hear the faraway voices of Brandy and Bailey, one of them squealing, the other laughing until Connie crunches up the stairs and shouts at them to shut up unless they want to deal with cops.

The sleeves of Eve's jacket hang down like long rabbit ears around Connie. "Stupid whores, " she mutters. She talks softly, confiding her grievances. "I never should've brought them along. It should've been just me and you." She's telling Eve what she wants her to do as Eve stands there trembling with cold, holding onto herself, not certain whether to be scared for herself or sorry for Connie.

"Me and Brandy did most of the work already," says Connie. "That Bailey is a lazy bitch. I'd ditch her if she wasn't related to Brandy." At the bottom of the stairs is a lopsided tunnel through the snow, which Connie says took them a day to shovel out, ending in a dirty vertical hole that reaches somewhere. "It's a cave, sort of," says Connie. In this cave are things worth something. "Stolen shit," she says. "Stolen by who?" asks Eve, but Connie says what does it matter, it was a long time ago, "before you

103

was even born."

She explains why Eve had been chosen, as if it had nothing to do with the keys or the money someone took. The problem is that Connie is too large to squeeze through the hole, while the other two are too large in places. "Their heads are too fat." Connie laughs hoarsely. Eve laughs nervously at first, her teeth chattering, then she laughs too hard, convulsively, out of relief. Connie tells her to chill, it isn't that funny, seeing through Eve the way you can see through a jar.

"Hey," she says suddenly, "You want a beer?" She pulls out an already open can of Coors beer that she had buried in the snow and they stand there passing it back and forth. The beer tastes like smoke, burning Eve's tongue, even though she's taking baby sips, letting Connie swallow most of what's left in the can.

After a while, Connie says they'd better get to work. Or, rather, Eve had better, while Connie stands guard.

"What if there are bats?"

"Once you're in, you get this." Connie shows her a cracked red plastic flashlight.

"How am I supposed to get back out?"

"You ask a lot of stupid questions." Connie shoves Eve backwards toward the hole and Eve realizes that the other, mean Connie is back. Her thoughts blink on and off, until they aren't thoughts at all, just hunger and fatigue and wanting the warmth of her jacket and hood. She realizes that she's being forced to do something that Connie can't, like doing a chore for Daddy, cleaning behind the commode, or fishing his glasses out from under the sofa.

In the dancing light beam, Eve witnesses brown creases and fissures, wrinkles like prunes. The cave looks small. She doubts she'll be able to move around much. Her left hand goes in first, grabbing blindly, until she finds a rough surface like beard stubble. She travels sideways, scraping her shoulders and the back of her head. The air in the cave smells like fungus, but it's surprisingly warm, which encourages her. Lacking breasts and much of a rump, she gets most of her top half through, but her feet are stuck in the hole with Connie, who yanks her back out.

"You'll have to take off those boots." Connie lays Eve's jacket on the dirty snow and Eve sits there, tugging. The gumboots make an embarrassing, sucking sound. She has the good sense to roll up her jeans, remove her socks and stuff them in her boots. Wet socks are death, Daddy had told her on a camping trip, back when vacations were possible, when Momma would come along with them and cook the food.

"You said I could have the flashlight."

Entering the cave feet first, Eve scrapes her face this time while pointing her little halo of light toward the cave floor to see what is there. Muddy water, mostly, with a skin of ice floating around. She has stood in chilly brown water before, in the brooks and creeks of her old life. Getting in is familiar torture, her jaw rigid with cold, a needling ache pressing down on the small of her back. Her feet prickle and sting. The stone floor gives her a foothold, not that she can walk very far. The cave isn't much bigger than her closet at home, knowledge she keeps to herself, moving far enough away so that Connie, whose face is pressed against the opening, can't see her. She has an inkling that she had been brought here to seize what she can, when all along her real purpose is to see around corners. Impulsively, she pokes the light beam into Connie's eyes and watches her go blind for a moment.

"You better not try that again."

"Sorry."

The wall bulges with comical shapes, jowls and buttocks, a giant earlobe, shining in heavy brown syrup. In a corner are folds, like stone draperies, chocolate, ochre, acid orange. Momma had once given her an antique brown slip to dress up in that had tiny accordion pleats around the hem, and the stone drapes are like this, ugly yet seductive. But no bats or spiders, or even rats. Nothing alive. There is a liquid sound, a pin-drop magnified by a beautiful, ringing echo. There are things only she can see, prying with the weak little light, and she thinks that if she weren't so cold, this place might be an adventure, or a refuge, or both.

Connie won't leave her alone. "Well?" she keeps asking, then "Hello" a few times and "Hey, you." Eve ignores her at first, then tells her there's a long empty hall that just keeps going down. Down to hell where you're going, she thinks. When actually there is just this little cubby.

It had been someone's once, she thinks. Someone who had left her stash behind. The stone had formed an eave with a basin in one area that someone had used to store things. Kitchen remnants, a few saucers and plates, an ancient cup, some forks and spoons, a can opener, a broken candle stuck in a crack. Funny-looking swollen cans, the labels mostly gone. A fat purse. She can tell it's a purse because there's an old-fashioned plastic handle, but the sack part looks right nasty, all bloated, and isn't worth the risk of touching. Something else shines. She encircles it with light, around and around again, to make sure. It has a row of holes in it like missing teeth and a familiar, compact shape. Recognizing what she's found, she is almost happy.

"You better come out and tell me what's going on." Connie sighs. "Look, kid, we gotta bounce."

Eve holds very still, thinking, "You can't make me." But her frigid body can make her. Her body does, stiffly wading toward the opening to grab Connie's outstretched hand. There is a bump on one side of her that makes getting out harder than getting in. "Push," commands Connie, but Eve is like a knuckle too large for a ring. Her face takes the brunt of it, then a leg, the jean material tearing as brute stone scrapes her from thigh to knee. Eve is too cold to cry, too cold to do anything but slide down and quake for a moment. She clasps her knees and sees the ugly tear in her jeans, worse, to her, than the scrape in her flesh. Shivering, she looks around for her boots.

"You could've froze," Connie reprimands, as if it's Eve's fault. She throws the quilted jacket, wet and soiled, over Eve. "You ok?" she keeps asking, then supplies her own answers. "You're okay, you're fine, you're gonna be fine." Her breathing is harsh and rank. "Oh, fuck," says Connie. "I think you're frostbit." She rubs Eve's feet, which triggers crying and moaning. "Hold still," says Connie. Then she unzips her jacket and wraps Eve's feet inside, in the frayed, steamy flesh of the lining, while Eve sits there letting go of an adenoidal wail that subsides into snuffling and ragged sobbing. She no longer cares what Connie thinks of her. Her only good pair of jeans is ruined and she may never walk again. She had heard what frostbite did to people dumb enough to rub snow on their skin. Her feet feel warm in the jacket, but sick, like a fever. After a while Connie dresses her in the socks and boots. In the dim light, Eve can see the long, adult-looking scar down one side of Connie's face.

"You better tell me what was in that cave." Connie's face is mean again

Shut your yap, Eve says to herself. Her jaw is shaking violently. But in the end, she tells Connie that all she saw was a boot.

"A boot? What kind of a boot?"

"I d-don't know."

"Was it a guy's boot or a chick's?"

"I told you I don't know. It was j-just a ugly old rubber boot." Eve begins to sniffle. "I did what you told me. I want to g-go home now."

Connie says that she's useless, a useless little baby, but she dresses Eve in her quilted jacket anyway. She stuffs Eve into her sleeves and zips her up and jams the hood over her head, tying it too tightly so it puckers in an infantile way around Eve's face.

"That's one dumb-looking jacket," says Connie. "I should've threw it in the cave with the boot." But she half-carries Eve home until she can hobble forward. The other two must have scatted, because Connie and Eve are alone under streetlights that have been on a while. The snow is long gone, having left a thin bridal veil on the hulking drifts around them and over the dirty faces of everything. The woods in back of it all etch the sky with a hairline precision that hurts Eve's eyes.

They limp and hop through neighborhoods that Eve has never walked in, past doors too close to the street, a bar with a blinkered Miller Lite sign, an abandoned auto body shop, a store that displays headstones. Next is a row of houses and hovels with several locks in each door and after that they cross over into town, where Eve recognizes places that ordinarily flash by from the car or bus, churches in dingy collars of snow, brownstone town buildings, a Masonic lodge squeezed in. Then a long gritty hill, flanked by billboards selling diamond rings and dinette sets, with bites taken out of the road by the snowplows. Cars rush past them, as if they were invisible, toward a quieter road she recognizes, with pastures on one side and disheveled little enterprises on the other, offering plate glass and septic excavation. Her street, Velvet Lane, is out there somewhere, Connie is telling her. "It's all downhill from here."

But downhill hurts and itches her feet as badly as all the rest of it, and halfway down, she realizes that she's alone. Turning around, she sees a hunched-over silhouette, with a curl of smoke, heading in the opposite direction. A truck with a loose fender rattles by.

Hunger keeps her going, despite her feet being on fire. She digs in her jacket pocket for whatever might be inside, a mint or a cough drop, but all she finds is the cigarette Connie forced her to take, now in soggy shreds. She has to turn her pocket inside out to shake it all away, the sticky, nasty little tobacco grits. Then she hobbles toward a street she knows must still be there.

13 / Arm

With March come boots on the ground, a war he'd been warned about, one he would just as soon ignore. But it seizes the media, the TV he tunes out, the dying radio in the dying car, the newspapers he no longer reads, Mark's battered computer, which he seldom flicks on, muddying the doorstep of his reluctant consciousness. Ground troops enter Southern Iraq just as Mark had predicted, which might absolve his lover of folly and paranoia. What if Mark also hadn't been wrong about nine-one-one?

"Cheney and the deep state did it," Mark had insisted. "The Saudi Islamists helped, and Israeli special ops assassins engineered it. Those planes that hit the towers may have been cloaked missiles." Mark had persisted with theories that had seemed to Arm, weary of the grind, like an excuse for not getting a real job at a real newspaper. It had been about the new world order, Mark had said, and a lot of other scumbaggery. It had been about gold in a basement and securities fraud, an attempt to loot and destroy America for good by creating the war on terror. It had been an insurance scam. "The guy who leased the buildings made a killing off the insurance proceeds," he'd say, reciting numbers Arm couldn't remember now, or much of the logic behind them in an argument that appeared to weave wild speculation with byzantine assumptions. He consoles himself with his own assumptions now, letting all his questions smolder and die.

He has a cold war of his own to tend. The head cold hangs onto him even as winter is letting go. All of them had caught it; Eve was next, then Rose. He nursed them both, guilty as charged. Slogging to the dollar store on foot, he had bought a jumbo pack of pink facial tissues in flowery boxes that he placed in strategic areas around the house. Then he made a cauldron of gumbo, knowing it was a favorite of Eve's. The gumbo required chicken, but he used turkey with a vengeance. And for filé powder, an herbal concoction made from sassafras leaves, he substituted the zatar he'd bought from Season. Zatar was crushed sumac leaves, close enough to sassafras, he reasoned. In the woods, he knew, they often grew together. But there was no substitute. Eve said it tasted nothing like her father's. "Yours tastes like seaweed."

In truth, he had taken quite a lot of guff from both of them. Rose had refused to lend him her car after the Incident, forcing him to go everywhere on foot. He had tried to mollify her with offers of gas money and dollars per mile, but she had remained aloof and adamant, slamming silverware in drawers and blowing her nose too hard whenever he entered the room. Until he had offered to buy the dying AMC Spirit. She had changed her tune then. And yesterday they had settled on the sum of one thousand dollars. But twenty-four hours later, he felt robbed and she felt short-changed, and the cold war continued.

He has had to remain in his dungeon or sneak around her, loathing himself. But today, despite a lingering cough and post-nasal drip, he feels unchained from his position beneath the floorboards. He is, for the first time in two weeks, alone in the house. Eve is back in school after a scary bout of chilblains all over her feet and ankles. And Rose is out on cleaning jobs. He is alone. He has a car. And it is March at last. The ice, the snow, the haughty winds have given way to sullen skies and rain, and winter has been made a joke of, forced back into its strongbox.

He is, for one day, what fate had never intended him to be: a free man.

He pulls on his boots before his pants, he's so impatient to burst his chains and begin his mission, what he had come to Swannboro for. This is contained in a rectangular box, a hand-painted Japanese cookie tin with rust along the edges. But it is lovely, showing a couple near groupings of pagodas, with the taller figure holding a parasol over the smaller figure's head. Both have Van Dyke beards. Arm had speculated that one of these beards is simply a flaw in the paint, and they had argued. Foolishly, he thinks now. It had all been about jealousy and shame and pride.

The box and its contents had been Mark's present to him the Christmas before he died. All Mark could afford to give him was time. Weekends in obscure libraries, nights alone with the computer, ferreting scraps, hours seeking FBI files about Taft's murder were inside the box, which Arm hadn't appreciated. Well, not nearly enough. Mark's death had changed that. He had come to Swannboro to make good on the promise sealed in his acceptance of the gift. It was a kind of guilt trip. The promise of his own time, the time it would take to follow breadcrumbs Mark had strewn down the murder path. His own complacent nature had blocked the path as surely as that turkey. But the Incident has begun to strip away certain assumptions.

Because it was fulfillment of a prophesy, really. Mark had warned him, which sparked bitter caviling, with Arm accusing Mark of paranoia and unwillingness to engage in a "real job," by which he had meant a respectable one. The feuds had led Arm to spend his nights on the couch and Mark to spend his in an Asian graduate student's dorm room. The young Asian, Arm suspected, was the source of the cookie tin. In those last weeks, he remembers now, great webs had been spun by each of them until they had become conspiracy theorists about each other.

Mark had warned him. "You won't think I'm paranoid the day you're up against the wall for being an Arab," he said.

And then it had happened just a few miles north of his hometown.

Justice would be sweet. Revenge would be sweeter. Arm recognizes that neither will be his. But just perhaps he could win some of both for Taft. There had been hints about police corruption in Mark's notes. If he could follow the thread, perhaps it would lead him to the murderer's threshold. And then what? He isn't sure, and isn't even sure he cares. Dangerous no matter what comes next. But what does he have to lose? His career has been botched, the love of his life is dead, he lives in the basement of a decrepit ranch house beneath a sister and a niece who despise him.

Arm pulls on his pants, then stretches his shirt tightly over his pelvis before tucking it in. There it is again, a worrisome sag around his middle, the sort of thing that Mark had overlooked, but which other gay men of his age would not. He has it coming; how many older gay men had he rejected in his prime? Nearly all, and now that he is a Gray, he recognizes that the real rejection he faces is that of his younger self. He threads his belt through his waistband, buckles, satisfied that he hasn't had to move up a notch. He eases a heavy fleece top over his head before making the final fastidious touches to his hair. Then he pauses the CD of Grieg lyrical piano pieces in his player, which he pockets. No Arab music today. He will travel with Grieg and Dvorak and Sibelius and Ravel.

The rain has abated, but he no longer trusts the weather. The car, his car, cooperates for once, and he is off on the itinerary he has plotted to avoid rural routes. The black ruff of snow around the perimeter of the road has melted, running down gutters and leaving behind tatterdemalion lawns. He feels as he always does after a cold, abraded yet wiped clean. The Grieg spins in the player and he is humming with the pleasure of knowing exactly where he is headed, which is a house about fifty miles away in the town of Ordwell on a street named Revere Lane. In this house lives the man that Taft was to testify against before he was murdered. The man is still alive, this he knows. Last night he had dialed the man's number, and when an offended, elderly voice had answered, he had hung up. What was there to say?

Mark had highlighted the man's name, which appeared in numerous newspaper clippings, in a brilliant primrose yellow. *Manny Manciani.* The name sounds to Arm like all of the small, sadistic, insecure men he has ever known rolled into a sausage. The citations Mark had found confirmed a life of petty crime. Gambling fines, car theft and escapades with lottery tickets in the late 1950s. Then, like Taft, Manciani had become an FBI informant, hindering trial witnesses and damaging property in the 1960s. And through it all, alleged narcotics sales. A drug charge that had never gone anywhere without Taft's testimony. Then an abrupt end to the crimes, but not to Manciani.

Arm rolls down the window as far as it will go, which is about two inches. The cool, damp air feels good on his winter skin. Dull highway scenery glides over melancholy music. He ejects the Grieg and inserts the Dvorak, a romance for violin and orchestra in F minor. He pins his speedometer precisely on sixty-five miles per hour, not a mile more or less. Whatever happens when he arrives, nothing will happen a moment sooner. He would just as soon that nothing were ever to happen to him again.

He keeps thinking, what would Mark have done? Would he have

protested, refusing to spread his legs, bend over and allow a cretin to enter his backside with a latex-gloved finger, searching for drugs? Would he have quoted, verbatim, the fourth amendment, the sixth? All the while, they had called him "Sir." Yet he had seen the mockery in their eyes, which gave them away, despite the false pretenses, the clinical room, the presence of a doctor. Would Mark have shat on them, wrestled them to the ground, kicked, punched, hollered?

Arm almost misses his exit and begins to hyperventilate. He's forced to pull over onto the shoulder and consult the map with shaking hands. He's relieved to see that he is minutes away from the correct exit, less than an inch away from the squiggle on the map that will lead him to Manciani. He squints, holds the map closer, could it be? Yes. Manciani lives not more than a half-mile from Ordwell's gambling casino. He turns the Dvorak off, then on again. He will need music to nurse himself back onto the highway. Cars race past, perhaps a dozen, before he finds his chink in the chain and can breathe again.

What does he expect to find when he arrives? An ancient gambler with a paunch and rotten breath. Manciani had used his FBI connection to defend himself against accusations of dope peddling and other felonies. His options in the crime world must have dried up after that. Arm expects his house won't be much to look at. On the other hand, people like that know how to hide their money. Perhaps Manciani is drawing a nice pension out of his floorboards. He takes the exit to Ordwell nice and easy, then takes a right by mistake and has to circle back through a Burger King. Ordwell, he sees, is just as sulfurous and dirty as he remembered it, yet is now smiling to itself intermittently with a small but cheery coffee shop or a façade painted lemon or fuchsia.

Ordwell had never been especially prosperous. Once a thread

mill town, it has suffered setbacks. Small businesses were bought up by opportunists who let them become down-at-heel and irrelevant, then selling them to franchises. It is now a chain of stained and smudged boxes, little cement-erprises with parking out front. Grim sixties ranches bite down hard on the suburban streets. Occasional dilapidated Victorians rise over them, but most of the remote past is long gone, relieved to surrender its insupportable beauty.

A few decades ago, when Arm and Rose would be dragged by their mother to salvage sales in Ordwell's retired factory buildings, Ordwell was still synonymous with a state mental institution. It's closed and boarded up now, but Arm can see its hull like a large black mood on an elevation in the distance. When he was growing up, the father of a friend was sent there after a quixotic fugue, knocking on neighbors' doors, nude, inviting them to "Have a 'Gansett!" Going to Ordwell had meant going insane. Now it means playing blackjack. The casino had been built feverishly, now churning out a large percentage of the town's tax base, chewing up the small paychecks made in Ordwell proper. It is a town of residents and strangers living in the meantime. As Arm rolls by sidewalks, he can see discarded lottery tickets caught in a storm drain.

Manciani's street, Revere Lane, is an easy right-hand turn off the main street. The setting is all wrong. Low-end suburbia with the sadness of broken drainpipes and rusted lawn furniture. An occasional shack painted parrot green or blue or pink as if only the most lurid colors can cover up poverty. A dead-end.

Arm turns up the street cautiously, passing several houses, all of them ranches with winter-straggled, struggling hedges. Manciani's is behind a tall row of arbor vitae with brown undersides. He drives slowly past, then circles around and idles at the edge of a short drive leading to

Manciani's covered side porch.

He parks in front of a modest nicotine-yellow ranch. It isn't the sort of house Arm expects. It looks like the house of a failing elderly person too weak to stand on a ladder or push a mower. Not someone whose livelihood was made in the backrooms of a corrupt town. A large chimney in the middle of a roof mottled with lichens sags over peeling clapboard and a forgotten lawn. Crime had not paid.

A small wagon wheel has been sunk into the side of the drive as a decoration or a sign. Doubtless before Manciani's time. Arm doesn't see him as the type who would rummage around in antiques stores for Americana. Wind pulls on the metal wind chimes hanging in the side porch over a pair of wood-slatted lawn chairs. Arm hears a tired clank. All of the windows are covered with yellowed shades, except one. What appear to be packing boxes fill up the blank space. The main sign of life is a red plastic receptacle out front where a news carrier had left Manciani's rolled *Ordwell Chronicle*.

A black sedan on a set of deflated tires has settled into the ground like an old dog. The one behind it is perkier, a Mazda in a bright aqua with a small punch in one side and an old *Virginia is for lovers* bumper sticker. Arm decides to drive around and have a peek at the backyard from the next street down. But there are even fewer signs there. A couple of metal garbage cans and a green garden hose looped primly on its hook. The back windows have the same mute look as the front.

Arm drives back around and parks in front of the hedges. The sky is starting to squeeze out drops of rain and he knows this means he'll drive home in a downpour. Bored with the music he's brought, he finds a fuzzy radio station playing Schubert's "Shepherd on the Rock." Fate, he thinks. A beautiful, silvery voice, soprano, echoed by a clarinet, edges up and down cliffs. It's the same duet he had been listening to when he and Mark had first met at an outdoor concert in Central Park. Mark had been serving drinks, and after spilling Arm's, had insisted on laundering his trousers. All in whispers, above German lieder. Charming, Arm had thought then. Sad, he thinks now. As he listens, he peers through obliging gaps in Manciani's hedge at a cropped view of his porch. The rain begins to plop on the windshield, when Manciani's front door opens.

A woman makes her way down the porch steps, turning back to say something to a figure framed in the screen door. The woman is large, black, her hair knitted all over like a sweater in thin rows. A nurse or home aide, thinks Arm, judging from the white pants, white top, white shoes as thick as tires. A red raincoat and umbrella are slung over her arm, and she carries a black case. She bends to talk softly to the figure in the door, then trudges down the steps to her aqua car. Arm slouches down in his seat, hoping she won't see him. But of course she does. She has one of those shiny, shut faces that reveal nothing, but while she's digging around in her raincoat pocket, Arm can see her lips moving. "Shit," she mouths, then trudges back toward the screen door in the slanting rain.

She shrugs at the figure behind the screen. The light inside is pale, outlining someone short, hunched over a metal walker. The door opens and the woman leans inside, using one square foot as a doorstop, searching for something, keys hidden by clutter. Then she enters the house, propping the screen door open with her case, so that Arm has a full view of the figure inside. A man.

He has the dwarfed proportions of someone no longer able to stand up straight. He seems both unlikely and familiar, with a stricken face, gaunt but wide, and eyes like pits in wads of loose flesh. A thin slick of gray hair is combed over his speckled head. His loose trousers are belted tightly over a sleeveless undershirt. Arm can see the sideways breasts that gravity has given him. He seems to be holding a half-smoked cigar.

Arm gets out of the car, locking it meticulously because he is in Ordwell. He is taking a risk parking here, but he knows now that he is in no danger from Manciani. No reason to hesitate asking a few pointed questions. What can Manciani do? He doubts he could lift his walker high enough to slam it down on Arm. The nurse exits the house, keys in hand, just as Arm reaches the steps. She looks at him with her poker face. "Talk loud," she says. "He deaf." Then she runs to her car with the red raincoat over her head.

"Hello," says Arm with false cheerfulness. He offers his hand to Manciani, but the little man keeps his hands glued to the walker and cigar. "Hello," Arm repeats, louder. After a few seconds, it's obvious that Manciani is having none of him. The walker balks as he tries to back his way into the house. At this point rain begins to pelt down as if a trap door in the sky had opened. Arm has no choice but to open the door and step inside.

The heat and orderliness of the interior stop him from saying anything. A space heater across one wall is churning out heat that would be suffocating enough without the heavy odor of Manciani's cigar. Arm feels the urge to cough and practically chokes. Apart from the heater, a cot in the middle of the room and a lamp, phone, ashtray and TV on the floor, there is no furniture.

The walls are blank except for scant rectangular outlines left by vanished pictures. It makes Arm feel sorry for Manciani; any other emotion would have been preferable. Only one picture remains, small and disproportionately high up in its gold frame. Arm can make out an old black-and-white snapshot of a woman with pale cotton-candy hair and a chiffon dress, posed on a barstool. Packing boxes are solidly ranked along one wall and the rest is just Manciani and his walker, hunched near one of them like a vulture, his small eyes focused on something to the left of Arm. Which Arm falls for, turning around.

"Gotcha," says the little man. His voice is pitched higher than Arm had expected, a toothless falsetto.

"Are you Emmanuel Manciani?" asks Arm. "I assume that's who you are." Nothing. The man remains where he is, waiting. He has all day, at least. Arm reluctantly approaches him, trying not to inhale the secondhand cigar smoke. He draws a picture out of his pocket, which is a crinkled wallet-sized black-and-white of Taft that he has carried around for decades.

"I wonder if you'd take a look at this."

Manciani looks at Arm instead of the photograph. "Everyone looks the same to me now," he says.

"You don't remember anything about him, then," says Arm, holding the photograph a few inches away from Manciani's nose.

"I don't remember shit no more. From what they tell me, that ain't a bad thing."

Arm reaches in his pants pocket and pulls out a newspaper clipping. He begins to read.

" 'Taft Said, the man whose body was found this weekend in a water-filled quarry hole, was to be a state's witness in an upcoming drug sales case --'"

"I don't know nothing about that," Manciani says.

" '... Said was a the key informant for the case, prosecutors say. At one time, he had been the kingpin dealer of heroin in the southeastern part of the --'"

"I don't know nothing about that, I told ya," Manciani said. "Whoever it is, I hope he rests in peace, but I didn't put him there."

Manciani draws on his cigar, wheezes and coughs up phlegm. Arm offers him a handkerchief, but Manciani shakes his head and slogs his way through the coughing fit. He clenches his walker, shuffling away from Arm, then he turns around and wheels back toward him.

"Who the hell are you?" he shrieks.

"I'm very sorry for the intrusion, Mr. Manciani. I should have called first," Arm said. "Well, actually I did. But … I'm truly sorry."

"You ain't sorry," said Manciani. "And even if you was, you got no right coming in here."

"Sorry," Arm repeats, smiling weakly at Manciani's quaint movie-mobster face. Manciani stares, his collapsed mouth working mechanically. Arm feels as if he's being gripped as hard as the walker.

"You look like him," says Manciani finally. He wheels closer, then he clamps onto Arm's shoulder with his armadillo hand and points to the framed photo on the wall. Arm feels sick with cigar smoke, but manages to keep his gorge down as he stares up at the oddly placed portrait of the woman. She is pretty in a fleshy, fifties way, sleekly coiffed, a smoker like Manciani, with the classic female cello shape of his generation, plump breasts, narrow waist, hips accentuated by the gauzy dress. Either Manciani couldn't bear to take her off the wall or he meant to leave her there.

"Up there's my wife," he says, pointing unsteadily.

"Died of the cancer two months ago. No point me staying here. I got a room at the Home. The boob who runs it can have the house." His laugh ends in one of the phlegmy coughs. The smile that follows is malicious mischief.

"You got kids?" he asks. Arm looks at him blankly, shaking his head.

"Mine don't come around much since she went. Anyways, they're all meaner than the Devil." He brings the cigar up to his lips without drawing on it, considering Arm. Then he leans forward, clamping the walker. He stamps it violently once, breathing hard. The cigar falls and smolders on the floor. Arm picks it up and hands it back, but Manciani lets it drop and crushes the burning end with his foot, small as a child's. He is wearing old men's brown vinyl bedroom slippers.

"You come in here, you ask me things I don't know nothing about no more, if I ever did." His voice hurries up the scale and his small sideways breasts shake.

"Let me tell you something. Ask your own people. Ask the cops. Bring lots of cash." Manciani's thin chest heaves as he coughs out of a deep cave. Arm holds out his handkerchief again, but Manciani shakes his head, his own bilge racking him. He coughs and pants and coughs again, bracing himself on the walker until he's silent. He stands there a while, staring at his feet until he raises his head again to give Arm a sad, quizzical look.

"You his son?" Manciani asks. Arm shakes his head, no. "No relation," he says.

"You look like him," Manciani repeats. He wheels and shuffles to the cot, then lowers and seats himself there, still holding onto the walker.

"You come here asking me things. So I'll give you something. Woman with a fancy name. Chelsea. Chelsea Fowler. Only he don't call her that. He called her 'Chesty.' Chesty Fowler. Big blonde with big white titties. Wife of a big shot he got mixed up with. Her on top of that other whore he lived with. Chesty Fowler. He carried on with too many women. It could have got him killed."

Arm clears his throat, hesitant. "Is it possible that he slept with your wife?" he asks quietly.

Manciani looks at him with hatred. "No. No, it ain't," he says. "I would've killed them both." He fumbles around in the cot's rumpled sheets and Arm is tempted to back away, thinking he might be groping for a gun, but it's just a dirty handkerchief. Manciani blows his nose copiously.

"Anyways," he says. "It was probably that rotten cop who put him down. There was plenty back then. More now. Glad I'm out of the, you know, the business." His bitter laugh turns into a cough, weaker this time.

"Do you happen to remember the name of the cop?"

"Happen to remember. No, I don't *happen* to remember." Manciani pokes at him with his hard little eyes. "You sound like a faggot. You know that?"

"Why did you tell me to ask my own people?"

"Did I? I don't remember now. Must have been talking in my sleep."

Arm turns around to go. He has no doubt that Manciani remembers everything, but knows he has reached the abrupt edge of his hospitality. "Thank you very much, Mr. Manciani," he says. "I appreciate your time."

"You a faggot?"

Arm keeps going, trying not to hurry, anxious to breathe again. The rain is gushing down; he will be soaked by the time he reaches the car.

"Hey," says Manciani. "Your look-alike was queer, too. All them women, but he never fooled me."

Once he's on the porch, Arm forces himself to keep his eyes on his car. He will not look back. He will not give Manciani the benefit of his self-doubt. Until he is seated in the car, his hair dripping, his hands shaking, his door locked, he doesn't look back at the house. And then he sees the little hunched figure standing there behind his cage, watching him.

Through sheets of rain, he can still see those implacable turtle eyes. He backs out slowly and drives away, and it isn't until the next town that he realizes he has overshot his exit.

14 / Rose

She isn't sure of her footing, but is sure of the place. The streets cross where the map says they should. To her left is a jubilant waterfall, part of Succour Brook, burbling like someone gagged all winter and happy to be free at last. Nearby, a sage-colored house with beige trim, a severely pitched roof and a twig wreath on the door. She has never ventured into this part of Swannboro; has never previously discovered its virgin parts. It draws her into a cloak of evergreens, a road milled by history, muteness. A postcard view. Yet thirty years ago, it was where Taft was murdered.

Arm had dropped her off near her destination this morning in civil silence. They had argued the night before about the car and Eve and some trifle she can't remember. Fine; she prefers silence, prefers, in fact, walking away to talking. Walking gets you somewhere. And today would be perfect walking weather, if it weren't for the callous on her left heel. She has walked here from a half-mile away, mostly uphill, after working all morning for Milly Beale, a balding, elderly sprite who can barely see, whose hearing has faded to exclude nearly all but the blare of a small TV she uses to watch videocassettes of her idol, Neil Diamond.

Milly has a Neil Diamond display that takes up most of a living room wall in her dark Cape. Rose had only just managed to handle the collection by purposely squinting, blurring the raw, glittering images of Diamond into impressionistic paintings. She'd spent the morning dusting and arranging the LPs and cassettes by date and enshrining new

Diamond memorabilia that Milly acquired on her recent trip to "Vegas," as she called it. She pronounced it half-mockingly, without the "s," like Degas. "I go there every year," she had confided with a baggy smile. "And, believe it or not, Neil remembers me." Rose had thought this sweet but ridiculous, worship of a celebrity with a false, cheap name.

But now she's thinking, with a pang, that Milly's obsession isn't too far from her own. She attempts to rationalize, to convince herself of differences. For one thing, Taft was not a celebrity. But wasn't he? He had made crass headlines in the local rags and in some of the bigger ones. Well, at least her relationship with him was real. But had it been? Rose has slept with more men than she can remember; yet all she had shared with Taft was a raw, failed encounter. This was not a relationship. At least "Neil" had remembered Lily. Rose doubts that Taft remembered her as he lay here, dying. She's getting closer, getting warmer, she is sure, to where they had shot him.

She limps along the road that skirts the brook, which is jostling free from the remains of ice and churning along, thinning to a stream near the house. Up ahead are more well-tended cottages with flower boxes and arbors and twig wreaths on their doors. Obviously here, anchored in Swannboro soil, for much longer than Rose has been alive. One has a plaque: "1889." Which means they were here when Taft was, presumably inhabited. Yet no one, according to the news clippings, reported hearing gunshots around the time Taft was murdered. The neighbors must have been as deaf as Lily. The stillness would have magnified the shots as it now does the song of a bird, whose liquid syllables reverberate out of nowhere. *Antiquity-tiquity-tiquity*. Rose cranes to see the maker of the song, but the pine trees obscure it and the beat of wings follows invisibly.

A drop between the road and the brook is steep enough to

weaken her knees when she looks down. The frontage is overgrown with carpets of weeds, weighed down by filthy crusts of melting snow. Below is where Taft's clothes were found, according to all she has read, by boys on bikes, in Succour Brook, pronounced like "sucker" by the locals. She tries to imagine the boys hunting for polliwogs and old bottles, and instead hauling up a grown man's jacket, punctured with a strange T-shaped hole, on the end of a stick. Laughing, she imagines, as the brook disgorged shoes, pants, a shirt, underwear. Most of the teenage boys in her remote past had laughed at death, at cruelty. Not Arm, of course. With him she had honored death, manners, nature, formalities. Twigs and snow crusts break beneath her feet like bones and cartilage as she walks along. The day is still and chill, the sky a mirage of spring with its changeable clouds on persistent blue. She can't remember the last time the sun had been this promising, but knows it will be over with tomorrow's rain.

The brook eventually turns and runs behind the houses along this road. Rose wants to stride across a lawn, to trespass her way to the brook, but she is far too obedient. A special kind of New England obedience that does not climb over walls has molded half of her. And what has molded the other half? Lies, betrayal, she decides. A stone border, low and easily hopped over, rambles along the road. She follows it past a barn and then, abruptly, sees the brook again. This time, it's defined by a little bridge bordered by two stone walls that lead over it to a road named after the brook. Succour Way, says the map, and the road sign agrees.

The bridge is a tidy arch, shoveled and sanded by someone over the winter months. Rose approaches it as if it were a shrine. There is a copper plaque attached to one of the stone walls: "WPA, 1942." Rose knows that WPA stands for Works Progress Administration because she had written a paper on it once, long ago, in a summer journalism class taught by a hairy-legged Marxist. People were given jobs building bridges, walls and barricades during the Great Depression through the WPA. Rose runs her hand along the rough inscription, verdigris now, wondering why the date seems odd. Then remembers it's the year that Taft was born: 1942. She remembers this because he had told her, and she had responded with disbelief. At the time, it had meant he was twenty-nine years old. "Believe it," he had said. "But don't tell no one." "Anyone," she had corrected. She had been sixteen and unable to restrain herself. Correcting her elders had normally ended in a rebuke or slap, but with Taft it had ended in laughter. His laugh was musical like the rest of him, and she had touched her face, and he had pulled her hand away.

Rose stops to listen. The brook swishes and tumbles. There is no one around this workday afternoon; most people commute to jobs downtown or in Hartford. Still, she's wary. If someone creeps up behind her, the brook would drown out the sound of footsteps. So she turns around, surveying the mild, soft palette of the foreground, old maidish as an apron spread across the ground, far from the obsessions of Milly Beale or a drug lord. Cold again, she rubs her hands together. Killing Taft here, on a bridge inscribed with the year of his birth, might have been meaningful, a message. Or it might have been a coincidence. Rose paces, huffing on her hands.

And then she sees where it happened. There couldn't be a more opportune place. Several yards from the bridge, a glade is sheltered by a low umbrella of trees. She walks beneath them with the certainty of an amateur, convinced that he had been here, forced to walk ahead of his murderer. He must have turned around suddenly, leaving them no choice but to fire five bullets. Perhaps Taft had been ordered to strip first, but had refused to go through the agony of removing shoes, shirt, jacket, pants, briefs. So they had done it for him.

Rose brushes off a clump of leaves and sits down on an ancient, rusted iron bench sunk into the ground beneath the trees, an old pile of brownstone slag at its feet. The glade is obviously someone's derelict outdoor sitting room. Spiky mosses that resemble miniature pines carpet the ground. A pile of split logs is neatly arranged at the base of a tree, which must mean that someone was here recently. Sitting still like this, she hears it, something almost musical, measured, in any case, carried by the wind. It must be her imagination. But there it is again, a ripple of minor thirds and perfect fifths that vanishes, then resumes thinly, the same phrases repeated. She sits there listening, snatching at the sound, holding her breath so she can hear it. After a time, she feels almost winded and puts her head down. Taft had been here, she knew. She remembers the way he had looked at her, sitting across the room in one of her mother's S&H green stamp chairs on a ruffled chair mat her mother had sewn from an old curtain. Everything about him so sharply defined that it cut into her.

Arm had been late to his lesson and no one was home but Rose. "Come here," Taft had said. "Sit here." He had patted his lap and she had hesitated. "It's okay, I don't bite." And she had sat on those hard thighs more because of not being able to move away, her legs by then what they were in her nightmares, sinking and unresponsive, as if they no longer belonged to the rest of her. "You should really be a singer," he'd said.

His presence whistles through her like the wind, which picks up, scattering leaves and pine needles. Logic tells her it would have been easy to drive across the bridge, to park Taft's car next to the enclosure, to put a gun to Taft's head and force him out. They would have nudged him along the way mobsters do in movies. Taft would have begged for his life; most people do. The glade would have sheltered them, indifferent to their actions. They killed him quickly, stripped off his clothes, discarded them in the brook, which would have swallowed and carried them off. They hauled him to his car and drove to the quarry, pitched him in, escaped in their own car, hidden in the bushes. Or perhaps, she thinks, they had lived within walking distance of the quarry. That would have been neater, cleaner. She checks the map. The trek from the quarry back to Succour Brook is only a few miles. Of course, they could have lived in that trailer park, whatever it was, housing for carnies, that used to be near the quarry.

But they had killed him here. She feels it, she *knows* in a way she'd dismiss coming from anyone else. Here, where Succour Brook has its marshy beginnings, pleasantly untidy with last year's bent reeds and a few fallen saplings. There are no little cottages this close to the marsh, as far as she can tell, so perhaps no one heard the gunshots. Perhaps the murderers had used a pillow to muffle the sound. Or the owners of the little cottages down the road had been out doing what people did back then, bowling, or drinking or attending a rock concert, high on drugs. Out cold. She stands and walks on the Lilliputian pine trees away from the bench and out of the glade until she has a view through complex fenestrations in the tall bare trees. And there is a house after all, on a hill past the marsh. She can see only a portion of the roof and the silvery blur of smoke hovering over a chimney. Someone must be home.

Rose looks around for stone fences, but none encircle or lead to the house. Nothing but a parting in the winter-dead tall grass. She thinks, why not? And limps uphill. When she reaches the top, there it is, a trim house like all the others, but this one is waiting for her, she feels. Even its colors are somehow hers, what she would paint a house, delft blue with cream shutters. Behind it is a peeling red barn, its roof beginning to cave, but still handsome, a bulwark of the past. And to one side of this, a pasture, where large buff-colored animals are grazing, confined by a wire fence. Their blunt, oblivious heads, bent to scrubby grass or a pile of hay, are crowned with horns of an elegance that doesn't match their shagginess, the filthy clumps in their undercoats, which Rose can see from where she stands. They seem, even here, anachronistic. Oxen, or some kind of exotic sheep, assumes Rose, ignorant about cattle. She approaches the wrap-around porch cautiously. A house like this, self-sufficiently remote, might contain people with guns or dogs.

But there's no mongrel to bark her away. She stands there listening, hesitating, rubbing her hands together, yet pulled. And there is the sound again, articulated now, lento, a plain-faced melody suspended over stodgy chords, pulling her by its strings. Someone is playing a piano. The tune is one she knows from somewhere long ago, a hymn or a folk tune, simple as a box.

She wants to knock on the door, to be admitted, just long enough to ask a few questions about the area and who might have lived here thirty years ago. But on what pretext? It might be risky to say anything about Taft. She decides on an offer of her housecleaning services, rummages a business card out of her purse and climbs the brownstone stairs slowly. Twig wreaths must be all the rage in this part of Swannboro. The porch is decorated with several twisted halos. Beneath them, an iron bench, similar to the one in the glade, except this one is freshly painted black. In a corner, a snow shovel cohabits with an old push broom, leaning against the wall.

There is no doorbell, so she knocks. Silence, except for birdcalls. Then she hears a bench scrape back and children's voices, immaculately high-pitched but too quiet, she thinks, for kids. When the door opens, she knows that her services will not be needed here.

The woman in the doorway is Mennonite or Amish, or one of those fundamentalist sects, Rose thinks, known for rigid rules about women's hair and clothes. She's wearing a faded blue check dress too loose and high in the waist, dowdy beneath a brown cardigan sweater, the effect accentuated by ankle socks and a pair of brown shoes with laces. But Rose sees that she's beautiful. A type. The kind of grave beauty pre-Raphaelite painters were mad about, the same liquid slopes and angles, the anguishing eyes, rosebud mouth, the frank, strong jawline. No makeup, no jewelry. She must be in her thirties, with a few strands of the hair that spills down to her waist going silver. Her hair is the russet Rose's used to be, glorious, lit from sunlight streaming in from behind her that catches on a fine mesh of wisps around her head and turns it into a picture that is somehow moving. That anyone could ever look that way. Rose is aware that she's staring. Not knowing what to say, she offers her card, ashamed of its worn, ink-stained edges. A sunny child, a girl, peers around from behind the woman and grabs it, holding it in the air above her head, as if she's teasing some other child.

"Martha," says the woman. It's a reprimand, but the young girl, who is a pale miniature of her mother, smiles as she hands the card over. Another child peeks out from behind the young woman, and it's clear from his sandy cropped hair that this is a boy, younger than the girl, but with the same fastidiously drawn features. Beauty of a kind that Rose finds most difficult to accept, wasted on a boy.

Rose touches her face. "I wonder," she begins, then drops the introduction she had mentally rehearsed. "I was walking by and saw your house, and wonder if you can tell me if there's land for sale. Here, I mean.

Or close by." She can feel herself blushing under the scrutiny of children, resentful of the lie detection she imagines people like this possess, pure enough to smell corruption. But all she sees in front of her is healthy curiosity.

The woman looks at the card, then at Rose, then at the card again, taking her time. Rose sees a long room with a kitchen in the foreground, banked by windows. The children are now standing to one side, looking Rose over without the usual fidgeting and torrent of questions. She feels freakish under their resolute stares. The girl is about twelve, a head taller than the boy, dressed like her mother in a long-skirted jumper with a sweater buttoned to her neck, which is long, supple as a lily, accentuated by hair that skeins down in loose waves. Sunlight frames the boy, whose face is somber yet sprinkled with freckles, a genetic toss of the dice that should make him less than what he is, a pixie rather than a Narcissus: Sapphire eyes, thick lashes, his mother's plush mouth. Ugliness can be disguised, but not beauty. He's dressed in a plaid shirt and a pair of khaki trousers that were obviously handed down, too large in the waist, cinched with a belt. Both are wearing leather shoes with laces, clean as new pennies.

The baggy pants and new shoes disarm Rose. The kids are sweet enough. The girl offers to take her coat, but Rose says no, she won't be staying. She looks warily at Bible verses on the wall. She can make out the words of one, from Isaiah 62:4. "Thou shalt no more be termed Forsaken; neither shall thy land any more be termed Desolate." The rest is in print too small to decipher. She had been tempted by religion once, in the parish house by the woman who taught her quilting.

"Do you like kittens?" It's the boy who pipes up. And now the mother is shushing him, telling Rose to come in, don't mind the mess. But of course, there is no mess, apart from children's textbooks and a mound of modeling clay on the kitchen table being sculpted into a boat by the boy, Rose assumes. A few playthings are scattered on the floor, which Rose doesn't see and stumbles over. "I'm so sorry," murmurs the mother, who grabs her daughter's arm and gets her busy picking up dolls and a bed someone has made out of a shoebox. The girl obeys silently, no sassing, none of the sullen commentary that Rose would expect from Eve. Rose winks at her conspiratorially, but the girl looks away and does as she's expected with a younger child's toys.

And then Rose sees it, a quilt, *the* quilt, hung to fill almost an entire wall. It is bait for her eyes, pulling her into its the pattern, one known to every quilter, a carousel of interlocking pinwheels. Someone long ago had named the pattern the Joseph's Coat. Whoever had needled this one was skilled, mastering the kaleidoscopic circles and petal points into a perfectly flat field of color. Rose steps closer to admire hand stitches that are tiny and enviably even.

"Some people would say it's too busy." The woman's voice is hushed, as if someone is asleep, but Rose detects pride. Which would be normal, she thinks, in the normal Neil Diamond world. She would be proud of the quilt if it were hers, but senses that pride is discouraged in this house. It makes her feel self-consciously vulgar in her makeup, her dyed hair and stretch pants.

"Mother did most of the work," says the woman. "I finished it. " She hesitates. "I'm Beulah." She offers a hand, which, unlike the rest of her, is rough and almost large enough to be a man's. You've already met Martha, and this is Jacob." But Jacob is heading through an open doorway to the other room, a den or bedroom, where he seats himself on a piano bench. Rose can't see the person beside him, but it's a woman, in a long white skirt with the same plebian socks and shoes as Beulah. Someone begins to play the piano. The melody lifts and lands, piloted with skill, then there is a pause followed by a few clumsy chords. A music lesson, obviously. Beulah shuts the door.

"So beautiful," Rose murmurs, still beneath the quilt's spell. More out of caution than humility, she decides not to reveal her background. She studies the quilt while flicking her eyes at the rest of what is there, a chest, a high chair, benches at the table, a sitting area with no TV, but instead a large Bible propped on a stand. Opposite this, a fire crackles. Nothing here that isn't necessary, except for the Joseph's Coat. And beneath a window, an aquarium, filled with a variety of fish that flutter and fold in slow motion, mugging at the glass. Pale pine boards, scored by use, make up the floor, and the walls are stucco, the color of butter. The house smells like sweet butter, too, and boiling milk.

Domesticity provokes boredom in her, the boredom of her own life spent chasing and taming chaos. But this woman's kitchen, hung with shining copper pans, makes her feel sadly envious. She thinks of her kitchen when she was married, with Randall flicking his ashes in the sink and blowing smoke up into the stove exhaust hood as if he were doing her a favor. The first house they had lived in was nothing like this one; it certainly hadn't smelled of boiling milk. It had been rundown rental that backed up to brambles engulfed by kudzu, situated on a hilly street with drainage problems. The lower floor had been inhabited by a large family of day workers and several dogs. On torrid summer weekends, the family would have a crawfish bake, tossing the remains in a pit they had dug in the basement. By Monday, the rotten odor would seep into Rose's kitchen in gagging wallops.

"There's been no land for sale here in decades." Beulah says it suddenly and Rose wonders what she means. Then she remembers the lie she had used to get herself into the house. She plays along guiltily. "Who owned it before you?" she asks, and Beulah tells her that for as long as anyone knew, this land has belonged to her ancestors.

"The Reids on my mother's side mostly. The Sneaths and Marches on my father's side added parcels," Beulah is saying. She pushes away a silk strand of hair from her face as if it were a fly. "Would you like something to drink?" Rose accepts a glass of what Beulah calls punch, garnet-red and too sweet, a child's drink, served in a glass with a straw. Rose sips it carefully, trying not to make a noise. Martha sits at the table and hums as she works on the clay boat, her whole, slow attention on it with her quick hands. *Her* boat, Rose can see now, a school project. But when Rose asks about it, Martha tells her in a polite tone that it's a Noah's Ark. "Ma'am," whispers Beulah, and Martha repeats it in her limp, sweet voice. Not the voice of her peers, the quick artificial patter learned from TV sitcoms. Not Eve's tartness either.

"Are your parents still alive?" Rose asks Beulah. She makes her voice slow and small.

"Mother is," says Beulah. "Father passed on many years ago."

Rose hesitates. "Is your mother here?" She suspects the woman in the other room is Mother, but Beulah looks away. Rose apologizes. "I just thought she might be able to tell me about, you know, the land. History, people, things like that." She hates needing to justify herself and wonders if she should go. She feels suddenly cold, suspicious, here with strangers who could be anything. Liars. But, of course, she is the stranger and the liar.

"Mother can't speak. She hasn't spoken since before I was born." Beulah flushes and a tiny vein pulses in her neck. Rose apologizes again, then Beulah gives her a sudden, radiant smile, like a light bulb before it flickers out. "But you know she can hear. She hears everything we're saying." She does what Rose had half-hoped, opening the door to the room with the piano, letting out a draft. Rose sees that both windows are open in the music room, keeping it cold, free of the scorched milk smell. The nervous silence stretches like a cat. Beulah bends down to give Jacob a whispered command and he heads off solemnly. All that remains on the bench is this small, bowed woman.

She must have been beautiful once. The bones in her face assert themselves against vacancy and lost contact with the world. She doesn't look at Rose but off to the side. Her eyes are milky with cataracts, heavy, as if they're turning to stone. At the nape of her neck is her one soft feature, a gray bun shaped like a cushion. Her clothes are all white, drifts of it over the ugly shoes, like Miss Havisham in the Dickens novel, without cobwebs or dust or bridal lace.

This is the way Beulah's flesh will go, thinks Rose. Mother is thin, almost wasted-looking, and her hands are large-knuckled and staunch, the hands of a laborer, incongruous on the ivory keys. Rose's smile is strained and polite and Mother sits there passively, until Beulah bends down to whisper something. Then Mother depresses a key silently and releases it. This goes on for a several minutes, the same whispering, then a silent march up and down the keys, until Rose recognizes what it is. A coded language.

She stands there nervously stirring what's left of her punch with the straw, trying not to stare at Beulah and Mother. There isn't much else in the room. Next to Mother, on the piano bench, is a black leather book with the title "Zion's Harp," but Rose sees no harp in the room. The upright piano is scrawled with scratches, with a wooden cross hanging over it. Broken-backed books are packed into a small shelf. There is a cot, neatly made up, next to a stern chair beneath one of the windows, and an even sterner clock hanging to one side.

Rose peers at the clock, but it had obviously stopped long ago at nine-something. Adagio, the pace of life in the house, has slowed to lento in this room. A waiting room. Who is Mother waiting for? Jesus, obviously. And Rose thinks she'll wait a long time. The long hair, she remembers from somewhere, is for the Second Coming, to wash Jesus' feet with, like wood nymphs in a fairy tale. It has a pretty, offbeat charm.

Beulah is whispering, this time too close to Rose's ear, and Rose has to restrain the urge to laugh, not out of humor but because of tension in her chest. All of this hissing and waiting. She supposes the silence is a way of letting go. She asks Beulah in a low voice if they should speak outside the room, and Beulah agrees. Then Mother begins to play something that sounds foreign and familiar. Something childlike, not from a hymnal. It skips and skims, like a feather duster all along the keys. And Rose realizes that this is for her ears, an improvisation. But when she looks at Mother with gratitude, there is nothing in those opaque eyes.

"She says the land belonged to the Reids from the earliest times, and they never sold any of it. But there were offers," says Beulah. She's not looking at Rose, her eyes darting from Martha to the stovetop, as if Rose's concerns are far from her own.

"So your family was here in this place thirty years ago."

"There were offers around the time I was born. The town wanted the land, but my grandparents refused. Mother says they kept coming back." Beulah moves to the stove and begins to stir what's in the pot. "Will you join us for lunch? It's corn chowder." With her back to Rose, she explains that her husband will be coming home soon and may have information about the land. "He's the family historian." But Rose declines, saying she's expected home.

"Who lives in those cottages down the road?" She slips the question in.

Beulah calls them *ancestral* homes. "The brethren live there with their families." This is all she will say, conscientiously stirring. Then Jacob comes back, carrying a younger child dressed in a flowered smock who looks half-asleep, her head nodding on his shoulder. When he sets her down, Rose sees this isn't a normal child. There is something odd about her eyes, set in her head at a slant with little pockets of flesh around them. The limpid lines of her mother's face are missing in favor of oddness, bluntness on a thick neck, with her tongue protruding. The girl's hair is sparse, standing up in birdlike tufts. Down's syndrome, Rose recognizes. She feels resentment as well as pity. She had said no to Down's syndrome, had refused to give birth to it, making up her mind. She doesn't want to see it in front of her, looking into her eyes, making her reciprocate. Then the little girl smiles and her elfin grace is set loose. She offers Rose the half-eaten biscuit in her hand, which Rose accepts.

"For me?" asks Rose, kneeling down, feigning delight. She puts the biscuit in her pocket. "For later," she says. "I don't want to spoil my lunch." The little girl reaches up to give her a wet kiss.

"This is Lydia," says Beulah.

"Do you like kittens?" Jacob asks Rose. He turns to Beulah. "Momma, may I show her the kittens?" Beulah says he may, and to bring Lydia, and to come back soon because Poppa is almost home and lunch will be ready. Rose glances at the quilt, a universe of wheels, as if she would rather be wrapped up inside it, but lets Jacob tug on her hand and lead her outside to the barn, where a huge animal smell of dung and piss crouches beneath the fragrant hay. The alarming smells and the cold bright air make everything seem ready to grab her and drag her back in time. And it seems to her that this place, these people aren't real, but a specter of the past allowed to materialize for a day, until she recognizes again that it is she who doesn't belong, who has dropped in from the evil present.

Whatever lives here, besides kittens, is out for the day. Rose remembers the oxen-looking beasts. Jacob leads Rose and Lydia to a cardboard box beneath a window where a blade of light has cut its way through, illuminating a swarm of dust motes. Beneath it, in a crate of hay, a small gray and white cat is nursing large-headed kittens, each fighting for a nipple. Jacob shushes Lydia. The cat's name is Skippy, he tells Rose, and Skippy doesn't like being touched. Rose is just as happy not to touch any of them. The smallest kitten has obviously been outweighed and outnumbered. Jacob helps it latch on by holding and petting a more aggressive sibling while Lydia coos and fingers each kitten head, then squeals and jumps back. She squats there like a mother hen, her odd hair coruscating in the sun. Rose forces herself to look at them both, the one who is conventionally beautiful and this other with her flat, primitive, impassioned face.

The children make her nervous with their backs to her, crouched over the nativity box. "Are those oxen you keep in the pasture?" she asks.

"No, ma'am" says Jacob, who is now cradling one of the kittens awkwardly against his chest.

She waits. "So what are they?"

"Highland cattle, ma'am."

"Do you raise them for their wool?"

"It's for their meat," says Jacob. "Momma says we can keep two. Would you like one?" He thrusts the squirming kitten toward her.

"I couldn't. My husband is allergic," Rose half-lies, and when Jacob asks her if she has a child, she says *no* to simplify matters, then feels both guilt and surprise. She wants to say she was joking, that there is no husband, but there is a child. But it's too late. She hears a car grind up the gravel road and both children forget her and the kittens in their rush to greet the driver, their father, judging from their cries. Through the smudged window, Rose can see Beulah on the porch. She's standing in profile without a coat, shivering, with her arms folded and her shoulders hunched forward, revealing what wasn't obvious before. Rose sees that she's wearing a maternity dress. She turns away, unable to witness the small reunion. There are farm tools hanging from rusted hooks on the barn wall, a scythe, some loppers, a row of other sharp implements she doesn't recognize. And she thinks how much she would like to shear all of that hair from Beulah's head. To slash away the trim house, with its copper pans and Mother and the piano and the high, exalted quilt.

Then she does what she has been doing since long before she fled from Randall. She steals away.

Skipping school in the South had been difficult, but here in the North, it's cake. No nosy next-door neighbors to see her climb aboard the bus, then exit at the next stop. Drac cooperates, letting her go with a wink, because Eve has been kind to him. When Momma asks her about school, Eve dismisses her with the same complaint. School here is boring. Life here is boring. Something Momma no longer argues about. The state of Eve's room, the style of her clothes, these are the bones they fight over, with Eve winning much of the time because she is tireless and Momma is not.

When she had chilblains, she was out of school for a week, which had been boring, but also a relief. It had placed her outside of Connie's reach, giving her a chance to think about Daddy, how she would get back to him. How she would never be cold again. She wouldn't even mind repeating a grade. She would settle for being twelve forever, to never be like Momma, working in other people's houses. It was embarrassing.

Of her earnings from back home, she had only seventy-five dollars and change left. To get back to Daddy, she would need a job, one that paid cash, enough to cover a cab ride and an airline ticket. Or even just a bus ticket. She has no idea how to find such a job in Swannboro. But she would find one. And when she had worked long enough to pay her way home, she and Daddy would start over. They would find a better house on a better street, and Daddy would teach her his trade. She would slip inside junk shops and angle up to consignment booths at flea markets like before, his "junior apprentice," to ask the ignorant about the price of rugs for which Daddy knew the value, but they did not. And she would surprise them with the cash in her pocket, the amount that Daddy was willing to pay. But they would never see Daddy waiting for her on the sidewalk, or ducking into a corner of the shop beyond view of the cash register. It was their game. Every item has value, Daddy would tell her. The trick is to make sure the price you pay is much less than what you can sell it for. Simple capitalism, he would say with a long lethal drag on his cigarette, depends on your knowing more than your seller, while never arousing suspicion. Otherwise, he might demand more. That was where she, Eve, had come in. "Because rug rats don't know nothing about rugs." How many times had he said it? It had a nice, smart-alecky jab, and she hadn't minded so much being called a rug rat, considering the importance of her role in the game. To "keep them guessing." To make them think they had the advantage.

He had taught her how to tell a hand-knotted rug from a machined one. And about the importance of provenance, which is proof of who owns an object over time. Without proof, Daddy said, and with ready cash, you've just as much right as anyone to ownership, even if the rug had gotten itself out of the Taj Mahal and flown across the ocean into someone's pawn shop. But if something comes with papers and labels and documents, that's a different story. Most of the rugs Daddy bought had no provenance, and he said that's what made it so much fun, imagining where each rug had flown away from. It was why he'd named his shop Flying Carpets.

She's decided that today will likewise be fun, a day without school spent tramping along with her find from the cave, a valuable item, it turns out. In the South, whenever she had felt sad, she had tramped around with something valuable on her, the whole stash of her money, or a thing that, if she lost it, would be more than missed. Mourned. Her diary. Her amber necklace. It had made her feel dire but in charge, possessor of a secret.

Once Drac lets her off at the next stop, Eve takes the valuable item out of her pocket, which technically she had stolen from Connie. But not really, since Connie doesn't know it exists and because she's a thief herself and a lowlife and a kidnapper. She brings the valuable item up to her lips and blows out a nasal sound. She had never possessed a harmonica before, but since this one is second-hand, she had taken precautions, polishing it with rubbing alcohol.

The harmonica is beautiful, neat as a comb, not a child's toy, but real, a musical instrument. It has ten square holes and two screws, and she had made it shine. On the top is a name, Hohner Meisterklasse, which sounds German, a language she associates with the girl whose diary she had read, Anne Frank in an attic, hiding from Nazis. When she had chilblains, she had found a German dictionary in Arm's room and looked up *hohner*, hoping it didn't mean something horrible. But it doesn't mean anything. *Hohn* means scorn. *Meisterklasse* means what it sounds like.

The bottom of the harmonica has another strange word scratched into it. It had taken her a while to see what it was. T, then A, then two Fs, then the part she had trouble with. It had turned out to be TAFFETA, a kind of cloth, she knew. What is this word doing on the back of a harmonica? She had swirled her name over it with fingernail polish, neon pink, but you can still see the original word if you look closely.

Taffeta, taffeta, she says aloud, testing the fussy sound, fabric you'd want in your wedding but not in your everyday clothes. She's walking into the woods where birds surprise her with their tapping and faceted shrills. "This way, this way, this way," one chants. The day is pure, one of the first undeniable signs of spring, still mercilessly cool, smelling of apples, and the beginnings of marsh marigolds are heading up along the path, although Eve doesn't know what they are. In the South, she knew the common names of wildflowers and weeds. Indian blanketflower, gayfeather, blue-eyed grass, broomrape, honeysuckle would show up in drifts so dense she never felt bad about picking them. Nature wasn't stingy the way it is here. She misses home like a food she craves. She misses the frank, warm, hospitable sky. Here everything is stony, cold, the path stuck with sticks, the sky always subtle, of two minds, gloomy yet hopeful, never just happy. And it has gotten into her, mixing her moods, making her sour and subtle. Keeping them guessing.

The path she's taking goes up to roughly where Connie had led her several weeks ago, but in a different circuit, one she had mapped out herself. A measly trail you have to keep mashing down because no one has used it in a while. But there is a granite boulder she likes, shaped like a turtle head, with lichens arranged in a pattern like a smaller turtle sunning itself. She sees it up ahead and thinks she'll duck behind it, maybe squeeze out a few notes on her harmonica, but as she approaches, she sees that the boulder has been marked with something red. Paint? Blood? Eve slows her pace until she recognizes that the red is a man's handkerchief. What Daddy would tuck inside his pocket and never use. Then, when Eve had a runny nose, out it would come, smelling of suede and smoke. He would grab her nose with his handkerchief and make her blow hard, honking along with her.

Eve pulls the handkerchief off the boulder. It's twisted and damp, probably full of germs, but she stuffs it in her jacket pocket anyway. A find, perhaps even a sign. Things that come to you like this are always signs, while things you take can be something else, she has found. Either good luck or bad. Eve believes in signs. This one means that Daddy is going to find *her*.

Her destination is the ridge overlooking the quarry, where she'd spotted the little crosses when Connie had marched her up there. She had forgotten them, but remembered yesterday. It's something to do, a mission.

She stumps her way up the path, which meanders in punishing slopes. The snowmelt has turned to spring mud in areas that would be hard to gain a foothold in even if they were dry, forcing her to climb on all fours like a beast. If there weren't so many stones sticking up like snouts, she would slide back down. In the myths she read about last year, a Minotaur waits for you at the center of the labyrinth. She wonders how far along she is in this one.

By now her palms are caked with mud, which she scrapes off on a boulder once she reaches the top, then wipes with the handkerchief. The ridge appears as a new world that lets her stand on its shoulders, showing off its height and muscular contours like a boy. She sees for the first time that it's handsome, that the place she had been dragged to by Connie is worth her attention. She stands there taking in the quarry cliffs, the lake flashing at her like a pocket mirror, until she has to sit down on the boulder.

Eve has never thought of a place as being herself, but now she does. It comes to her that she is the land she grew up in, its swimming holes, its hot afternoons ending in tantrums of rain, only to switch back to a smile as big as the sky, its forests draped with kudzu and lined with brambles and glades so lush it's embarrassing, Daddy used to say. The chanting cicadas, the mosquito hawks, even the taint of the drains in summer. She is all of that, too. And this place is someone else, someone opposed to her, cold and secretive, twisted, with a sour work ethic and accusing sky, making you crawl to its top. The quarry cliffs are beautiful, but they are not hers.

She chews on a thumbnail, despite the dirt, working on the little ingrown spike that has in turn been gnawing at her for days. All of her nails are now gnawed to the quick, making the tips of her fingers appear slightly clubbed, but vanity doesn't stop her. She chews semi-consciously, lulling herself with the pointed pain. Up in an oak tree, somewhere to her left, a bird tattoos a branch, making Eve jump. Another reason to distrust where she is, the way things scold and lunge at you for no reason. The woodpecker resumes its hammering, which feels like a beat in her chest. She tries to sight the bird among the bare tree snarls, walking in the direction of its racket. If it's a woodpecker, she wants to see what kind.

The path up here is well-trodden and defined in places by glum-looking boulders, mini quarry cliffs mostly of the same monotonous color. Why is so much of the stone in Swannboro the same boring brown? *Put-tut- tut- tut-tut-tut-tut.* The woodpecker's hammering is closer, but still no sight of what she imagines to be a black head with a red cockade attached to a stout, striped body. Now and then, she hears a scuffle in the brush. Squirrels off on business, taking advantage of the mild-for-Swannboro temperature to dig out what they'd buried last fall. At least, she thinks, the squirrels up here are the same as ones back home.

The path narrows and begins to climb, so she has to be careful, clinging when she can to tree trunks and boulders. The woodpecker knocks again, directly at the sky above her, it seems, where the path levels. Craning, staggering around with her face to the sky, reveals nothing but an agitated squirrel rushing from one tangle of twigs to the next. Dizzy, she falls to the soggy path on her rump, panicking that she has lost her harmonica. But when she feels inside her pocket, there it is, warmed by her body.

Put-tut-tut-tut-tut-tut. There is something else this time, a dull after-sound, so close now, she can't believe its maker isn't visible. She wishes she'd brought the set of binoculars she'd rescued during a science field trip after a boy on the bus had been sick all over the seat and left them behind. She's on her feet, one hand in her pocket to guard the harmonica, the other to grab what there is along the corridor, a thorny bush clinging to a brown edifice.

The path swings abruptly, and Eve slows because the gradient dips again. *You never know what might be down there.* The worry words of Momma, not herself, but she obeys the warning, flattening herself against the brambles and walking down sideways. Then stops, because here is the sound of pounding, but not the put-tut of a woodpecker. It's the sound of Daddy in his workroom, building frames to mount tapestries on. Her heart thuds before she recognizes the impossibility of what she is seeing. Daddy pounding a stake into the ground with a mallet. Daddy, or someone wearing his cowboy hat, his cowboy boots and suede jacket and jeans, squatting there, mumbling in a voice that is not Daddy's. Eve can make out only a few words, "money" and "Jesus," and "dang." The voice cracks a lot with a sad, gargling sound. A small shovel is stuck upright in the ground nearby, and beyond is the fire pit with the tramp trash that Connie had said held the remains of a cooked rat. At least now she knows where she is.

Eve crouches behind a boulder. If it isn't Daddy, then at least she'll have the pleasure of spying on an adult. Worth the filthy crawl up the hill and the guilt she feels, which is only a nick, from stealing privacy away from someone. This is theft, she admits, because the person thinks it is alone. Whatever it is, male or female. Its maleness could be an optical illusion. It flings the mallet down and rises to its feet. Like an old cowboy it stands there, head bowed, gloved hands folded, rigid. It could be a tramp. It could be the *Minotaur*. But, of course, Minotaurs aren't real.

    The person takes Daddy's cowboy hat off its head, and Eve sees that it's some kind of woman. Old, for sure, nearly as old as Momma, with thick salt-and-pepper hair in a long braid. Ugly, with a witch nose and eyes too close together, like the face of a large bird. As if to agree, the woodpecker hammers again and the person – the woman – looks up to a snarl in the treetops and Eve sees it, finally, the pileated woodpecker, which laughs shrilly, like an imbecile, flying off as if this place had never been worth its labor or time.

    Eve watches the old woman pull her hat on and the shovel out of the ground, then crouch to adjust the stake and pat the earth around it. Then she stands again with her hands folded. Something chirps keenly, a chipmunk, and the old woman's shoulders shake and her head is bowed, and when she looks up again, Eve thinks this old woman sure has the sorriest face she has ever seen on a person, the big, hooked foreign-looking nose and moping eyes perched above a hard little mouth chock full of teeth. As if someone had pinched her whole face. Trudging stiffly and not looking back, the old woman moves off with her shovel.

    Eve waits, just in case, but the woman doesn't return, so she sneaks over to the place with the stake. Across it, midway down, is another stick affixed neatly with twine. And from this hangs a metal tag. *Beloved Dustin,* it says. But there is no phone number or address. Eve flips it over to find: *T.A.G Signs*.

    It must be the grave of a pet. The woman's pet, a cat, maybe a small dog. And judging from the number of other stakes in the area, the woman had buried lots of them. Eve wanders, stopping to look at what is there. Most have lost their tags and some their crosspieces. One has a stake as tall as Eve, too close to the cliff edge to investigate. Of the tags, Eve can find only five still dangling, and all are the same. *Beloved Someone,* they all say, with *T.A.G. Signs* on the other side. There is *Beloved Scrap, Beloved Kooty, Beloved Yoko, Beloved Doughboy, Beloved Musetta.* Now there is also *Beloved Dustin.*

Eve loiters, scratching crosses in the dirt, then sits on a rock near the fire pit. She has never owned a pet, but knows what it would be like to lose one, because she has lost everything: Daddy and them, the people in the shop, the lava lamp on the countertop, her jars of feathers, rocks and marbles and shells, and the two friends her age she had, Hootie and Mary-Alice, who lived around the corner, and even Aunt Fleurette who was a mess but a good cook. She hardly thinks of them anymore, only of Daddy. She takes the harmonica from her pocket and runs her finger along the holes, then puffs tentatively on it, trying for *You Are my Sunshine.* All that comes out are clown noises, like noses being blown.

She expects harmonica-playing is one of those things you need someone to teach you. Pulling a loose branch off a naked shrub, she sweeps the path, which consoles her. It's something useful to do, scooting the brown leaf skeletons out of the way. Sweeping had been one of her jobs in Daddy's shop. Much of the path around the fire pit she clears this way, then begins working on the surface of Dustin's grave, where a few twigs and mashed acorns have settled. Her good intention is to tidy up all of the animal graves.

After a few minutes, the branch catches on a rock and snaps. Eve reaches down to pick up the rock. How satisfying it would be to toss it over the ridge and listen for a small gulp as it hit the quarry lake below. Skipping stones across lazy ponds – how long has it been? Chucking a rock into a lake would feel almost as good.

But the rock turns out to be the old woman's mallet. Eve thinks a mallet would be a good thing to keep inside her backpack, if she ever returns to school. She swings it in one hand and feels its weight. The handle is dirty, so she wipes it with the bandana. But there is something scratched into it. She polishes and polishes until she sees the familiar seven letters. TAFFETA. The same word, obviously a name, on her harmonica. She sets the mallet on the grave.

The harmonica is different, she thinks, fingering it in her pocket. Left for years in a damp cave, gulped down, lost and forgotten. Then found and paid for with her own skin. Bigger than provenance. The reward for all she has lost, her friends, her jars, her daddy. The mallet belongs to the old woman, Taffeta. But the harmonica belongs to nobody but herself.

He's found a better gig. Nothing to brag about, but to whom
would he brag, with only himself to face in the morning or, recently, early
afternoon? The new gig, tacked onto his old ones, has meant later hours.

The venue is Harpo's, a spaghetti restaurant on the main strip of
a neighboring town, an eroded brick rectangle with big greasy vinyl
booths in front, a dance floor in the middle, a gleaming bar in back with
No Smoking signs. But smokers from all of the river towns come anyway
for the music, which is homegrown and loud. Solid musicians imported
from nearby colleges along with locals, day drinkers with talent. Most of
them younger than he, if one cared about that sort of thing. No one
starving because Hank and Horace, the twin brothers who own the place,
feed the strays.

Arm feeds his lower and middle chakras. Taffy had whacked
habits into him that Julliard had reinforced with sado-masochistic
pettiness, a hair shirt with a frill, which he knew lay beneath the
formalwear of all classical musicians. "You bow like a hillbilly," one of his
instructors had criticized, which had mortified him then, but which
delights him now. Despite the hair shirt and a year of listlessly twanging
on a guitar, his whole body wants to jam, a reflex against recent events and
realities, an attempt, on the one hand, to fling away the mission Mark has
imposed with his theories. On the other hand, to shrug off the straitjacket
of fear that this is where his life will land, in a suburban cave with an
audience of beer drinkers. He recognizes what he is doing, allowing an act

to usurp the throne of art, but he needs the money and, more than that, a substitute for the oblivion he craves.

He's found a worthy contender, a cellist named Moby who looks his name. White, scarred, whale-bellied, with the arms of a pugilist. Yet what flows from his bow would melt a prison warden, and Arm suspects it has. The faded tattoo of a goat leers from under his shirt cuffs, looking like it was inscribed on the inside. Moby had approached him one night while he was playing alone. His shaggy buffalo head down, he had mumbled something unintelligible that seemed complimentary. Arm had smiled and nodded, giving him a thumbs-up and Moby had gone away, then returned with his cello and delivered himself in a tone so liquid and gorgeous, that Arm had stopped playing. Since that time, Moby has spoken only a handful of sentences. "Where's the loo?" "You done with that?" "Back in a flash." "Pass me the salt." "Sorry I'm late." Arm doesn't know where he lives or works, and doesn't care.

He thinks it can't be a bad thing to be seen with a bruiser like Moby. Because he suspects, but cannot say for certain, that he is being watched. Tailed, actually. Just a feeling, nothing more, with the occasional glimpse of a familiar, vaguely reptilian face in the crowd. Whose face, he really can't say.

Arm and Moby are sitting in one of the greasy booths, a plane of gray, well-thumbed formica between them. Outside their window hangs a string of gray grist, the remains of last year's spider web. Against the wall is a miniature jukebox that still accepts quarters but refuses to play anything but "Boots" by Nancy Sinatra. Arm flips through the selections. As a joke, he had been using it to line up his themes, but has found to his surprise that it suffices, and actually works better than a premeditated set. For tonight, he selects "water music" – "Yellow Submarine," "Bridge Over

Troubled Water" and the theme from "Titanic" – which he intends to mix up with Handel.

"You hungry?" One of the twin brothers is peering at them. Hank, it must be, who whistles between his teeth and wears a hairnet. The other one, Horace, chews a cud of gum and wears an earring. Both are healthy eaters, short and stout as teapots, with frontal characteristics from the era of their childhood: the mustache of Adolph Hitler and the 'fro of Harpo Marx, for whom the restaurant is named. Arm says he ate already, but Moby says, "I could eat," so two steaming plates of spaghetti and sauce are set before them and Arm has no choice but to dig in. He doesn't wish to offend anyone; in a new gig especially, he takes special care. Using a spoon as a twirling platform, he pirouettes spaghetti strands around his fork, while Moby spears his and shovels. Hank whistles one tune while Horace hums another. Arm tries not to think of his waistline and the effect Harpo's will have on it. He sets down his fork, only to pick it up again when Horace arrives with two smudgy glasses of Chianti. "On the house," he says superfluously. No one who plays at Harpo's pays. It had been the first rule of engagement.

This will be his third jam with Moby, and already the crowd is thickening. Arm watches Moby commandeer his plate while he picks at his mound of pasta and gingerly fingers the stem of his wineglass. He knows what will happen if he takes a first sip. Sliding the glass toward Moby, who has emptied his, he feels more treacherous than generous. But Moby ignores the wine, focusing instead on Arm's plate. "You done with that? Wordlessly, Arm pushes his plate across the table and Moby tucks in.

Before they're up, Arm hits the head which, at Harpo's, consists of two urinals and a stall, a claustrophobic arrangement he detests as it forces urinaters to become a couple, unrelieved by the usual phalange of anonymous non-spectators. So he is happy to see that the urinals are unoccupied and the stall is empty. He enters the stall, latches the rusty hook and stands there singlehandedly peeing into the bowl, shins against the chilly rim, glad of this private, unheard interval, which is impossible at home unless he takes his business outdoors.

Things there have worsened all around between Rose and himself, their arguments devolving from the car to the plumbing. This afternoon, they had feuded and he was accused of clogging the sink drain with whisker shavings. Furiously snaking the drain, he had liberated long sopping pelts, which he had then laid out on paper towels across the kitchen table as proof that he was not the culprit. This had provoked screaming by Eve, who came into the kitchen unexpectedly. His futile attempts to calm her only worsened the enmity of his sister, who spat out the insult that he was just like Randall. And he had swallowed the pill for Eve, who was just as insulted as he. "He is not, he is not!" she had screeched in her father's favor. By self-sacrifice, he had thought, he could pay his indulgence to his sister, while clinging to that most vicious optimism, that things could not get any worse. He realizes that her resentment goes deeper than any puncture wound he might inflict with his absence or presence, down into a hole of unhappiness and envy he can't fill. Down, down past his own presumed happy childhood and her professed unhappy one. Whether or not his childhood had truly been happy was not of any real concern for Rose. Nor did it matter that it had been the precursor to a disappointed adulthood. From his perspective, it would have been far better to be ignored than clasped to large-bosomed relatives, treated to violin lessons on the porch and birthday parties at local bowling alleys. But his sister would never accept his version of the truth.

On his way back to the booth, he tightens his muscles against the old nausea that arrives with a crowd. And this one promises to be larger than any he has played to since his short-lived career in the orchestra, when he still had a compliant nature, determined to beat down that part of himself that wanted to play outside of the lines, to cheat the score. Tonight, his talents will be dispensed on unruly talkers and laughers, who pay only half-attention. Moby hands him his instrument and they take their places before the mike, Moby slumped on a beaten-up barrel and Arm trimly standing. As they tune up and test the mikes, the audience ignores them, tough locals, weary yet talkative, most of an age that blurs the line between the sexes.

And yet, when he keens out the first few measures, even the men lower their voices and glasses. Middle-aged women, he knows, are his musical prey. Even gay men don't come to him as women do, not that there are any to be found at Harpo's. He caresses aging females with the oboe solo in the first *Water Music* suite, jazzed up, playing as he would if one of them were his, aiming his bow at a bottle-bodied Auntie Mame clubbing with three other older girls dressed in jeans, high-heeled boots, short, bottom-revealing jackets, the attire of their youth. And somehow she believes him, and because she does, the rest of them come along, blind to Moby, who steers.

By the time Arm sinks into "Yellow Submarine," they are his, and few of the men in the room are grumbling. He sneaks in more Handel, a bourée, the rigaudon and the famous hornpipe without boos or rotten tomatoes. He keeps them going with more seventies candy, riding the wave of their sugar high, unabashed when one of the balder men bellows nastily for Pink Floyd. He obliges him with a few depressing measures of

"Comfortably Numb," wishing he had his guitar, and the man sends him a beer, which he sets aside for Moby. When the set is finished, he bows and receives the kind of standing ovation Harpo's discourages, in which chairs are kicked over and tables are mounted. Two of the women are standing on one of them, blowing him kisses. The men holler and pound the walls before heading out for a smoke in the parking lot. And that is when he sees it, the one face in the crowd familiar to him, but which he can't put a name to, the hardboiled face of a bald man, with a trim, steeply arched nose, deepset eyes and a curt-looking mouth, a likely slot for a pair of fangs. Then the face disappears, whether into the crowd of chain smokers or into the damp, wooly jumble of bodies headed for the loo, he can't be sure.

Near the men's room, Arm stands in line to receive blunt male nods, an occasional thump on the shoulder, then is detained by a barstooler who wants to impress him with his knowledge of jazz. But mostly he's ignored. When it's his turn to enter the small room, the bases are loaded. He stands there, pretending to read graffiti, the usual juvenile nastiness, nothing worthy of the rapt attention he makes a pretense of. He misses the gay bars of the city, but not their loos, where there was often nastiness of an adult kind. He remembers with revulsion a loo that had a single trough as a urinal and the man he found lying in it once, prone, waiting to be showered.

The flushing sounds intensify his urge to pee, and he is glad once again that the stall is vacated first. As he eases past a brown leather belly, one of the urinaters zips up and turns slightly, and Arm realizes it's the face, again, of the man who has been following him. He feels absurdly cold, frightened, and for a moment cannot get his equipment to cooperate. He stands there, glad of a barrier between himself and the face,

trying to make his body obey, when a crumpled piece of paper is kicked
under the stall. His bowels seize. He smoothens the paper and reads it
sitting down. But it's nothing, a pentameter line from somewhere,
Shakespeare, he thinks, as vaguely familiar as the face. *The instruments of
darkness tell us truths.*

" Hey, bro." A heavy fist is pounding on the stall. "Shit or get off
the pot, man." Certain the voice doesn't match the face of his stalker, Arm
obliges, then flushes the crumpled paper down and experiences one of
those moments of frantic regret. Because there was something about the
handwriting, an odd way of slanting left first, then right, with lofty upper
strokes, which might have made it possible to identify. No matter, he
thinks, he would recognize it if he saw it again.

But he hopes *never,* as he saws his way through the second set to
a restive audience, taking them into darker woods with voluptuous
Arabian arabesques, and a few of the women who whistled at him before
begin to churn, contorting their bodies and thrusting out their arms
angularly like belly dancers. And then he is belted by a scream. At first he
thinks he is the cause; in a way, of course, he is. He sees that one of the
mouthier, alpha-male drinkers has seized the breasts of a belly dancer.
The scream is followed by more unpleasantness, a burst of violence that
Horace and Hank are forced to break up, their bodies going straight into
the center, staunch as jugs. Arm sees a hairy arm rise then come down on
a bald head and suddenly there is a pile-up of bodies. "Back in a flash."
Moby sets his cello down and rushes into the fight, and Arm knows the
set is over. Out of loyalty, he slumps in the background, instead of beating
the hasty retreat he desires. It isn't that he doesn't want to help, just that
violence, like football and most contact sports, repels him slightly and
bores him a lot.

Arm stealthily packs his violin and slips into his jacket. It's obvious that he won't be missed or even noticed, except perhaps by the women. In times past, one or two female audience members had come on to him, resulting in embarrassment for them both, Arm backing away politely as the women hovered. In truth, he had been flattered and felt badly for having created a false impression, if it was that. He knew for some women, pursuit of a gay man was an endless, unwinnable yet tantalizing sport, in others a sickness, and he supposes, in either case, he only had to be there, an unwitting mouse blind to the elaborate arrangements of bait. In all cases, it had been his playing that had attracted them. *Playing.* The term had always bothered him, as if music were merely a way to toy with and trap its victim, the listener. And he admits to having committed his share of musical flirting. Tonight, for instance. But it was hardly the same as real seduction. Sane, normal women would know the difference between playing and foreplay, he rationalizes. He has far too much respect for the gender to think otherwise. Besides, had he been a player in its most vulgar sense, a mere tease, he would have chosen a different instrument. The saxophone. Drums. Guitar. Well, in his case, of course, the guitar had been temporary.

He steps into a soup of mist and smoke. The smoke wreathes a group of barflies and the tall, slack figure of the cook, all inhaling and flicking their ashes. Yet another reason Arm hesitates to eat at Harpo's. He heads off in the direction of his car, his compass compromised by visibility he guesses is less than four feet. His boot crunches down on a discarded beer can and he struggles for a minute, hopping at first, then kneeling on the damp asphalt to remove the dented metal from his heel. He wants to throw the thing at whoever left it in the parking lot, but now it has become his burden to dispose of properly, with no recycling bin in sight. Irritably, he stuffs it in his pocket, rises to his feet, shivering, hugging his violin case closer to his body as if it could protect him. He may as well go back inside, the fog has become so thick. Then he hears a car door thump shut and thinks it might be possible to get his bearings once the driver switches on the headlights. As his retinas adjust, he views the hulls of cars moored in a milky harbor with the usual topography of cigarette butts, broken glass and crushed cans. Ghostly and ghastly. And there ahead of him, parallel to the curb that defines a fishing pond on the edge of the property, is his car with its corroded muffler and loose tailpipe. He really should have them replaced, he thinks, before a cop notices.

The mist parts and lifts for him as he walks toward his car and enters a small island of clarity, fairy-misted and half-mooned. Then his heart sinks. An unidentifiable female person, a smoker, is leaning against his car, one of the belly-dancers, he sees, as he approaches. He has half a mind to tell her off; he'd be within his rights. People shouldn't lean against other people's property, however humble. But then he sees, above the knoll of her quilted jacket, the sort of face common around Swannboro, roseate and puffy with alcohol and junk food and maybe a boring job, yet out of it shines a pair of eyes that seem to him more human than most. Loyal, friendly, sad. He dithers, digging inside his pockets, pretending to search for something, but in that same moment something propels him forward.

"Hi," she says. Already he can see where this is going. "You played awesome tonight."

That's very kind of you," says Arm, clutching his violin case.

"Ignore those guys. They're a bunch of animals. I mean, pigs are much nicer than them." She smiles, draws on her cigarette, crushes it out on a high-heeled boot, then cradles the butt in her hand awkwardly when she could more easily toss it in the pond. It makes him like her a little.

"Me and the girls were wondering if you'd like to come to our reading group sometime."

"A reading group?"

"We meet every Tuesday night. It's my house this week. We each bring a covered dish. But you don't have to bring nothing." She pulls at her jacket zipper and tucks her hand, the one without the cigarette, into her pocket.

"Palm-reading or book-reading?" he asks, smiling indulgently.

She giggles. "Books. We belong to a book-of-the month club."

"I see. Well, I'll have to think about that. I have gigs most weeknights and --"

"I forgot to say we meet on Saturday afternoons sometimes." She hesitates. "We read fiction last month. This month, we're doing nonfiction. One on alien abductions by this guy, a professor."

"I don't … I'm afraid I'm illiterate nowadays. Too busy working. Gigs, practicing, you know how it is."

"Well, it's a good book. Scary, though. But you'd like it." She pulls off a pair of owlish glasses perched on her head. Then she fishes in her purse. "Look, I just happen to have my card." She hands him a card with her face from at least ten years ago on it. "I sell real estate. You can call me anytime. Our next Saturday meeting's in two weeks."

"Thank you." He squints at the card in the dim light. "Sable," he says appreciatively. The last name is something Polish and unpronounceable. "What an unusual name. Lovely."

"My grandmother's on my father's side. She owned a riding ranch down the road in Doringham. Sable's Stables, she called it." She laughs. "She was a ticket."

He chuckles wearily. "Ha, ha. Well." He pulls his keys out of his pocket. "It was nice to meet you, Sable." He nods and ducks into the bomb, glad for the narrow escape from whatever rude thing he might have been forced to say if the conversation had taken disagreeable turns. An invitation to a movie, cups of tea, mall-strolling and potluck dinners in moldy church basements, whatever middle-aged women do with men on dates in Swannboro. He does not want to go there. As for UFOs, he does not want to go there, either.

Driving home, he remembers the dreadful arguments that had erupted out of the subject whenever Mark had brought it up. It had been one of their lowest points, just before the end, when Mark was devouring books about Roswell and claiming to have seen a disk in his backyard as a boy and another over the Brooklyn Bridge just before nine-one-one. And Arm had cruelly accused Mark of mistaking various ordinary phenomena – a helium balloon, Venus, or perhaps his ocular floaters – for UFOs. He had made unkind jokes about rectal probes. This had resulted in days of silence and brooding. Over fiction, Arm thinks smugly. Science fiction, the lowest form, in his opinion, lower than a romance off a vanity press. Yet the *reality* of their relationship was something that Mark could never fully acknowledge to co-workers, his family, even some of his friends.

From this interstellar distance, Arm can see that most of their disagreements had been over *factitious* matters. Imagined seductions and abductions, imagined conspiracies, imagined affairs. Imagined "craft" – how he hated the word – hovering over ordinary humans in their pajamas, stalking them over lifetimes, stocking up on their eggs and seminal fluids. Over such grotesqueries they had probed each other's motives, laid out each other's beliefs on the steel table of suspicion and doubt, and alienated each other forever. And for what? He is nearly halfway through his lifespan. If UFOs were real, he would have seen one by now.

But he would never see his beloved again. What would it have cost him to suspend disbelief for an hour or even a day? To tell Mark he believed him? He had lied about other things throughout his life to avoid complications. A bit of harmless dissembling might have given them back what little time they had, time now lost to shame. The shame of being in love with someone whose worldview was suitable for tabloids, not for the conversation of serious people, their friends, Arm himself. Shame over what most discarded as blarney, paranoia, offensive political incorrectness, presented as "the truth." Underneath it all, Arm has to admit, is something else about himself that he doesn't like very much. Worse, in a man, than hypocrisy.

Arm begins to weep. He swallows hard and coughs, but his efforts to distract himself are overcome by a hot cataract. He sobs and gushes until his nose drips and his vision blurs. He grapples with the steering wheel, refusing to do the sensible thing, to pull over and wait it out. Groping for a tissue in the glove box, he disengages a hoard of roadmaps and sunglasses, flashlights and CDs and a disembodied red thermos cup, an artifact that has floated along with him since he had been in high school. A ridiculous plastic object, with a chewed-up rim and broken handle, with a crack down one side, yet the sight of it pangs him. It seems to represent all that he is, broken, childish, displaced, incapable of giving or receiving. He takes it in his hand and tries to crush it, but only succeeds in swerving dangerously toward the other lane and a driver whose angry horn blasts him. But at least it stanches his self-pity.

He doesn't even know where he is, whether the hill ahead is a landmark he remembers or evidence of a wrong turn he had taken miles ago. But he soldiers on, driving at a crawl, enduring the censure of other drivers, who tailgate, then charge around him.

Arm flips on the windshield wipers, as if they could wipe away his tears. The sound of the wipers calms him. He breathes like a woman in labor all the way down a foggy road that he tells himself must be right, because it is the only road. Eventually he comes to Swannboro's town center, grateful for the first time to see the familiar grubby sidewalks, billboards, gas stations and the friendly squalor of rooms for rent above a chain of fluorescent-lit storefronts.

Coasting toward a stoplight, he sees that something is caught beneath his left wiper blade. A piece of paper, perhaps a parking ticket? No, logic tells him. Parking at Harpo's is free and frequently overnight.

Then he thinks it might be a note from that poor woman, Sable. He has received this sort of thing before from women. Love poems, sometimes, but most often wine-stained propositions. The crumpled paper flicks back and forth in a teasing manner. He hopes it will fall off and be carried away by the wind. With the tenacity of the trivial, however, it hangs on.

He's too exhausted to investigate once he's home, anxious to tuck himself and the violin inside. He blows his nose as quietly as possible. Cocooned in his smoky clothes and an extra quilt, he falls hard into a dream that crackles with metallic noises. In it, he is chased down a rabbit hole by a flying saucer, which divides endlessly into smaller versions like a cell.

On waking, his head is full of the previous night's fog and a crushed beer can cuts into his thigh. Caffeinated but still rumpled, he goes outside to piss in his bucket, prepared to greet the early afternoon with an open mind. In the east, vast white worms are being sprayed from the engines of a jet, slowly whiting out a delft sky. Squinting, sore-eyed, he observes the chemtrails slowly spread and fuse. Yes, yes, he sees that. It's a fact he can accept because he can observe it: someone is seeding artificial clouds. But what could it mean? And if it's true that the world is as Mark portrayed it, a chessboard ruled by soulless aliens who control the kings, the political pawns, then what exactly can he do about it? All he can do is play the violin.

And then it dawns on him that this may be exactly the point. As he stumbles across the yard, he nearly tramples the signs of someone's planting, whether Rose's or a previous tenant's he isn't sure. Here at his feet are tulips, their perfect tips entering the world with the promise of color. He wonders if his contribution is as vital to the scheme, an act of unfolding beauty that is only partially predetermined. Anything can happen because natural life, including his own, is full of surprises.

One of these surprises ends his reverie. A front tire on the Spirit is flat. He rushes over and kicks it. "Shit!" His entire day will now be spent comparing prices and sitting in a dingy shop while a new tire is installed. Pulling out the car keys still in his jacket, he staggers toward the trunk to begin the sweaty process of removing the flat and replacing it with the spare, grateful that Mark had initiated him in this mystery. While rolling the spare around to the front, he notices the piece of dirty paper still clinging to the wiper blade, and isn't sure which of the two is more disagreeable, reading the note or changing the tire.

The question is irrelevant. Scrawled across the lined paper are two ten-digit phone numbers he doesn't recognize in a cursive hand that slants first to the left, with tall ascenders, then capriciously to the right.

17 / *Rose*

She had heard somewhere that touching your own face is a sign of insincerity, or even deceit. She can't remember if it was a psychology text or some know-it-all on TV. Most likely, she thinks, it was her mother.

She's sitting in her unbuttoned coat on the edge of Natalie's antique sofa, trying not to touch the antique-looking pillows, fleshy rolls of damask and velvet. Natalie has opened the blinds, exposing the flawless skin of her parquet floor and the gleam of every object on surfaces that Rose has most recently dusted, the chiffonier, the curio cabinets, the walnut buffet. There is an aura of lemon oil over everything. And when she touches her face, there is a whiff of lotion, which she'd been rubbing on her cracked hands.

Spread before them on Natalie's marble-top coffee table is the quilt, halfway to completion, with all of the unfinished portions neatly pinned so that Natalie can see Rose's ideas and progress. And so far, so good. Natalie has made noises of appreciation, sighing and caressing the finished areas with her smooth oval fingertips.

But she has questions. Why, for instance, is the border of the quilt a river? It is a river, isn't it? And why does it contain what appear to be doll-sized shoes, a jacket, pants, a shirt? And what is the miniature quilt pinned to the top right? It's very sweet, of course. But what does it have to do with the quarry? Rose must understand, says Natalie, that she is playing devil's advocate. "Others will ask." She smiles and shrugs. "I would hate to have you tear out stitches."

Natalie concedes on the river, which Rose lets her believe is the Connecticut River when actually it is Succour Brook. And the miniature quilt can stay because it's Rose's artistic signature, a falsehood Rose delivers while touching her face. But the "doll clothes," these must go. Rose nods her head submissively as she does always, inwardly protesting. She doesn't like people mussing with her art. It's their quilt, they are paying, but art isn't a sport and she isn't a player. If they don't like what she's doing, they ought to try doing it themselves.

There are now many symbols of Taft in the quilt, remnants that Natalie has allowed her to keep. His violin lies at the pit of the quarry lake. His bones and brain are in the cliffs, his headstone at the top, his body, disguised as a blood-stained flag, droops over the shallows of the lake. And now the landmark where his clothes had been found, symbolized by the stream and the Joseph Coat quilt, have been worked in. Here lies Taft. Clever. And yet, homely, homespun, what one would expect. No one would suspect that she has turned the quilt into a shallow grave, what the quarry had once been, embroidered with clues. The original Greek word for "clue" meant thread, she knows, retaught to her by Eve when she had been learning the old myths. Theseus had gotten himself out of a labyrinth by retracing his steps with a thread. And here she is doing the opposite, working herself in deeper by the thread of her needle.

"We'll plan for an unveiling in early July." Rose agrees, but doesn't agree to stay for lunch, which Natalie has brought home from a local deli. And this is because she has a canker sore on her tongue that shoots a needle of pain whenever she eats or drinks. Folding the quilt into her backpack, she tells Natalie that she must run, literally, to her next job.

Free at last, she runs, but not to a cleaning job. Where she's going, all is dust. She pulls her jacket collar up to her chin and slots her hands in her pockets. She's wearing old clogs with knee socks and can feel her heel through the hole in one of them. Cold world. But not as cold as last week. Spring is winning the war and, already, crocuses are standing up in cheery crowds in the gardens and near the sandy deltas that border Swannboro's sidewalks. Rose walks with her head down in order to see them.

A block from her destination, the cemetery behind St. Stephen's Episcopal Church, she spots a gathering on the sidewalk. People holding signs, marching in circles, some of them lunging at cars as they drive by and accosting pedestrians. Religious fanatics? She shudders. Whatever they're doing she can easily avoid by cutting down a block before the church and taking a footpath into the cemetery. And this holds out the tip of spring, as the churchyard has been freshly raked and there are green shoots of what she guesses are tulips, perhaps iris and hosta, alongside the crocuses.

The cemetery is built around a hill. A wrought iron gate is open, like death, accommodating and polite, holding the door. Although she expects it isn't easy getting into this particular cemetery. The newer headstones are abstract sculptures, expensive-looking, and people have left little cairns on them instead of withering bouquets. A sign near the entrance forbids artificial flowers, along with dogs. Another outlaws skateboarding and sledding. But there is nothing that outlaws hunting. She hunts for Taft in the contemporary section, scanning every headstone. She hunts for a small, embedded square with his name. But after thirty minutes of searching, nothing. If Taft had a stone, it isn't here.

Rose hurries to the oldest part of the cemetery, where brown stones lean like chair backs draped with lichens that resemble torn, dirty doilies. The inscriptions are shallow and badly eroded, some filled in with moss-colored velvet. Rose can still make out several stiff, dressy names. Lavinia, Evangeline, Silence, Bethiah, Asa, Sherman, Jerusha, Ebenezer, Noadiah. The Swanns and Russells and Hills have whole mausoleums, built like miniature manor houses. But the names she's looking for aren't here.

Rose threads her way over coarse grass around crooked slabs shaped like crib headboards and carved with grim-faced angels. The life spans on these are pitifully short, some inscribed with sad verses for children born in the early 1700s. *God finished thy page in the fourth year of thine age.* Death had every reason to claim the young back then. Consumption, smallpox, scarlet fever, typhus. Rose thinks of Eve. Since the bout of chilblains, she has spent too little time with her. A wave of guilt sucks at her and the sore on her tongue aches.

She looks around for Reids, Sneaths and Marches, the surnames Beulah had given her, but instead finds the first names of her past lovers attached to the dead. There are Elihu *Taft,* Peter *Percival,* Roger *Talmadge,* Abigail *Fritz,* Tulip *Dabney,* Margaret *Randall.* There is a small Italian section in the cemetery, and in it she finds Lucia *Alfredo.* And beyond, the plethora of *Marks, Jameses, Paulies, Allens, Jakes, Richards, Thomases* and *Jeffries.* Everywhere she looks, there is a former lover's name. Except for Taft and Randall, she doesn't know whether they're dead or alive. The names make her feel homesick and a little ashamed.

And to think where it had started. It had been so cold in her parents' finished basement, on a braided brown rug beneath a sky of floating ceiling tiles, that her teeth had chattered. "You should be a singer," Taft had whispered. His attempts to possess her had felt like a rope burn and after a time, he'd given up, lying on his back and telling her about her brilliant future. He knew a woman who could train her voice for practically nothing. He knew of schools and scholarships. "And you should get some experience with men," he had said offhandedly, as if it were knowledge anyone her age already possessed.

Afterwards, she had shivered back into her underpants, her private parts burning, and he'd gone upstairs to give Arm a lesson. She'd cleaned up after herself, fetching a washcloth from the laundry room, blotting the rug with water and Ivory soap because, despite her impenetrability, there had been some blood. Kneeling on the rug, cleaning, she'd listened to a flighty dance by Vivaldi being played above her. Her mother had called her to set the table and asked what she was doing down there, sitting all alone, reading in the dark. "You'll ruin your eyes."

She should have grown to despise him, an older man preying on her teenage hopes and delusions. If he hadn't disappeared and died soon afterward, she might have. But she doesn't think it's likely. He was the only one to find her beneath the bad skin. The only one to say who she really was. If someone had asked, she would have offered these reasons for love.

Though I give my body to be burned, but have not love she recites mentally, *I have nothing*. Her only take-away from that other basement, in a Rockton church where she'd attended Sunday school.

As she walks away from Elihu Taft's headstone, the sun invades her eyes, transforming everything into a spill of gold. The trees, the church, the street are molten and she has to turn around to blink their silhouettes away. Down the lane of headstones, someone is coming. A ghost, she thinks impulsively, assessing the black blur. It's thin and is wearing a cowboy hat and a fringed jacket. Not a ghost.

She turns around and walks briskly back into the sun. If the person is Randall, she would only invite his attention by running. Don't look back, feign nonchalance, *pretend* you know the people on the sidewalk. Only a few remain, and the one coming toward her she recognizes from Stone Circle meetings, Eve's teacher, Albert Warner, the man with the abraded skin and bow tie. He extends his hand and she is shaking it, straining not to look behind her. Albert Warner, is telling her about the anti-war demonstration, which he calls "a vigil," but she's hardly paying attention. "You're welcome to join us," he's saying. She agrees reservedly, taking one of the large homemade signs on a stick, which exclaims, "U.S. Out of Iraq!" She had half-watched a televised report about the ground invasion and agrees that war is bad. The report had disgusted her, presented like sports event or a Christmas special. But beyond this, she has no knowledge, no opinion.

She's using the sign to hide her face. To take refuge from Randall, if the person in the hat is Randall.

In the meantime, she's receiving an education from Albert Warner, who is telling her about George Bush and Daddy Bush and Colin Powell and Condoleeza Rice, and how Saddam Hussein had not been complicit with Al Qaeda. "There was no uranium yellowcake imported from Africa or anywhere else." She nods her head, saying nothing, disguising her ignorance. "Laurie Mylroie was wrong about Islamic radicals and Saddam Hussein." Yes, yes, nods Rose, who has never heard of this person, Mylroie. Off Albert's tongue rolls a torrent of facts and dates and places and names. His pitted face is red and his authoritative, bullet voice is at war with the "Pray for Peace" sign he's holding. A murmuring group of elderly women and a silent, middle-aged bald man are standing to one side, collectively holding a banner that says, "Stand up for Peace." The women have short-cropped nun hair. They have shrunken, inward-looking eyes, sagging mouths and they look sick and tired of standing, much less standing up for anything. All are wearing heavy orthopedic shoes. One of them drops back and sits on the stone wall behind them next to a torn, nearly empty bag of donuts. She shakes her feathery, bird's head sadly. "Tell her about the Patriot Act," she says in a quivery voice. "Tell her about the depleted uranium," snaps another woman whose angry anti-war buttons date back to the Vietnam War. Albert tells Rose about shock and awe and the Kurdish front and Jessica Lynch. He snorts. "That poor kid was used."

Rose is ashamed of not being able to reciprocate. She offers what platitudes she has. "War feeds the corporations." "War solves nothing." The canker sore needles her. She comes to realize that Albert expects no response at all, that she is serving his need for an audience as he is serving hers for cover. Men like this are familiar to her; she has slept with enough of them to pack a graveyard. The silent bald man looks at her sympathetically. "Would you like some hot tea?" he asks. She smiles and darts a furtive glance over her shoulder. No cowboy hat, no fringed jacket. No one is there but a couple of wiry boys in trousers that have ridden down below their underwear waistbands. With skateboards tucked under their arms, they're heading up the cemetery hill. The bald man knows them by name and asks them to join the vigil, but they avoid his eyes and shake their heads no, bent on their illegal, secret slide.

The bald man is at her side with a steaming cup of tea from a thermos. "You look as if you could use a warm drink." His eyes are kind, pewter-colored, but one of them lists. "I'm the priest at this church," he says. "Father Andrew." He offers his hand. She hesitates, then chafes his hand with hers. "You can call me Drew." The good eye looks straight at her while the listing eye looks beyond. "Just don't call me Andy." His smile is directed toward something to the side. Like most people, Rose assumes that the clergy can read minds. Her fear of exposure outweighs her desire to be civil, until the silence feels heavy. "I'm Rose," she says. She senses an affinity, what has always turned out to be false.

The tea is sweet and comforting, despite the canker sore. By swallowing carefully, she manages to circumvent the pain. They stand a little apart from the others, sipping out of paper cups, and when he asks her where she's from, she tells him she lives in Swannboro on Velvet Lane, and before that in Rockton, skipping the South and Randall, and the many places she had lived before him. Funny, he says, I detected something in your voice. His fingers are bare of rings, or even the telltale incision of a past ring, she notices. But perhaps, she thinks, it's because Episcopal priests make vows of celibacy. She isn't sure.

And then it occurs to her that the business of a priest is life and death. She takes the plunge, asking him about the missing dead, the Marches, Sneaths and Reids she had hoped to find in the cemetery. *I met this strange family.* And he laughs in a way that surprises her. They aren't here, none of them is, he says, they have a private cemetery of their own in "Reid land." He isn't making fun of them, but to Rose it sounds like "storybook lane," and she laughs. What a luxury, she says, to have a cemetery of your own. He looks at her, inscrutable and sober, as if she had said something offensive. "It's on Reid Hill Road," he says.

Albert is talking to her again, explaining the difference between Sunnis and Shiites. His face is red, as if scalded by his words. She thinks, *I don't want to know.* He corners whoever will listen, prophet-style, badgering and shooting his mouth, but finds the only ear in an old man, obviously homeless, with greasy gray hair and pants that bulge at the crotch and pucker at the waist, held up by a belt with too many notches.

His pants hems drag along behind him. "Screw Bush," says Albert, "Fuck Cheney," and the homeless man nods his head in agreement. The elderly women shake their heads at Albert's profanity and begin packing up their signs and tote bags. Father Andrew brings the homeless man a cup of tea. Rose can hear the swift slicing and scudding sound of skateboards in the background. Some crows strut toward a half-doughnut one of the old women left for them on the sidewalk.

She looks at Father Andrew, "Drew," whose pristine head is bent close to the greasy head of the homeless man. His saintly attention triggers something in Rose, a desire to be charitable. She piles the signs that remain neatly, as Albert stalks off. Then she follows Drew and the homeless man into the church, carrying her clattering signs. Drew thanks her, tucking the signs beneath a broken pew in the narthex. He introduces the homeless man as "Clark, our sexton," who offers a worn, heavily veined hand. The group meets here Wednesdays and Saturdays for the vigil, Drew tells her. She should feel free to join them.

"Don't mind Bert," he says. He has an accent that buries his consonants and keeps his vowels wide open. Massachusetts? Maine? She has lost her knack for placing northern speech.

"He seems to know it all," she says lamely.

"Knowledge is a burden." His good eye stares at her while the other is off somewhere. "The more knowledge, the more grief."

"He does seem sad," she says. "But mostly angry."

Drew shrugs. "We should all be sad and angry. But most of us prefer not to."

"You mean about the war."

"I mean about the desecration." He turns toward Clark and they open a creaky closet, where brooms and mops have been stuffed and keys hang off little hooks next to a conundrum of electrical breakers. Clark unlocks a door to the sanctuary, then pushes a broom down the long aisle, his shuffling steps making a lofty echo. The sanctuary ceiling looks like an upside-down boat with tall, pale green windows arching up to it.

The narthex is being used as a charity corner, with boxes that contain cans of food. One is labeled "fellow humans," another, "cats and dogs." Drew sits on the one labeled "cats and dogs" and offers Rose the other. He says she looks rather sad herself. "Like you lost your best friend." Maybe I have, she says, seating herself delicately. With the door open to the sanctuary, her voice echoes a little and reminds her of singing in halls and lavatories with high ceilings in school. How she would find empty rooms just to feel her voice peal around her. And this makes her want to tell him things. Not to confess. To be heard, to draw her own lines and fill them in on the fresh page she's been given. She doesn't tell him about Randall or Arm or the murder of Taft or her work as a housecleaner or the names of her lovers in the cemetery. She tells him about her quilts while he looks into and past her with his mismatched eyes, as if there were two of her, one seated and the other standing to the side.

"I have a daughter," she says, "who's also very artistic. I decided to move north for her sake, to give her a better chance in life." She clasps her hands tightly around her knees while a light clove fragrance floats and fades in the air, and she realizes that Drew must be wearing men's cologne, which seems odd to her, a vanity.

"It must be hard," he says. "On your own, I mean." Rose nods gravely. He wants to know about her interest in the Relds and Sneaths, what had brought her to seek them out, and she tells him about her commissioned quilt. "They've been in Swannboro a long time. I thought they could tell me more about quarry history." They sit quietly as the sun pulls at the clouds and the sky begins to hang down. In back of them, the soughing of the mop, the tramping, the echoes that seem to her funny and sad all at once.

"What religion are they anyway?" she blurts. "I don't know much about that sort of thing." He tells her they're a strain of Apostolic Christian. "They're isolated here in the northeast, just one church in the whole state, and it happens to be in Swannboro. But they manage to keep it going. Like a spider's web, some say."

"What do you mean?"

"This town used to be a hot spot for Mormon missionaries. A few never left. Caught in the web. Converted to Apostolic Christianity and married in. Disaffected Amish, Mennonites, Baptist fundamentalists, others have trickled through. The Reid family has a long history. Stricter than other fundamentalists in some ways. Not as strict in others. They allow certain kinds of art."

Rose leans on her elbows and cups her chin. She knows what she wants to ask, but the moment rolls away like an egg she doesn't want to crack. The church is colder than outdoors and she finds herself shivering. Beneath her, the box has caved in and soup cans are cutting into her legs, but she remains sitting there primly. Her eyes are on the sky, but return to him at discreet intervals. He has the bald man's habit of bowing his head and laying his hand on his forehead as if he were blessing himself.

"Tragic," she says softly, "what happened to Beulah's mother." He rubs his head and she looks at him as she would any other attractive man. Olive, slightly seamed skin, a lean nose, square jawline, the bone structure not needing the embellishment of hair to be handsome. A fit body, almost muscular. Mid-fifties, no more, she is guessing. Both eyes are observing her now and she drops her gaze.

"Do you know what happened?" she asks. He looks at her in his double-sighted way again and laughs. Everyone in Swannboro would like to know the answer to that question, he explains, and nearly everyone has a theory.

"What's yours?" she asks, looking away. Stone stairs twist toward what she imagines must be a belfry, and she flicks her eyes upward.

He shrugs. "It was just before Beulah was born. I've always assumed it had to do with that. Post-partum depression. Or something worse. A transgression. Incest. Or even something she imagined. But, you see, it isn't my business."

"People don't lose their ability to speak because of something imaginary."

"People like that do. To them, a thought is real. Well, technically, it is. It's possible to commit adultery in the heart."

"You think she committed adultery?" The word sounds archaic, like "conjugal" or "illegitimate." She makes a face.

"I wouldn't presume. I think something profound happened that changed her and made her silent."

"Well, she still plays the piano. She and Beulah have a language."

"The piano, maybe, but not the violin."

Rose gives him a look.

"She was a very talented violinist. If she'd come from a different family, she might have had a career."

It could be a coincidence, Rose is thinking. There are violinists in many families, even mine. "Who was her teacher?"

"The Reids home-school their own. All of them do."

"I mean, who taught her music?" He explains that music is taught, along with everything else, at the kitchen tables of the faithful. This keeps her quiet for a while, enough to create the impression she intends, that she isn't really interested.

"How do you know so much about her?"

"She would have been my classmate in high school. I was from Swannboro originally." He has stood up and is looking into the sanctuary. "I came back here when this post opened." He admonishes Clark to be careful of a loose board in the choir, and Clark says he's got it. The space resounds with his rough voice.

Drew sits back on his box. "Her name is Lilah. Lilah Reid, before her marriage to Oliver Lamb. Beautiful. The most striking girl in Swannboro back then. The Reids couldn't keep her in a bubble. People, boys her age, would see her at the grocery with her sisters and brothers. It would have been hard to miss them in the nineteen-sixties and seventies. And Lilah was friendly back then. She played where she could outside of the home. Outdoor venues mostly. Country fairs, like that."

"Did you date her?"

"Me?" He laughs. "No one dates a Reid. Suitable mates of the same faith are approved by the elders and they are married. Very simple. But, of course, nothing is so simple."

"Haven't any of them defected? I mean, you'd think some would."

"Maybe. Probably. I seem to recall a girl, a boy who ran off together once. But I doubt they got very far. That sort of life. Hard to break away. I mean, it isn't just belief that holds them, but family ties. It's how they survive.

"How do they survive? I mean, how do they make a living?"

He smiles. "What does all this have to do with the quarry?" he asks, and she blushes to her roots. When she swallows, her tongue feels like a nail has been driven through it.

"Farming," he says. "Cattle-raising. Soap-making and farm goods, cottage industries, family businesses. Not as much as before, of course. Some are educated professionals. Many of the younger men have jobs in insurance now. They commute to Hartford along with the rest of the herd. But most of the married women stay at home."

The attraction would never be mutual, she is thinking about Drew. She's glad to see Clark shuffling back, his pants dragging. He's deliberate, taking his time, the church hall magnifying the smallest sound he makes, his ragged breathing, the loose change in his pockets. As he returns his broom to the closet, it knocks keys off the board and he is crouched on the floor, picking each one up with rapt, agonized attention. And she can't think of a less likely setting for what she is feeling.

But now Drew is inviting her to the Easter service next week. "It's all downhill from there." And she is saying, "Well, maybe."

The light in the narthex changes and she sees what she had missed before, that the eye staring straight at her is the glass, false eye, while the other, which glances past her, is the real. It peers behind her, to something she can't see.

"You trip me out, Yowl," says Connie. "You know that?"

Eve is walking several paces ahead of Connie, who is trailed by Brandy and Bailey. They're on the sidewalk bordering a main strip in Swannboro during a low traffic hour. It is Thursday. Eve can't remember which class she is supposed to be in. The road ahead of her would be full of trouble if the adult drivers pulling into muddy parking lots knew who she was and where she belonged. But no one who amounts to anything knows her in Swannboro.

She stares straight ahead, ignoring the voices in back of her. She's pulling a little red wagon that says "T.A.G. Signs" on one side and "Signs for Every Purpose Under Heaven" on the other.

"Hey," yells Connie. "I said, hey! Sucker bitch!" Eve can feel Connie walking faster until she overtakes her, and then she's right next to Eve, breathing hard for someone her age.

"First you're a pussy, afraid to go down into a wet hole," says Connie. The B sisters giggle. Eve can hear them talking behind Connie in their twin way. "Pussy hole," says one. "Pussy hole," snorts the other.

"Now you're hanging out with a bridge troll." Connie has passed Eve and is walking backwards in front of her. "Admit it."

"I don't know," says Eve, "what you're talking about."

"Ah dunno what yoh-er tawkin' about," imitates one of the sisters and they both laugh hysterically.

"You all are crazy, or something," says Eve. She digs her free hand into her windbreaker pocket, reassured by the smooth feel of the harmonica together with the starched surface of dollar bills.

"Or sump-mm," Bailey imitates. Brandy has her arm over Bailey's shoulder. "Sump-mm," she repeats. They sputter.

"We seen you there last week. And now you're pulling her wagon. You and that troll are buddies," says Connie walking backward.

Eve waits for Connie to back into the telephone pole behind her before she says, "Careful." But if Connie feels the crack on the back of her head, she doesn't show it in her face, which is even bonier than Eve remembers. Connie stands there against the pole as if it were her destination. Across the street is Lucky's Feed Store, which is Eve's destination, but she has no intention of letting Connie know, so she turns the wagon around and walks the other way. The other two lazily make their way toward Connie like two blobs in a lava lamp.

"You better watch yourself, Yowl," says Connie. "Because we're watching you. And that cave is ours. That hag thinks it's hers, but she's wrong. You go near it, we'll be on you."

Eve turns around. "I told you there was nothing in that cave but an old boot." But Connie and the sisters are already walking away, toward the feed store at first, then Connie changes her mind and crosses onto a dusty street that splits Swannboro down the middle between commercial and residential and leads down to the river. She's pecking away at something in her hand, which Eve recognizes as a cell phone. It's 2003, and Eve still doesn't have one, and prospects for the future don't look bright, considering who-all she lives with. "We can't afford cell phones," Momma has said too many times. Well, here is evidence against that. If Connie can afford one, anyone could.

The man at the feed store is slow-moving, shaggy and big as a bear. He eyes her suspiciously as she lifts two big sacks of dry cat food onto her wagon, then starts building a little tower of canned cat food. He scuffs around the aisles pretending to be engrossed in birdseed and fertilizer. "Aren't you s'posed to be in school?" he grumbles when she wagon-wheels over to the register. Eve tells him she's home-schooled. It had worked with the old woman, Miss Gates, and it works with the man. She takes her sweet time counting out cash Miss Gates had given her, as if she's doling out cards. It makes her feel happy and grown-up to handle money again.

And she realizes, pulling the heavy wagon back across town, that she is happy for the first time since moving here. Happy to be alive on a day when the sky isn't growling for a change. She had been a mess without a purpose, without a paying job, and now that she has one, it couldn't hurt to smile. She grins at the first person she sees, a bald priest crossing the street, and is rewarded with a smile made tentative by the sidewise way he looks at her, as if he's not sure she's really there, or as if she's taller or farther away. Or maybe the man isn't a priest at all, she thinks, but just some pervert dressed up like one. But it's a smile from another person, something she has not wanted in a long time. Miss Gates doesn't smile, not even at her cats.

She'd found her the hard way, in the Yellow Pages. Eve knew no one would hire a twelve-year-old except as a babysitter or grass cutter or maybe a papergirl, but she had been brought up in a shop. So she looked for shops that sounded ragtag or cheap or too small to matter. She looked for T.A.G. Signs and found it next to a bigger ad for a tackle shop. The sign shop had a funny address: 1 Shirley Gates Lane. But it was real, a squiggle on a Chinese restaurant placemat street map she had found folded up in the phone book. It was just a hunch that the old woman might need help.

Eve could run errands, put sales flyers under car windshield wipers, sweep, empty ashtrays, dust shelves and counters. She had a whole speech prepared, but by the time she arrived at Miss Gates's, she was so unnerved she just stood there with her mouth hanging open.

The place of business was two trailers, one a caravan home on wheels, with curtains in the windows and a door with several locks on it. The other was a metallic Quonset hut. On neighboring lots, a few dented trailers hunkered, off their wheels and sunken into the soil. They would all have had a perfect view of the rusted underside of the Swann Bridge, except that most of the other trailers had no views at all because of the junk piled to the top of each window. But they all had the traffic noise, an interminable low roar. Nearby was a warehouse with painted-over windowpanes and a small For Rent sign on one of its doors. Loose gravel smudged the borders of each yard.

Someone had recently raked the old woman's yard, leaving tidy parallel lines in the soil, sprinkled with grass seed. There was a whiskey barrel near the caravan door, full of pansies in tart shades of yellow, orange and violet. And there were signs up and down. One with the words "Keep Off" in curly capital letters, like what might be found inside an ancient book. Another sign announced "T.A.G. Signs – Signs for Every Purpose Under Heaven." And on the trailer door was a hanging sign that said "Wipe Your Feet," red on yellow, which seemed more like a warning than a friendly reminder. There were more signs arranged in a row near the front path with quotes from books, Eve guessed, or Aesop fables. "Attempt not impossibilities," said one, and the rest were similarly bossy. "In serving the wicked, expect no reward." "Every man should be content to mind his own business." "Those who suffer most cry out least." "Do not attempt to hide things which cannot be hid." And there was a sign with chapters and verses, PSALM 40:1-2 and ISA 13:19-22 and HOS 4:6 and LUKE 19:11-27 and 1 COR 1:27-29 and EPH 5:8-20 and REV 3:7-13, with no other words beneath them, as if you were expected to look them up.

Seeing a tire swing hanging from a scraggly tree out front, Eve had tiptoed around the grass seed and sat there a while, trying to work up her courage, until the door in the house trailer opened and the old woman came out and asked her what she wanted. She wore a pair of blue overalls over a plaid shirt and a look of suspicion, one of the few expressions at home on the stark topography of her face. An orange tabby with a huge one-eyed head appeared and sat beside her. Then a small gray cat sprang around the tabby and hunched down in front. The tabby cat spat, and the old woman said, "Easy, Sledge."

"Are you Taffeta?" asked Eve.

"I used to be," said the woman, "Who are you?"

"I was just wondering if you're looking to hire someone," said Eve. "To do chores."

"Chores?" The old woman said it as if it were a foreign word.

"Yes, ma'am."

The old woman stood there, looking at Eve with her long bony hand over her mouth. "Come back tomorrow," she said. Then she turned back inside her trailer and shut the door. The cats stayed where they were, eyeing Eve languidly. It had seemed a good idea not to interfere with them, so Eve had walked the two miles home and checked the mail.

Letters, two so far, had arrived from the school, which Eve had stored underneath her mattress. She hadn't opened them, but she knew what they contained, knowledge that became a sharp pain in her stomach whenever she thought about it. She tried not to, pushing the thought beneath her mattress with the letters. The next day, when she returned to Shirley Gates Lane, something green was flickering around the yard. It looked, at first, like a salamander, but she knew such animals did not appear this far north in a cold month. It danced along the edge of the yard on the wind and she chased it around until she saw it was only a ten-dollar bill folded up in no particular way. She was holding it out in her hand when the old woman opened the door.

"I think this must be yours," Eve said.

The old woman had her cowboy hat on and a pair of heavy gloves. Her suspicious eyes were red around the lids, as if she hadn't slept. "What kind of girl are you, anyways?" she asked. Eve stood there with the money and a feeling of having been caught red-handed.

"Most girls your age are smart-alecks, flirts or snitches. Which kind are you?" The old woman waited. She folded her arms across her chest. "You a taker?" she asked. "Or maybe you're a bully."

Eve felt her heart drop down into her shoes. A smart-aleck, she thought.

"You don't seem to be much of a talker, anyways." A motorcycle blasted over the bridge, then a car that thudded with the radio turned up too high.

Eve made herself look into the old woman's eyes. "I'm a worker, ma'am. I'd only be two dollars and fifty cents an hour."

"Well, you seem honest. I can see that." She snatched the bill out of Eve's hand. "What's your name?" They had gone down the steps and around the trailer a few times with the old woman asking questions and Eve answering. "How old are you?" "What kind of accent is that?" "Why don't you get a paper route like other kids your age?" But mostly, the old woman talked. She would grab a handful of leaves or twigs caught in the underside of the trailer and crush it in her hand and complain about weather messing up her yard. She hated wind and cold, but mostly, she hated rain. "If I was God, I would have quit while water still come straight out of the ground. Bet you didn't know that, did you. A long time ago, it never rained." Eve said she didn't know, but that would be just fine with her, too. Miss Gates said Genesis ground water must have been better than the kind that comes out of her well. "Half the time you can taste the diesel from the plants next door and the sulfur from hell. I have to go up to the public library to brush my teeth. Or waste my money on bottled water."

The old woman had introduced each of her cats. All four, she said, had begun their miserable lives in the empty warehouse behind them, which was full of feral cats she fed whenever she could. "Some are floor cats, living mostly indoors, others are mud cats like Sledge here was. Some of 'em come from good homes and got lost, but most never had a home. I'd take more in, but it gets to stinking with more than four of them sharing a cat box."

Sledge had stalked them around the trailer while his sad life was being narrated. "Found him on my steps one morning with his balls chewed off, one eye hanging by a thread and his belly dragging. His life was a tragedy before he got here, but it's been a comedy ever since. For him, anyways. The rest of us still got to suffer." Slinky, a low-slung black cat, had gotten in through a vent hole ("sprayed my bathroom so bad I had to replace the vinyl") and capable, gray Henrietta had always been around, a former mud cat plagued by "fertility" and "a bunch of rotten kids" who had stuffed her down a storm drain. The old woman said she had chased them off with a stick, then had to crawl down herself to rescue the pregnant cat. "Got pregnant after she was spayed, too," the woman said. "Twice. Kept the kittens until they overrun me, then found them all homes. I kept Pindrop, though, and now Pindrop is pregnant. She got out one night and that was all it took. She looks guilty, don't she. The little tramp." Pindrop, a white cat with a pudding shape and a gray cap and vest, just sat there, looking glum rather than guilty.

"Anyways, you're hired," said the woman. "My name is Tag, but I prefer people your age to call me Miss Gates. You can start tomorrow cleaning up after the weather." Eve had raked up old leaves, picked up acorns and swept the front path the first day, while Miss Gates shadowed her and talked. She used strange words like "lollygag" and "mollycoddle," which Eve had never heard of before. "Never mollycoddle a cat," she said. "Never lollygag on an errand." It was easy to tell what she meant. After a while, Miss Gates said she had to go make signs and trudged over to the Quonset hut with her elbows out. No one came out of the junky trailers in the adjoining yards and Miss Gates remained inside the Quonset hut all morning with her cats. While she worked, Eve could hear her over the traffic, humming and talking to the cats, asking them questions, then answering for them. "You hungry, Pindrop? She says, 'Of course I'm hungry, I'm pregnant aren't I?' " Eve wasn't invited inside the hut or the caravan and was paid in dollar bills and change out of a cigar box while standing outside on the caravan stoop. She left before noon. The next day, she had been handed a pair of yellow rubber gloves and told to scrub the sides of the caravan with a kitchen sponge and a bucket full of ammonia and suds. Then she had to pick out leaves from around a lonely-looking carousel clothesline anchored in the grit of the backyard. When she was finished, Miss Gates had appeared out of nowhere as if she'd been checking her progress all along. "When do you go to school, anyways?" she asked, and Eve had told her she was home-schooled. "Well, self-help is the best help, I always say. Or something like that. You better come inside now and have a sam-widge."

By then Eve was hungry, but entered the trailer with a sense of dread, expecting spider webs and a cat piss odor. Instead she beheld a tidy collection of furniture, books and bric-a-brac, arranged tight as puzzle pieces in the caravan. Metal lockers with doilies on top stood next to bookshelves filled with paperbacks, an old set of Encyclopedias Britannica and fat hardbacks that still had library labels on them. Other books were ranked by height from a world atlas down to a thumb-sized field guide. The art on the walls consisted of photographs of cats, framed and hung cheek by jowl. Sun-faded striped curtains hung in the windows, and the same fabric sang out its vivid original primary colors on a narrow bed at the far end of the caravan. The air smelled slightly fishy, of cat food and pine chips, a scent Eve liked better than ammonia. All four cats were on the floor with their heads bent over separate bowls, lapping up food, while an old mantle clock clucked from one of the bookshelves.

Miss Gates had set the dinette table with flatware on cloth napkins and plates that had a farmy-looking picture in the middle of wheat bending in the wind. There was a platter of egg salad sandwiches on white bread, isosceles triangles with their crusts trimmed off precisely. When Eve reached out for one, Miss Gates grabbed her hand. "One of us has to say grace first," she said. "Which one of us will it be?" Eve said nothing, her hands folded in her lap, a slow flush creeping up her face, while Miss Gates said grace. "Dear Lord," she said, "Thank you for lunch. Thank you for my cats. Thank you for work orders and helpers who fall out of your blue sky. Keep us all in your hands. In Jesus' name, amen." Eve watched her out of the corner of her eye. "Well," said Miss Gates. "Dig in."

Miss Gates made an odd clunking noise while she ate and drank, as if she were swallowing coins. Between them, they ate all but two of the egg triangles and drank most of the chocolate milk poured out of a crystal vessel Miss Gates called a "picture." "This old picture was my grandmother's on my mother's side," she said. "And these old plates are all I have left of my mother. She broke or drank up everything else." Miss Gates drank more chocolate milk, *clunk, clunk,* then she pointed to a framed picture of a pretty woman with a big globe of ratted blonde hair, pale blue eyelids and a pink lipstick smile. Her eyes were half-shut, the way they might be if someone were expecting to be kissed. "My momma's name was Shirley. Shirl for short. She was a flirt and a taker. She got to have the road I live on named for her after the town took our land. That was a long time ago. I wasn't much older than you. My father was already dead, so my grandma come here from out west to do the rest of my raising. She was a talker." She reached for another triangle, took a bite, chewed solemnly, swallowed. "She was a worker, too. Got me started in the sign business." She pointed to a picture hanging next to the sink. "That's her over there." Eve could see a face that looked more like Miss Gates, a narrow mountain range of a face, but instead of a long graying braid and overalls, she had a cloud of hair arranged in tidy white curls, and she wore a shapeless, puff-sleeved dress that fell below her knees.

For dessert, there were sour apple slices with peanut butter and brown sugar, and after that, Miss Gates cleared the table and washed the dishes with her shirtsleeves rolled up and rubber gloves that nearly covered her red, wrinkled elbows. She hummed and sloshed water while Eve sat and petted the cats. Henrietta hogged her lap. Sledge one-eyed Eve warily from a stool near the sink while Slinky and Pindrop alternately paced and posed on the floor like big pincushions, until the dishes were dried and it was time to stop lollygagging.

Returning home after work, Eve had found another letter from the school in the mailbox. Stuffing it in her jacket pocket, she scuffed to the kitchen, but was stopped by a smell: a jolt of vinegar. And she saw him there at the table, fussing, as he always seemed to be doing about something, while she aped a look of disgust. "What stinks?" she asked, and her uncle looked up with that face, the one that always made her want to hurt his feelings. His eyes always smiling, his mouth pursed and prim, the bags of age beginning to show around both.

"The vinegar helps set the dye," he said. "Sorry about the odor." He had laid out his doings on the kitchen table over newspaper, several bowls of dye, a box of cheap crayons and a pan of boiled white eggs in water. She watched as he daubed each of them with a kitchen towel and nestled them in the cups of their brown cardboard container. He palmed an egg and began drawing on the shell with a red crayon.

"Your mother and I used to do this together every Easter when we were kids," he said. "A family tradition." She could see that he was decorating the egg with polka-dots, drawing circles, then fastidiously coloring each in. "Of course, mine were never as good as hers, but--" But what? She hated the way he ended almost everything he said with an open flap, a "but," as if she were supposed to sew up his thought, to know what he was thinking. Well, she didn't know. Next, he would want her to dye a stupid egg. He lowered his egg delicately into a bowl of purple dye.

"Would you like to decorate one?" he invited. He had that other sneaky adult look on his face, his eyes cast down, suppressing mirth, the one that made her want to walk out and slam the door.

"Sure," she said. Eve slid out a green crayon from a box on the table and took one of the boiled eggs. Carefully and, she thought, cleverly, she covered the egg with stripes, then wrote "Dumb" in the middle. She dunked her egg in a bowl of garnet-colored dye before Arm could see what she'd done, then picked up another and began a similar design with the word, "Stupid." There followed four more, "Boring," "Lame," "Old" and "Ugly," each dyed a different color. Somehow she resisted swears. When she was finished, she let him think she had enjoyed herself; in a way, she had.

"They'll be ready in about five minutes if you'd like to help me take them out," he said. He looked pleased with himself, with her, which only intensified her dislike.

"That's okay," she said and made for her bedroom. She spent the early evening cleaning up her mess, bunching dirty clothes into her hamper, making up her bed and piling up dirty plates and glasses from the week before. She arranged the unused books on her desk in a neat hierarchy, like a staircase. She didn't have a doily, so she spread across her dresser the man's red bandana she'd found in the woods and had later washed with hand soap in the bathroom sink. Then she emptied her pocket of the coins and dollars she had earned from Miss Gates and placed them in her money jar. Thinking better of it, she dumped the cash out on her bed and counted. What else was there to do? She had no homework. *One-hundred-fifteen dollars and seventy-six cents.* At this rate, she might get home before the school term was out.

When she thought her uncle was back in his cellar, she had tiptoed to the kitchen sink with her dirty plates and glasses. Then she had padded to the fridge to make herself a sandwich. She hadn't flipped on the kitchen light, and it was past dusk, so when she opened the refrigerator door, that was all the light there was, a rectangle of cold glare. And the sallow interior looked starker and meaner than usual, with a stain of hardened Worcestershire sauce that a former tenant hadn't wiped up in time, and a puncture in back, patched with duct tape. Her uncle's fancy coffee, Momma's ugly bean casserole, sticky jars of pickles and preserves and condiments, apples, half a quart of milk, a sack of discount bread, almost used-up butter with an unappealing blob of jam stuck to it, a tub of yogurt, unappealing, too, because of its watery top, and then his profusion of green things, which took up most of the bottom shelf.

But there on the middle shelf were her Easter eggs in a clean bowl, cooling, with a breath of condensation. Pastel, untouched, sweet, unless you were to read what she'd written on them.

He must have seen what she had done, must have known her insults were intended for him, yet here they were on display in Momma's brown speckled pottery bowl that reminded Eve of home. She wanted to throw the eggs, bowl and all, on the floor and smash them, but instead returned to her room and tidied up her closet. A monstrous, vacant feeling plagued her as she picked her few things off the closet floor and hung shirts on wire hangers and clamped her few skirts together on a wood hanger the previous renters had left. The letter from the school had fallen out of her jacket pocket with the money, and she slipped it beneath her mattress. By the time Momma came home, she was in bed, hollow and hungry, pretending to be asleep.

The next day, the temperature dropped to a coldblooded forty-five degrees that persistent drizzle rubbed in her face. "Sky's spitting at us again," Miss Gates had said first thing. "Just do what you feel like, then you can go on home." She had shut herself and the cats in the Quonset hut, same as before. Eve had to wear one of Miss Gates's baggy sweatshirts to stay warm enough to work outdoors, yanking plantain weeds out of the backyard and filling the potholes they left with soil from a bag, then sprinkling grass seed. It was better than schoolwork, but worse than office work, and punishment for what she had done the day before. Together with the sweatshirt, which smelled like Ben Gay, the work helped shoo away the hollow feeling.

"Come back tomorrow and you can run an errand for me in town," said Miss Gates. "Save me a trip up that rotten hill."

Eve is fighting her way back down the asphalt and gravel hill now with the loaded wagon, past the diesel and propane drums, past the bleak wreckage beyond, where cracked masonry and exposed rebar poke up out of the weeds like skulls and bones. The wagon takes the path of least resistance, becoming stuck in ruts and requiring frequent stops to yank it around and keep it heading toward the trailer park. Eve is sweating halfway down, but once she's over the railroad tracks, an opposing force takes over and the wagon wants to pull her.

Trucks lumber over the bridge, farting and groaning and jittering. In the distance, she can see someone step out of one of the junky trailers without his shirt, exposing a large, shaky belly on a lank frame. He stretches, swigs down something from a can, then goes back inside his trailer and lets the metal door bang shut on its own. Eve thinks she recognizes the person. Mr. Keith, the janitor? Or is it Mr. Drake, the bus driver? From here, it's hard to tell which is which, one man kind of bad and the other kind of good. She is trotting to stay ahead of the wagon when she loses control and the wagon is bumping down the hill in full spate.

Eve chases it, but when she bends to seize the handle, she skids and scrapes and lands on her side as the wagon overturns and cat food cans bounce out, along with loose change and the harmonica from her windbreaker pocket. Some of the cans roll or pitch down the hill, but most just land in craters. Sickened and ashamed, she begins picking them up, the ones with dents and the ones with torn labels. One food sack is perfectly intact, but the other is torn, spilling out kibble everywhere, and it is all her fault.

And then, Miss Gates is there, helping her pick up cans and making too much of the tear in her windbreaker. "I shouldn't have let you go alone. I should-a met you halfway." She rights the wagon and makes Eve sit on it while she rescues cans. Eve feels foolish and guilty, sitting on top of a sack of cat food while Miss Gates does the work she is paying Eve to do. Eve sits and watches Sledge come out from under the caravan and sit on the stoop, waiting. His shape is that of an empty sack, but his head is like carved wood, too heavy with distinction for the rest of him.

Out comes the man again, but when he sees Miss Gates and Eve, he retreats inside. Eve cranes her neck as he peers over the garbage in his trailer window. She thinks he has a nerve spying on them and not offering to help. She wonders again who it is, Mr. Keith or Mr. Drake. It's hard to tell who a person is from a distance, especially an old man. *Dumb. Stupid. Ugly. Boring. Lame. Old.* The words pick at her. She feels hollow, and there inside the pit of her are those barbed wire words picking and stabbing, the words she has said and the words she hasn't said. But they are only *words,* she reassures herself. She wants to cry, but nothing will come out.

Her thoughts are broken into when her shoulder is jabbed by a finger. And she's looking up at a face that is deformed by surprise, fury, fear or grief. It's hard to tell which on such a face. But there's no mistaking what is in Miss Gates's hand, though it is coated with dust and some dirt has lodged in its blowholes. She can see her name across it in an artificial shade of pink.

Miss Gates wags it in front of her face. "Where'd you find this?"

19 / *Arm*

A lukewarm Saturday afternoon in late April, the day before
Easter. Arm is in his basement sorting laundry. He has the radio on, which
is full of Iraq War news in the military lingo that so-called embedded
journalists now use as they travel and sleep with military units, allowed to
see bursts of the war, but not the politics behind it. Not the people either.
Mark would have hated that. "Embedded," Arm thinks, a word generally
reserved for thorns, splinters, bullets, other undesirable things. He
switches the radio off.

His Sunday afternoons are what they have always been. A stretch
of time still tinged with guilt for his sins of omission, or as Mark used to
say, "sins of no mission at all." Weekday afternoons are for practicing and
sleeping, so they are better, in some ways, than the anxiety-ridden rush to
concert halls and classrooms they had been.

But Saturday afternoons are the worst, he thinks, because they
are empty, and he is supposed to be doing something with Mark. In for
unhurried, uninterrupted lovemaking. Out for a virtuous run, a visit to a
gallery or museum, a walk from their cluttered, narrow studio on East 94th
to the park, just to ogle people on sidewalks that never failed to supply the
full expression of the human genome. It had been their game to give male
strangers names having to do with bedroom furnishings and accessories.
Caspar Sheethogger. Rufus Pillowbane. Wilt Fourposter. They had
secret names for scores of strangers, yet he can remember only a handful.
Like so much else, they have been stripped from his memory by grief.

Arm strips his bed, filling a laundry basket with linens that don't need washing. If nothing else, he can spend his afternoon at the laundromat.

In truth, he had hated living in Manhattan, in lower East Harlem, or the "Upper East Side" as the brokers liked to call it, where a block or two made the difference between prosperity and squalor. He had hated the way the city made him feel, just another talented queer clinging to his tiny portion of it, worked up about the grime, the crime, the trash, the noise, worried about the rent. At Julliard, he had learned that talent was not rare, as he had been spoiled into believing, but shockingly common. The city had taught him it was also cheap, that it was possible to be gloriously gifted and homeless. But unlike here, in the city there was always someone to see, some accent or personal history to divine, some new block to explore, which, when he was with Mark, had always seemed less threatening. Mark had carried a concealed weapon wherever he went.

He unlocks a trunk where he stores fresh linens and feels around for the familiar shape. And there it is, still buried in flannel, the cowboy of hand tools, "Clint," Mark's name for the dark gray revolver now in Arm's hand. He assumes the stance of the gun initiate, balanced on two feet. He swings open Clint's empty cylinder, swings it shut, cocks the hammer, grips Clint with two outstretched hands, sets his sights on a crack in the grubby basement window, pulls the trigger. *Click.* A dry run that he had repeated countless times with Mark in back of him, guiding, coaching, easing him into that slot within the political spectrum he had never wished to occupy, that of a gun owner. Cock, sight, *click.* Cock, sight, *click.* He repeats the dry sequence a dozen more times. The gun is a Smith and Wesson .45 Colt revolver, currently unregistered because, instead of turning it in when Mark died, Arm had wrapped it in a flannel pillow sham, locked it in the linens trunk, and smuggled it over the New York border to Connecticut.

Ever since he was pulled over and medically raped by the police, Arm has been tempted to strap Clint to his leg. But he wraps it back in the pillow sham instead, selects a set of clean sheets and pillowslips, blue Tartan edged with red piping, and makes up the bed he must lie in alone, which he does now, on his back, buttressed by plaid pillows. He settles back, sighs, inhales a complex draft of mildew, coffee grounds, aftershave.

The paper with the phone numbers is on his nightstand, in the Chinese cookie tin filled with Mark's research. He pries off the lid, fishes out the folded scrap that had been left under his windshield wiper weeks ago, looks again at the dancing scrawl of numbers that remind him of something he can't place in his memory. At a computer café in town, he had reverse-searched both numbers, one of which turned up the name of a man: Anthony B. Streeter of Somerbury, a town over the bridge from Rockton. Taft's hometown. The other number must have been unlisted, because it had turned up nothing, always busy. The person was either a chronic talker or had taken the receiver off the hook to avoid telemarketers, collection agencies, other chronic talkers.

Yesterday, he had bought two cheap red pay-as-you-go cell phones, one for Eve and one for himself. Eve's phone will be a birthday gift in August, a sincere effort to establish good will through a bribe. He breaks in his red phone now with Anthony B. Streeter's number. He has already decided what he will say.

Anthony Streeter takes his time getting to the phone. "Streeter residence," the voice crackles. It is deep-throated, dry, elderly, androgynous.

Arm clears his throat. "Hello, I'm looking for an Anthony B.

Streeter."

Heavy, winded breathing. "I'm sorry, but Mr. Streeter is indisposed."

"I'm sorry to call him at an inconvenient time. When might he be available?"

The voice is pitched differently this time, lower down the scale, a rasp against steel. "*Who* is asking?"

Arm shifts the pillows in back of him, sitting up. "My name is Arthur Guest," he says. "I'm writing a book about something that happened many years ago to a man I believe Mr. Streeter knew."

The voice turns away from the phone to cough. It's a dry cough, tired-sounding, the kind that hangs on.

"Excuse me," the voice apologizes. "I've never heard of you. What else have you written?"

"Actually," says Arm. He endeavors a warm, confiding tone. "Actually, this is my first book. I've been a journalist for most of my career."

The steel edge in the voice sharpens. "A *journalist?*" Arm detects suspicion, or worse, and decides to change tack.

"Journalist in the sense of keeping journals. I have an interest in old diaries, scrapbooks. History. Anyway, I'd be interested in speaking to your … to Mr. Streeter about the diary of someone he might have known a long time ago, about thirty years, give or take --"

"Who?" the voice interrupts. It turns away from the phone, hacks a few times, comes back and repeats itself. "Who's this man Mr. Streeter knew?"

Arm had not planned on revealing Taft's name, but can see no alternative with this elderly voice, whom age has made perceptive and suspicious rather than feeble-minded.

"A man named Taft Said." He exaggerates the two syllables in the surname.

There is a long pause, then a clatter like dishes in a sink. "Taft Said was my brother," says the voice. "A journalist helped put him in his grave." The voice turns away and coughs. "So if you're a journalist, you can go to hell."

"Not that kind of journalist," repeats Arm. "I don't work for a newspaper. I'm more like a collector of stories, diaries. I'm writing a book about --" He realizes that he is talking to a dial tone.

So Taft has a surviving brother. Arm rummages in the Chinese tin and brings out what had sufficed as Taft's obituary, one half-column in the *Somerbury Day* wedged between town news: "Former Somerbury Man Slain." It says that Taft was the son of Solomon and Ghada Said formerly of 23 Hilltop Road and was survived by an older sister, Mrs. Anthony B. Streeter of Somerbury. A *sister.* How careless of him, how stupid. Had he checked his research against Mark's, he might have understood whom he is seeking, the woman mummified in Anthony Streeter's name.

Arm is about to secure the lid on the tin when he sees the business card he'd thrown in with the face of the woman at Harpo's from two weeks ago. *Sable Budziszewski,* Realtor. On the back, she had scribbled what is now today's date and the time of her book club meeting, with her home address in evenly spaced, guileless penmanship. Arm flips the card over. Why not? It would be better than nothing. There would be discussion on a book about UFOs through which he might hear Mark's ideas, vicariously experience Mark's presence. Is this pathetic or simply ridiculous? He doesn't care.

He may as well launder his load before he attends the meeting, so he settles the heavy laundry basket in his car. For brunch, he runs back inside the house through the bulkhead and up the stairs to the kitchen as quietly as the creaky stairs permit. To the refrigerator, where he selects one of the last three boiled Easter eggs, the one labeled "Stupid," white lettering on pale yellow. He taps it on the countertop and rolls it around, then removes the delicate crackled shell in nearly one curl. He rinses it under the tap and eats it standing up, biting through the soft, flabby white engulfing the rich golden sun of yolk, like body and soul. "Stupid," he mutters. Yes, he is Stupid. One by one, he has eaten all of Eve's eggs, swallowing her judgments with his own. They are remarkably similar.

He drives to the nearest laundromat, The Suds Mama, in a neighborhood where shoes dangle from telephone wires and the parking out front is skid-marked. The place is humid, brightly lit, with huge anthropomorphized bubbles painted on the walls. Ironically, it is also dirty, with lint, candy wrappers and used dryer sheets littering the floor near a regurgitating trashcan. Arm loathes laundromats, but better this than swallowing the egg of Guilt while using Rose's washer and dryer. She had set her boundaries; he is not one to trespass.

He feeds clothes, coins and laundry soap into two washers, dusts off a pink plastic chair with a clean dryer sheet, seats himself, crosses his legs, fidgets with his cell phone. Eight out of ten washers, including his, are churning and jittering and spinning, yet no one else but a sad-looking mother and waif are here, guarding what's theirs. The thirtyish mother is pale as dough with eyes made up to look Gothic, well on her way from overweight to obese, wearing stretch pants beneath an ample pink hoody. The waif, a static-haired blonde child still dressed in a winter jacket, is her mother's physical opposite, with porcelain features and fairy-thin legs. She has a severe cold. Her upper lip is a red welt and her nostrils bear a perpetual blob of yellow mucus despite her efforts to wipe it off on her sleeve.

The mother offers comfort in the form of pound cake that must have dropped out of the vending machine across the room. She serves it in its cellophane wrapper as the child snuffles and whimpers, clinging to her mother's ponderous legs. Arm looks around for a magazine, but the dated specimens on a chair appear germy and, anyway, not his thing, *People* and *Us* and *Star* with curled, damp pages. The mother wants something from him. Out of the corner of his eye, he can see her smiling at him, craning. Poverty of this kind, disparate from his own, both annoys and shames him. He observes it furtively and, he knows, uncharitably. It amazes him that a giantess could produce such fine-boned china. Well, unhealthy air and junk food will take care of that soon enough.

He pretends to be absorbed in the tempest of suds in the washer's porthole when the woman waddles over. And it becomes obvious that she isn't a customer, but the attendant, her pink hoody matching the sickening hue of the place. He thinks how depressing it would be to work here, saturated in pinkness and the dryer sheet odor. She is asking him if he would like her to dry and fold. "Ten dollars a basket," she informs him, smiling. Her smile is oddly immaculate beneath the fleshy, pierced nose and sooty eyes.

He hesitates because of the germs, but charity persuades him. "Actually, that would be grand," he says. "I have an appointment in an hour and my load may take a while." Out of guilt, he offers twice her asking price.

"You sure?" she asks. He presses two tens into her hand.

Despite losing his way to Sable's twice, Arm arrives early. He pulls into a small condominium complex done up in Shaker shingles that have been painted olive green, now in varying stages of flakiness. "Buttercup Croft" has a hobbit-like, seventies feel to it, low to the ground, with brightly painted doors that clash with each other, and ivy just beginning to wake up and resume its mission of obliterating the brick garden walls. Knowing that these places with silly names are notorious for towing cars, Arm heads for the guest lot and lodges in a space. Twenty minutes to kill.

The sun has arrived, teasing open the buds on a colossus of forsythia, the citrus color so intense it makes Arm's mouth pucker. Across the greening lawn beyond the parking lot are flat clusters of pale violets and bluets, alive more by neglect than design, but the effect is charming, like a long green table with elfin tablecloths dropped on it. Arm opens his car windows the meager two inches they permit. But by some mechanical anomaly, the window on the front passenger side abruptly drops into its invisible slot, allowing a mild breeze to enter the car.

Arm leans back against his headrest. The front seat can no longer be forced into a reclining position, but the moment, the wildflowers, the open window, the dawning warmth are enough. He leans over, pulls out a CD from the glove box, Tallis's *Spem in Allium*, a motet with forty vocal parts, and slides it inside his disk player. He leans back again, listening as each voice arrives, floating, spinning, looping, hovering, soaring, parting and converging, the vocal equivalent of several mumurations of starlings. If only life were like this, he thinks, not a forced chorus, but a polyphonic gathering, each clear voice making way for the next. He closes his eyes with pleasure. In a few minutes another car arrives and parks to his right. Beneath the weaving voices, he hears a car door open, feet on gravel, a curt *thunk*, more footsteps, then silence, which eventually pries Arm from the arms of Tallis. The person does not move on, but seems to be standing there, possibly staring, possibly planning something unpleasant. Nervously, Arm opens his eyes.

The man leaning against an old white Impala isn't the one Arm expects to see. Nothing sinister, nothing reptilian. His eyes are closed, for one thing. Like the Stranger, he's bald, with a shadow where hair had once been. But this man's face is honest, long and lean, a handsome kind of face that, if you had to draw it, would not yield its complex symmetries easily. You might never get the wings of his nose or the hollows of his temple or the arches of his eyebrows right, Arm thinks, they are so subtle and supple and of one piece across his bones. Yet, the face is old enough to be firmly stamped with the lines of its owner's dominant mood, which must be something sonorous, disappointment or doubt. There are shadows beneath his eyes. And beneath the light beige jacket and loose navy trousers he's wearing, a well-maintained, muscular body. The trim hands are free of rings. Only when the man opens his eyes does Arm discern something off kilter, one gray eye fully mobile, while the other appears fixed, strange, not real. The bald man nods gravely at Arm.

"Sorry to intrude," he says. He stands there motionless, private, giving no clue.

"Beautiful," the man says. "Is it Tallis?"

Arm nods. "Forty vocal parts," he says. "Can you imagine? It should sound like a heap of coat hangers rattling around in a garbage can. Instead, it sounds like the music of the spheres."

The man looks at his watch. "Sorry I'll have to miss the rest of it. But thanks. Thanks for that." A brief, mannerly smile. He starts off across the lot with a zippered pouch under his arm, veers toward a staircase and disappears halfway down. Arm watches him resurface, cross the lawn toward the condo units and disappear again around a corner. Settling back against the headrest, he listens to the balance of the motet, then fumbles around on the back seat for a spiral notebook he had thought was there. Nothing. He has forgotten the title of the book up for discussion. He hasn't read anything on UFOs since Mark force-fed him articles, nor has he brought a covered dish. He has nothing to bring but himself.

Sable's unit is on what the residential marketers would call a "knoll," and the short uphill climb by railroad tie stairs brings Arm to a vivid plum-colored door. Pansies in a pot on the porch echo the color in their merry panda faces. On the porch rail is a purple ceramic ashtray, gleaming, recently wiped clean. Arm uses the tarnished knocker to announce himself. He can hear voices, giddy female laughter. The door is opened by a short, slump-shouldered woman in her stocking feet, fortyish, with bushy black hair cut Cleopatra-style, which makes her interesting, angular face look drawn. Her pants are black balloons, her bosomy blouse a splashy lime and lemon floral print, and she's wearing a citrus fragrance to match.

"Hi," she says, scowling up at Arm. She is one of those dark women who always look angry. Sable is suddenly at the door with her, in a flowing purple paisley dress, emitting a little squeal of delight. Her short silvery hair has been freshly styled in cherubic curls. High-pitched introductions are made and Sable takes Arm's old navy windbreaker. Cleopatra's real name is Alexandra. She offers her hand, hot and sturdy, carefully manicured with square nails that match the lemonade color in her blouse. Arm enters a room that is a sensory overload of purple. Planters, the woven shawls that drape faded old furniture, gauzy curtains, knick-knacks all belong to the grape family. Family pictures of Sable with what appears to be her parents, a bright-eyed young woman in a cap and gown (daughter?), are framed in violet. Even Sable's perfume, the dense aromas from her kitchen, seem to issue from this end of the color spectrum. There are only two other guests, one of them a tall, freckled auburn-haired woman with a weak chin named Aisling, wearing a frilly top over silky lavender trousers fastened with a drawstring. She has a precise little mouth, with a long monkey-like upper lip, which gives her face a comic mask. Shaking her hand, Arm feels conspicuously under-dressed, in jeans, shirt and running shoes. But who the devil would ever think to dress up for a book discussion group?

The other guest, seated on a purple couch, is the bald man. "Drew Matteson," he says, standing and extending his hand. "We met in the parking lot," he explains to the women while looking at Arm with one eye and, with the other, at a busy, provocative framed print of a woman in purple by Klimt. Arm introduces himself to Drew as "Arthur Guest." Sable giggles. "The *guest* of honor," she says brightly. Her profound, sad eyes contradict the tone in her voice.

"Arthur is a great, *great* violin player," she adds. "Me and Aisling heard him a couple of weeks ago at Harpo's."

"Aisling and I," murmurs Aisling, who is elbowed and shushed by Alexandra.

Arm bows operatically. "If only I were worthy." Aisling and Sable assure him that he *is* worthy, that he is *great,* and Alexandra agrees, although she has never heard him play, her eyes on Drew. She is the odd woman out in the purple scheme, slipping on a pair of high-heeled lime-colored sandals. The other two women still tower over her in their bare feet.

Several other book club members have "pooped out," explains Sable. Penny and Ann-Marie because of spring colds and Stephanie because of a grandchild. Another, Albert, hardly ever comes anymore.

Aisling rolls her eyes and Alexandra pretends she is about to kick her. "Be nice," she commands with a scowl. Sable pours glasses of burgundy and offers Arm one, which he declines. "Just water for me," he says. Drew, he sees, is drinking Evian.

Sable dominates the chatter, which is mostly about Arm's talent, which Arm finds pleasing, even touching, but embarrassing, while Alexandra steps inside the kitchen to stir a pot and contribute her two cents about people she knows in the "music biz." They begin to talk as if Arm isn't in the room. "House concerts," says Aisling, "That's what he ought to be doing. I knew a guy, a *great* uilleann pipe player, who toured New England, going house to house. He ate free and slept free, too." She opens her comical mouth wide, to one side, and winks. The women laugh uproariously.

Only Drew seems less interested in Arm than the book up for discussion, which he pages through as the banter continues. Sitting on the purple couch with his reading glasses on, his legs crossed, he wags his foot irritably. Arm looks at him secretly with a misery he cannot name, feeling tugged between the women's bustle and naïve interest and Drew's disinterest. He wonders what lured Drew into a roomful of extroverts, all women for whom he shows no particular attraction. Is he gay? Like his memory, Arm's sexual radar has been dulled by grief.

Alexandra serves everyone bowls of something dark, mysterious and multi-ethnic. "Braised eggplant, chard and purple rice with quinoa, almonds and mango in coconut sauce," Sable announces gaily. There is a leafy salad, a cheese board, various dark, seeded breads on a purple ceramic tray and grapes in a lavender bowl. Everyone munches and exclaims while Drew begins to talk about the book, which is "The Threat," based on UFO abductee interviews by Dr. David Jacobs.

"I *know* that book," blurts Arm. But when Drew asks him what he thinks of it, he is flustered, and confesses that he's never read it. "It was my deceased partner's, actually," he says. There. He has said it, using the sexually ambiguous term while making his single status known. But it registers no reaction in Drew's impassive face. Sable and Aisling women observe Arm with hopeful pity in their eyes.

Alexandra looks at Drew. "Would you like more water, Father?" she asks. "I'll get it," says Drew, self-sufficiently. He stands, stretches, visits the kitchen, returning with a several small bottles of water. *Father.* Arm is afraid his disappointment, his doubt show on his face. He calculates that Drew can't be a Catholic priest anymore than he could be Alexandra's father. No collar, no black cloth. Lutheran? Episcopalian? He checks again: no wedding band. His mind races while the others talk.

"I found it too negative," Aisling is saying. "He made the aliens sound like sex maniacs. I'd rather see them as helpers. Raising our consciousness. Helping us evolve."

"Not sex maniacs," says Alexandra. "Did you even read the whole book?"

"I skipped around a lot." Aisling winks at Arm.

Sable looks uncomfortable and chilled as her friends cavil. She swings her bare, fine-boned feet up onto the couch and huddles with her knees up and her arms tight around her shins.

"Well, you missed what Jacobs is saying," responds Alexandra tartly. "He's saying that of the seven-hundred abductees he interviewed, most are forced, most are subjected to painful, humiliating, awful procedures involving--"

"Sex," Aisling snipes. "Not sexy sex, of course." She tears off a cluster of grapes and pops a purple globe into her mouth. Her eyes are downcast, but mockery slips through her calm facial expression.

"Excuse me, may I finish what I was saying?" Alexandra scowls. "The point isn't sex, but creation of a new breed. Something to replace *us*, the human race, with." Aisling flips around in her book, munching.

"Can you blame them?" Aisling asks. "Look around you. Land wars. Religious wars. Drug wars. Too many people plundering Gaia."

"*Gaia?*" Alexandra makes the word sound ridiculous. "Do you mean planet Earth? Please, at least try to speak English."

"Those poor abductees," says Sable in a placating tone. "I can't imagine how they live with their memories after hypnosis. It's like being *raped.*" Arm flinches. "*Serial* rape," says Alexandra.

"Maybe it's for our own good," says Aisling. "For our collective evolution." She purses her simian little mouth. "He says here, oh where is it, anyway, he says it's like going to the dentist --"

"*He* doesn't say it," snaps Alexandra. "Others have said it. The New Agers. Charlatans, followers of Adamski, Billy Meier, Steven Greer. Worshippers of these disgusting, gray, demonic --" She searches for the right noun: "*Meddlers.*"

"Alexandra is right," says Drew. "Jacobs is no apologist for aliens." Alexandra nods moodily. "Thank you, Father."

"I was only saying --" Aisling shrugs and pours herself another glass of burgundy.

"But isn't there such a thing as false memory?" asks Arm, looking at Drew. "I mean, isn't it possible that what the abductees are remembering is something awful from their childhood?" He doesn't want to use sexually charged words like "molestation" or "pedophilia." The others are staring in silence, Aisling with a little smirk, Alexandra with a frown. Sable blushes.

"Yes. Yes, of course," says Drew. "Actually, Jacobs devotes much of one chapter to it. And provides a convincing analysis of how false memory and abductee testimony differ. Here," he says, handing Arm his book. "Take my copy. You may find it worth your time. Jacobs is a history professor." Arm accepts the paperback, embedded with scraps of newsprint that have served Drew as bookmarks.

"And you might also check out the work of Dr. Jacques Vallée," Drew says confidingly. "He compared alien abductions to medieval stories about encounters with demons. I agree with his views." Drew reaches out as if to touch Arm's hand, but instead collects his empty glass. "I believe so-called aliens are demons."

Drew clears bowls, forks and glasses off the coffee table while the others talk. Aisling calls Alexandra "humorless" and Alexandra calls her "naïve." "Now, now," says Sable. Arm hears them in his auditory periphery as he listens for the object of his attention, a controlled clatter in the sink, the gush from the tap, the baptism of glasses. Then Drew is back, and they all agree that their next book will not be Jacobs's latest, but a novel, something with its feet on the ground. Drew suggests a new novel slated for release in May: *The Kite Runner.* He reminds them that tomorrow is Easter. "I hope to see you then," he says genuinely. He turns to Arm. "I'm the priest at St. Stephen's," he explains. "At the corner of Forest and Main." Arm feigns indifference, disguising hope. Sable brings everyone her or his outerwear, a slim purple sweater for Aisling, a fringed black shawl for Alexandra, and beneath it all, Arm's blue windbreaker, ratty, he thinks, in comparison. Drew is still wearing the immaculate beige jacket he arrived in. As they exit, Sable goes out with them, cigarette in hand, and lights up on the porch. "I'm so glad you came," she says to Arm, taking his warm hand in her cold one, clinging to it, and at nearly the same time, Drew turns, touches Arm on the shoulder briefly and says, "Thank you."

"Thank you for the Tallis."

Arm tenses at his touch with a rush of desire, then Drew is heading down the stairs, flanked by the women, whose airy garments billow around him. Arm is left to thank his hostess, who delays him with her earnest eyes. She manages her cigarette neatly and considerately, flicking her ash into the purple ashtray, blowing bluish smoke away from Arm, but a breeze blows it back toward him before it collapses and vanishes. "I'm sorry," she apologizes. "My nasty habit." He tells her there is nothing to apologize for, with the unvoiced thought that he doesn't want debts on either side. "You're perfection personified, the perfect hostess," he says, feeling generous and buoyant and alive.

He forgets to stop at the laundromat on his way home and is forced to make an awkward turnaround in someone's driveway. When he arrives, the woman and her daughter are gone, and a shifty-eyed older man with slicked-back gray hair is feeding uniform shirts into a washer. But Arm's laundry basket is there beneath the glaring fluorescence, seated on a chair. All is well, crisp, warm, neatly folded. On top is his spiral notebook, left behind in the laundry basket, apparently, in his haste. He flips through the notebook, nervously expecting to find some new message written in the psychotic cursive hand. But nothing is there.

He stares at the notebook's cool blue empty lines. Yes, truly, he thinks: He has been handed a fresh page.

20 / Rose

Tree pollen is descending on everything. It litters the streets and cars and porches and catch basins with its corpses. Catkins, puffballs, needles and capsules, silken tassels, propellers, tiny oval envelopes, infinite flecks amass in body piles. It's one great dust storm, making Rose's paying jobs more difficult, because it enters homes through cracks, screens and on shoes. It punishes her eyes and throat. She leaves her shoes outside when she arrives at her clients' doorsteps and pads around in a pair of old hospital socks.

She's been going to St. Stephen's whenever she can to stand with the protestors and hold one of their signs. She still thinks of it as "their" demonstration, not yet hers. Her part is to learn and, primarily, secretly, to see Drew. For two Sundays, she has meant to attend a service, but cannot drum up the courage to face him as he must be on Sundays, dressed in a cassock and stole. To be lured into chanting a faith she does not have; to tithe money she does not have. How would she feel about him then? To see him on the street is enough, to be seen by eyes that ought to frighten her, but which she craves, like two opposing forces, gravity and elation, that she must have equal shares of to remain standing.

To keep him, to keep up with the others, she must know about the war, and allows herself to be de-toxed of ignorance and re-toxed with regular accounts of its serpentine maneuvers. Albert is only too glad to perform this service for her. He stands too close, talking to her without looking at her, his eyes on the street, filling her ear with facts about

Baghdad, which, having fallen in April, is still seething with insurrection, he says, despite the American general that the Bush administration appointed to run the country.

"It didn't work out with that first Bozo, and it won't work out with the new one either," he says. "Paul Bremer," he snorts. "Did you know he's from good old Hartford? A Yalie. Kissinger's ass kisser. He has a big fat neocon's ego. But don't they all?" He chuckles, then pokes Rose in the arm. "Colin Powell has one of those, too, transplanted from some heartless bastard's chest. But they let him keep one ball and half his own brain. You wait and see, he'll figure it out. He'll bail."

Rose nods. What can she say? She wouldn't presume to know more than Albert Warner about this war or past wars. She doesn't like him, his elbowing, his bombshell words and abrasive voice, his excoriated skin, as if burnt by his own stomach acid, which reminds her of herself turned inside out. Last week he had told her all about depleted uranium that the U.S. used in weaponry in the first Iraq war. "Then they left the projectile shells behind and let the dust storms carry depleted uranium to the lungs, gonads and wombs of the entire population. Fucking everyone in Iraq is poisoned." Albert had described the horror that resulted. Newborn babies whose heads supported massive inoperable tumors, or whose heads, faces and limbs had either been modeled by radiation into surreal atrocities, clown mouths and stumps and raw-looking horns, or taken out completely. It had made her stomach slide, but she had listened to all of it, and later had forced herself to read about it, shivering, sick at heart, on a computer at the library.

Dust, she thinks, is her enemy. Uranium dust, pollen dust, everyday dust, the dust of the twin towers. She won't ever escape its arid inevitability. In back of her stands Drew, whose warmth she can feel while clouds temporarily slide the sky shut. The weather has swung from hot and damp to cold and clammy all week. Even human warmth is more reliable. Drew taps her on the shoulder. "Are you cold? Would you like something hot to drink?" It seems his role is keeping his troops watered and fed. She thirsts for his attention and accepts a steaming cup of tea, bitter despite all the sugar.

He asks her how her week has gone and she tells him that the quilt is "coming along," that she is "fine." In truth, the quilt has cost her in guilt for all the time it has sucked away from mothering. She has torn out pieces, rethought others, stitched and re-stitched, second-guessing her critics. Exhaustion has become her excuse for neglect of Eve, who hides herself at school and in her room and, except for one tedious squabble, has been seen only in passing. To Arm, Rose has spoken hardly a word beyond asking for rent money and an infrequent ride, which each of them had suffered through in bumpy silence. She was sarcastic with one of her customers, costing her a day's work. But she hides these private failings from Drew. What she wants to tell him about is the miracle.

Two days ago, after cleaning out Milly Beale's closets, she had trudged over to Succour Brook, taking Reid Hill Road past its mouth, past the little bridge and Succour Way toward enigmatic pines and a meadow rustling with wild phlox. There was hardly any traffic, just an anorexic-looking man on a recumbent bike, pedaling with his knees to the sky, and a couple with their convertible top down.

Woods were filling up with vivid ferns and skunk cabbages. Beyond, Rose came to a gated area on a little hill. Brown headstones scabbed with lichens stood behind them, belonging to Reids, Sneaths and Marches with long lines of marriage partners and their begotten. A hand-lettered sign expressed the pious sentiment of their survivors: "Blessed are those who Mourn."

Fine-stemmed grasses grew out of moss around the stones, their red tufted tips forming a pink haze. Aching from work and the hilly walk, Rose was tempted to be on the grass, to lie down in it. She had removed her shoes, opened the gate, and walked across the grass in her hospital socks.

A simple oblong stone toward the front of the cemetery bore the inscription, "Oliver Lamb, b. 1921, d. 1974." Lilah's late husband, Rose remembered. Beneath his name was his wife's still incomplete life, "Lilah Reid Lamb, b. 1947." Rose did the math: Oliver had been Lilah's senior by nearly thirty years. Rose glanced around cautiously to see if anyone alive was there, but there were only a few mercurial little birds. The earth around the Lambs' stone was cushioned and inviting. Rose couldn't resist it; she was so tired. She surrendered, lying on her back next to the stone on the earth's forgiving mattress.

Across the sky, complex clouds drifted. Some looked quilted, with flyaway wisps like feathers escaping through seams in a down comforter. Rose took a dust rag from her fanny pack and laid it over her eyes to block out the intensity of color and light.

Exhaustion and the soft, warm compress of the sun intensified a feeling of being pulled downward. As she lay there under the celestial quilt, it came to her that quilt-making was sky-making, each little stitch a connection to the next star in a blanketing constellation. Was it also a secret desire to lie down permanently, to sleep, to dissolve and be absolved? Over this question, sleep came. She drowsed with her left hand across her chest and her right hand clutching a handful of grass.

Then a roar shattered the stillness and a chain of motorcyclists blasted by. Rose awoke, thinking at first that the war had arrived and it had come for her. She bolted up, terrified and exposed, pulling her shoes on hurriedly.

"Assholes," she cursed later, heading back down Reid Hill, crossing the little bridge to Succour Way, passing the glade where she was certain Taft had been killed. The trees had leafed and grasses had filled in since her first visit. Vines were sneaking over the slatted bench and through its iron lace.

As she walked up Succour Way, then the uphill path, she could hear children's voices singing, but the singers remained invisible until she reached the clearing. And there they were, all three, Martha, Jacob and Lydia on the porch, snapping beans into a wooden bowl as they sang. *"Wondrous! Glorious! Sweet and cheering to our hearing is the singing."*

Martha and Jacob waved as she approached and Lydia stuck her hand up. "Momma!" called Martha. "The lady is here." *The lady.* Rose felt both touched and ashamed. She could see Beulah's face in the window, but she retreated into a back room before coming out of the house.

Beulah was showing. The pale green maternity dress she wore, smocked at the top, belled over a small mound. She looked beautiful, her hair twisted into a bun, but tired lines appeared on either side of her mouth. Her beauty ended at her wrists; her hands were reddened, the knuckles raw, clutching a piece of rolled-up cloth. And there was a faintly scolding, admonitory edge to her voice when she told the children to go inside and finish their homework.

"You'd better lay Lydia down for her nap," said Beulah to Martha. Martha uttered an inaudible stiff-lipped remark, her eyes lowered, but took her sister by the hand and led her in. Lydia offered Rose a private smile over her shoulder, elfin delight spreading across her face. Her smile entered Rose like an arrow, but she turned away, focusing on

Beulah. It was Beulah and Lilah she'd come to see.

Rose apologized to Beulah for not calling first. "I didn't know how to reach you."

Beulah shook her head. "No, no. It's a welcome break." She tilted her head toward the door. Her beauty outshone the annoyed look on her face. Rose thought that she had seldom met a beautiful young woman who was also kind. The few others she had known had used their gift to rob, stealing attention, boyfriends and promotions.

Rose tried to think of something kind and neutral to say. "Your children have lovely manners."

"Martha is beginning to sass me," Beulah said. *Sass!* If only she knew, thought Rose. Beulah shrugged. "It happens. It's not easy being the oldest." She looked back over her shoulder. "There are fresh diapers in the linen closet," she called out. She invited Rose to sit on the porch, leading her to the bench, which looked recently painted. Beulah settled on it heavily, with a sigh, and when Rose sat down, the seat slid backwards. She made a sharp, flustered noise. "It's a glider," explained Beulah with pride. "My husband built it." The two of them glided back and forth together haphazardly at first, then with uneasy regularity. The springs in the glider made a soft scissoring sound, as if they were snipping through a page.

"How is your mother?" asked Rose.

"Mother is well," said Beulah. "Her heart is weak, but she doesn't complain."

"I was wondering if … " Rose broke off. "Would a short visit be too much for her?"

"Mother is resting now," Beulah said firmly, pressing her lips together. She quickened her gliding and Rose went along, *Snip, Snip, Snip.*

That the two of them, so different, should be sitting together at all was odd. Their only shared virtue, if it could be called that, was diligence, Rose thought. But in Beulah it was driven by piety, while in Rose, by necessity, by fate and money problems. Faith was at the root of Beulah's life. What was at the root of Rose's? Art and love, she had once thought. Now it was money and trouble.

"I'm glad you stopped by," Beulah said, "because I've been meaning to ask you something." She cleared her throat, stalling, shy.

"Of course," said Rose hesitantly. She feared that she was about to be asked if she had accepted Jesus as her personal Lord and Savior. She had been ambushed like this before and knew it was in her best interest to answer, simply, "yes." She sat there, silent, prepared.

"I was wondering about your business," blurted Beulah. "I want to have my own business, like yours." She flushed. "Here at home." Her eyebrows were drawn together in a pleading expression. Rose let out a deep, constrained breath. The poor woman, she thought irritably, actually wanted to clean houses for a living.

"That's wonderful," said Rose with a forced smile. "But if you clean, you know, you'd have to go into other people's homes."

"Oh, no," said Beulah. "I would *never* clean other people's homes." She looked wide-eyed, caught inside language's trap. Her cheeks reddened. "I didn't mean --" she said. "I only meant that I'd never compete with you, with your business."

"Believe me, there's enough work to go around," said Rose.

"Well," said Beulah, "I wouldn't clean. I would sew, embroider, mend hems, things like that. And I'd make these." She unrolled the piece of cloth in her hands and held up a pink baby quilt.

It was a miniature replica of the Joseph's Coat that hung inside the house, with pinwheels in various rosy calicos, ginghams and geometric patterns. Each swirl of hand stitches was rendered with precision and delicacy. Beulah looked down at it with love, holding it against her belly.

"How lovely," said Rose, touching her face.

Beulah beamed. "I can make them in blue, or any other color. I would charge more for the hand-stitched ones like this, but I can machine them for less." She draped the quilt on Rose's lap nervously. "Here," she said. "You can examine my hand work if you like." Beulah sat there in a supplicating way, her hands folded. Already having seen that the tiny stitches made her own look clumsy, Rose held the quilt away from her, at her arm's length, and squinted. "Perfect," she said, returning the quilt to Beulah.

Beulah chattered happily about how she would personalize her quilts and price them while Rose listened in silent misery. She could easily imagine every member of the Stone Circle lining up to buy Beulah's baby quilts for their grandchildren, while picking her own difficult, blood-stained art to death. *Snip, snip, snip.* She kept the glider going while Beulah talked about her prospects. In the background, Rose could hear a blunt wail from inside the house.

"It isn't our way to advertise," Beulah was saying. She stopped gliding long enough to slip her hand inside her pocket. "I don't mean to be forward." She drew something out of her pocket and handed it to Rose. "But would you be willing to hand out a few of these? To your customers, I mean." Rose looked down at a white business card with the pinwheel pattern squarely in the middle and a needle and thread suspended over it. Across the bottom was *Beulah Lamb Kingsley, Mending, Tailoring and Baby Quilts,* with her address and the unlisted phone number. "I made them on the computer," Beulah said meekly. "It took me a good week to figure it out. But Jacob helped." She laughed sweetly. *"He will render to each one according to his works,"* she quoted. Rose started gliding abruptly, which jerked Beulah backward.

"Sure, I'll pass them around," said Rose, accepting Beulah's cards. "You never know." She blinked hard, avoiding Beulah's eyes. Overhead, the clouds now looked like rumpled sheets across a bed someone hadn't bothered to make. The same treacherous sun that had lulled her to sleep earlier was revealing every detail on the porch, the fresh paint someone had recently brushed over crackled floor boards, the carefully reconstructed newel posts at the bottom of the stairs, the sets of miniature handprints in the cement below it, the close-cropped grass beyond that had become an emerald shimmer, and framing this, the fields and pastures and tenebrous forest. Sunlight touched the heavy, twisted roll of hair at the nape of Beulah's neck, the prim part at her crown, the radiant curve of her profile.

Beulah gushed on about her plans. She would work up a few sample quilts, enough to fill a market basket, and take them to crafts stores, little gift shops around Swannboro and the river towns. She would leave one behind for each shopkeeper to display. Orders would come in and she would cultivate a small but satisfied customer base. People were starting businesses online now; she would be one of them. "My husband told me how it works." My *husband.* What was this husband's name, anyway? Rose didn't bother to ask. *Snip, snip.* The two of them were gliding along, Rose falling in with Beulah's rhythm.

"But how will you find time to do this kind of work when the baby comes?" Rose asked. It was an underhanded question, spoken to cast doubt. But Beulah only laughed and said that everyone would pitch in. "Mother will help. Martha will learn."

Rose felt a rising resentment that seemed to come from

somewhere far beneath the glider. What had her works "rendered" her? She thought of all the free and paid labor she'd performed over her lifetime, the housework, the shit jobs, the education acquired in fits and starts through loans and all-nighters. The art she had tried to needle out of old dresses, skirts, blouses, the cloaks of a body that had so often betrayed her. In all this time, she had received help from no one. Not from her parents, not from Randall, and only a pittance from Arm, whose presence negated his help, whose attempts to cozy up to Eve were pathetic and, she judged, a sham. She had seen his Easter eggs, the degrading, self-pitying words he had written on them. What did a vain, selfish gay man know about raising children?

Knowing that help would never arrive, she had arranged her life, cutting, stripping, taking down all that was not within her circumference, her power or her means. *Snip, snip, snip.* Rose glided along, straight-faced with Beulah, listening to her plans, reflecting that her own had never yielded much. She could hear Martha singing to Lydia, in a voice thin and lucent.

Raising a child with Down's syndrome would have been impossible with a drunken, vaguely unsavory husband, with all she had to do. She knew how it felt to be helpless, but unlike those women in Iraq forced to carry their monsters, she had drummed up the means to help herself. It had saddened her, she had wept, but she had done what she believed needed doing, as she had always done. Now here she was, without a car or a partner, without a real income, without a respectful daughter or the soft, fertile ground of social approval. All of the usual human transactions had been shattered. But she had something after all.

"I'll help you," she said suddenly to Beulah. "I'll help you, if you'll help me." Later, as she walked home, her shoes crushing the reproductive surplus of trees, she realized that this was the first time she had held a position of bargaining power with anyone in her working life. Normally, she was cast as the pawn. Only here, as a stranger, had she formed an agreeable contract. The fact that her business partner was naïve and, to her mind, backward, didn't matter, nor did it weigh on her conscience. She saw only the irony of her position, that this pious girl should have the world of commerce on her side while she, Rose, legs open to the world, should have it set against her.

As Rose walked, she felt the letdown of success, the hard pit inside, which was failure. She would concede to the Stone Circle all of their demands, setting aside her art and supervising Beulah in making a neat, plain-faced quilt no one would question. She would pay Beulah a portion of her commission, and in exchange, Rose would gain the time to begin a series of her own art quilts. In her mind, she had already begun sketching out life-size mothers holding the kind of children no one wanted to see.

The road became hillier, bordered by banks of crisp ferns, a fairy-sized forest, and drooping pines with branches as long and heavy as bell pulls. The road narrowed under the loose embrace of dense trees, then it widened and gently dropped. She could see a random cluster of farm buildings ahead. They were built too close to the road, she thought, each sided with broad, worn planks, painted red. Was this still Reid land? No sign, no doll-faced woman with long hair in the yard. She approached the buildings cautiously, seeing that a few of their small paned windows were cracked, a malicious gape in one of them. Too close to the road, thought Rose again, an easy target for stone throwers. The lower building, likely a henhouse, had missing planks. It slumped against a small barn with one window boarded up. Both buildings had the warped, weedy look of disuse.

Behind them, on a hill, a barn-red house stood up straight in a meadow. Rose observed it through green traceries. Why were so many New England barns and farmhouses painted red? She'd asked this question while researching the quilt and found the same secret ingredient she'd discovered in brownstone: iron. Farmers had mixed linseed oil with rust or blood and brushed it across their barns to discourage mildew and mold. The slaughter of pigs, chickens and bullocks assured a fresh supply of blood on farms. Blood, Rose thought, was at the bottom of everything.

The road curved around a gravel driveway, which led up to another red barn, nearly as ramshackle as the others, but with its middle garage door wide open like a mouth. In and out flew swallows in frenetic arcs. On either side, similar, closed doors bit down on the weeds growing in the gravel, their white paint peeling and small windows glinting despite the dust.

Through the open door, she could see more windows in the opposite wall that the sun hadn't reached. Even here, from the front, it seemed reluctant to enter. What light there was traced large, nearly colorless hulks. Rose stepped closer to see they were farm machinery: tractors, ploughs, combines, threshers; she didn't know the difference. Mechanical pachyderms, one yellow, the other red, with rusted appendages and sagging beds. Rose squinted and looked. The sun wouldn't cooperate, crashing into her eyes from any angle, so she squatted there in the gravel, straining to see.

Something moved. Something that might have been many things, it was so long, floating horizontally with a strange dipping motion. She shielded her eyes with a hand, squatting, moving back slightly, feeling a needle of fear until her eyes adjusted.

From darkness emerged a peacock, dragging his dressy train across the dirty cement floor. He strutted along, swerving carefully to avoid catching himself on the farm equipment. Then he turned around with a kind of clumsy grace, and went the other way. Several times, the peacock paced, dipping his head and dragging his train. Each time, Rose witnessed the inner rainbow, the odd procession of brilliant, maddening, inward-seeing eyes. Then it ended. The peacock managed to heft himself onto a crate and suspend his tail, his magnificence dulled by shadows.

Rose sat with her knees drawn up, her arms around her shins. She sat there in silence, in the dirt among weeds in front of a mundane barn beholding the improbable.

And now all she wants to do is tell Drew about it. But even if she could find the words, she sees that there will be no time. Drew is already distracted, talking in low tones to the young people who have begun to straggle in, joining the anti-war group. And there will be no time to tell him what she'd witnessed.

21 / *Eve*

She's seated on the metal floor of Miss Gates's Quonset, helping her pack boxes. There is an illogical order to what she is doing, similar to the way a library numbers its books. She likes this, along with everything else in the close, tubular space. The plywood shelves on each side, with their fragrant, alluring knots, are heavily packed with boxes of nails, screws and smaller pieces of wood, with paint and varnish cans and brushes. A row of jars, suspended from the ceiling where Miss Gates had glued their caps and screwed them in, carry loose sequins, tacks, pins, grommets and other articles that Miss Gates calls "notions," as if they were thoughts.

Eve has already swept the sawdust into a single crumbling peak. She had to crouch and reach beneath the saw to get it all, with the vicious, jagged-toothed wheel above her. And the other machines, the routers and engravers, whose purposes she imagines must be important and permanent. Above them hangs a huge black and gold sign of a hand pointing its index finger toward the back of the shop that reminds Eve of Miss Gates's finger. All that's really missing, Eve thinks, is a lava lamp.

"Why are we packing?" she almost asks, but doesn't push her luck. The last time she had been told to pack, it had meant leaving home and moving to Swannboro. By not asking questions, she is safe from the future.

Miss Gates is busy with a small order of signs, which has something to do with a war, and is meantime doing her thinking by questioning her cats and answering for them. She asks Henrietta if it's warm enough for her. "She says it's warm enough for alligators," says Miss Gates.

Eve is packing only one portion of the shop, the front part that gets a breeze. The rest of the Quonset, where the cats sprawl in frowsy, belly-up heaps and where Miss Gates works, is warm and damp, lit by a long fluorescent tube that hums tensely. A dusty metal fan is plugged into a socket in the ceiling, but Miss Gates has switched it off because of the noise. "Can't hear my own self think," she'd said.

Into each box, Eve must place a certain number of smaller boxes containing sharp things, as well as loose blunt objects, gritty sheets of sandpaper, brushes, mallets, hasps, nail-guns, hammers, screwdrivers. Then she must label each box precisely, using initials. N is for nails, P for paint, T for tools, and so on. Under tools there are other initials. She must account for the number of boxes and cans, and here is where illogic sets in, because there are large and small boxes and cans. But Miss Gates says this doesn't matter. "Just count them and make them fit good so they don't joggle around."

Eve suspects that the labeling is what Daddy would call "make-work," but she doesn't care. After all of the flap over the harmonica, she feels lucky to be here at all. The harmonica is back in her pocket. She can feel the edge of it nudge her as she works, along with an old machine manual she'd salvaged after Miss Gates threw it away.

Miss Gates hadn't said anything after asking her where she found the harmonica. Eve had begun to cry and that was bad enough. Miss Gates had gotten her off the wagon and taken her inside the trailer without saying a word. She sat Eve down at the table and delivered a cup of milk and a red handkerchief like the one Eve had found in the woods. Then she went over to her bed at the opposite end of the trailer, where she sat and waited. "Take your time," she said, and then Sledge had come up to Eve and curled around her feet and Slinky jumped on her lap.

Eve didn't like milk without chocolate syrup, but she drank what was in the cup. She would have drunk eggnog to get back in Miss Gates's good graces. The cats purred. She blew her nose on the red handkerchief and got the rest of the milk down her without gagging. When she looked up, Miss Gates was sitting on her bed with a book in her lap. Her feet were on the floor, squared up together in man-size boots. Eve cleared her throat and patted Slinky.

"Think about what you mean to say before you flap your lips," said Miss Gates. She turned a page in the book she was holding and Eve could see there was gold around the edge of the page, which meant it was a Bible. This was not a good sign, Eve suspected, even though no one she knew owned a Bible except for Aunt Fleurette, Daddy's sister, and Fleurette had been kind to her that first time Daddy disappeared. It had been the hottest summer of all, and she had gone down for a week to Natchez where Aunt Fleurette lived alone with her hound dog and pictures of an unsmiling square-jawed man in a military uniform. It was so hot and damp that everyone had fleas in their houses. You had to bomb the living room once a week, and Aunt Fleurette did hers on Sunday, which meant you went to church right afterwards. What advice would Aunt Fleurette give her now?

"I found it in a cave," Eve said. She waited politely for Miss Gates. She picked up the cup of milk and gulped the few drops that remained.

"No," said Miss Gates quietly. "You found it in *my* cave." Eve looked at her blankly, a vague feeling of disbelief traveling from her throat to her stomach. She tried to remember something Connie had said about Miss Gates.

"You found *my* harmonica in *my* cave," said Miss Gates. Several seconds passed while Eve patted Slinky. "What else did you find?" Her voice was quiet, neutral. Used to her mother's emotional outbursts, Eve was struck silent. Clearly she could not tell Miss Gates that all she had found was an old boot.

"Things that wouldn't fit through the hole," she said finally. It was true, but seemed lame and incoherent. "In my pocket," she corrected herself. "I had to put it in my pocket so Connie wouldn't see." She sniffed. "Anyways," she said. "You can't own a cave."

Miss Gates's face didn't change. By now Eve was used to the way Miss Gates looked, her buck teeth, the rest of her face crowded into a fierce little mask of knowledge and disappointment. She looked at Miss Gates and felt ashamed. She had caused offense with her careless words. She looked at the portrait of Miss Gates's Grandma, who looked back through her just like Miss Gates. She looked down at Slinky. Sledge had gotten up and huffed over to where Miss Gates was. Eve wanted to crawl under the bed but felt herself too large even to get out through the trailer door.

She began to talk, rapidly at first, telling Miss Gates the story of what had happened before the cave. She told her about the keys she had stolen from the school gym and tried to return, about the stolen money and how Connie had accused her at first, then turned around and done her a favor. And how she'd dragged her through the woods and forced her into Miss Gates's cave. And what she, Eve, had seen, but hadn't revealed. The china saucers and plates and cup, the utensils, the broken candle, the swelling cans and the big old lady purse.

"I only took the harmonica," Eve said.

"Because that was all you could fit in your pocket." Miss Gates no

longer looked mad, just tired and puckered. There was a fly buzzing
around in the trailer, but Miss Gates ignored it when it landed on her
head, then it took off and defined a haphazard path to its destiny, the
kitchen sink where cat bowls were soaking. Miss Gates took a peppermint
lozenge out of her pocket, unwrapped it and stuck it in her mouth,
without offering one to Eve. "How do I know what you'd-a taken if you'd
had a bigger pocket?"

"I wouldn't have taken anything else," said Eve. It was the truth.
Nothing else in the cave was worth risking her life for.

"That how you found me?" Miss Gates nodded her head
thoughtfully, sucking on the lozenge. "You got my name off the
harmonica." The fly was back, and this time landed on the Bible. Miss
Gates waved her hand and smacked it off the Bible onto the floor, then
stepped on it. "You felt guilty and thought maybe you'd return it to its
rightful owner."

It wasn't exactly true. Eve nodded her head cautiously while
patting Slinky.

"So you asked around about a person named Taffeta. Wouldn't
be hard to find. Nobody else here but me named that, thanks to my
mother." Miss Gates went on about that a while.

Eve let Miss Gates dig her out of the hole she'd dug herself into.
Slinky stretched and loosed himself from Eve's lap, so it became harder to
conceal her emotions. Her hands were shaking. She folded them up tight,
ready for a sermon, but Miss Gates talked just like her normal self. Where
were Findrop and Henrietta? Looking down, Eve scanned the lower
regions of the trailer.

"Point is, you brought the harmonica back," Miss Gates was
saying. "That means you're good as new." Miss Gates put her finger in the

Bible then brought it over to Eve. "See here where the Almighty says it."

The Bible was directly under Eve's nose, the strange words above Miss Gates's bony brown finger. "Sit up straight and read it out loud."

"Repent you therefore," said Eve, in an unwilling, hollow voice, "and be converted, that your sins may be blotted out."

"That's right. The Almighty said it first. You turn yourself around, so you can go back to where you started." Miss Gates took her finger out of the Bible and placed a red ribbon inside, then tucked it on a shelf next to her bed.

Getting back to where you started, in Eve's estimation, involved money and train tickets. There would be no getting there without Miss Gates's cooperation. She nodded her head in agreement.

"Good," said Miss Gates. "Your reward is you get to keep the harmonica. And now I'm going to tell you about my cave." She used a blue handkerchief to clean up the remains of the fly. Then she scrubbed her hands over the sink with a slip of soap. Her fingers were long and thin, but her knuckles stuck out like rope knots.

From her kitchen cupboard she took out two large cans of tuna fish, opened them up and used the cut tops to strain the juice into cat bowls. The fishy smell in the trailer intensified. "Come on out, all of you," called Miss Gates. Pindrop and Henrietta squeezed out from under the bed; the other two already owned the bowls. Miss Gates set two more bowls down. She turned her back on Eve and made their lunch with a fork and a jackknife, stirring up the tuna fish with mayonnaise, celery, salt, pepper, walnuts and cane sugar inside a see through bowl with scratches all over it. Eve watched passively as sandwiches were assembled from rough bread slices Miss Gates cut off a loaf that looked homemade. The bread was white with holes you could almost stick a finger through.

"No one ever tell you some places in the world belong to you?" said Miss Gates. "You may not like them, but they're yours all the same." Eve watched Miss Gates's back. The pigtail she always wore was tucked neatly inside her overalls.

She set the sandwiches on a plate without bothering to cut off the crusts. Eve folded her hands and Miss Gates said grace. "May the good Lord turn all of us around and convert us, so that our sins may be blotted out," she said. Eve took a half-sandwich and ate it with her eyes on the red-check tablecloth. Miss Gates began to talk.

"You told me your story. Now I'll tell you mine." She bit into her sandwich and chewed a while. "My people were carnival workers on my momma's side. *Carnies* is what we were called, but don't you call us that. On my daddy's side were people I never got to meet. My parents never married, and back then, well." Miss Gates shrugged.

"My daddy was bad, but not rotten. Not mean. Just bad in what he did, working for the Devil, like your chum, what's her name." Miss Gates paused. "Connie," she announced.

Eve saw what she thought was a flicker of amusement in Miss Gates's face. "Connie isn't my chum," she said sullenly, and the look on Miss Gates's face got swallowed up in a bite of her sandwich.

"Good," Miss Gates said. "My daddy, he was a dealer and an addict. Street drugs, heroin mostly. You know what that is?" Eve did, but shrugged. "It's a drug you put inside your veins with a needle." Miss Gates's eyes narrowed and she pursed and worked her mouth. "Picking at your skin. Making a terrible mess of your insides, too. I found out all about my daddy by reading the papers. His name was Taft, but most people called him Taffy. I guess my momma wanted me to have one of his names, anyways. So she named me Taffeta. Stupid name for a girl who looked like me." Miss Gates scowled, and Eve had to agree, but said nothing. "It would-a been some other trashy name if it hadn't-a been Taffeta. Desirée, Tiffany, something like that. Momma liked fancy things of no use to anyone. Except for her bit of land. She knew its price indeed. But they took it from her anyways." Miss Gates stopped to take a bite and diligently wipe her mouth off. Bits of sandwich stuck to her front teeth.

"My daddy's business started paying off and that meant my momma could afford to drink more. And she had her own trailer and the land beneath it, finally, in the park that used to be tip-top of the ledge over the quarry lake." Miss Gates stuck her sandwich up in the air and pointed northeast. "That meant we could stay put during the off-season. Worse part is we stayed poor as dirt. My daddy had his money holes to fill. Good part is we had the prettiest view in Swannboro. I had it, anyway. Momma hardly ever saw the outside of her trailer. Always waiting inside for him, my daddy, and sometimes other men. I waited, too, but not inside if I could help it. I was busy being a squirrel on that ledge, exploring. School bored me, except for art, but the quarry had what I needed." Miss Gates patted her lap and Slinky jumped up, making himself as comfortable as possible on bony thighs and knees. "I had a cat and eventually a paper route, and my momma never even figured it out." Miss Gates looked at Eve and winked. She patted Slinky on the head, her head tipped to the side, chuckling to herself. "I'll never forget that cat. Name was Chiclet. Smartest little cat in all the world." There was a toothpick holder in the middle of the table, a little red china pig with its mouth wide open. Miss Gates took a toothpick out and worked on her teeth diligently as if Eve weren't there.

Eve looked away politely and waited. When she looked up again, Miss Gates was still digging at her teeth. Eve made herself stare at her lunch, which was mostly gone. She had a feeling that the story would last only as long as the rest of her lunch, so she kept what remained on her plate. She watched the three cats on the floor lick their bowls with their eyes closed. Finished with his bowl, Sledge butted Henrietta out of hers. "Sledge," snarled Miss Gates with her teeth clenched around the toothpick. "Get your noggin out of that bowl!" Henrietta returned to her bowl with small neat steps after Sledge slinked under the bed. "Never mollycoddle a cat," said Miss Gates. Pindrop moved on to the tattered mat beneath the sink that served as a scratch post, and ripped at it obsessively with her claws. Then she lay on her side so it was impossible not to see her swollen, sparsely furred belly with its two rows of pink teats.

"The quarry ledge had look-outs. I could see people, but they couldn't see me. That worked out real well. And the quarry lake had hiding places. You found the one I owned, but there were others. Other caves and cubbies cut out of the rock long before my people were around. The one I owned was mine because no one else could get inside it. I was skinny." Miss Gates held up her toothpick. "Like this toothpick. I could get inside places other kids couldn't, not that they'd want to. The entrance to that cave stunk. Boys coming around, pissing like dogs."

They resumed eating their lunch in silence, Eve taking small nibbles, then Miss Gates swept the crumbs from the tablecloth into her palm. "You gonna finish your sam-widge?" Eve stared at Miss Gates, unable to explain her reluctance, so Miss Gates snatched the last bite off her plate. "For the birds," she said. She scraped back her chair, opened the door of the trailer and tossed out the leftovers. A trailer truck blasted a single note from the bridge.

Eve looked around for a cat to take up into her lap, but all there was by then was Pindrop with her swollen nipples. She squatted down, patting Pindrop's silken edges, her ears, her gray cap, the stretch of her neck, paws that splayed contentedly.

"You have a father?" Out of the corner of one eye, Eve could see that Miss Gates was sitting on a dinette chair, her elbows on her knees and her long face cupped in her hands. Eve shook her head, yes.

"Well," said Miss Gates. "Is he a good father?"

"He's the best father." Eve hesitated, then sighed. "But I haven't seen him since we moved."

"That's awful sad." Miss Gates squinted her eyes and jutted out her lower lip. "My daddy was good when he was with us, and bad when he wasn't. I've heard what it's like the other way around and I guess I got lucky. When he was with us, he played the fiddle. That was mostly what he did. He played the fiddle. Heck, he could make your heart jump up and down inside your feet. Wasn't anyone in the park didn't stop and listen. He could draw them. Yessiree."

Miss Gates took another toothpick out of the pig and dug around in between her teeth while she talked. "I was proud of his playing. Proud of his good looks, too." Miss Gates sucked her teeth. "Bunch of rotten kids treating me like their dinner. Townies plaguing me something fierce. They were in awe of my daddy, though. When he was around, they wouldn't have dared. But you don't want to hear about that. Point is I was proud of him. And pride is poison. Pride makes you stupid. Don't you know that yet, Sledge? Just look at him there, getting ready to jump Pindrop." Sledge had bellied his way out from under the bed and was crouched near the sink, one eyeing the mat Pindrop owned. Pindrop ignored him, stretching her limbs and splaying her paws hypnotically. When Sledge made a move, she was up on four paws in an instant, her back arched, her head low and flat as a snake's. The hard rasps seemed to come from another corner of the room. Sledge backed up, his large, wounded, hostile head upraised.

"Gotcha," said Miss Gates. She nodded at Eve and reinserted the toothpick. "Now you come over here, Sledge, and sit with Momma." Sledge recovered his stature, then beat a path around Pindrop and lodged beneath Miss Gates's chair defensively, his ginger face registering something not wild, but not tame either. Eve felt sorry for him. "You stay put and listen," said Miss Gates. She reached down and patted Sledge, who craned his neck. A tuft of fur floated off of him. "Says he's sorry. Sorry is the story of his life."

"My daddy must-a been feeding his veins every day," Miss Gates continued. She shook her head. "I never saw but once. I got a look at his arm and I about threw up. After that, he made sure he was covered up around me. That didn't make him good, just secret. He didn't like his stuff showing, always giving me something to hide for him. Like I told you, I had hiding places. So I hid the things he gave me. Things that most of the time I didn't know what they were for. I kept 'em hid and fetched 'em when he wanted." Miss Gates reached down and scratched Sledge. "It was a way of keeping him." Eve looked up from Pindrop as a shaft of light cut through the curtains. It smarted her eyes and she looked back at Pindrop, who blinked and purred out a snore, then stretched her legs out straight before tucking them all into a neat loaf.

"One day after my momma had been drinking hard for a week, my daddy shows up and hands me a bag. Says you need to hide it somewhere safe so your momma can't find it. It was money, you see. I hid it in the cave. Already had my own stash of coins in there, plus other worthless stuff I'd found. Well, you saw most of it. Next time he come, he wants his bag, so I get it for him." Miss Gates reached behind her shoulder and pulled out her braid, wagging it around and pointing at Eve as she spoke. "Next I know, he shows me a handbag big enough to hold a couple of bowling balls, except it was light as a feather. So I ask him if there's more money inside, but he says it isn't money. It's something that could burn your nose right off your face." Eve looked up at Miss Gates, who closed her eyes and nodded.

"He said it was a relic come from another world. It's the truth, so help me God." Miss Gates clamped her hand over her breast pocket. "It come off a spaceship that landed on top of someone's barn, then crashed on a neighbor's cornfield. He said it was made of poison, but worth more than gold. Take the bag and hide it good, he told me. And be sure and keep your nose out of it. He'd be back for it soon, and then we'd buy a boat with money we'd make off the space relic, and we'd travel, me and him." Miss Gates leaned over and pointed her pigtail at Eve. "Then he gives me the harmonica that's in your pocket. Never had time to teach me how to play it. He was dead a month later. Well, a lot sooner, but it took a month for his body to float to the top."

Eve bit her lip and a flush crept over her face. "Here," she said. She pulled the harmonica out of her pocket. "You can have it back." Miss Gates put her hands up as if to surrender and shook her head. "It belongs to you now. And, anyways, I never had it with me much. Once I knew he was dead and the police went away and things got back to what they were, I brought it to the cave and stuck it in there with the rest. It would-a made me sad to keep it." She tucked her pigtail back inside her overalls and picked up Henrietta who'd sneaked out from somewhere. She made the cat lie in her lap then kneaded her reflexively. Eve saw that her bruised-looking eyes had lost their harsh light, blinking down at Henrietta.

"I left it all in there. Once I knew he was dead and gone, I figured

I was to blame for hiding what he'd taken from someone. Could-a been a relic off a space ship. Could-a been someone's money or drugs. There's drugs that'll burn the nose right off your face. Didn't matter anymore. It was all vanity, a lot of stuff that come to no good. I left it where it was and never went back."

"But weren't you curious?" asked Eve. "I mean, if it really was from a flying saucer."

"If it was," said Miss Gates, shaking her head. "He wasn't meant to have it. None of us was. A thing like that got itself on the wrong side of the Lord. And there's some things you're better off not knowing."

She poured Henrietta off her lap as if the cat were honey. Then she stood up halfway and headed stiffly toward a bookshelf with her back bent. She got down on her knees and tugged at a tall book that stuck, then suddenly came loose. The bookcase shook and spilled out other books, but Miss Gates ignored these, wetting a finger and paging through the tall book. Its jacket crackled and Eve recognized it as a library book from the label stuck to its spine bearing a decimal number. Kneeling, Miss Gates whistled through her teeth while thumbing pages. When she found what she was looking for, she beckoned to Eve and they both sat on the floor looking at one of the sorriest paintings Eve had ever seen. "This pitcher is a *vanitas,*" said Miss Gates, hissing out the word. "It's a warning to me and you." She held the book straight up and stood it on the floor so they could both study the painting.

It looked like someone had gone out of his way to make beautiful objects appear mean. There was a conch that the artist has taken his time with, making the whorl gleam and diminish in a melancholy way to a pearl at the tip. To one side, a snuffed-out candle sat in its waste of wax. There were long pipes for smoking and one for making music. There was an old leather wine bottle, a vase and the hilt of a sword and books posed every which way. On one of the books a yellow skull had been made to stand on its few remaining teeth. All of it was grouped on a table in a way you might arrange a science project, thought Eve, but not your favorite things. An unfriendly light glared all over it.

"Nice loot," said Miss Gates. "I bet you wouldn't mind having some of it."

"I think it's ugly," said Eve.

"Good. You're supposed to," said Miss Gates. "Next time you're tempted to go inside my cave, think of this pitcher. It's a warning to me and to you."

"But I thought you said it was your cave," said Eve.

"That cave," said Miss Gates, "is a *vanitas* same as this pitcher. It's a warning. And now I'm warning you. Don't you go back in there." Miss Gates's face was set so every bone in it showed through her skin. Eve thought it was the closest a person could come to looking like a skull.

"The Lord found a place for things like that relic, and it's not here on this earth."

…

Eve finishes packing up a box for Miss Gates, who has gone to do her laundry in a large metal tub outside. The humidity has caused Eve's hair to stick to the back of her neck and little black flies have entered the Quonset, which require vigilance. She has been smacking the side of her neck, and now she sees the small scrawl of a dead one in her hand with a smear of her own blood, which gives her satisfaction. She wipes it off on her shirt and tapes the box slowly. It's time to end her workday, but she doesn't want to let it go.

The cats have made themselves invisible, high up on shelves or down beneath tarps that Miss Gates uses to cover projects not yet finished. Miss Gates is out in the yard with clothespins, hanging identical denim overalls on a clothesline carousel. Her cowboy hat is pitched back on her head as she snaps a pair of overalls. She takes two clothespins, slots one in her mouth and hangs a suspender from the other pin. The overalls are worn denim, faded almost to white along the seams, but they are vibrant, somehow alive. The carousel sighs as Miss Gates works. A breeze lifts the wet pants-legs up and slaps them down again. Eve thinks it's odd to see Miss Gates's clothes without Miss Gates in them, resisting the breeze like so many same, hardy selves.

She thinks she would like to take one of them with her when she goes, to steal it right off the clothesline.

Owl Hollow Court is almost as hard to find as it is to pronounce, the last turn in a neighborhood of look-alikes. The house is a tidy white suburban ranch with gray shutters, set back from the street with a gate on one side and a garage on the other. Multi-colored pansies crowd the stone flower container in front. Like other ranches in the neighborhood, it has a breezeway, a picture window, and like them it's distinguished by diminutive trees, red buds, a Japanese maple, lilacs in bloom, planted by someone who has likely since passed. Arm guesses the house was built in the 1950s, brought into the current decade with additions that mask its original modest footprint. And there are gray-and-white birdfeeders built like miniatures of the house; Arm counts four. As he parks in the driveway, black-capped chickadees make a fluster before rushing away and blue jays stay long enough to rebuke him. He looks around warily: no barking, no domesticated pit bull on a chain. In the distance, a lawn mower drones.

Mrs. Anthony Streeter had agreed, finally, to an interview. What had changed her mind was a truth and a lie: Arm confessed that he had been Taft's music student, exaggerating his success.

"Come to my home," she had said in her female baritone. "Bring your credentials. Then we'll see."

The Streeters have a car, a Buick sedan, gray and of roughly the same age as Arm's AMC Spirit, but that is where the similarities end. The Streeter car gleams with recent polish and a long history of upkeep, tires clean and plump, a rear deck empty of clutter, the tailpipe rust-free and aloft. Arm turns off the CD player and parks two car lengths behind it, then disembarks cautiously. As if the blue jays aren't enough reproof, the whole neat roll of lawn and swept walk leading to the front door suggest that he hasn't taken enough care of his appearance and should retreat.

But he is punctual. That much of him aligns with the Streeter standard. He raises his hand to knock, sees a carved owl-shaped wooden doorbell, presses it once, then waits. Old people take longer to respond, and this one, from the sound of her on the phone, may be on a cane or a walker. When the door finally opens, however, he stares down on a tiny, theatrical-looking woman, out of breath but standing unassisted. Arm guesses she is in her mid-seventies.

Mrs. Streeter is vividly made up. Her lips are outlined in coral and her complexion has been revised with tanning from the neck down. But her face is cosmetically beige with spots of rouge on her cheekbones. The features beneath the makeup are large-boned, almost mannish. Arm resists the temptation not to stare at her eyebrows, which have been plucked out. A pair of imposters, sienna-colored accent marks, are penciled in midway up her forehead, making her eyes appear lost and stark. Her hair has been dyed the same sienna color, upswept into curls and sprayed in place. The effect is very odd, thinks Arm, as if the top of her head belonged to someone else from a long-ago time, a Sybil or an augur.

But Mrs. Streeter is conventionally dressed in coral trousers, a white silk blouse, a gray vest with pearl embroidery, gold, open-toed sandals, which she wears with lace-edged anklet socks on her diminutive feet. A pair of reading glasses on a chain swing and skim her birdlike chest as she moves forward to open the door and stretch out a tanned, spotted hand with coral fingernails. Arm is about to grasp it, but she claws him away. "Wait a minute," she says in her chesty voice. "Let me see your credentials."

He had forgotten. He'd brought with him his driver's license, of course, but also his diploma from Julliard and a bill from the dentist. He runs to fetch them from the backseat of the bomb, hoping she won't notice its condition. But when he rushes back, there she is, taut on the porch, her chin raised and head cocked.

She examines the evidence, shakily drawing the coral nail of her index finger across each page while breathing audibly. Then she peers at him over her reading glasses with those sybilline eyes, half-shut as if against smoke. "You can come in, Mr. Guest," she says finally and he follows her into a tiny mirrored hallway, where he checks his reflection for disarray. Smoothing his hair, he steps carefully across a carpet that is immaculate despite being cream-colored. Obviously, no pets in the house, neither cat nor dog. If she had a pet, he suspects it would be a parakeet – or a lizard.

As if hearing his thoughts, she stops suddenly, turns around and asks him to remove his shoes, forcing him to struggle precariously. "It isn't necessary to take off your socks," she commands. "Just your shoes." She takes each from him huffily as he removes them, then she places them somewhere out of view. It's her way of snaring him, he thinks, keeping him shoeless to keep him where she pleases: a sitting room with a coffee table and a floral couch. He can smell the coffee, already brewed, in the white porcelain set she has made ready for him.

He sits where she invites him on the couch, against too many cushions. She's drawing up a tufted velvet chair and he stands up awkwardly to assist, but she says to sit down, she is "capable." The room is a narrow rectangle with a hearth at one end and a built-in mirror-backed shelf on the other with groupings of figurines (camels and birds), a

Venetian glass vase, a set of classics and several elaborately carved boxes. On the top shelf an antique hookah is displayed, two green pipes snaking out of a clear glass belly. There is an ornate desk and two low-backed armchairs with slipcovers in sherbet stripes of lemon, peach and cream. Cream-colored sheers have been looped and draped over the picture window, framing a view of other well-groomed yards, porches, trees fussily articulated against a sky knitted up with chemtrails. A perfect day, otherwise, with a promising early summer beginning to simmer.

There is no sign of accommodation for an elderly male, apart from the hookah. No pipe rack, no newspaper, no leather slippers. If Anthony Streeter still exists, thinks Arm, he is seldom in this room. Boredom and anxiety collide in a yawn he tries to stifle. Was Taft ever in this room? He tries to imagine it. Taft ducking through the door, stooping to take off his shoes, slipping past the sentimental prints on the wall of children and dogs to light upon the sweets on the plate. Sugar had been another of Taft's addictions. He hadn't lived long enough to have to worry about his waistline.

"You'd like some coffee?" Mrs. Streeter pours steaming dark liquid into cups before Arm can answer, providing a saucer and napkin. "Help yourself," she says, pushing a tray of cream, sugar and cookies in his direction. He sugars, stirs and hesitantly accepts a cookie, a jellied shortbread, which he places on a napkin and doesn't touch again.

"Thank you for taking the time to see me," he says.

"What else do I have to do?" She's looking down into her cup, stirring in sugar, and Arm has an unimpeded view of those artificial eyebrows, each a pure brushstroke if he has ever seen one. He can't help staring, they are so obviously not her own, so symmetrical, so highly placed on beige furrows, (Could they be tattoos? No, he decides) and when she looks up at him finally, he is still staring. "You have the same eyes," she says sonorously. "Same as Taffy."

Arm smiles, says "thanks," pulling a notebook and pen out of his pocket. He thinks he'll have to probe her with questions, but she begins without him. As she speaks her hands flutter and clasp and smooth the cloth of her trousers.

"My brother was a devil," she says. "But he started out a good boy. My mother raised him the best she could while she was married to Solomon, Taffy's father. That was her second husband. My birth father, David, he was a good man, he owned a barber shop and died when I was ten. My stepfather, I don't like to say it, but he was a devil just like Taft. You know what I mean? He was no good. I wish't I could say otherwise."

"I understand." Arm lifts his cup, sips. The coffee is so strong he wishes he had added more sugar.

She leans forward and holds her hand to one side of her mouth. "Solomon was a polygamist," she says confidentially and, Arm senses, triumphantly. There is a terse, bitter smile before she sits back against the cushions. "A bad man." She wets a finger with her tongue neatly and opens her napkin, which is a little floral square, the sort used for cocktails. She spreads this over her lap, plucks a cookie from the plate and nibbles at it with her head bowed.

"What do you mean by bad?" asks Arm. Looking up, she shoots him a look of suspicion. "I mean besides the polygamy." He knows next to nothing about polygamy. It seems repugnant, committed by Mormon mountain men, Muslims, animals. But as someone with a stake in keeping bedroom matters private, it isn't the sort of thing he'd pick a fight over.

"I was fifteen when my mother married Solomon," she continues, clasping her hands. "Taffy was born the next year and he was a handful. Sick all the time with the croup, then rheumatic fever. Solomon resented him. As Taffy grew older, Solomon wouldn't touch him, wouldn't even talk to him. 'Weak,' he called him. Solomon, he was a small, mean man. A bully. He'd beat my mother just for talking to the mailman. Made her cover her head with one of those black hoods. Then off he'd go to see his other wives somewhere up north, only we didn't know it then. And he had his dirty mind on me. I knew it, but my mother didn't." She breaks off to slurp her coffee. Bobbing over the cup, her head with its elaborate hair appears too heavy for her frame.

"My mother, she was a beautiful woman, but she wasn't vain. She wasn't *shrewd*. I wish't she had been." She reaches across the coffee table for a small, cloth-bound album, slips a thick nail beneath the Velcro fastener and shakily rips it open. The miniature scratchy overture, the contemporary sound of undressing, clashes with what he sees. "This was my mother," she says. Pearly olive skin, swart, delicate features, the controlled yet voluptuous hair of her day. "Stunning," he says. Mrs. Streeter flips to the next page. "And this was my father." In a doorway, a man dressed in the barber's white frock and to one side the classic candy-cane pole. The man's expression is solemn with deep grooves, reminding Arm of a tobacco shop Indian.

"I favor him." Mrs. Streeter turns away to muffle a cough with her napkin. As she does so, she crosses her legs and her pants leg rises and puckers so that Arm can see the veiny alabaster of the skin above her sock, markedly different from her other skin, more like that of the woman in the photograph. The coughing fit goes on, to his embarrassment. He sits there helplessly, waiting, looking around the room for the oxygen tank he suspects she needs. When the coughing fit is over, she looks at him with accusatory eyes. "Never smoke," she rasps, and pours herself another cup, then tops off Arm's cup, which he has barely touched.

"Mr. Streeter rescued me from Solomon," she begins. "The usual way, by getting me pregnant. Back then, you married when that happened. We married and I miscarried." She stops to breathe. "But it was a done deal. I was married, by golly. Even Solomon wouldn't cross that bridge. And afterwards, that made it easier." She fidgets and sets her cup on the coffee table. Elongating her coral-tipped pinky finger, she meticulously sweeps invisible cookie crumbs off the table and into her napkin.

"It's chilly in here, or is it just me?" She looks at Arm critically, as if he were responsible. The room is warm and stuffy, but he agrees with her.

"You were saying that your marriage to Mr. Streeter made it easier." He squares his eyes with hers, resisting the temptation that drags them upward to her forehead. "What did you mean by that?"

She hunches over and frowns, her near-perfect posture collapsed into a round-shouldered cave. Her blouse makes a silken swish of sound.

"We took Taffy in as if he was our very own son. That was years later, after Momma died having another one of Solomon's big-headed sons. Solomon threw Taffy out of the house and he ended up down by the river living underneath a box. He was twelve years old then. The real trouble began when he was thirteen." She clutches her vest, pulling it around her hunched shoulders.

"Do you mean drugs?"

She snorts and coughs darkly, looking downward, shaking her head. "That was later. Got himself in good with some bad boys first. Petty crimes, you know. They broke into a Catholic church, through a window. Taft fell in and landed on his head. The police arrived. It was stupid of him."

"Is that why Solomon kicked him out?" Arm tries to engage her eyes again, but she's looking down, folding the napkin.

"I tell you, I wish't it was. Solomon wouldn't have cared much about that. All he cared about was carrying on with women and music. He kicked Taft out for not practicing. He was a tyrant. *Mean.* Taft couldn't please him, and he was gifted. A gifted young man. That beautiful boy could bring you to tears with his music. He had this sponsor, I believe it was a woman, who got him lessons." She looks up at Arm. "I guess I don't need to tell you."

Arm nods uncomfortably. Solomon wasn't the only mean one in the family, he thinks. His son had administered many hard raps to Arm's knuckles, torture likely drummed into him by his father. Arm pulls his leg up carefully and neatly poses it over his knee. He is self-consciously aware of his stocking feet in the lifeless, pet-free room, and is relieved his socks are clean. He wants to ask where Mr. Streeter is keeping himself.

Mrs. Streeter keeps talking. "Once he moved in here with us, he began hanging around with that crowd. Bad boys. He had messy habits, too, I have to say. Leaving his dirty laundry in a pile, mildewy towels, gum wrappers, soda cans and dirty magazines everywhere. I think he must've been smoking pot then, but of course, I didn't even know what pot was. Mr. Streeter didn't know either. Solomon knew. But by then, Solomon was back where he belongs." She gives Arm a thumbs-down deformed by arthritis.

"Dead?" he asks.

"Hell," she replies, then shrugs. "Saudi Arabia. Went right back where he came from." She shifts position and her eyeglasses swing on the thin chain.

"We were the only people Taffy had. Mr. Streeter had a soft spot for him. Not me, by golly. I was the disciplinarian. The bad cop." She mugs a mean face. "But he talked me into letting Taffy have a birthday party here. Right here in this room." She eyes the room with as much incredulity as Arm.

"I didn't have as much décor then," she explains. "Even so, you know what teenage boys can be. These boys weren't normal. Tough, using that language. It was the sixties. Kids had smart mouths, but these boys had something … *Hatred.* You could tell they hated you. I didn't want to be around them, so Mr. Streeter says to me, 'Why don't we go for a drive?' soon as they arrive, looking like hoodlums. And we did. We went for a nice drive along the beach. But I was too nerved up to enjoy it." Mrs. Streeter bows her head and shakes it slowly, twisting the napkin in her lap. The tiny motion disturbs something in her chest and she coughs deeply, then she struggles up and staggers out of the room. For the oxygen, Arm thinks. He looks around the room again for signs of inhalers and sees her cup, with its bright coral lip smudge.

A door shuts and the coughs become muffled as if she'd entered a small box. When she returns minutes later, she's holding one, delicately carved and inlaid with mother-of-pearl, a cousin to the ones on the high, mirrored shelf. She catches Arm standing up in mid-stretch, but upon seeing her, he sits down immediately.

Mrs. Streeter is fluttering, patting cushions and setting the box on the coffee table. Arm expects some new revelation, but she continues her story. "I have to say, I hit the ceiling when we came home," she says hoarsely. "Everything strewn. Empty, spilt bottles, potato chip bags, pillows crushed and all over the floor with their drunken bodies. Ketchup everywhere, torn up lampshades. I don't know what I was thinking. They'd snuck in beer and their girls, fast numbers, you know. Mr. Streeter

had to intervene. He found Taffy in our bedroom closet, sick as a skunk."
The faux eyebrows arch farther up on her forehead. "He stank of pot. I
nearly fainted. Mr. Streeter had to carry me out to the car and I sat in there
while he dealt with them all. Hell to pay."

She lets out a bronchial-basso laugh. "Long story short, Taffy
spent many of his high school years in a reformatory. One of his drug
buddies was brutally murdered a few years later. It was so brutal what they
did to him, the police wouldn't tell his own mother how it happened." He
senses this is her measuring rod for many things.

"Meantime," she says, "After an arrest and prison, Taft got lucky.
Some liberal prison program. I suppose his sponsor, that woman, helped
him get in. He got a degree in music, just like that." She laughs joylessly
and snaps her fingers. "Compliments of the taxpayers. Or someone. Who
knows who? Then Taffy gets out, and starts teaching violin. Took up with
women, just the same, like his father. But that was better, we figured, than
the alternative. Mr. Streeter worried about that a lot, too, if you know what
I mean."

Arm knows, and nods.

"We hardly saw him at all after he moved up to Swannboro. Now
and then a call. No news was good news with Taffy. Anyways . Mr.
Streeter got sick around that time. Parkinson's. I was his full-time nurse
until he passed away several years ago. I had a lot going on. Too much.
And you have to take care of yourself, you know. I didn't have time for my
little brother. I wish't I had." He waits for her shrunken eyes to well up, but
there is no change, the dam she has put there holds, all passion plucked
away and replaced by those impassive brows. He's relieved of the duty to
console. It would have done no good anyway, he thinks.

She wheezes, then suddenly switches gears, seizing his hands in both of hers, which makes him flinch at first. Her breath is an odd combination of death, confection and a chemical odor he can't identify.

"It wasn't the drugs that killed him," she says, her drama mask contorted, the ruined eyes catching fire. "It was a reporter for the local newspaper. He identified Taft as a police informant. The police informant for what's-his-name's trial."

"Manny Manciani?"

"That's the one," she says. "Right in the article. Everyone read it, everyone knew. So I called him up at his big-shot desk." She releases one of Arm's hands from hers to sip lukewarm coffee, then manacles him again. "I says to him, 'you're going to get my brother killed.' And do you know what he said?"

She wears an expression that commands a response, but his answer will never be right, he knows.

"I'll never forget it," she says, releasing him. "He says to me, *'That's the news, ma'am!'*" She leans forward and looks at Arm intently. "What do you think of that? *'That's the news, ma'am.'*" The sun, which had moved behind a cloud, suddenly enters the room bearing a drift of sparkling motes, making Arm squint.

"Anyways," says Mrs. Streeter to his blind silence. "Anyways, they never report the *real* news."

Arm looks down at his freed hands, ashamed of himself, of his misgivings about Mark, who had made a living telling other people's stories until giving it up for the reason Mrs. Streeter has cited. It's because of Mark that he's in this room with her now, probing a past he'd been content to forget about.

"Anniversary of his death was a couple, few weeks ago," she murmurs, her breath whistling. Arm had forgotten, of course.

"Mr. Streeter and I buried him in our plot. His name is there on the headstone next to Mr. Streeter's and mine. They won't have long to wait now – for me." Mrs. Streeter looks down at Arm's feet, frowning.

"I'll tell you a little secret," she says, brightening. She bends forward, crooking a finger and motioning to him. "That reporter, turns out, he had his eye on this woman. Big bosoms, big hair, the Marilyn Monroe type. Married to a local big-shot, but that didn't stop Taft. I think it was jealousy. I think the reporter was jealous, and that's why he put my brother in the news. To get him out of the way."

"Do you know the woman's name?"

"Yes, sir, I do. *Chelsea Fowler.* You don't forget a name like that, now do you? Other names should be that easy. Chelsea Fowler, married to a big-shot in cahoots with other big-shots. Anyways, she's in a rest home now, I think, with the other mental cases. Wish't I could remember which one." Her little sandaled foot wags tensely as she finishes her cup. "Could even be dead by now."

It isn't until he's about to leave, toiling over his shoes, that Mrs. Streeter remembers the box. She rushes to the table in her haywire way, both hands in the air. "For you," she says when she returns, pressing the box into his hands. "Mr. Streeter was a woodworker. He was good at it, I think." She huffs nervously as he examines the box, which bears the mark of mastery, plainly cut and polished to reveal the fine grain, perfectly joined. The design on the top is a yin and yang, a mother-of-pearl swirl joining a masculine teak one. As perfectly matched, he thinks, as Mrs. Streeter's eyebrows.

"Are you sure?" he asks.

"I wouldn't have offered it if I wasn't." She clenches her jaw, but he sees no other sign. The dam has held. The danger is over. "It's lovely," he tells her genuinely. They shake hands on a promise he knows he'll never keep, to send her a ticket to his "next concert," and he enters the exposing summer light as he had entered her home, on a truth and a lie.

He opens his car door to a yawn of heat. An anonymous bird sings "tree, tree, tree, tree" over another's trill as he looks back to the doorstep. She's vanished, no longer invested in sizing him up. But he's relieved when the car starts up without a stutter, and he doesn't bother to let the fan cool off the interior before backing up, guiding the hot steering wheel with his fingertips. He's anxious to be away because Drew has consented to attend one of his gigs at Harpo's. The thought of him is balm on the blister that the ride home will be as the day heats up.

As he rounds a corner, past shuttered ranches, a dog rushes out of a yard and he hits his brake pedal with tragic awareness. The brake shoes are soft and insufficient. The car lurches, spilling everything he has piled on the passenger seat, but the dog, a tousled terrier, makes it across the street and into a leafy orifice in a neighbor's shrubs.

Sweating, he begins again, this time accompanied by miniature music that seems to have been shaken loose from time itself. He looks at the floor of the passenger side, and there it is, Mrs. Streeter's box, open and prone; the tiny embedded brass key he hadn't seen previously was moving slowly. He picks the box up and winds the key full measure.

He would have expected an old cliché, *Fur Elise* or something from her time, a Bing Crosby song, *White Christmas* or *To-Ra-Loo-Ra-Loo-Ra*. But instead he hears the chimes of an old gospel song that he actually recognizes. Taft had played it and had forced him to play it. What was it called?

He finds his way out of the suburbs at last, but a turn he takes is the wrong one, and now he's committed to the view ahead of him, which is squalor. Crumbling old tenements with front porches where old people sit staring and rejected indoor furniture has been piled. Then a fast food wasteland and the prodigal acreage of one used car lot after another.

Beulah Land, he remembers, as he passes a showroom that takes up an entire block. The song is *Beulah Land.* Why would Streeter have tucked an old gospel hymn inside one of his boxes?

Too many questions. As he stalls and burns his way through the hardcore strip, he wishes he'd asked his hostess for the reporter's name. Why the devil hadn't he? And *her* first name, too. A whole afternoon in her parlor, and he'd forgotten to ask.

23 / *Rose*

The quilt shop is in the village of Barnham, located to one side of railroad tracks that split the tiny village in two, like a zipper on a pocket. Beulah had found it through the phone directory and her husband, Joseph, has driven them there in his station wagon, with Beulah in the front passenger seat and Rose in back with Jacob, who had stoically read a book. Rose could feel his dark blue eyes race toward her and back to his refuge of pages. They had to stop twice at convenience stores to allow Beulah to use the restroom, and Jacob had held the heavy glass door open for his mother, ignoring the hard stares and smirks from boys his age.

Rose had expected Joseph to be a Bible-thumper, but discovered instead a sweet male goofiness. He has neat, freckled features on a head too large for them and fine, brown hair shaved to a military bristle. Every so often, he rubs one of his big, freckled hands over it. All the way to the shop he had joked and punned. "So if we're going to a quilt shop, does that make this a quilt trip?" he had asked. No one had answered. Beulah had giggled, looking back nervously at Rose. She wants me to like him, Rose had thought, touching her face.

The boys, as Beulah calls them, are eating their lunch on the shaded bench near a confectionary shop across the street, while Rose and Beulah browse bolts. More than three thousand of them, according to the ad. The building that contains them is an old clapboard with an impressive arched entrance and apartments on the second floor. Entering, Rose can hear bumps, scrabbling, creaks and pitter-pats from above and an occasional child's whine soothed by a muffled voice.

The shop interior is homey and clever, with masses of tulle bunched into roses and stapled to the walls. Rose takes in the color array of bolts on shelves and racks like a rich diet she has long denied herself. Above the shelves, finished quilts are displayed: Star quilts, Jacob's Ladder, Joseph's Coat, Irish Chain, Bow Tie, Tree of Life, Sunflower patterns, all expertly rendered. A trio of antique pictorial quilts, straight and prim as *American Gothic*, look weary next to their bold successors. Rose pays homage to these, then heads for the remnant table at the back of the shop, while Beulah plods to the restroom.

Near the remnants table is a picture gallery arranged across a cloud of white tulle. Postcards from afar and hazy framed photos of smiling women, it appears, holding up their finished masterpieces. Curious, Rose puts on her glasses, and the faces clarify and converge into the same woman, a redhead with a short, dumpling shape and broad smile. Clearly, she's big on charitable work, the queen of raffles. Local do-good organizations have all received quilts by this woman for their fundraisers. Nice, Rose thinks. And here she, Rose, is pawning off her do-good work on Beulah so that she can make her art. She can see Beulah now, heading from the restroom toward a shelf of demure pinks.

Rose immerses herself in remnants. To her, their draw isn't in the cheaper price, but in the hunt. You never know what ravishing beauty might lie beneath the rabble. She's holding up two yards of a glorious cerulean when she sees the woman from the raffle photographs make her way toward Beulah like a bee to a rose. At first, they appear to chat about Beulah's pregnancy, with Beulah rubbing her belly. The raffle woman listens and responds with a stack of bolts they examine together, heads bent, out of earshot. *Secrets.* Beulah is good at keeping them, Rose thinks.

"Mother says she's never heard of him," had been her answer to Rose's question earlier while they were getting ready to leave Beulah's house. It was too hot to sit outside and the whole kitchen was an oven, despite a small fan rotating on the countertop.

Martha had been placed in charge of Lydia, who was happily washing her dolls in a metal tub on the floor. "Don't splash," Martha had pleaded, but Lydia had splashed deliciously, the soapy water dripping from her chin and sopping sleeves. Beulah had been packing lunch while Jacob helped his father out in the yard with something that growled and racked, a farm tool, Rose guessed. Lilah's door was closed, but Rose could hear her in there, rustling and tapping.

Beulah was unmistakably pregnant, but the hot weather had compromised her dress code only slightly, with three-quarter-length sleeves beneath a limp yellow smock that outlined her navel. Rose guessed she was unaware of it because it had seemed, to Rose, overtly sexual. But everything about Beulah was sexual now, whether or not she knew it. Her astonishing hair had grown thick as a pelt and her skin gleamed with perspiration appealingly, like the sheen on the freshly washed nectarines in the dish rack. These she packed into brown bags with the cheese and pickle sandwiches she'd made for all of them.

"So did you have a chance to ask your mother my questions?" Rose had tried to sound nonchalant.

Beulah had looked up from her work, then back down again. "I was going to ask her before we leave." But instead of knocking on Lilah's door and obliging Rose, Beulah had continued packing unnecessary items into lunch bags. Thick slices of a blueberry pie, requiring multiple wrappings of wax paper, and radishes that Beulah had taken her sweet time cutting into tulip shapes. She took hard-boiled eggs out of a bowl, their lucent skins salted and peppered, and wrapped them in foil. "These are Joe's favorite," she'd explained. Rose hoped she wouldn't be expected to eat one.

The questions she wanted Beulah to ask Lilah were about Taft. *Did Lilah remember a handsome man of about her age who played a violin and taught music? Did she remember a man named Taft Said?*

She had put the questions to Beulah a week ago, and had been made to feel that she was asking for a set of house keys. Beulah had frowned and said, "I don't know if Mother should be expected to remember such things." *Such* things? *What things?* It was exasperating. When Beulah had finally knocked on Lilah's door and slipped inside, Rose hadn't been invited to join them. The door had shut and Rose could hear only murmurs and key-tapping, not a normal conversation. Then Beulah emerged from the room and said, "Mother says she's never heard of him." Her eyes had shifted. *Liar,* thought Rose. *Liars.* But, of course, to lie would break the ninth Commandment.

Then Joseph had stomped in to say that a woodchuck had gorged on his carrot patch. "Ate all the tops off the north end, then just took his time polishing off the ones in the middle." He had rubbed his large, baby-like head with exaggerated dismay. "A dang woodchuck," he had kept on saying, not a "lawn fucker" as Randall would have. He hadn't cursed, hadn't pounded his fist on the table, and Beulah had held her belly and laughed. Joseph had fidgeted, greedily rubbing his hands together, contorting his mouth into buckteeth and impersonating a woodchuck. Lydia squealed with delight. Joseph had lifted her onto his shoulders and was lumbering around the room, pretending to snap at and eat her dangling feet. Even Martha, sober-faced from duty, couldn't suppress her amusement. Jacob had stood on the porch, bent over laughing. Through the blurring screen, Rose could see his sapphire eyes and wasted beauty, and found that she had to smile along with them, at their foolish happiness. A ruined garden, she thought. They must know better than most how it will end.

Now Rose is cloistered in garden patterns of every color. The women in the shop browse companionably, but from the apartment upstairs a family's noises escape, footsteps and murmurs, the beat of a rocking chair set to a child's wail. And Rose thinks these are both her stories. The top floor is life with its noisy needs and compromises, and beneath it all is art with its ideals, endangered by commerce. A woman in the aisle smiles and admires a bolt she's examining. "That looks like summer," she says.

Rose agrees. "Summer squash," she replies, but actually, what it calls to her mind is one of those ripening yellows in a Vermeer painting, in the bodice of one of his maidens.

Then Beulah is there, tapping her on the shoulder. "Look!" she exclaims girlishly, her eyes dancing, handing Rose samples of baby-sized prints, her hair tumbling richly over her yellow smock. And Rose sees at once who will be the model for her mother quilts. Why hadn't she seen it before?

The spell is broken when the raffle woman seizes Rose's hand and introduces herself as "Velvet" in a faint Scandinavian accent. She's wearing a sleeveless quilted top, like an oven mitt, with the word "Grandma" embroidered across her middle.

Velvet proceeds to market the fabrics to Rose, addressing her as "Ma'am" and Beulah as "Angel Face."

"All on sale, Ma'am," Velvet is saying. "And it's a good thing you got out here today, because the sale ends at midnight." Her smile is all cheek, exaggerated by hair pulled back tightly and rolled into a bun.

"I was telling Angel Face we do long-arm quilting out back," Velvet continues. "The demo is free, then we charge a pittance." She tacks a deliberate hiss on the end of the word. Her puffy complexion makes her eyes look pressed in, and her mealy nose has a reddish cast. Rose takes an instant dislike to her. "No, thanks," she says.

"Angel Face here says she wants to take part in our sewing circle. We sew pinafores and shorts for poor Haitian girls. We get a lot of help from the local churches, but I'm always recruiting new angels." She is one of those who sometimes refer to themselves in the third person. "Take it from Velvet, Ma'am," she says. "It's mostly *fun*." The cheeky smile again.

"No, thanks," Rose says abruptly, forced to be uncharitable. Beulah blushes. "I mean," says Rose, "I don't have a car, so --"

"Joe could drive us," entreats Beulah softly. Rose blushes and asks to see the fabrics, so they spread them out on a table, the bouquet of one against the stripe of another, as Beulah explains her choices. As if it mattered. Rose has agreed to pay Beulah for her work on the quarry quilt by purchasing yards of floral, checked and striped fabrics for the baby quilt business. The two of them vet yards of pink, fuchsia, indigo, lavender and gentian, as Velvet unrolls bolts, aligns them with a metal yardstick on the cutting table and snips like one of the Fates allotting life spans. Her scissors make a sonorous sound, final as a tonic chord.

Rose hums nervously and touches her face. Beulah's fabric decisions for the quarry quilt are fine with her, all passion spent. Like dirty linen, the quarry quilt is now rolled up in a laundry bag. Beulah will complete the quilt now, based on a simpler block design Rose had sketched in about an hour. Most of her original imagery is gone, with the exception of the violin at the bottom of the lake. Natalie had lobbied hard for that; no reason to abandon it now. But the little flag man is missing, along with the quirky bones, the brain whorls stitched into the cliffs, the headstone and her own dried blood. Let the Circle women have their quilt; let Lilah have her secrets. She has moved on.

She's decided to stitch a peacock into her three mother quilts using remnant brocades and silks. Velvet pokes at Rose's resplendent finds as if they were damaged fruit in a grocery. "These are nice," she hisses. "But I just got in some gorgeous new bolts with colors like these. Would you like to see?" She walks away from the cutting table, but Rose doesn't follow her. Beulah is rapt in what Rose has purchased for her and doesn't notice. Velvet returns with several more bolts, each priced beyond Rose's means. "Sorry," says Rose, shaking her head. "They're lovely," she adds warily. *"Tack,"* says Velvet with the smile. Rose knows the word means "thank you" in Swedish or Norwegian, but senses an attempt to make her feel cheap.

"You be sure to bring that angel baby back here to see us," says Velvet to Beulah after she bags their purchases. "And," she advises Rose, "Take it from Velvet. Being a grand-maw is going to be *fun!*"

Rose can feel the flush rise from her neck to her cheeks. She touches her face. "She isn't my daughter," she mutters on her way out the door. Beulah is rushing toward her and is there by her side on the sidewalk suddenly, taking her hand and telling her it was a mistake. She pants along with a gait that is becoming a waddle, which forces Rose to slow down. "She didn't mean anything," Beulah is saying to Rose. Then she thanks her, right there on the sidewalk, with a pregnant hug. "Oh, Rose, you've made me so happy!" And Rose surrenders, hugging Beulah back against vanity and malice.

The "boys" are eating pastries when Rose and Beulah find them outside the bakeshop. "You'll both spoil your appetite," scolds Beulah, but her heart isn't in it; it's in the bag of fabrics. She opens it to Joseph and they examine the cloth together, mutually invested in quilts. Rose feels a stab of otherness. She looks away to meet Jacob's starry gaze. "We saved some sandwiches for you," he says shyly, holding up his lunch bag. Rose shakes her head at first, but noting his disappointment, accepts a heavy packet. The cheese has melted in the sun, the bread is springy, yeasty, homemade, and a sweet tang surprises her. Pickles, she remembers. Rose savors it during the road home, an excuse to remain silent. Beulah and Joe chatter about nothing, the trees along the road, quilts, carrots, the wish for rain, the rattle in the station wagon.

Jacob reads his book, but doesn't turn pages. When they stop for gas, he slips out of the car, fills the tank and pays the swarthy little man with cash that Joseph gives him. Behind a cash register, the man smokes and slouches in his service garage full of rusted, twisted metal, a fake Christmas tree with a grubby red sash, an Evinrude boat motor. Everything, including the man, appears to be from the wrong time and place, missing from somewhere or lost to someone.

"Thank you, sir," Rose hears Jacob say. When Jacob climbs back in the car, Beulah pats his head and Jacob doesn't duck or shrink or smirk. As Eve would, thinks Rose.

It's been months since she's touched her own child. Eve has made herself scarce since Easter, returning from school to withdraw to her room and "study." The studying involves faded *National Geographics*, library books, as well as her stack of textbooks. Once, on Eve's nightstand, Rose had found a crumpled and spotted old manual about a heat press machine. What on earth is a heat press machine? "Where'd this come from?" she'd asked and Eve had shrugged moodily. No last-minute, late-night pleas for help with math, as there once had been. No projects involving felt markers or craft supplies, just "homework" Rose is never invited to read. No friends, either, but this eliminates the cruelty of girls, the groping of boys. Whenever she peeks into Eve's room, it's breathtakingly tidy. What mother could possibly object to that? A snugly made bed, and, on the dresser, a brush, comb and a harmonica, of all things, arranged across a red handkerchief that Rose suspects had been Randall's.

Yet it's a repudiating tidiness. There are no mother-daughter secrets, no confessed crushes, no menstrual signs so far. Rose, who checks Eve's dirty laundry, is relieved, yet anxious. When Eve had requested to eat supper in her room, Rose had agreed, hoping her respect for Eve's privacy might bring her daughter back to the table. But Eve has persisted in eating alone, the door shut with the sulky strains of her cassette player marking her territory. The only other sign of her is in the kitchen, with the plates and cups she once habitually left in the sink now innocent occupants of the dish drain. And in the bathroom, her towels are neatly squared and draped over the rack.

"Let's not go home the same way," Beulah is saying. "Let's meander."

"Will that make us meander-thals?" jokes Joseph. No one laughs except Beulah. Joseph ferrets back roads, narrow passages parallel to the highway and the river, densely treed and ferned, with occasional houses and barns that peer through profuse foliage or stand naked in trampled clearings. It's Reid-like land, thinks Rose, but impoverished and beaten up by the economy and the sun. A sale-by-owner sign sags in front of a house seized by vines. Some of the homes look abandoned, but there are still curtains in windows with Christmas candles, satellite dishes on roofs.

Somehow all of this is connected to the bridge that takes them back to Swannboro. Somehow, she and these people from a strange mooring are together, heading to the same town. She is the alien, traveling in a station wagon with a happy family. Her place is in the world of unhappy ones.

They drop Rose off, at her request, on the sidewalk a few blocks from the church. She doesn't want Drew to spot Beulah for reasons she isn't willing to examine. And she doesn't want Beulah and Joe to see the church, the peace vigil. It would raise too many questions in minds she judges to be closed. "Thank you," she says simply. "I'll be in touch." They let her go, driving away with a friendly rattle.

Drew is there. Rose sees his bald head bent in conversation with an elderly woman, and she feels the warm glow he arouses in her, which she senses is reciprocated. They have had exactly two dates. For coffee once, in a musty hangout downtown full of hippie posters and old pinball machines. She had ducked in to escape a man in a hat who turned out not to be Randall, and there Drew had been, alone with a book. It hadn't been a date exactly, more of a coincidence. But weren't coincidences supposed to be God's way of pointing? The second date had been her offering to help him move a collection of coats for the homeless out of the church basement and into a cedar closet upstairs, hanging countless bulky shoulders on wire hangers that had slumped under their weight. In the summer heat, the old leathers and wools had an exhausted, burnt body odor, but she hadn't minded.

She hugs the bag of cloth, forcing herself to walk slowly. She can't wait to show Drew, to demonstrate her worth as a purveyor and creator of beauty. But she recognizes that this may not be the best timing, given today's news and, for that matter, all of the past month's. No weapons of mass destruction have been found in Iraq, yet Blair and Bush remain adamant about the bombing campaign, revenge for an unattributed act. Rose has seen this before in nearly all of the women she has known, and most of the men. Recreating history to rationalize their selfish desires. Blaming someone, anyone. She doesn't understand why people should be so surprised, so disappointed, so shocked and outraged. *Where have they been living all their lives?* People lie all the time, Rose thinks, about sex, about money, even about their do-good impulses. Why not about weapons of mass destruction? Yet, everyone in the peace vigil group is expressing shock at national leaders who are as immoral as anyone, and much worse in most respects. Drew patiently inhales what one of the Quaker women is saying about Bush.

"… betrayal," Rose overhears. She listens as the usual words file past.

"… Yellow cake … hubris … hegemony … Jesus --"

Jesus? Well, the last time she heard, Rose thinks, Jesus wasn't running the country. People should expect the usual, the lies, the betrayals, the power games.

She stands there, waiting for an opening, but Drew doesn't look her way. He's sucked down into the milky storm of an elderly woman's face. Rose looks around for a poster to hold and finds "Bush lied -- Innocents died" lying by the curb on top of a grassy patch. As good as any.

She heads for a spot at the edge of the group and raises her sign, keeping Drew within her peripheral vision, just in case, setting her face in a mask of impassivity. She doesn't want to appear obvious, and forces herself to gaze at passersby, who mostly ignore the vigil. Blind business people, looking down into the cell phones, solipsistic gazing balls, that are beginning to proliferate, she has noticed. And mixed with the gazers are homeless walkers, people who intrude with their eyes and ask inappropriate questions. "You got a cigarette?" asks a shaggy, sunburned gnome in a Marlboro Lights tee shirt. His eyes burn blue above a cancerous nose. Rose trains her eyes on a distant spire until they water.

But here is Albert coming for her and there is no escape. She braces herself for the contemporary history lesson about to erupt like Vesuvius from his inflamed face. Why had she insisted on coming here? She pictures Velvet slicing through fabric and imagines Albert to be in on it, colluding in her destiny. Ignoring him won't work, but she does her best until he's upon her and she can hear his breath and feel his heat. He's wearing jeans, they all do, with an open-collared shirt exposing a chest with a healthy field of hair.

"Your daughter," he says. "You have a daughter, right?" She stares at him and touches her face. "You have a daughter in my class."

"Eve," says Rose. "Her name is Eve."

He turns around to greet a fellow activist, one of the young men that Drew recruited, and Rose, relieved, steps off the sidewalk onto the street. She searches for Drew, for the shortest distance to him through the scramble of signs and faces.

But Albert steps in front of her, blocking her path. She steps away and he steps forward in a dance she has been a partner to before. Randall had this same way of holding her captive. She looks at him acidly to voice her objection, but he takes the words from her mouth.

"You've got a problem with Eve," he says, looking down. "I'd say a big one."

24 / Eve

It's hot, so hot she feels almost at home. But what had been comforting during the long hours in the school's detention room is punishing here in the woods. Swannboro has smaller brambles and mosquitoes than Millsap, but, just like the ones at home, they seldom miss their mark. She slaps her way up the trail, stopping occasionally to scratch, avoiding poison ivy and sumac. She knows where they hide in plain sight. The trail leading up to the cat graves has changed. What had once been dirt is now moss and fern, creeper and bittersweet.

Several paces ahead, Miss Gates tramps and swash-buckles with a long stick, and Eve is glad, because it isn't likely she'd find her way otherwise. She tries to make conversation with Miss Gates in small, self-conscious nudges. "I can smell pine," she says. "Do you think we could go swimming after?" She offers to carry something for Miss Gates. But it's no use. Miss Gates is giving her what is called the cold shoulder, which Eve knows she deserves. The forest rattles with cicadas that drop off and leave silent blanks that make Eve's ears ring, but Miss Gates's silence is worse.

It's a fine, torrid Saturday morning with a cloudless sky, tight as a sheet over a well-made bed. The previous three days, it had rained hard, so the way is wet. There are brown puddles, each of them occupied. One has a struggling bee with a big black patent-leather-looking bottom, another has a crushed can, and another has a strange gelatin that turns out to be a cellophane wrapper when Eve roots it out with a stick. She wonders when she'll stop seeking lost things, putting her hobby away forever like an old toy. Nature, she thinks, is full of odds and ends for the taking, but she isn't tempted by any this morning. This morning, all she craves is forgiveness.

Mr. Warner had betrayed her to Momma. She knows this now. Momma has other spies and these had tailed her to Shirley Gates Road, where Miss Gates has her shop and caravan. Who were these spies? Not Connie and the twins. Not her uncle; Momma hardly speaks to him. That doesn't leave much of anyone, except the queer old dragons that Momma cleans for. What does it matter? The damage has been done, with two weeks of detention to pay for it and a sentence to serve in Swannboro's summer school with the dumb and the delinquent. She had cried, apologized, made offers of chores and yard work, salvaging only Saturday mornings with Miss Gates as "community service." There would be no more money, Momma had ruled. Instead, Eve would pay with her time for what she'd done.

Blasts of sunshine have dried areas up ahead where wildflowers emerge and begin to lift up soggy heads. Eve recognizes them as Queen Anne's lace, Dame's rocket and butter-and-egg because Miss Gates had told her what they were. Hoping to please Miss Gates, she pulls a few to throw down on the cat graves once they get there. A thin path scored through the weeds by someone has begun to emerge and the going here is easier, with well-worn footholds of brownstone. Then grapevines scramble a fence of low shrubs and Miss Gates has to whack her way across with an angry gusto. Eve had seen it before in Daddy, on the rare occasion when he had chopped wood.

Momma had gone in person to see Miss Gates. Eve had been dragged along in the old gray bomb, then made to sit on the tire swing in front of the trailer. Momma had sniffed when she saw the saying signs in the yard, as if they had an odor. She had marched up Miss Gates's steps and knocked on the door. "She's in her workshop," Eve had been about to say, but then the door had opened and Miss Gates's head had popped out, with the rest of her trying to keep the cats inside. But it was no use, all but Pindrop had escaped, Sledge heading straight for Eve. Eve had sweltered with Sledge on her lap and Henrietta at her feet, her legs stuck to the tire, while Slinky poked around the yard as if there were something to hunt, then stretched and lolled in the dust. A small, bright disk had gleamed in the scorched grass. A dime. Eve had let it lie where it was. Now she wishes she'd scooped it up and put it in her pocket. It would have been her last dime from Miss Gates.

They've come to the place where solemn brown boulders guard what's beyond. Hadn't she found the red handkerchief on one of them? No, that was farther down. The forest has been rejuvenated by foliage, needles, vines and leaves weaving a massive canopy. Even the birdsong is different, keen twitters against the long buzz saw of insects. Like home, almost. She would be happy if she weren't so miserable.

Squirrels clown around on the ledge ahead, where trees hang on like acrobats, and she has to be careful to dog Miss Gates. Here are hairpin turns and sudden, steep, damp dips. At one point Miss Gates turns around and pulls her up with iron insistence, making Eve lose her grip on the wildflowers. "Ohh," she groans as they fall away from her and drop onto trampled weeds and mud below. Miss Gates barely looks at Eve and says nothing, her mouth a steadfast pucker.

The sun takes turns with tree shade blinding them all the way up and down, until they come to the fire pit, still heaped with ashes and tramp trash. Eve knows they've arrived. She sees what she'd missed before, a dark, wooden sign on a dark tree. The words *Gates Cat Cemetery* are carved in a fine curly script but there's bathroom graffiti all over. *Cemetery* has been crossed out and the word *Piss* hangs over it, and to one side is a caricatured penis with a cowboy hat. Eve thinks this would make her mad if she were Miss Gates, but instead Miss Gates is mad at Eve.

Everyone but her daddy is mad at her. During meals, she's forced to sit with others who shun her. Lunch with the dorks at school is like eating with a row of cows. Supper at home is worse, each of them feeding off mismatched plates. Well, the three of them, Eve, Momma and Arm, *are* mismatched. She doesn't belong with Momma any more than her uncle, each of them made from different clay. Still, she feels bad about what she's done, her meanness to Uncle Arm, her lies to Momma. But she expects it's too late for feeling bad.

A mosquito bites her thigh, and the wallop she gives it brings forth a radiant smear of blood, which she wipes off on her shorts. Already, her legs bear bites in various stages, from fresh welts to scabs. She hopes for more bites this morning as a good excuse to scratch. She scratches now and Miss Gates shoots her a poisonous look. "Quit that scratching," she says. Then she shakes her head and mutters, "Worse than a cat."

They are the first real sentences Miss Gates has spoken to her since that hot day on the tire swing, with Momma in the trailer. Eve is jubilant. It isn't forgiveness, but it's talk. Miss Gates removes her cowboy hat and shakes out her braid, then lays out the tools and tags she's brought along in a large green knapsack. There are screwdrivers, trowels, a wrench, wire cutters, a small electric drill, a jar of screws and lots of metal tags, plus a sack of what Eve assumes is lunch.

Eve folds her arms with her hands tucked under her pits, and manages to scratch the mosquito bite by rubbing her left leg with her right. "You gotta go to the bathroom or something?" Miss Gates asks irritably.

"No, ma'am," says Eve. "I went before."

"Then quit lollygagging and get over here so I can show you what to do."

They have to take the old hanging tags off the crosses that mark each grave, Miss Gates explains. Some of the crosses had lost their tags altogether, but the cats' names are scratched into the wood. Eve's job is to screw new tags on so that rotten kids can't remove them.

"We start over there." Miss Gates is walking and Eve follows her to an old cross with no tag close to where the ledge begins to drop. "This one here is Chiclet," she says. She kneels and furiously digs around the base. The stake doesn't come out of the earth easily and sends Miss Gates sprawling, but she doesn't go over the quarry cliff the way Eve fears. Eve offers a hand to help her up, which Miss Gates ignores. She picks herself up and dusts herself off, same as always, but there are damp stains in her tee shirt, beneath her armpits and in the skinny valley between her shoulder blades.

After that, it's the same thing over and over again. Miss Gates removing one cross at a time, drilling holes in the crosspieces and Eve screwing in the right nametag, which says Beloved *Somebody.* Then Miss Gates planting the cross again, patting the earth around it and muttering a few words Eve can't hear. Eve screws in the tags of Chiclet, Scrap, Kooty, Petunia, Yoko, Doughboy, Bosch, Musetta, Skippy, Ether, Sly, Molotov, Wrigley, Salt, Hamster, Pudge, Lola, Tilly and Dustin.

"We might could just pull a bunch of them and line them up on the ground and do them all at the same time," says Eve, feeling bolder. "I bet it would go faster."

"What kind of fool idea is that?" Miss Gates wears a sour

expression. "You think this here is an assembly line?" She speaks in a high pitch that her voice seldom achieves. Eve looks down at her filthy sneakers. "This is sacred ground!" exclaims Miss Gates. She takes a checkered handkerchief out of her pocket and mops her brow. "Anyways, it's enough for now. Time for lunch."

They sit down on a blanket of pine needles beneath the tree that shed them. Miss Gates closes her eyes, folds her hands and says, "Lord, bless this food to our bodies and help us be good stewards to your creatures, even the ones who are no longer with us. And especially the ones who are with us, but get themself in trouble by not being where they're supposed to." After a long moment of silence, she opens the knapsack and passes Eve a warm peanut-butter-and-banana sandwich. Then she pours cold lemonade from a thermos into paper cups for each of them and it's almost normal, almost what it had been between them before she, Eve, had ruined it all. But it was already ruined, she realizes, even before she met Miss Gates, even before she saw her that day here in this place. A vireo somewhere flutes out musical brushstrokes and she can hear the tiny beat of wings. A jay bird squawks "Ah-ha!" as it picks up a crust Miss Gates throws to the wind, then flies off with it.

Eve chews glumly, careful to take small bites and keep her mouth shut. Once or twice, she peers through her lashes to see Miss Gates observing her with her usual face, two stern eyes over a leathery landmass of skin and bone. Miss Gates takes a long drink of lemonade, *clunk, clunk, clunk*, without breaking her tragic gaze. The mosquitoes have calmed down, but Eve wouldn't scratch even if one bit her on the eyelid

"I'm sorry." Eve whispers the words at first. "I'm real sorry," she says. Her palms are sweating and what's left of her sandwich feels like a wet sponge.

"Oh?" says Miss Gates. "What're you sorry for?"

"I'm just sorry." Eve takes a bite and chews, feeling like her mouth is bigger than the rest of her, every bone and tendon and tooth, with enough food in her mouth to fill a cave.

Miss Gates says, "If you ask me, I think you're sorry about having to sit in that ugly school all summer, and now you have to repeat a grade. I think you're sorry for yourself."

Eve's face gets hot, then crumples. "I'm sorry about not getting home and seeing my daddy."

"Well," says Miss Gates. "Homesick is an awful good reason to be sad. But it isn't the same as sorry."

To her horror, Eve begins to shake and sob, clutching herself. No words come out of her mouth, but instead crowd inside her. Yes, she is homesick, so homesick that she hears their accented voices in her head, the voices of Daddy and them, Mary-Alice and Hootie, Aunt Fleurette and the rug people. She can hear them all, the sweet, leisurely chorus of Southern talk. Even the appliances, the doors, the cars, the birds and trees in her head have Southern accents, sounds that linger with an extra beat before melting away. Eyes shut, she can still see the floating, slow-motion dance of the lava lamp on the countertop of her childhood. She sobs openly until a clean, blue handkerchief arrives on her nose and her whole face is being daubed and wiped while she sobs. She can feel Miss Gates giving her a big squeeze. "Let it all out, lamb," she says. "Have yourself a good cry."

Afterwards, Eve sits there on the pine needles, blinking. She has cried herself dry, but there is still a stuffy nose and swollen eyelids. In a little while Miss Gates sets a napkin down between them with something wrapped in wax paper. She opens it delicately. Eve sniffles, looks down and sees that she is being served brownies, homemade with chocolate icing that has melted in the sun and stuck to the wax paper. She waits for Miss Gates to take one before she does, then they each eat silently, the rich chocolate like a shared emotion. They must lick their fingers and the wax paper, there is so much, too much, a dark, melting excess.

"Come on over here," says Miss Gates afterwards. "So you can see what I'm about to tell you."

They walk farther into the woods along the ledge until they come to a flat area where trees are scarcer and roots poke up like hairy handles. Here you can too easily see the quarry lake below and Eve hangs back. Then Miss Gates is talking to her again, telling a story. She's pointing toward spears of light in the lake below with her pigtail, telling Eve that's where she first spotted her daddy's dead body. Eve squints and when she turns away, her vision has darkened.

"All blown up like a balloon. There were two men fishing out there who thought they were the first to see it. But it was me, not them. I saw it first. No honor in that. I didn't even recognize him. Too blown up with water and the wind of his innards." She pulls on her braid thoughtfully. "It changed me, though. It took a while to piece it all together. My mother carrying on the way she did about everything. The police coming to our trailer. I overheard what they said about a body floating in a lake. And I knew it was him, my own father, I'd seen. I would-a been twelve that year. I remember because Chiclet was with me. It was on our first day together."

Eve looks back at the lake, shielding her eyes, but now Miss Gates is pointing somewhere else, up beyond to where there are buildings.

"That land up there belonged to the carnival my momma's

family owned. Then, after my daddy died, the town come and took it all and built a shopping center on it. Right of eminent domain, they call it, but there isn't a thing right about it. It's just thieves helping each other. We got that bit of land I live on now and a little money. Don't ask me how much." Miss Gates chortles. "But they never interfered with my cat cemetery, I'll say that much for 'em. I just kept burying and they just kept ignoring. Except for those rotten kids. They got to it first. Soon, the rest of 'em will, too. So I may as well --" A sound makes Miss Gates freeze, duck and place a finger to her lips.

Eve squats where she is. Peals of female laughter seem to come from the forest, but Miss Gates is looking down, down into the quarry lake. Eve moves toward her, stooping, then squats on all fours. What she sees below is a perfect little theater made of quarry-stone walls, the surface of the lake and behind that the promontory. The balcony view nearly turns her stomach upside-down. She hangs onto a nearby root to steady herself.

There are three females down there, a tall, skinny, red-haired one and a pair of identical Buddha-shaped ones, the latter seated with their legs dangling over the edge of the promontory. None of them has on a stitch of clothing, but the tall one has something dark stretched tight around her neck, over her stomach and thighs and all the way down one arm. She's throwing what appear to be bottles into the water. "Hey, don't get my hair wet!" Eve hears. Then "Shut your yap!" after one of them screeches. The voices have the empty echo of school.

Eve watches Connie move back a few paces, fling out her arms, then run between the twins and enter the quarry lake on a belly-flop. The twins screech at first, then one by one flop in and float around on their backs like little empty jugs. They have put on weight since Eve saw them last. She can see their breasts and belly flesh from where she's crouched and the dark patches of hair between their legs. But Connie appears to have no body hair at all. And Eve suddenly realizes that the dark, stretchy thing that clings to her skin is a tattoo.

From an unseen distance, Eve hears the furious blast of a motorcycle. It arrives on the promontory with a snarl, then the motor sputters and dies and the man on it dismounts. Eve can see it's an older man because his hair is gray, slicked back, and he walks old, with a paunch and puffed-out chest. The sun glints off something metal on his chest, a chain or pendant. Eve recognizes him even from a distance: Mr. Keith, the school janitor. He's reaching into a saddlebag on his motorcycle and removing a box of some kind or other. All three girls swim over to him as he bends down to hand them each a bottle. The twins squeal and one of them launches onto her back with the bottle still in her mouth, scooting around backwards so that all of her parts can be seen, then dunks her whole self and resurfaces without the bottle. Connie and the other twin drink their bottles stark naked on the promontory with the man between them. Eve looks on in dumb fascination.

"That's enough," says Miss Gates in a nervous but stern tone. "Time to stop gawping and help me get packed up," she says as she begins trudging back down toward the cemetery. When Eve doesn't budge, she stops dead without turning around. "Come on now," she says. "Those fool kids won't be needing your help where they're going."

Eve tears herself from the view, backing away on all fours before rising and reluctantly following Miss Gates. Miss Gates is stomping off in a way that reminds Eve of Momma about to pitch a fit. High and mighty, as if everything was beneath her. Miss Gates is muttering to herself as she goes, her jaw working, her elbows out and her thin hands clasped. Eve watches her keenly until the resentment she feels flares like a little match inside of her.

"You won't be needing my help either," Eve murmurs. "Where you're going."

Miss Gates turns around with a mad-red face and a cautionary look. "What do you mean by that?"

"All those boxes you had me pack. It just seems you're going somewhere."

"Look here." Miss Gates crosses her arms and juts her chin into the air. "What I do and where I go is nothing to do with you. I'm not the one who wasn't where she was supposed to be. Lying about home schooling. Telling tales. Getting yourself into the trouble you're in now. Do you know what kind of trouble you nearly got *me* in?"

Eve feels her stomach plummet, as if she's back on the precipice standing full height all by herself this time. "I'm sorry," she says. "It was real dumb."

"Could-a got me arrested for kidnapping or something. Aiding and abetting a truant minor. If it wasn't for your mother and that one-eyed priest, I'd be in jail."

"I'm sorry. I said I was sorry." Eve wishes she hadn't said anything at all. In the distance she can hear them all still laughing down there in the quarry hole as if the roles are reversed and she is the one on display.

Miss Gates tugs on her pigtail. "Well it's all done and said now. Time to move on is what I say."

They pack up the tools and tags and the remains of lunch in silence. Miss Gates goes around and pats down the earth over a few of the graves, clasping her hands after the last one and standing there the way Eve had first seen her. A peal of human laughter is carried by the wind until the cicadas come up full clatter and drown it out.

"You aren't really leaving are you?" Eve's voice is scarcely above a whisper.

"I haven't made my mind up about that. When I do, I'll be sure and let you know." Miss Gates tugs her cowboy hat on and adjusts the drawstring. Then her face softens and she squeezes Eve on the shoulder.

"You never know what you'll lose and what you'll be carrying around the rest of your life. Could be something you thought was something else. A body. Or an old harmonica turns up in your pocket." She peers at Eve under a stormy brow, but her eyes are kind.

"Your own heart will lie to you. And the things you wish for end up biting your hand."

"You mean like a *vanitas?*" Eve tests the old word, hoping to please her. The sun unrolls their long, faithful shadows before them, like carpets, as they make their way down.

Miss Gates chuckles mirthlessly. "Whole world is a vanitas," she says.

25 / Arm

He tunes up in Sable's bedroom. He opens his violin case on her bed, which is draped in purple satin, looks around, takes in the *feng shui*. The only mutiny against purple is a canary-yellow scarf that sings from a hook on the bedroom door. The furniture and frills adhere to the purple scheme: a garland of artificial violets along one wall, lavender prints in curlicue frames, shapely amethyst glass bottles posed on the top of an old armoire. The rest is shabby chic wicker, which crackles when he sits on her vanity chair. He switches on the tiny fan clipped to her vanity table, animating the purple sheers hanging over a small window. A moth batters itself between the glass and screen and he wants to liberate it but the window has been painted shut. Poor thing.

Sable had offered him the spare room at first, but it was stuffed with boxes, Christmas ornaments, old lampshades, paperbacks, decades of accumulated clothes. She had giggled and apologized. "I really need to have another tag sale." Her lavender bedroom must do. He doesn't like tuning up before an audience unless the venue is large, and her charming living room is filling up with guests, his audience, mostly women judging from the timbre and levity of their voices. Everyone seems to be laughing, and he imagines that life, his life, would be far more terrifying otherwise.

He has brought his good instrument, the '68 Scrollavezza, for tonight's concert, a gift from Mrs. Cauliflower long ago when he'd won his place at Julliard. Unlike his bar violin, it's worth enough to insure, but he wouldn't take a chance with it at Harpo's or any other bar because, in fact, it's irreplaceable, an extension of himself or, at least, his best parts. Complex to be sure, capable of a ringing brilliance as well as the darkest of his moods, with a human throatiness that has made him wonder if the Italian master had metamorphosed into the spruce tree sacrificed for the body of his instrument. Scrollavezza was said to have loved his instruments so much, he had given them names, but this violin isn't one of these, likely made by a gifted protégé. Still, it sings with temperament, and Arm is willing to give the dead old master much of the credit.

He tucks the violin under his chin, bows his A string, tunes it precisely, then keens a perfect fifth by tuning the D string. He does the same with the other two strings, bowing and plucking and bowing with a patience he lacks with most other manual tasks. The fine-tuning he will save for the last gong against the accompanist, who isn't Moby but someone Drew had suggested. "Talented but ornery," Drew had said, and the latter had turned out to be true.

Hunched over a plate of beef stroganoff at Harpo's, Moby had declined the invitation to play with him a month ago. "I don't do house concerts," he had said, spearing a forkful of Arm's congealing dinner. Moby's shirtsleeves had been rolled up, and the goat tattoo on his arm seemed to be grinning at Arm, refusing to tell him the secret joke. Arm had explained in the terms that usually convinced Moby to stay an extra half-hour, that there would be food, wine, that he'd split the money plate in half, but Moby had just chewed and swallowed. "I don't do house concerts." Arm could see that the thinning area on the top of Moby's buffalo head was filling in with what looked like quills, and it occurred to him that Moby was undergoing hair replacement surgery. It must have cost some serious boodle.

A knock on the door, then Sable pokes her head in and her

outstretched hand offers Arm a plate of hors d'oeuvres arranged in a little island. "Hungry?" She sets the plate on her wobbly wicker desk. "The living room is packed. It's a good thing I put folding chairs on the porch." She looks at her watch. "Ten minutes and you're on." She smiles, crosses her arms and gives him two thumbs up, but he can see she's nervous. For herself or for him? He supposes for both of them. Sable is chewing gum, a habit he abhors, in an effort to quit smoking, and he supposes that is for both of them, too. Knows it is. The dress she's wearing, a silky kimono with a spray of Japanese irises, accentuates her small but shapely bosom, and the fact that she has any waist at all at her age is remarkable, Arm thinks. "Madama Butterfly!" he'd exclaimed when she had opened her front door to him earlier, which had caused a rich flush to spread across her cheeks, and as she gave him one of her fluttery hugs, he realized that this made him Pinkerton – the seducer, the exploiter, the deserter.

But he dismisses the recurrent thought now, in favor of complimenting Sable. "You look ravishing, sweetheart. I think you should wear kimonos every day." She mugs a happy, poppy face, bowing her head, batting the air with an invisible fan, then snaps her gum.

"There was only one of these at the consignment shop," she says. "I'd've bought more if--" She shrugs. "I splurged. I don't buy nice clothes much anymore." Her eyes brim with feeling.

He looks away. "Well," he says, picking up his bow.

"I should let you get back to it," she says shakily. "See you soon." When she closes the door, the yellow scarf slides off the hook and puddles on the floor.

The audience is middle-aged, mostly female, chattering while balancing china plates and cups on their laps. He recognizes some regulars from Harpo's, who compete for his eyes with cleavage and raised plastic wineglasses. Alexandra is there with Aisling, each costumed in colorful halter-tops and yoga pants, Alexandra casting a smile out of the pessimism of her face while Aisling smirks and blows him a kiss. Grouped behind them are the Harpo harpies, then two rows of people he doesn't recognize and behind them the front door, which opens onto a porch full of people seated on lawn chairs. He doesn't dare look. He isn't sure what he fears most: Drew's presence or absence.

They had been on exactly two dates, if one could call them that. One at Harpo's after a gig, when Drew had lingered to join him for dessert and coffee at a greasy booth. Arm had barely touched his danish, he was so intent on Drew, watching, listening, latching onto every show of friendliness and palming them all for closer inspection later. The other date had begun at the laundromat where Drew had been washing and drying donations of clothes for the homeless. Arm had offered to help him schlep back to the church, and afterward they had sat in Drew's office and talked. Nothing special, yet, somehow, everything special, every pause, every word Drew had spoken new and surprising and renewing. Yet he can remember little of the actual conversation. It had been about the bloody war, most of it, and Arm had agreed with everything Drew said, contributing only a few faded words from Mark about oil fields and warlords.

It's a sunny, sultry evening, the evidence for which stands out in beads of perspiration on the forehead and around the collar of Arm's piano accompanist, Roger Roile, a square-headed, pink man in his fifties who glowers at Arm. Arm knows that Roger isn't angry about anything in particular, just angry in general, which has smelted his face into a block of bad mood. During the week, he is an insurance manager of some sort, but on Sundays, he is a competent organist, and tonight he is what he should have been all along. Roger swelters in a stocky summer suit and bowtie, while Arm glows in a white shirt with rolled sleeves, a sleek pair of navy linen pants with suspenders. An odd couple, Arm thinks, as he fine-tunes the Scrollavezza to Roger's keyboard, which had been a bitch to haul up the porch and into Sable's living room with Roger huffing and hovering as if the thing were a baby grand. Feeling eyes on him, Arm glances toward the kitchen entrance, but it's only Sable, leaning against the wall primly yet seductively, waiting. Behind her he sees the platters she had prepared, the purple punch bowl, the string of lights she has draped over the table and the rose petals strewn across the tablecloth. Poor thing, he thinks, she had put out every fragile china plate and cup she owns.

Alexandra is standing before the audience with an index card, reading off Arm's credentials, which requires all of twenty seconds. Most of the audience applauds politely while the harpies pound away. The floor is his and Roger's, and he feels the beeline of adrenaline rush from his bowels to his chest.

They begin with Fauré's "Après un Rêve," a vocal piece transposed for violin and piano, and he has slowed it down to a prayer, letting the harpies know that this is serious music, and if they don't like it, they can leave. Roger plonks along steadily, leaving Arm to carry the lyrical line up to its full height, then spin it down into his audience's laps. He doesn't have them yet. Most are still shyly eating and drinking, applauding with cups and plates clattering on their laps.

But he won't give them exactly what they want. There will be no rock classical fusion this evening. Wordlessly, he begins the tango he had selected by Astor Piazzolla over Roger's objections. "I am not a dancehall musician," Roger had argued, but Arm had won and now "Vuelvo al Sur" floats from his instrument, over their heads and out the door to where

Arm hopes Drew is seated. That's more like it, the audience tells him, smiling and clapping. Two of the harpies give him their thumbs up.

He gives them a minute; no words, not now. Then he breaks them with Bela Bartok's "Roumanian Folk Dances." He digs into the first measures as if his bow could move earth, then it is a feather, a quiver on grace notes and staccati. He wails and implores, swooping and teetering over his strings, his eyes closed until he must glance over his shoulder at Roger, whose red face is dripping, shoulders up in anticipation. Arm pounces, making every double-stop break the wall between himself and them, between himself and his source. In the third dance, when he's on the precipice, the sound sluices through its high, narrow passage and he knows they are breathing with him. A lone someone begins to clap and a few others join in. He nods and quavers on. Everyone's breath now belongs to the music, weaving its way from a lament to elation. During the sixth dance, the harpies are tapping and stamping, and he lets them, leading them out of their skin. When they applaud, many are on their feet and he can see that their eyes are shining.

He shares the praise with Roger, thanks them, delivers the patter he'd prepared about each of the composers. "And now for something American," he says. "A tribute to this sultry evening." Coughing, shifting, rustling, clattering. Someone lights a candle, releasing a taint of sulfur. Arm and Roger converge on Gershwin's "Summertime," ending the set with a waterfall of notes. Most are standing, with some of the women in tears. He bows deeply, having finished the set, then flees with his violin to the untouched plate of food in Sable's bedroom, which he eats like a wolf. It's stodge, fat and sugar, but he's famished, not having eaten all day, his response to nerves.

In a tiny bathroom adjoining Sable's bedroom, he splashes his

face with tepid water. Looking up, he finds his accusers in the mirror –
dark circles, little puckers across his upper lip, the beginning of a wattle
beneath his chin. And behind them stand Mark's sentiments about his
superficiality. *Look beneath the surface.* He examines his teeth, rinses, spits
out. He's dabbing his face with a scented guest towel when someone taps
on the door.

      Who? He wants to ask first, but since it may be Sable needing her
private bathroom, he cracks open the door. His heart thuds at the sight of
white curls held in place by a hairnet, a fleshy moon face. *Mrs. Cauliflower?*
Guilt pangs him for having failed to invite her. *How the deuce had she
managed to find him?!* He hasn't been to see her since the Incident. But the
face before him resolves into that of an elderly neighbor of Sable's in
search of the powder room. Her perfume is strong, a ripe musk. He points
her toward the main bathroom down the hall over her effusive apologies
and praise, then bobs, thanking her, before shutting the door and locking
it this time.

      He picks up the Scrollavezza, bows the first few measures of his
next opener, an Americana string of old hymns he had arranged himself.
Beulah Land is the anchor, a tribute to Taft he tells himself, but he knows
it's for Drew, to draw him out, to convince him that he, Arm, is capable of,
if not belief, then fervent desire to believe. But Mark will not leave him
alone this evening. *Look beneath the surface.* What Arm finds is doubt and,
the usual culprit, desire. He stops to tune, plucking, bowing, perfecting. *If
only.* If only he could do the same to himself.

      The crowd in the living room has swelled by the time he enters.
No one appears to have left, even the gruff Harpo men. He sees a few
more faces from Harpo's, friendly, raw, deferential, not the one he seeks.
And then as clouds push west and the sun steps aside, he spots Drew,

settling into a lawn chair on the porch, looking down, brushing crumbs from his lap, talking to someone out of range. The sight of him banishes the doubt that might have ruined everything, pitch, timber, dynamics, the purity of his phrasing. But all is well. Arm sings his hymns to Drew on the Scrollavezza, eyes closed, with grace, as Roger glumly rolls chords and arpeggios. During the applause and the piano solos by Roger that follow, Arm perches on a windowsill, contemplating the enigma that is Drew, whose gaze encompasses Roger and something to his left that is not Arm. At one point, Drew closes his eyes and shuts out the possibility. Like a man stranded on the moon, Roger does what he can with a Tailleferre piece Arm had insisted upon, then settles back into a song without words by Mendelssohn. When it's time for the last duet, Arm is ready.

He had selected Vaughan Williams's "The Lark Ascending," scored for piano and violin, for its melodies. Modal scales come closest in his mind to pure longing. That morning, he had reread the Meredith poem that had inspired the Williams piece. *"He rises and begins to round, /He drops the silver chain of sound."* He wants to bring his audience, not to their feet, but their knees, to convert them from the solid world to something; he isn't sure what he would call it. The firmament. Higher planes. Nirvana. *"And he the wine which overflows/to lift us with him as he goes."* He has often thought that he will never come closer to belief in a Creator than music will take him. He ribbons upward, feeling their eyes on him, liking them, almost liking himself.

It happens following phrase after phrase of flawless execution. Of course it does, because that is what his life is. Like Orpheus, like some fool playing for cash in a subway terminal, he looks up, sees Drew. Losing his grip on the string, he loses his audience. A note goes south with a mournful blort. He recovers quickly to send his listeners back on the journey to the sky, but he knows what they will remember in the end, after the beefy applause that follows, the bows, the teary-eyed hugs from the women, their maudlin praise. He bows deeply to them while cringing, unable to forgive himself.

Sable is before him with her infinite eyes. *Look beneath the surface,* Mark tells him. Arm returns Sable's flighty hug, kissing the air above her head, then looking over her shoulder, he sees Drew, the straight, lean back, the bowed, bald head. At first, it appears that he's speaking to someone. Aisling? A woman, in any case, with a monkey mouth and a lounging way of standing. Then he turns and just when Arm is sure he's making eye contact, Drew retreats, as if he never knew him.

The rest of the crowd demands an encore, but Roger is already collecting his music and Arm has lost whatever it was that drew him here in the first place. "Excuse me, dearest," he says to Sable. "I left something in my car." Off he hurries, pausing to accept praise, cutting through to make his way down deck stairs, then crossing the endless lawn to the endless path leading to the parking lot. What will he say once he finds him?

The lot is almost full with too many white cars, but Drew's aging Impala isn't among them. Arm paces along the sand pit that borders the hot lot, craning, retracing his steps, but he knows without looking further that Drew had left. Why? Had Drew been offended by that one small, fatal flaw in the *Lark*? Some people are like that, he knows, cruel perfectionists, among whom he counts himself.

Or had his other fatal flaws caused Drew to retreat? He can name them all. Vanity, stupidity, cupidity. Perhaps even his sexuality. He pushes the thought away as he walks to his car, which simmers in a bath of heat and grit. As he searches his pocket for car keys, he discovers that he still has his bow in his hand. How ridiculous he must look, dashing around the parking lot like Cupid.

No sense sitting in a hot car. He must go back, retrieve the Scrollavezza, face the music . He's about to turn, when he sees a white envelope beneath the right windshield wiper. His heart gallops as he seizes it, tears it open. But the note it contains isn't from Drew. He recognizes the Stranger's handwriting, the same reedy ascenders and insinuating slant. This time, another phone number with a scriptural reference, *Genesis 4:9.* He stuffs it in his pocket.

As he heads back, he can see Sable there on the porch with some of her loitering guests, the kimono tracing her curves, the modest bosom, the still trim waist and generous hips. He can hear their casual voices, a laugh, another laugh, everyone laughing to fill empty space. She doesn't raise a hand to wave, but he can tell she sees him, waiting there, as women have always waited, for him to return.

When she rolls the quilt up, she finds that she must unroll it to
see it again. The woman depicted isn't herself, of course, it's Beulah, but
there is no better mirror.

It isn't what she'd planned; nothing ever had been. Her
marriage, her career, her life, not even this kitchen. She surveys it as she
tacks the quilt on the wall for the last time, she promises herself. Radiance,
she thinks, not dust, has been her gift all along. And here is living proof
spread out against dingy, peeling cherry-blossom wallpaper she should
have removed a month ago after the landlord finally gave his consent.

She touches the quilt, tracing the topography of her own tiny
stitches. All of her plans for the quilt had dropped off like petals from a
rose. Her quilt wasn't to be about mothers or children or even the war.
Her subject is a peacock, with its fantail spread in blazing colors – ebony,
turquoise, emerald, gold. In the background are the three crosses of
Golgotha, which she had stitched in by hand to please Drew at first, until
the crosses became an essential detail, like the violin in the quarry quilt.
Beneath the peacock is the figure of Beulah, looking up. "Why me?"
Beulah had asked, and Rose had said it was because of her hair. "It's very
good," Beulah had said, staring impassively at the peacock. Rose waited
for judgment, repudiation. A peacock, she knew, was a pagan bird, yet she
had given it a sacred context.

"Joe calls them rainbow birds," Beulah had turned and said to
Rose finally. "The rainbow is a symbol of God's promise never to destroy

His creation with a flood again." Well, Rose had said, relieved, I guess that leaves plenty of other options.

When she had told Drew about it, he had laughed and told her about the peacock angel, a deity worshipped by the Yezidis, an endangered Kurdish sect in northern Iraq. "They consider the peacock to be their Creator God and savior," Drew explained. "Of course, your peacock could be a Christian symbol of the second coming." It had been for Flannery O'Connor, why not for Rose Strang? And she had said that her peacock was a miracle, appearing out of nowhere, when she was at one of her lowest points. "That's grace," Drew had said.

Eve had asked about the peacock this morning after breakfast. And Rose had said, "I saw one in an old barn once." Who's the girl? Eve wanted to know, and Rose had told her it was a friend.

"A friend? You have friends?" Eve had on a pair of dirty, once-pink rabbit slippers that she wore around the house.

"You'd better throw those in the wash," said Rose. "They look like you dragged them out of a hole."

"I thought you just had customers and those old bats who made you sew for them."

"They didn't *make* me do anything. Take those slippers off now." Rose stood with her hand out.

Eve ignored her. "I didn't know you had any friends."

"Yes," said Rose stiffly, rolling up the quilt. "Actually, I do have friends." She placed the quilt on the table and touched her face.

"Well, how come you never invite them over for supper, Momma?" Rose looked hard at her inquisitor, standing there in a pair of rabbit slippers. Her long hair was mussed from sleep and the old tee shirt of Randall's that she'd worn to bed hung inside-out on her small frame.

Her eyes still had a dazed, visionary look.

"Because that would make them real," Rose said. "I'm not sure I'm ready for that."

"Momma, can we have Miss Gates over to supper sometime this week?" Ever since Eve had been grounded, she had been asking. Nagging. Rose had said "no" at first, then "maybe," then "sometime perhaps." It was inevitable. That peculiar woman was going to sit in this kitchen staring at her with those eyes, the windows of a train wreck. It was obvious she'd been through hell, with that unfortunate face, living as she did in a trailer with feral cats and saying signs, wearing the getup of an old hand in a rodeo. Brushing her teeth in public lavatories. She was "harmless" according to Drew, a hard worker, but not a churchgoer. What had he called her? "A true believer." Regardless, not the sort of person a mother could want her daughter to befriend. But who was she to talk? She was long past scoring points for looks or clothes.

"Please? Momma, please?" Eve had taken her slippers off and was holding them out in her palms like a sacrifice. "I'll cook."

"Oh, well, in that case," Rose had said, taking the slippers, and had spent the next five minutes being quizzed on what they'd cook and whether it would be alright if Arm could give Miss Gates a ride home afterward. "You better ask him," Rose had said. She wasn't going to do it. But the impulsive hug she'd received had thawed her. She tried to prolong it, smoothing her daughter's silk hair, but Eve had caught on, disentangling herself with the excuse she had to get dressed "for work." Work with that woman. A couple of weeks before, it had been in a pet cemetery. Rose sat down in her broken chair, listening for the sound of Eve brushing her teeth and the innocent pat of her bare feet on bathroom linoleum.

Eve had grown an inch this year, her body beginning to announce the subtle, dreaded appearance of the young woman who would soon take over, shedding childhood like a skin. When Eve was ready, in a pair of shorts, a shirt and dirty sneakers, she said, "Bye, Mom," and was out the front door. No seconds on hugs. Through the window above the sink, Rose watched her, the lissome way she moved, pausing before crossing the street, then passing out of view. She would turn thirteen in two weeks. *What would she become?* When Rose had moved her hand up to touch her own face, she saw that she was still clutching the rabbit slippers.

Now Rose is packing the quilt in a bag with an umbrella and heading out the door herself, into the moist heat.

As she walks on the shoulder, memories flash by her like cars. She's in her mother's kitchen, being instructed on how to use an eggbeater. "Never put your fingers in the bowl," her mother is saying as Rose watches the egg white she's beating stiffen into snowcaps. Now she's in the backseat of her parents' old blue Chevy, being driven home from a summer theater musical performed inside a circus tent. Arm is asleep next to her, his head slumped on his chest, his black eyelashes against the pure drift of his cheek. And she, Rose, is singing softly the music of the evening. "Rose, simmer down," her mother says wearily, and Rose obeys until she sees her mother's head droop and hears the soughing of her breath, then she hums the songs all the way home and no one is the wiser. As they pull up in the drive, she can see her mother's flower box, brimming with impatiens, a bright profusion by day, depleted in the evening light. Her parents fuss over Arm, picking him up and carrying him inside the house, while Rose follows them by her own power, secretly humming.

Next, she's sewing a potholder on her mother's Singer. The cloth is gray with yellow, pink and blue roses, scraps from an old slipcover. Her mother stands to the side in a quilted bathrobe, fretting. She hasn't combed out her hair yet, and the curlers she'd worn to bed had shaped her hair into abrupt little rolls. "Don't put your fingers in there," her mother is saying. "Be careful of those pins." When Rose finishes the top stitching and breaks the thread, her mother examines her work, magnified by bifocals, and Rose can see the mole on her face that will kill her within a few years, right after Rose finishes high school. Her mother's expression is stern yet approving. "Nice straight lines," she says. "Not bad, kiddo." Praise of the highest order from her mother.

Next, she's standing by her father's armchair four years later, attempting to awaken him. They're in the basement room where Taffy had tried to plunder her without success. The same brown braided rug on the floor, the same ceiling tiles above, the same red, nubby couch and the brass-based lamp she had scratched her name into with a safety pin as an errant toddler. Her mother's wobbly ironing board stands where it has since her death. And her father sits where he also sleeps, slouched in his recliner, his face crumpled and mild, but there is something odd, a urinary odor, and his belt is loosened, exposing the elastic waistband of what must be his boxers. Her father hadn't finished his dinner; a greasy aluminum container with a fork, the remains of mashed potatoes and a chicken bone litter a metal TV table next to him. Rose had arrived home late after a night class and had heard the TV, louder than usual, with the laugh track of a sitcom chorusing. "Dad, wake up," Rose says more and more desperately, trying to awaken her father's dead body over parroted laughter. His large domed head is balding, the thistledown that's left arranged in a kind of swirl. She shakes him gently, then takes his hand, but its flaccid coldness makes her jump back. The TV laughs. Sobbing, she fumbles with the dials and buttons to kill the TV, but instead flips to more sitcoms, more canned mockery. The best she can do is to punch every button until the screen suddenly goes black, all of its false light sucked in.

Rose steps up onto the sidewalk of Swannboro's main street, shuffling her bag onto her left shoulder. Besides the umbrella, she had packed cheese and tomato sandwiches for a lunch date she had never actually set up with Drew. But she'll arrive during his office hours and present him with the quilt as a gift to the church. Offering him lunch will seem offhand, but providential. It will be the natural unfolding of their friendship to share the blazing peacock, a symbol of grace, and the lunch, an expression of her *caritas*. She hesitates to think beyond caritas, yet she fancies him, and hopes to be fancied back despite being, technically, married. That she should feel anything at all for a man seems a miracle. All her men lie dead in the cemetery of her mind. Even Randall. She no longer balks at men in hats.

Natalie is pulling weeds in her yard when Rose passes, trying not to be seen, but Natalie calls out to her. "Hello, you," she says brightly, running over to swoop on Rose with a hug. She's wearing a yellow sunbonnet with an oversized brim that resembles a duck's bill. Rose gives her a lukewarm smile in return. "How are you?" she asks politely. Natalie tells her she'll be better once this heat wave breaks. "How do you manage to stay so cool?" Rose says she's used to it. "I lived in the South," she reminds Natalie.

"The Circle is so pleased with the quilt, Rose," says Natalie. "Not a stitch out of place. And the design is perfect." Natalie's face lights up as she waves to someone passing in a Buick.

"Thanks," murmurs Rose.

"It was a team effort, of course," says Natalie. "Either we hang together or hang separately." Natalie laughs. "And we'll be hanging it in the library in two weeks. Will you be there? I'm counting on you." The phone rings from the shaded interior of Natalie's house before Rose can answer, and Natalie excuses herself, kissing the air as her hat pecks Rose on the forehead.

"It was nice of you to stop by," Natalie calls back as she hurries onward. Rose watches her rush up the stairs, hands raised, flighty yet overbearing. She has on loose yellow culottes with large splashes of white, which adds to her duck-like appearance. Rose doesn't want to dislike her, yet dislikes her all the same. Affinities, she thinks, are like social castes – you're either the chosen or the not-chosen. Why should she, with her sour disposition, have an affinity for pious Beulah and Joe, but not worldly Natalie? No answer comes. She touches her face and moves ahead, past the houses of customers and potential customers.

The sun has scorched the grass and all that remains of most lawns is straw. But ahead is a flower garden that dazzles Rose. Lush mattocks of marjoram clipped into geometric shapes, several rosebushes, hidcote lavender standing upright, gypsophila, sea lavender, dragon's head, the coppery remains of astilbe against a grouping of hollyhocks. The kind of garden she had always hoped to have, instead of the straggling bed near Arm's piss bucket. Yet she's created such flowerbeds in her quilts, a whole series that may still be hanging in an art gallery on the only really good street in Millsap, Virginia. Why not reclaim what's hers? It has never occurred to her until now. The gallery owner was an aging hippie whose chaotic past had gone into remission, then burst and metastasized into punctilious habits. Rose had signed a contract in three places with legal language between them. Perhaps she's been cast out of her gardens forever.

The church is up ahead with a clear sidewalk, thanks to Saturday. No Albert, no Quakers, none of the rabble that arrived at Drew's peace vigils. Rose approaches tentatively, entering the church on tiptoes. She doesn't feel that she belongs in a sanctuary, any more than she *feels* that her sins will be forgiven. Too many of them, all repeats with baroque variations. She had expressed this to Drew once. "Put your faith in Christ. Name your sins and sincerely ask God for forgiveness," he'd said. "You'll receive it. You'll be born again." Tell me something I haven't heard before, she'd said capriciously. They had been carrying coats for the homeless down to the church basement when the lights began to flicker and their conversation had been snuffed out by the effort to locate a breaker box in the dark. Rose had bumped into a cold wall and the edge of panic, but Drew had found the breaker after a long minute. They hadn't even touched hands in the darkness before the light had bolted on.

Now the hall is dark and Drew's office is locked, yet the office hours posted on his door say otherwise. She can hear typing from the office across the hall, and she knocks before she enters. The aged church secretary looks up from her work under fluorescent tubes glaring from a high ceiling. Her short ruff of hair is nearly transparent and she has a papery, spotted skin that reveals veins and capillaries. The room is no bigger than a closet, packed with stacks of paper, supply boxes and massive oak furniture carved into whorls and fleurs-de-lis. "May I help you?" asks the woman in a tremulous voice. She doesn't smile, but her tired eyes are sympathetic, and when Rose tells her why she is here, she says that she's sorry. "Father Andrew is no longer with us. He left last week for another parish." Rose explains that she had seen him the week before and the woman apologizes once more. "What is your name?" she asks, her dry voice fluting upward. "Father Andrew may have left you something."

She repeats Rose's name under her breath as she searches a file drawer. When she hands Rose a cream-colored envelope, her hand shakes. Rose takes it from her and is about to rip it open when she senses a knowing disapproval, the woman's back, painfully humped, turned against her. "We were friends," Rose explains to the woman. "I attended the peace vigils." The woman nods and goes back to her work, as if Rose owes her no explanation. Her body language is appropriately guarded, but Rose senses reproof, as if the woman had read her mail. It silences her questions: *Why had Drew left? Where had he gone?*

For a moment, she feels compelled to offer her quilt to the woman. She had meant for it to hang in the church, after all. But something stops her. The quilt belongs to the person who made it – and to its intended recipient, which is Drew. And Drew is gone. Rose turns and leaves.

She trudges home, dodging the bullets in her mind. At the library, where a bench has been set beneath a shade tree, she sits and eats her soggy sandwich. For dessert, there is the envelope. She opens it with care, trying not to rumple and tear the tidy flap. She had forgotten her glasses, so the typed words on the page slide and blur.

Dear Rose ~

I'm sorry to leave without saying good-bye. My work here is done and I must attend to other matters.

Bless you for all you did to help our parish.

Yours in Christ ~ Fr. Andrew+ (*Drew*)

Ephesians 1:7 "In whom we have redemption through his blood, even the forgiveness of sins."
Ps. 103:12 "As far as the east is from the west, so far has He removed our transgressions from us."

"Other matters." Clearly what has been removed is Drew, not her transgressions, Rose thinks. Or perhaps they are one and the same. She crumples the note, then smoothens and rereads it, then replaces it in the envelope and tucks it inside her backpack. His signature, *Drew,* is the only personal remnant. No forwarding address. Her throat aches, her jaw trembles, her eyes well; she fights it back.

By the time she arrives home, the air is still heavy, but cooler. No one is there. Eve isn't due back for an hour, Arm is off to who knows where, and she has the luxury of her own chastened company. Normally, she enjoys being alone, but not here, not now. From somewhere, Eve's room she discovers, a radio is playing "Forever Man," a Clapton love song from her past. *Forever* man, she thinks, what a joke. To silence it, she trespasses on her daughter's sanctuary, switches off the radio, then furtively looks around at the blinding perfection. Nothing out of place, the bed made, the books aligned, the dust of the day chased from each surface. She leaves, shuts the door, returns to the kitchen, sets her backpack on the counter. Her own slovenliness greets her in spicy wafts. The sink stinks of the drain; the fry pan on the stovetop reeks of onions and grease from last night. And there is the wallpaper. Since she'd left the house, a portion had loosened and curled, exposing the uneven, scarred surface beneath. Rose tugs at it and off the wall it comes, like a skin. She stands there with the flap in her hand and thinks, *Why not?* The humidity will help.

Rose rips wallpaper, stripping the wall naked. What color will she paint it? A fresh buttermilk, she decides. She pauses in her work to unzip her backpack and hold against the exposed wall her portrait of grace.

Grace – is that really what it was? Yes, she thinks, rolling up the quilt. That is what it was.

Eve chooses a rainy day because it will wash away the filth and keep away kids and people.

Miss Gates doesn't like rain any more than Eve does, it keeps her at work in the trailer or the hut, away from the library and the cemetery and the few other places worth walking uphill for.

The afternoon rain will keep away Connie and Brandy and Bailey, and hopefully fend off Mr. Keith. She hadn't seen them since that day in the pet cemetery, but you never know with lowlife. The rain beats a pattern. It's a Southern kind of rain, warm and sudden and drenching, but it's a northern rain, too, determined to last for days.

She had planned her clothing carefully: a two-piece bathing suit beneath a tee shirt and a ragged pair of jeans. Sockless, sitting on her well-made bed, she pulls on her old winter boots. It's either those or a pair of sneakers, but the boots you could rinse off in the bathroom sink. From her closet she selects the ugly yellow slicker with the metal clasps that got packed up when they left Millsap. The sleeves have grown shorter, like everything else. One of the pockets contains a pen that becomes a flashlight when you press a button. There's an umbrella around somewhere, too, but she doesn't rummage around for that. It would only get in the way.

Uncle Arm is in the kitchen when she enters. "Off to the trenches?" he asks. She nods *yes*, then hesitates. She had meant to rummage in the silverware drawer for a butter knife, but here he is, and she must use her manners. She and Uncle Arm share one of those scary silences. Momma had peeled away most of the wallpaper and it looks hideous but clean. Eve runs her hand over it to fill in the silence.

"There are granola bars in the pantry," says Uncle Arm cheerily. "And peaches in a bag." Eve murmurs, no thanks, then changes her mind and says she might actually like a peach. Uncle Arm's face lights up that way. Why does his happiness make her so sour? He isn't ugly or dirty, he doesn't have bad breath or other smells. He's a homo, Daddy had made sure she knew, but there are worse things, creeps, like Mr. Keith. He's wearing a goofy checkered shirt over shorts that reveal hairy legs, his sleek ponytail giving him a coolness that would appeal to some girls her age.

But he's needy in the way of adults who don't like themselves and want you to like them anyway. Other adults she knows are like this. *Daddy is like this.* It flushes her with angry blood because Uncle Arm isn't like Daddy in any of the ways that matter, the jokes and adventures, the lessons about warps and wefts, about who owns what-all and the endless little war over prices.

She accepts a peach from the bag Uncle Arm holds out to her. It doesn't hurt to be kind, to be grateful. "Thank you," she says, slipping it inside the rubbery pocket of her raincoat. From a distance, Miss Gates is tugging on her conscience. *Say you're sorry,* she's saying. *Do it now.* Eve takes a deep breath and obeys. "I'm sorry." She stammers at first, then blurts. "I'm sorry I wrote those nasty things all over your eggs." Her voice has flown south to where "eggs" rhyme with "plagues."

"Which eggs?" asks Uncle Arm.

"The ones you dyed for Easter."

"Oh, those." Uncle Arm is leaning against the fridge. "Well, they tasted exactly the same as regular Easter eggs, didn't they?" He smiles too much, she thinks, with all those many crinkles around his eyes.

"Yes," she says. A nervous laugh comes out of her. Her eyes go from his hairy legs to the wall and back.

"Next year, you'll dye the eggs and I'll do the decorating."

"Sure," says Eve. "If you want to." She has given up on the butter knife. "I got to go," she says. She knows no other way to leave than to abruptly turn her back on him and walk out the door, but he catches her like chicken wire.

"Wouldn't you like a ride? It's pouring rain." She hears the floor creak as he walks toward her. "Where are you going?"

"To a friend's house." She blushes. "We're going on a treasure hunt." She clops backward. Her bare feet feel tacky in the heavy boots.

Again, he offers what a good father would, which rankles her. "It's okay," she says. "I can walk." But he's fumbling in the coat closet anyway, bringing out an umbrella in a boring beige color. "Here, take this," he insists. She accepts it politely. It's one of those miniature umbrellas you can slip inside your pocket. Now she has two raincoat pockets full of things she doesn't want. She opens the umbrella once she's outdoors to make a show of compliance. Splashing down the street, she knows he's watching her. To her annoyance, she needs the umbrella after all as the rain becomes a downpour, beating down on the dinky beige canopy. Cars sizzle past, sloshing her boots.

She takes the route past the school, where Connie had dragged her that first time. It isn't the good way, the one that Miss Gates liked, or the measly other trail she'd found, but it's safer, less exposed. She follows a dirt path, now mud, past her school, the window blinds all drawn, the summer inmates released. Her school in Millsap had been older but friendlier, with a cupola on top like a cupcake. It had hedges so thick you could sit right down on top of them, and there was a row of fragrant rosebushes. This school is just a flat-topped wedge attached to a rectangle with a mean field around it. But in back of that are woods, which she enters now through a hole in some bittersweet brambles. The trees provide shelter from the rain, but she holds the umbrella aloft anyway.

She finds the trail, then loses it. What had been snow craters when she was last here are now trampled leaves and bent twigs and earthy mush, but her memory hasn't changed. Rocks, trees, the pitch of the land lead her back up the trail. Up she goes and down, then higher again. Weeds have gained a chokehold on everything, slowing her down, giving her enough time to change her mind. But she doesn't change her mind.

Since that day in the pet cemetery, Miss Gates had kept her busy doing yard chores. She'd been close-lipped about her plans, but Eve knew the signs of someone about to get out of town. It wasn't just the boxes, it was the pricked up shoulders and pursed lips, the nervous whistling. Miss Gates went around with her arms folded, hunting for things that didn't lie straight or needed watering or pulling. Looking for the right wrong thing, but never finding it. Eve figured she needed to make everything look nice to sell the place, but there wasn't a sale sign in front of the trailer, just the saying signs and the tire swing, the same old gritty lawn with cats.

Slinky and Henrietta had followed Eve around while Sledge got himself inside a box to keep the sun off his pumpkin head, and Pindrop lollygagged in the dust, preening herself. It had turned out she wasn't pregnant after all. "Had a clog in her milk ducks," Miss Gates explained. "Cost me a fortune to get it all cleared up. And look at her. You'd a thought she'd done something special, instead of putting me in the poorhouse." Eve knew the poorhouse wasn't an actual place, but Miss Gates talked about it as if it was. She had felt stupid for not realizing it long ago: Miss Gates is poor.

That weekend, the poorhouse had been on top of Miss Gates's kitchen table. Bills and busy documents of the sort that had cluttered Daddy's office desk each April. But mostly, Eve had seen the poorhouse all over Miss Gates's face. She had followed her around with her eyes.

"Why don't you take a pitcher?" Miss Gates had said. "It'll last longer."

"You're leaving, aren't you," Eve had said. "I know you are."

"You don't know anything at all," Miss Gates had responded, but her eyes had scatted around. She had made each of them a peanut-butter-and-jelly sandwich, same as always, but Eve knew.

Eve can smell the fire pit's pleasant stench even before she reaches it. The rain has beaten it down, but it's still filthy with discarded yuck and beer cans. Of all the nasty things in the world, she hopes she'll never see a hobo, and leaves a wide margin between herself and the fire pit. The path squishes beneath her boots, threatening to suck her into snake holes or traps. She uses the umbrella to scrape aside suspicious areas before tramping ahead. When she hears a noise, she ducks, but it's only a squirrel. No one here but herself and, up ahead, the ghosts of cats.

She finds the skinny path along the ledge from where you can see the cliffs, slick with rain, and the big fuel drums and the basin below that time's wicked claw had reached down and scooped out. She makes herself stand there despite jelly legs. The view below is cursed. It had been where Miss Gates had seen her father's corpse floating around in the lake, and where Connie and the twins sat naked-assed on the promontory drinking beer with Mr. Keith. Eve steps back. You could get swallowed up by a view like that. Hadn't Miss Gates said? A *vanitas*. She slogs down the path with the rain, which downshifts to a delicate mist, unable to make up its mind.

Her foot catches on a tangle of vines and she nearly loses her balance. Leaning against a trunk, she returns her foot to the mucky sanctuary of her boot. Once she passes the rock with the haggard cleavage and the old headstone, the rest is downhill. Trudging on gravel, she approaches level ground, then stops. Somewhere ahead, an engine is idling. She drops on all fours and squats behind a shrub.

An old navy blue truck shakes and splutters near the oil drums. Eve can make out two dark, close-cropped heads in the front seat belonging to the driver and a passenger. The passenger window slides down and a muscular brown hand tosses out a plastic grocery bag, then the truck growls and skids away. After a good minute, Eve heads toward the bag, which is the remains of a lunch. Crumpled foil with a scrap of hamburger bun, an empty plastic container of chocolate pudding, and a cheap carpenter's tool pouch with the words *Take this job and shove it* across it. Eve takes the tool belt and shoves it in her pocket with the peach and pen-light.

The rain stampedes again, then lags and plops steadily. By the time she reaches the promontory, the sky has turned, a fist of sunlight punching through cobbled clouds. She hesitates to look down the staircase toward what she fears will be sodden dog turds, but sees instead the slick, washed surfaces. There's still a rogue ammonia odor, despite the rain.

The fear of being observed is on her like a thief. Eve turns around and looks. No one in any direction, just the gaunt cliff heads. Holding onto the wall, she steps down into the well. At the bottom, she's up to her ankles in brownish churn and begins to shake out of fear. It isn't too late to go back.

But it *is* too late. She's come this far; Miss Gates needs whatever is in the purse. She had thought about it. If it's money, she could leave it on Miss Gates's table. If it's drugs, she can sell it to Connie. If it's an alien artifact, Daddy had taught her how to sell old things.

She checks the entrance to the cave with her pen-light and is met by warm mist. Has the water in the cave risen? With the pen-light in her mouth, she begins to undress, then realizes there's nowhere clean and dry to put her clothes. Her sweaty feet torture her. She clops up the stairs, plants the umbrella in a crevice near a straggle of wild grass, spreading her raincoat beneath it. Then she tugs off her winter boots, stuck to her bare feet worse than if she'd worn socks, and strips down to her bathing suit, laying her clothes on the raincoat. The rain has ceased, but the sky is still stern enough to discourage dumb-enough kids and grownups with nothing better to do than make their way to the quarry. Eve shoves her boots back on, then, thinking better of it, yanks them off and leaves them with her clothes.

Her business requires four hands. She discovers this after attempting to squeeze through the cave entrance, the pen-light clamped between her teeth. What she would give for two extra hands, Connie's hands, even. She nearly gives up, out of breath, her eyes stinging, her skin raw. Then she finds that by angling a certain way and making herself long, she can drop down into the pool of the cave and slowly drag herself in.

The water reaches to her waist now, cool and salty-bitter when she accidentally tastes it. Her pen-light picks out the cave wall's weird body shapes, the same buttocks and jowls and giant earlobe as this winter. Here is the basin shelf, undisturbed, with the kitchen table things, the naked, swollen cans and the fat old lady purse, where she'd found Miss Gates's harmonica. "All I saw was an old boot," she'd told Connie.

A drop of water plops down on her shoulder and she jumps. Pointing her pen-light, she sees a trickle of water shivering down the cave wall. Another drop, then another. *Poing. Poing.* The drops make beautiful, disquieting tones. She listens for a moment, standing still, then swishes her way to the purse.

The purse looks something awful, bloated, with a kind of furry crust. What if there are worms inside? She holds the pen-light over it, over the funny plastic handle, a bag you could use as a weapon, shut tight with a metal clasp.

After a deep breath, she touches the clasp, drawing her hand back quickly. Nothing happens, so she uses both hands to open the clasp while holding the pen-light in her mouth. She jumps back nervously, but nothing jumps out. The blood pounds in her wrists and her insides grip. Then she hears muffled noises coming from somewhere outside the cave, murmuring and crunching like feet on gravel, a single splash, and she can't restrain her bladder. She had never peed in a pool before.

The feet and voices fade after a few minutes. Miraculously, no one scuffs down the stairs. Eve breathes again. Like the way Momma had pulled out her baby teeth, fast and giving her no time to think, she yanks open the purse with her eyes closed. Then she looks down. At first it looks like a shiny nest.

Then she realizes it's plastic wrap, big bunches of it, wrapped around something and tied with string. She's drawing it out timidly when something else from the purse falls out and she nearly pees herself again. The weakening beam from her pen-light reveals three tiny skeletons floating on the cave water near her, the bones of salamanders or fish or, more likely, the bones of frogs –how had they gotten inside the purse?

Aliens, she thinks. The wobbly, goggle-eyed skulls look like them.

She swishes their bones away from her and the backbones float off, fragile twigs, then the rest of the skeletons break up like eggshells. Eve pulls the wad of plastic wrap free of the purse, which falls apart, too, like an old balloon, and there's nothing she can do about it.

Getting out is even worse than getting in. She tries to hold the plastic wad between her teeth, but ends up stuffing it through the hole, then, hastily, she wriggles through like a tadpole. Her shoulder blade takes the brunt of it, and the stone roughs up her bathing suit bottom, tearing out one of the seams. She has to hold it together with one hand on her way up the stairs, the wet plastic wad bunched under her arm.

The sun is only half out of the clouds and already it feels hot as hell, despite her near-nakedness. No one is around. She squints, making her way onto the promontory and wonders why her clothes aren't where she put them. No boots. No umbrella. Her heart skips, but the cliffs are mum and vacant. Whoever'd stolen from her is long gone, not a soul here but herself. She finds the carpenter's pouch stuck to a clump of wet grass. After shaking it out, she knots it to her bathing suit bottom, then ties it around her waist. Sore and spent, she sits on the promontory, dangling her legs over the edge the way Connie and the twins had that day.

The quarry lake is smooth and wrinkled like the palm of a giant hand, holding all of its secrets and throwing out a few sparkling treasures you can't ever catch. And here is one of them, Uncle Arm's peach, bobbling around on the lake with exactly one chomp taken out of it. Dumb kids, she thinks, probably boys. If it had been Connie, she'd have waited and jumped Eve the minute she was out of the cave.

From the look of the sky, it's nearly dinnertime, but she doesn't relish walking home half-nude in a bathing suit. Other girls did it all the time, but not her. She hunches her thin shoulders and folds her arms over her breast buds. She's skinny, but lately she's noticed that her body is going soft in places and sticking out in others. She was lucky to make it in and out of the cave. The sky glares down and she decides to hunker here until it darkens up a bit. So there's nothing left to do but what she'd come here for.

And now that the moment has arrived, she loses her nerve. What if it's drugs? She isn't sure she could make a deal with Connie after all. If it's drugs, it might have gone sour or rotten maybe, and then she'd just have to chuck it all. But how could you tell? She isn't sure. An old artifact or money would be easier. She chews on a nail, obsessively working, then picks up the treasure and begins.

After several minutes of teasing knots out of the string and carefully unwinding the plastic wrap, she discovers that the treasure is none of these things. It's just a packet of old letters. Nothing she could sell, just a bunch of love letters in a dainty lady's hand, all of them addressed to "Taft Said" at a post office box. The letters are on unlined pages, yellowed and mottled with brown spots and blotches. And the bottoms of the words are either flat or cut off altogether, as if the lady had written them on top of a ruler. The ink is faint, but Eve can still read most of the words. The lady had signed the letters "Lilah" or "Lil," or, in some cases, "L" with a fancy squiggle.

Her letters are sad and scared and serious. "I fear for your safety," the lady had written. "I fear Oliver knows." In one letter she'd written, "I fear I'm pregnant," and that's what the rest of the letters are all about, figuring out what to do about a baby that the lady and Taft had made, and how they'd get away from old man Oliver, and where they'd go next. Then, in the last letter, the lady had gotten cold feet. "I'm afraid they'll kill you." There's a lot more about that, which Eve doesn't understand. Her shoulder blade hurts. Peering around to look at it, she sees that it's weeping. She reaches down, scoops a handful of quarry water and attempts to wash away her wound.

She rereads the last letter. It's all about men coming around and asking Oliver a lot of questions about Taft. "Oliver is suspicious." The lady wrote that Taft must never see her again because of Oliver, but mostly because of the men. ""I'm afraid they'll kill you." There's a part Eve doesn't understand at all, about state's witness testimony and confession and absolution. "Fear no judgment but God's," wrote the lady. She'd changed her mind about old man Oliver, too. Now he's a "good man," and the letter talks about that for a couple of pages.

The rest is about the unborn baby and baby names. The lady promises to name it after Taft if it's a boy. And if it's a girl, she'll name it after somebody else. Eve can't make out who because there's a brown blotch over the words.

Then there's just *Good-bye, my heart.* Beneath those words, the lady had written her name on top of the ruler.

Eve folds the letters and tucks them into their envelopes, then wraps them up again. The sun is slipping in and out of clouds like a button through a hole, and all she has on is a bathing suit. She feels different somehow, ashamed, half-sad, half-angry about the letters, because they are the same old story. Secrets, lies, then some poor little kid without a daddy. She'd traded her clothes and Miss Gates for some worthless letters. And she's stuck with them now. She wants to return the letters to the purse inside the cave, but her pen-light is almost dead and her shoulder stings.

Chucking the letters would be wrong; they are hers to carry and keep. *Finders, keepers.* Eve tucks them inside the carpenter's pouch before picking her way around twigs, sharp stones and gravel in the parking area in front of the promontory. Streetlights haven't popped on yet, but it won't be long. She'll have to keep to lit-up streets and sidewalks to avoid cutting her feet. The woods are darkening already. At least the summer air is warm and solacing, as if Millsap had come and put its arm around her.

The damp sidewalks stab her heels with little knives of grit as they lead her through town and then past a two-lane highway. Cars whip around with their windows rolled down and trashy music blaring. A carful of teenagers slows down like a shark and a white boy leans out. "Hey, baby," he says. "Wanna fuck?" She ignores him, but she's shaking. Older boys like these have never even noticed her before. She tightens the carpenter's pouch around her waist until it hurts, then folds her arms in front of her, and looks straight ahead. *No,* she whispers. The driver, a dark-skinned boy, shoots her an angry torrent of Spanish. At least she doesn't know what he's saying. They speed up, backfire and blast off, shouting what she assumes are obscenities. Once they're gone, she cuts down a side street, then another until she reaches one she recognizes from the bus route. The houses here are old but tidy, with shade trees and flower gardens, and they have lawns that cool her bare feet.

Despite the rain, the air smells scorched with sun and barbecue. She can see families through windows and trees, washing up after dinner or shaking the rain off a patio umbrella or just sitting on porches big enough for rocking chairs, where they talk in hushed tones, laughing confidently and warning their kids not to shout. Above the houses, all of the sky is displayed like an abstract art exhibition she will never understand, but is supposed to admire. She wonders if the story is the same everywhere in the universe.

A big shiny RV splashes toward her with its headlights on. It's one of those silvery boats that could hold a troop of boy scouts, but this one just has a mother and a father inside and what looks like one thin kid rattling around in the back. The mother is round and ruddy with dangly earrings and the kind of short, unruly adult hair that humidity turns into thatch. The father has one of those blunt buffalo heads beneath a baseball cap.

The RV considerately avoids the puddle near to where Eve is standing, then it makes a U-turn and pulls up beside her. The back window rolls down and Eve sees the shiny forehead of Jill Rathbone from school. Jill has on a white halter-top, accentuating her inflamed skin and making her head loom large. Her hair has grown and Eve sees that it's unfashionably bushy, but prettily braided like a medieval maiden's.

"Would you like a ride?" Jill speaks with her lips stuck together and doesn't smile. Eve guesses it's because of her braces. It's okay, Eve wants to say, go ahead and smile. Instead, she nods her head and says, "Yes, please." Jill opens the door and slides over.

"So you're Eve," says the mother, who turns around and rests her chin on her elbow. Eve nods, but doesn't look at her hostess.

The whole car smells like the mother's perfume, which is orangey-raspberry-rose. The father is one of those silent ones who make cowboy noises at other cars. "Whoa," he says when another car approaches too closely.

"Where are you headed?" the mother asks. She has a sweet, chirrupy voice and her earrings swing.

"Home," says Eve. "I want to go home."

"Well," says the mother. "You came to the right place." Eve sits stiffly with the carpenter's pouch cutting into her. The mother furrows her brow and looks at Eve expectantly. "So, where is home?"

It takes a while to find the house she wants and all the way there, the mother is pumping her with questions. "Do you like to swim?" "What do your parents do?" Eve tells her they have a shop in a nearby town. "How nice," the mother says and Eve agrees. "Did you go away to summer camp?" Eve says not this year, she went and stayed with her auntie instead. Then the mother says, "It's kind of late to be out walking alone, isn't it?" And Eve says yes, ma'am, it is. She looks at Jill, who rolls her eyes, something Eve is sure she doesn't do often.

The mother is talking again on top of her elbow. "What do you say about getting you two girls together sometime soon?" Jill looks down and Eve looks away, because she isn't in Jill Rathbone's class anymore, and would never be again.

Eve leads Jill's father up and down roads along her school bus route until she finds the house she's looking for. At one point they take a wrong turn down a dead end and the father says *Whoa* again. Then finally, there it is, white with blue shutters and the same funny kind of gambrel roof they had in Millsap, only Eve had called it a "gamble" roof and Daddy had laughed quietly and said, "I expect all roofs are a gamble."

The house sits on a hill as houses are supposed to. Its porch light is on and there are miniature lights flickering all along the hilly drive. The father is about to trot them all the way up, but Eve says it's okay to drop her off here on the street. And by the time she climbs halfway up the asphalt driveway and turns around and waves, the mother and the father look convinced. Jill knows, and unlike most knowers, she keeps her yap shut. Eve waits until their RV is a faint chug in the distance.

Her house on Velvet Lane is a good quarter-mile away. Before she heads back down the drive, she makes a little picture frame with her thumbs and fingers and holds the house with the gamble roof inside of it. *Why don't you take a pitcher? It'll last longer.*

Peepers and crickets from a nearby pond are jawing away, just like the ones back home. She could be home, for all she knows. Maybe she *is* home, after all, carried there by losing everything she had. Carried there by the horseman. There is only one real way she might be able to find out, and that is by closing her eyes against the impenetrable night sky and holding her breath, and then inhaling deeply.

If she's really home, the smell would be unmistakable, the smell of hot, sweet honeysuckle against the taint of the drains. But all she can smell is orangey-raspberry-rose.

28 / *Arm*

It was in the news clippings. It had been there all along.

Two-hundred-fifty-five American casualties in Iraq and still no weapons of mass destruction. Arm doesn't know how many civilian Iraqis had died, because they aren't counted in the *Times* article he's reading by someone named Phoenix O'Connor, an improbable name, a strange marriage of Greek to Celt. Who actually *writes* these news articles? Are they researched and written by a person, or some sort of media overlord? Arm rummages, trying to retrieve what Mark had said on the subject, but it floats on a distant, cluttered shelf where memories go to die. *Sausage grinder.* That much of Mark's lecture he remembers. Everything goes in, including a few of the facts.

Sitting on his couch in the basement room, he decides to take Mark's revolver, Clint, to where he is going. Mark had left him only one bullet, which he loads into a chamber clumsily, giving the Stranger five chances out of six. Struggling as he does with anything manual that isn't musical, Arm straps on Mark's leg holster. It has the awful intimacy of anything elastic. Once inside the holster, he knows, Clint becomes his temporary life partner. He puts the moment off.

Lacking one at home, he had bought a paperback Bible at the dollar store to look up the scriptural reference, *Genesis 4.9*, written by the Stranger on the note Arm had received after the house concert. *"Then the Lord said to Cain, "Where is your brother Abel?" "I don't know, he replied." "Am I my brother's keeper?"* The phone number underneath had a prefix he didn't recognize.

He sits in his sweaty basement room, heavy with incongruity, an aging gay man clinging to a gun and a Bible. He half-laughs, half-cries, a good emotional spasm in any case, something he hasn't experienced since his ride home from Harpo's that faraway evening when he'd first met Sable. He tries not to overthink it, the need to protect himself against the unknown coiled inside of a Bible verse. Yet he also feels he is meant to take this one personally, that he is being cautioned - or threatened. What did Cain and Abel have to do with anything? Taft hadn't been his brother. Neither had Mark. They had been antipodes, and yet, he recognizes, so have many brothers.

Unable to restrain his curiosity, Arm had called the number the Stranger had left him. The talker on the phone had one of those boy's voices in a man's chest, made for sarcasm and ghost stories. "Hello," it had said heartily. No sooner had Arm introduced himself than the voice continued, obviously a recorded message. "This isn't me, but if you want to reach me, please leave your name and a credit card number. *Haha.* Just kidding. You know what to do." *Haha.* Arm had waited an hour before calling again, and this time the phone was busy. It took two more calls to get to the man who, it was obvious, had been roused from a sound sleep. But his voice regained its clarity as soon as Arm had stated his name.

"Mr. Guest, at last," said the Stranger. That it was the Stranger hadn't been clarified by a name or an admission, but it was obvious to Arm. The Stranger, at last. They had circled each other.

"Who am I speaking with?"

"It's whom," said the Stranger. "I believe you mean whom."

"Just tell me who you are, you don't have to play games."

"This isn't a game, Mr. Guest. It's really very serious. I mean from the beginning, I've tried to--"

"Thanks for the calling cards," cut in Arm nastily. "I haven't received so many notes since I was in finishing school."

They had agreed to meet, but caviled about where. Arm wanted a restaurant; the Stranger insisted on his residence. "You don't want to be seen in public with me." Arm had sneered at this and suggested that perhaps he did. "So you won't try anything."

"I assure you, Mr. Guest, you're in no danger. Not from me anyway."

"Why should I meet with you at all?'

The voice had laughed humorlessly, then cleared its throat. "Well, that's a question only you can answer. But I will say I'm one of your biggest fans. That Bartok you played … the dances … truly ravishing. One of the most convincing renditions I have ever … well … honestly, words can't do music like that justice. If they could, there'd be no real need for music at all."

"I don't meet with anyone, especially fans, unless they identify themselves," snapped Arm. In the end they had agreed to meet on the front porch of an address that the Stranger disclosed along with his first name. *Ian.* "Call me Ian," he had said, pronouncing it with a long, accented "I." The name had rung no bells.

Arm makes up his bed and ties back his hair, killing time. He's wearing nothing special, a polo shirt, an old pair of jeans over the leg strap, and a pair of thick-soled sandals. The mirror exposes his facial crinkles and puckers in the low-hanging fluorescent light of the basement, his face being stolen from him like something, a favorite toy, carried away by the ocean. Well, he is not his face, nor even his arms and hands, and time's ocean will certainly drag them all away, leaving, he hopes, a few vague memories of music, Mark, and even Drew, but not much else. Perhaps one or two of his sister from the old days.

He can hear her creaking around upstairs as toxic wafts of the paint she's using on the walls seep into his den. His desire to be away is waylaid by a guilty conscience, urging him to poke his head upstairs and offer help. The stairs wince beneath him and the door sticks, and here is Rose behind it holding a roller of cream-colored paint.

"Go back down," she says testily. "It's wet." He offers his help anyway, but she says she's almost done with the first coat, that he can help her with the second. He loiters on the top stair to praise the transformation. "You've brought in light," he says, to which she answers sourly that it's about time, isn't it, that they had lived in darkness long enough. "Maybe I'll paint the whole house." She's wearing a pair of coarse overalls over a sheer blouse, gathered at the top, accentuating the fragility of her shoulders and neck. No makeup, which flatters her, despite the porous skin, her mortal enemy. Certain men would like the languor of her eyes, imagining them inside of a bedroom. He sees in her their mother's fine-boned grace before the weight gain that had plagued her in the end. He wants to tell her where he's going, just in case, but doesn't want to freight the moment with death or even doubt. So he says, "I'll see you later" with an offer to make dinner. Before he goes, he unites with Clint, checking the safety several times.

He's driving to Brook's End, a town in the northwestern quadrant of the state, where the Stranger lives. It's eleven o'clock, hours past the morning rush, but people still drive as if they were late to work, while Arm drives as if he prefers not to arrive anywhere at all. Dodged around by trucks and RVs, he hugs the shoulder of the right lane, determined not to be nudged over the guardrail and down into one of the road construction pits along I-84 where idle tractors and cranes sear in the sun. Relieved to see his exit, he slips a CD of Italian arias into his player to celebrate, and settles his nerves in vocal ambrosia.

Miles of trees and occasional shopping strips roll by before he's forced to think again. He would rather not; the thought of Drew still draws a vial of blood. The whole matter was like an addictive secondhand novel one wolfs down only to find that some jackass had removed the final pages, so one is left with guesswork.

After the concert, he had learned that Drew had left the area for good, not from Drew himself, but from Roger Roile, whom he'd run into at Swannboro's one grocery in a tiny organic foods section. Desperate for information, Arm had humbled himself before Roile while reaching for a box of quinoa. "Have you heard from our friend Drew?" Roile was the sort of man who feigns deafness, and did not answer, so Arm was forced to repeat himself. "Have you heard from Drew?" His voice had nearly cracked. This time Roile had coughed into the fold of his fist. "If you mean Father Andrew, no, I have not." Arm made a desperate attempt to conceal his interest and embarrassment, which Roile sensed as a shark detects blood. His large, square teddy bear head had been freshly razored, and his words were precisely clipped.

"Father Andrew returned to his old parish in Northern Idaho." With cold-blooded curiosity, Roile had stared down at Arm through the magnifying halves of his bifocals, as if into a fish bowl. "Back to his family."

It had occurred to Arm that perhaps he should visit St. Stephen's Church for the real story, whatever that was. Perhaps Drew had left him something there besides the cracked-open door of salvation. A memento. A word of farewell in a note. Roile's words had crumpled up any such idea.

Arm turns before a different sort of church, a Jehovah's Witness, up a hill where the height of the pines suggests that the road hasn't changed since the last world war. Tidy homes and manors behind granite walls confirm it; perhaps he had underestimated the lapse of time since the last bulldozer had paid a visit. Despite his destination, he enjoys the ride. Meadows rustle with tall grasses and wildflowers – mulleins, wild carrot and New England aster. Purely sculpted and laid out with classic white buildings, the town center begins with a columned Protestant church, then a pleasingly worn general store, a few lone restored homes, white as sugar cubes. Beyond, the road disappears down a hill, then emerges like the silver lining of the future, or the past.

The stuck window of the car won't budge to admit more air, but Arm feels refreshed. He has noticed, on his rambles, that his tiny home state offers an embarrassment of uninhabited forests, farmland and open spaces, making him suspect that the calculus of overpopulation is wrong. But who would lie about mathematics? *They* would, comes the answer from Mark, but Arm can never be sure. Reasonable doubt is his mantra. Above in the distant blue, a jet like a tiny needle is dragging its poison thread across a sky already seamed with chemical trails while Cecilia Bartoli sings "Voi Che Sapete." Nothing like cheerful lovesickness to signal that all is not well. He passes a barn, then another meadow, then a tiny ancient cemetery with a wrought iron gate that couldn't keep out a mob of weeds. Order has succumbed to chaos.

When he's a mile from his destination, there it is, another white church, sinking into a bed of tall grass, starkly vacant, but with tall windows overlaid with diamond-shaped lattices. Attracted by the church's lonely stature, Arm pulls over and gets out of the car to stretch his legs. Fearful of ticks, he doesn't wade through wild grasses to get a better view

of the church, but sits on the warm hood of his car and looks. A portion of
the roof had collapsed some time ago. Or perhaps, he thinks, believers
had been violently seized and borne away through a rupture in the ceiling.
The *Rapture*. And here he is, left behind, on the hull of the Spirit, a rust
bucket. He checks his watch, sees that he's going to be late and reluctantly
leaves the warm hood for the hot seat.

      The roads that follow are inhabited mostly by conifers, with
natural streams and berry bushes, a deep-shadowed terrain that now
makes him nervous. The tree canopy is high, but lower species have crept
in, creating lush brocades. He looks around for turkeys as the car shudders
down a long lane with occasional cabins and ramshackle cottages. An
asbestos-sided wreck is hung with ironic road signs: Bates Motel, Merry
Christmas, Captain Hook. The shack is a wart that can't diminish the
beauty of the forest, but still fills him with dread. *Mountain men,* he thinks.
Was the Stranger a mountain man? Not likely: he had sounded like a man
of developed tastes.

      Two hard lefts on a bad gravel road take him to nothing but a
mansion of trees, undergirded by thickets of bittersweet and mountain
laurel. At first, he thinks he's been had, then sees the form of a house
behind curtains of vines and masses of ferns in the foreground. Not a
shack, merely worn, with a sagging, mottled roof and brown paint that
needs renewing. But the structure he can see is otherwise sound, with a
wraparound porch and dormers in the front and a brick chimney to one
side. Perched on high haunches, a truck of some sort is parked on the
other side. There is no driveway, so Arm parks in front on a scrabble of
leaves and trudges with his shoulders hunched toward the shuttered
entrance. Black flies land on him, but don't sting or bite when he swishes
them away.

Something brown lurks to one side of the porch, stopping Arm in his tracks. Stiff-necked, he can see the crude form of a bear carved out of a tree trunk, its paws around the shaft of a raggedy American flag, its mouth in a grimace. He heads toward it with morbid curiosity. And as he approaches, the door opens and the familiar bald head pops out.

The Stranger is wearing a dew-rag, giving him a piratical appearance. Once again, Arm is seized by a sense of recognition. This is a face he knows, yet a stranger's face. "Well, hello," says the Stranger. "Can I offer you a mug of grog? *Haha.* Just kidding." Arm trudges forward with suspicion, rubbing past weedy bushes that prickle and snap. "Nice garden," he says. "Thank you," says the Stranger. "There's more out back."

The Stranger is dressed in the uniform of his generation, a tee shirt, a pair of cut-off jeans, boat shoes with frayed leather laces. He stands on a threshold that isn't exactly clean, but swept, surveying the forest and Arm with a pair of eyes that are gray, yet intense. There is something about the way they are set in his head, pushed in deep like nail heads. The cast of his bald head, entirely devoid of facial hair – no eyebrows, no mustache – is clearly defined, seamed, hard-boiled, yet candid.

Watching his step on wooden stairs that have been worn thin in the middle, Arm is comforted by the chafing presence of Clint. His eyes can't pick out details in the dark interior behind The Stranger, but take in what is obvious. There is a strong fragrance coming from the house, not sweet, not dank, but resinous and masculine. Linseed oil, he decides, or something like it. To the right of the door is a Shaker-style bench; to the left, a wooden mailbox with a rusted metal nameplate. *I. Castleman.* A funny coincidence: Castleman had been Mark's last name.

"You're Mark's father," Arm blurts. He sees the resemblance now, clear as day. The eyes, of course. The sculpted nose, the slightly

Neanderthal brow, the boy-chin. "You can go straight to hell." When Arm turns to leave, he's restrained by a sunburnt hand attached to a burly arm. "Actually, I'm his brother," says Castleman. "The haircut makes me look older."

Arm turns around and looks at him with loathing. He isn't sure why he should feel such antipathy and gropes around for an insult. "You didn't even show up after he died. Mark told me you were estranged. I can see why. A loser who stalks prey like a lovesick girl. Who doesn't even have the courage to --" He's cut off by the impact of being knocked to the floor of the porch. The shock of it prevents him from moving as Castleman shoves a hand up his pants and pulls Clint out of his leg strap. Arm covers his face instinctively and feels his body shrink, knees to chest, balls to bowels. A minute passes.

"Get up, Mr. Guest. *Haha.* Disarmed and still dangerous. " The voice is eerily quiet. Arm tightens his knees against his chest.

"I haven't seen Clint in forever. Years. Let me see, it must have been Mark's eighteenth birthday. My gift to him. There's nothing like a good revolver to set the tone of a conversation." There is a click, then another and another. Arm opens one eye. The Stranger is over him, holding Clint's one bullet between a thumb and forefinger. "Only one bullet," he says. "You must have been feeling lucky."

Arm sits up with a cautionary raised arm. When Castleman hands him his empty revolver, he seizes it and tucks it back inside the leg holster, then scrambles backward, teetering. He considers making a run for it, but given Castleman's height and muscle mass, he doubts he'd make it as far as the stairs.

"Mr. Guest, you seem to have mistaken me for someone else. Your mortal enemy, or is it your immortal one? *Haha.* You really should get up, brush yourself off and come inside. You look much better vertical, like most middle-aged men." Arm sits and glowers at his captor. Then he shrugs. What else can he do? He rises and follows Castleman.

It takes several minutes for his eyes to adjust to the murky interior, which is overwhelmingly brown. Knotty pine paneling, exposed ceiling beams, the brown propellers of a ceiling fan circling lazily. The pitted floor has been painted dark chocolate and along every wall are ranks of brown chairs in various stages of repair, from peg-legged wrecks to shining examples of Americana. He recognizes them as Hitchcock chairs, stolid rush seats with somber paintings of flowers and fruit across the backs and tops.

"Welcome to my workshop," says Castleman. "I'd say my castle, but as you can see --" His voice trails off as he gestures toward his workbench and tool rack in one corner. "Pull up a chair, Mr. Guest. Make yourself at home."

Arm grabs one of the finished specimens and sits with his legs crossed, trying to look nonchalant. To steady his shaking hands, he crosses his arms. He is sweating heavily now beneath the weak breeze of the fan.

"A marvelous choice," Castleman is saying. "The button-back crown top is my personal favorite. Early nineteenth century classic Hitchcock. Anyone who was anyone owned one." He crosses over to a cooktop stove on a table in a corner where a teakettle is beginning to whistle and pours hot water into two brown mugs.

"Why have you been stalking me?" says Arm. "What the devil is all this about? I demand to know. If you don't tell me, I will –"

"Call the police?" Castleman's eyes register pity, not ridicule.

Arm forces several deep cleansing breaths. So Castleman knows what had happened in Rockton. What could that mean? The trick is not to panic. Castleman, he thinks, is just a bigger, clumsier, older version of Mark, someone Arm knew how to talk his way around. If he can reason with Castleman, perhaps flatter him, he may be able to talk his way out of the cabin.

"That line you wrote, the one from Shakespeare, was very clever," Arm begins. "And sending me to the old woman, I admit, the joke was on me. But what could you possibly care about Taft Said?"

"Patience, Mr. Guest. Let's have tea before we have the inevitable. I brew a very good orange pekoe. Sorry I can't offer you anything more exotic. Cream? Sugar?" He hands Arm a scalding cup, which Arm sets down on the floor. Castleman carefully slurps as he pulls a chair up, then sits, crossing one thick-calved leg over the other. Mark's legs, Arm sees. Both brothers had powerful builds, but Mark was shorter and not as formidable. His brother's hands are huge and red-stained, human lobster claws. And there is something not right about his knees, encrusted, Arm sees, with psoriasis.

"Robust yet mediocre," Castleman is saying. "That's what makes orange pekoe so special! Sir Charles Lipton came up with the Chinese-sounding name. But did you know that the orange portion of the name is thanks to the Dutch? Marvelous hucksters, the Dutch. When the Dutch East India Company brought the tea to Europe, they marketed it as orange to suggest the House of Orange."

No, Arm did not know.

"Tea drinkers were hooked. The Dutch were good at hooking people on things. They hooked the Chinese on opium, of course."

Castleman yucks a few times, then he leans forward with a lurching movement, his eyes nailing Arm.

"Speaking of the Dutch East India Company, I didn't start out in the furniture stripping and repair business. Mark tell you?" Arm shakes his head *no* cautiously, wary of a trap.

"Well, I wasn't a drug dealer, if that's what you're thinking. Nothing so respectable. *Haha.* I was a newspaper reporter."

He sits back, letting Arm take it in, propping the brown mug on his barnacled knee.

Arm shrugs. "So. So what?"

"So, everything. In the early seventies, I was a reporter for a local paper, *Somerbury Day.* You ever hear of it? No? I was sure Mrs. Streeter would have told you." Castleman's look of disappointment takes up the entire region beneath his brow.

Remembering, Arm stretches forward to grab his mug. "You were the idiot who revealed Taft's name before the trial?"

"My first big byline. How could I refuse? You know what they say, if not myself, then someone else. Thinking back I realize, of course, that I could have refused. Should have. By quitting my job, I mean. But, no, I was in love with the big bad world back then." He rubs his jaw. "That tea must be lukewarm, let me get you another cup."

Arm puts his hand over his cup. "I'm set." Castleman gulps his still steaming tea and continues. "Drink up, Mr. Guest. Hot liquid is a marvelous way to cool down." He raises his mug in the air until Arm takes a wary sip. The tea is surprisingly good and is certainly not orange pekoe.

"Mrs. Streeter called me several times. Of course, I took her calls. There is something very bracing about a righteous indignation. Plus, no caller ID back then. But eventually, she stopped and I forgot about her and Taft Said, to be honest. It wasn't my fault that he died, not directly. Not even indirectly. Still, it was a matter of human decency, something I lacked --"

"I'm not a priest. I didn't come to hear your confession," says Arm irritably. His eyes, having adjusted to the lighting, can make out the built-in bookshelves on one wall and a cot. And on the walls hang oil paintings of garden scenes, small but good, all apparently by the same painter, someone who knew how to render shadow and mood. Limp white curtains that end and meet in modest ruffles are fluttering at the window. A set of stairs leads up to what must be bedrooms. The linseed oil reek is wafting in from outdoors through a torn screen door in back, which is also admitting several flying pests. They buzz around randomly, lighting on chairs and remaining anchored, then darting and reeling through the room. Castleman doesn't seem to mind. "Sorry about the flies," he says. "The working man's enemy. Let us hope they aren't spies in disguise. *Haha*. It wouldn't be the first time."

He frowns, gulps more tea and continues. "I wanted to report on the big and the bad, like Woodward and Bernstein, so of course I went to New York City. I starved for a few months, then I got a foot in the door of the *Herald-Tribune,* which didn't work out exactly, due to my, shall we say, attitude. I started to take freelance assignments with, well, with the CIA." Castleman pauses again and nail-guns Arm with his eyes, his mouth twitching. He shrugs. "Operation Mockingbird, they called it. They paid you to write stories with a certain slant, and I was desperate. I was also awfully good at it. After a few years of it, I hated myself. So I became an ad copywriter and hated myself even more."

"I don't see what this has to do with --"

"With Mark? I'm getting to that, Mr. Guest. All in good time. Careful, there's a wasp on your shoulder." Arm freezes while eyeing a peripheral blur. Is he allergic to wasp venom? He thinks so and emits a barely audible moan while Castleman flicks it away as if it were dandruff. "*Apis mellifera*," he says. "A common honey bee. I have a garden out back and they're shopping around. Sorry to alarm you unnecessarily. You must be sweet. *Haha*." He reseats himself, crossing his foot over his knee. Trickles of sweat make tracks down his large, bare face and his mouth twitches as if he's attempting not to smile.

"Where were we? Oh, yes, my brilliant ad career. I won't go into all the dead bodies, since mine was one of them. It paid the bills. It put young Mark through university where he majored in journalism. I suppose that's all that matters. I did what I could and he did what he wanted. He came out while he was living with me in the big city. You might say, he came out all over my couch. I didn't like knowing he was homosexual. But what led me to kick him out wasn't that. It was his atrocious, infernal *gay* lifestyle. My apartment became his brothel. There is nothing like a young gay man in heat. Well, I don't need to tell you. Never knowing what new bass-ackward coupling I was going to walk into." Castleman is staring unapologetically at Arm above the shield of his tea mug.

Arm stares back, taking refuge in his fury. "I just hope," says Castleman, "that you won't take any of this personally, Mr. Guest. Mark was my brother. I loved him. I supported and educated him in the absence of willing, sober parents and did so, I might add, under no obligation. But he was a libertine by any standard. He made an ass of himself at my expense. I had every right to kick him out." Castleman's mouth is twitching badly.

"So … With Mark gone, there was no reason to continue living in the filthy city. I'd made enough money to float a while. I left, rented this place, eventually bought it, and built up a chair repair business. Honest work, but I guess the chemicals didn't agree with my hair. My girlfriend didn't mind. We married, she died, I mourned. *Life.* And I guess around that time, Mark had hooked up with you and discovered the marvelous coincidence. The one that has brought us together, Mr. Guest."

"You can call me Arm," says Arm, and immediately regrets it, despite cringing at the repetition of his surname. Castleman ignores him, gets up, solemnly pours himself another mug, then brings the teapot over and empties what remains in Arm's cup. "Drink," he says. Arm, who needs to empty his bladder, says nothing.

"Mark figured out where I lived eventually. He wanted a truce, I guess, and money. He knew about my short-lived journalism career. The CIA gigs, the drug trafficking stories, all of it fascinated him. How he figured out that Taft Said was your musical mentor, I will never know. Perhaps it's what drew him to you? Hm? Why the long face, Mr. Guest?" Castleman wags the foot on his knee and stretches his arms behind the chair. With pursed lips, he leans back, assessing Arm, who sits rigidly, his hand on Clint.

"Never mind," says Castleman, making a chopping motion with his hand to bat away a fly. "Mark began sending me articles fetched off library microfilm to remind me of my failures. Then he began sending me something altogether different." He gets up and saunters over to one of the bookcases, squats and groans in an old-man way, contradicting his obvious agility. He searches, muttering to himself. "I've become the keeper of my brother's theories." Several books and binders thud and one falls, spine up.

He selects a thick black ring binder from the bottom shelf, then holds it up in the air on one hand like a waiter with a tray as he approaches Arm. "For you, Mr. Guest," he says with a silly, sweeping bow, then hands

Arm the binder.

"What is it?" asks Arm ungratefully.

"Exactly what each of us deserves."

Arm places the binder on the floor next to his chair and folds his arms. Thanks to olfactory exhaustion, he guesses, he can no longer smell the linseed oil, but some other scent is infusing him, sweet, fussy, ethereal. If he were blind, he'd assume a woman had entered the room. "What is that fragrance?" he asks.

"That is jasmine. My wife, she --" Castleman pauses, shrugs. "I do what I can to keep it going. She liked scented flowers, aromatic herbs. This time of day, out in back, it's a perfume factory. So often, I think she must still be out there." The jasmine scent fills up the silence.

Castleman pushes the binder toward Arm with his foot. "Why not take a peek, Mr. Guest? Dazzle yourself gradually, as the poet wrote. Come, now, you're a great champion of the truth, the gospel according to Mark. *Haha.*"

Arm opens his mouth, then shuts it. Let Castleman harbor his illusions. He picks up the binder, which holds innumerable pages, each preserved in a plastic sleeve. Some of the contents are familiar to him, either because they're in Mark's small, incising hand or they are newspaper clippings he has already seen on the drug trial that Taft was to testify in; now he sees them beneath Ian Castleman's byline. Other articles on Taft's murder are by someone else, and there is an obituary of the married woman Taft had fancied, Chelsea Fowler, who died two years ago. Then a slippery plastic avalanche of other pages, in the Stranger's idiosyncratic hand, with records and photographs. One of these is a blurry black-and-white showing a young Mrs. Cauliflower in her butcher's smock and hairnet, stooping, with one hand cupped beneath the chin of a young boy.

"Where did you get this photograph?" Arm asks sharply, holding up the binder.

"The boy isn't you," says Castleman. "It's Taft. Amazing likeness, though, don't you think? Before he developed a habit, he was her best boy. I guess that makes *you* much less than her best. You should be grateful, really."

"What does she have to do with Taft?" Arm snaps.

"Well, Mr. Guest, that is the reason why you're here. To listen and learn. I'm sorry to say the news is not good, as usual. The news is almost never good, have you noticed? To sweeten it up, I suggest that we go outside and partake of my wife's pride. There is shade and a breeze. And thou. *Haha.*"

While Castleman talks, Arm observes a charming cottage garden, a late bloomer, it seems, since many of the plants are still flush with flowers despite the ripeness of the season. The garden has been laid out around a neat, circular lawn, defined by brick retaining walls that hold perennial beds and shrubs. A herringbone brick path lined with flowerbeds leads to a cupola, and behind that is what appear to be a series of miniature chairs set on poles. Near the house is a lichen-mottled shed, which Castleman must use as a workshop judging from the tools and machinery wedged inside. Arm suddenly understands how Mark inherited his repertoire of man-skills.

"My wife was the horticulturalist and *artiste*," Castleman is saying cheerfully. "I was the digger of holes and layer of bricks. Someone once wrote that in every relationship, there is a peasant serving an aristocrat. I wonder, Mr. Guest, which one were you? No, don't tell me. *Haha.*"

Castleman snatches the binder out of Arm's hands, herding him by alternately walking backwards, then pivoting and chummily marching by his side. Their destination is the cupola, which Arm assumes Castleman had built, and they sit in its shade while Castleman narrates the story of Zillah Khouri, the woman Arm knew affectionately as Mrs. Cauliflower, but whom, it seems, he had not known at all. He sits defensively, his arms crossed against the delicate fragrances.

" … a drug kingpin masquerading as a cultural doyenne," Castleman is saying. "Until she became the asset of a certain alphabet soup agency. A quid pro quo arrangement. Then she became the queen. The queen of heroin. The queen of child procurement. And some suspect she's a queen in that vulgar other sense. *Haha.* But I believe she's got two X chromosomes, same as Madeline Albright or Mata Hari. Just that sort of woman. You have to consider the various appetites that drive a person. In her case, it wasn't just money."

Castleman reaches over the cupola rail and plucks at a tendril of jasmine. "For some," he says, "the beauty of creation suffices, with all of its flaws and, well, *you* must know. The fallen world disappoints. Certain people crave more, they desire to be gods. She wanted the beauty she envied, the culture she lacked, a way to turn little ruffians into artists, to bring the world to its feet. The heroin trade allowed her to do it, but at a cost to the children. Most of them exploited in multiple ways, you understand." Castleman is avoiding his eyes. "And if you don't, get yourself educated," he says harshly.

Arm receives the bad news in a daze. A pale butterfly with brown and orange markings traces a haywire path from one flower to the next. After it lights on a stem of lavender, its wings pulse slowly before they close in a taut fan. It reminds Arm of Sable, of all she has been to him and all that she hasn't. "I don't believe you," he says mechanically.

"And that is why you are now the proud owner of the facts. Take and eat, Mr. Guest." Castleman nudges the binder toward Arm with his lobster fist.

"If it were true, she'd be in prison right now. And besides, she never did anything inappropriate--"

"To you? Ah, Mr. Guest. You were one of her trophy boys. Too good for the street. You were destined for scholarships and the rest. A life of fiddling. But she misjudged you. In the end you couldn't cut it in an orchestra, nor were you made for the solo circuit. You were made for the recording studio and the parlor. *Haha.* No offense. But others, they were bound for back alley sales after they finished their gigs or lessons. A violin case is a marvelous way to transport heroin."

"I don't believe you," repeats Arm unconvincingly. A warm breeze is beginning to pick up, showering the terrace below with jasmine petals.

"Then go and ask your bud what's-his-name, the cello player. She lured him out of some dreadful roach haven, bribed the lowlife parents, gave him lessons and encouragement, but he liked heroin more than Bach. Twice he's served time – for her. Zillah's boys eventually do a little time, but she gets them out so they can go back to work for her and inform for her friends in high places. Or do much worse as honey pots for the control grid. Only one of them I know of has ever betrayed her. She's kind to them, in her way. Like Fagan was kind to his thieves."

From the garden shrills a blue jay: "In-dig-nant, In-dig-nant, In-dig-nant." It seems to be on speaking terms with Castleman, who gets up ("Excuse me") and hurries to his shed. For a minute, Arm fears that he has gone to grab a shotgun for the bird or for himself, but Castleman emerges with a bag of birdseed, which he pours into a feeder that resembles a miniature Hitchcock chair. After cocking its head and screeching, the bird is on it immediately. Castleman fills the other feeders as he talks.

"Taft betrayed her and he paid the price. He was about to insert her name along with the names of numerous police and certain elected officials into a big drug trial with a judge who couldn't be bought. Much easier to kill off Taft than a judge, I guess."

Songbirds, two titmice and a wren, arrive to peck at seeds on the fringes of a feeder, but are driven off by jays. Castleman ignores the small border war, filling chairs until seeds spill to the ground.

"What about Manciani?" Arm asks. The question makes Castleman snort.

"What about him? A waste of flesh. One of the few useful idiots she had in her talons who didn't play the fiddle. He got off scot-free."

"But why would Taft *betray* her as you say. What on earth did he have to gain?"

Castleman stops filling feeders. "A question I can't answer for you, Mr. Guest. Some say he found Jesus. Who knows? It may have been a woman he wanted to impress. Or just that he was tired of his life. Mere speculation. The facts are in the binder. Mark did most of the work and I finished it. I suggest that you--" He pauses, sets the bag down on the stairs to the gazebo. His bald, seamed face looks gaunt, too small and worn for the robust body it crowns.

"Look, Mr. Guest. I'm giving you what I have left of my brother because you believed in him, which I did not. At least, not while he was alive. I know what you're thinking, and you are wrong. True, I didn't approve of his sexual leanings, but it was his slumming and mooching and drunkenness that ended it for me."

"Sexual leanings?" snarls Arm. "He was *gay*."

"Ah, *gay*." Castleman sings the word. "Yes, gay. And you think that excuses everything. He was not gay, he was *miserable,* Mr. Guest. A miserable little reprobate. But he eventually became a damned good researcher. It's not just a matter of ferreting around in library dungeons and the Internet, you know. People would talk to him. And he had a sixth sense. He knew, to his detriment. And he was right about most of it. Nine-one-one. Chemtrails. The shadow government. Aliens." Castleman's eyes are off somewhere, watching birds. The laugh lines that define his face look like scars in the afternoon light and he is dripping with sweat. He turns and faces Arm, his mouth twitching.

"You're a gifted musician. Don't ask me why God settled so much on you. The world settled the rest. It doesn't matter how or by whom you were taught. But I think everyone deserves to know those facts. Because living in an illusion is a kind of second exile. Take the binder. Discover for yourself who murdered Taft Said. What I'd like to know is who murdered my brother. At least now I know it wasn't you."

"Mark wasn't murdered," Arm answers without conviction. "It was an accident."

"Mr. Guest. I'm in the furniture business, for Pete's sake. Expensive armoires do not fall on top of people's heads unless other people want them to."

Arm hears, but cannot stumble down the path that leads to more doubt. All he can manage is to watch Castleman, the brother of his friend, going about his odd work, filling miniature chairs with birdseed. His stride is like his handwriting, long, sloping, extravagant.

In another thirty minutes, Arm will be far from this place of fragrances and birds, the enigmas of the forest where turkeys can suddenly emerge and filtered light can make you see what is not there, or not see what is. He'll stop to pee behind a laurel bush, relieving himself of the tea as much as tension. He'll get back inside the car, reach the place where the sinking church had been, half-expecting to find that it had vanished. But it will still be there, vacant and alone. He'll stop to survey it again, watching for signs.

It will occur to him suddenly that the gun attached to his leg might once have killed a man. Could this be? The coward in him will want to say *yes,* an excuse to lob the gun out into the meadow grass along with Mark's binder. Amputating his arm, his true identity. Putting the past behind him. Letting God sort it all out there in the oblivious field.

Beaten by sun and fatigue, he'll sit inside the car and be tempted. Then Castleman's words will come back to him. *Second exile.* And he'll start up the engine and drive himself, his life and his inheritance, home.

29 / Rose

For the second time since selling the Spirit to Arm, she drives. The first time had been to meet that solitary woman, Taffeta Gates, with the saying signs and feral cats. It had been only a month ago and, ever since, time had done nothing but rob her blind.

The steering wheel is hot and damp and the wind rushing through the stuck-open window of the Spirit blows hair in her face, but she feels oddly inspirited. She laughs at her bad and silent pun.

"What's so funny?" asks Arm.

"Everything and nothing."

"I'll settle for nothing," says Arm. He'd been depressed for many days, which had helped cement a partnership between them in painting the walls of the house. Arm had purchased trays, brushes, rollers and paint they'd selected from little chips to contrast with the buttermilk wash of the kitchen. Celadon for the living room and a deep plum for the bathroom. They had put off the argument with Eve about her request for a silver bedroom. For the basement, still in progress, they'd agreed on eggshell to bring light in, as if it were possible.

Long-faced, Arm had lapped on thick but precise strokes with his paintbrush, blending with her work. She consoled him with her silence at first, the communion of handiwork. But after a day or two, she'd hummed some of the old songs from their childhood, "numbers" their mother had called them, "Mares Eat Oats," "I Wonder Who's Kissing Her Now," "Let Me Call You Sweetheart." And he had joined her eventually, singing duets from *Oklahoma!, Camelot, Porgy and Bess,* until Eve had protested. "Y'all are too loud. I can't hear myself think," she'd announced, emerging from her bedroom barefoot, with a book in her hand. She had started to read again, a habit Rose was happy to oblige with a vow of silence.

Once the paint was dry, Arm had gone away for a few days. "It isn't what you think. I just need time alone." She'd been relieved at first, not having to walk on eggshells over her brother's tricky moods. Eve needed school clothes and she needed to work, trudging to her day customers to clock in her time on their dust. At night, while crickets cheered in the yard, she had sewed like a madwoman on the kitchen table, speeding through simple patterns that she and Beulah had designed for a business they still hadn't named. *Baby quilts.* If someone had told her this would be her passion a year ago, she would have laughed until she cried.

And then one night Fleurette had called. The phone had rung as if it were anybody. "Hi, Rose, this is Fleurette," said a soft, worried voice with a Mississippi accent. "Do you remember me?" Of course she did.

"I didn't want to call you," said Fleurette. "I don't know how to tell you." There had been a long silence and Rose had thought, wishfully, that the line had gone dead.

Today she'd suggested to Arm that they take a drive. "Just somewhere, anywhere. Let's be Meantherthals." High summer is upon them, holding its hot breath inside the car.

"What if you suddenly discovered that everything you once believed about yourself were untrue?" he asks her now. "Everything. Your view of the world, the facts about your early life, the people you treasure. Fill in the blank with anything you believe."

Rose hesitates. "Is this a hypothetical, or is it for real?'

"Could be either. Or both."

"Well, I'd say that's the state we live in perpetually," she says. She likes the misty wisdom of her statement.

"Then it's true. We're already in hell," says Arm.

The road ahead offers exits north and south, so Rose slows down, turns to Arm and asks, "Which one?" He shrugs. "Go south, old woman. I'll tell you where when we get to it." She says *thanks a lot* and heads south, noting the golden bursts of ledge on either side of the highway and the dense, still-green forests that rise above them. Ferns dominate the shadowy undergrowth. Connecticut in August promises another shock of fertility before it fades, making her reflect on her own. She is forty-eight years old and will not have another child. She feels sad and sadly relieved, left with whatever time will reveal in the only child she has.

"Fleurette called," she says abruptly.

"Fleurette who?"

"Randall's sister, from Natchez. One night while you were away." She waits for Arm to register the name and for the sarcasm that usually follows, but he says nothing. They rush past road signs that would take them to idyllic river towns, but Arm looks straight ahead. Out of the corner of her eye, Rose can see him driving from his passenger seat, pressing his left foot on an invisible brake pedal as she accelerates. A silent rebuke, she thinks, or is it a silent prayer? She tests him a few times, accelerating, then slowing down when his foot moves. Stealing a glance at his face, she sees the deep shadows beneath his closed eyes. A few months ago, she might have squawked at him, but with Drew gone, her brother is the only man she can trust with her news. Can she trust him with her feelings? She takes a deep breath.

"Randall is dying," she says. "That's why Fleurette called. He has growths all over his lungs. He wants to see Eve before he goes." She's aware that her voice has thickened, but she is not going to weep.

"Fleurette is sending plane tickets. For Eve and me. She says we should come next week, because--"

"Take the next exit," interrupts Arm. At the end of the ramp, he tells Rose to pull over into a restaurant parking lot. The restaurant is a Greek diner with a shiny exterior, a hall of windows. Most of the customers in the lot are families in vacation campers with children who dart around as soon as a door opens. One of the plump, harried mothers is bent over a baby, changing its diapers on the front seat of an RV while her husband minds a sleeping toddler in a stroller. Rose carefully steers the Spirit away from the families into a space near some trash receptacles. The flies are having an orgy and there is a ripe odor, but Rose's eyes are on the dragonflies, soaring, tilting and vanishing in silver maneuvers. One of them lands, spreading its stark wings against an old hat mashed on the ground. It isn't a cowboy hat, but a filthy red and black check aviator cap with clumsy earflaps made for the head of a large man.

"Rose," says Arm. He touches her hair and that is when she breaks down. She allows him to nestle her awkwardly, the brake handle between them. "Rose, I'm so sorry." Rose sobs, disarmed by the depth of her feelings. She had always assumed she would feel relief to be rid of Randall, his appetites and rage, but instead is shaken by an insatiable grief. It forces open a small, sealed box containing all that love had brought her. It had brought her, finally, this far, and all except Eve is now gone. She weeps, allowing herself to revisit a time and place she had shuttered, a rented vacation cabin on a pond where they had once been happy. Randall had found an old, leaky canoe and had laughed when she paddled the wrong way; they had floated gently backward into a tangled fringe of pond grass. She pats Arm on the shoulder, as if he's the one being consoled, and bends to rummage in her purse for a tissue. She weeps again until she's spent, this time turning away from her brother, and afterwards, when he quietly offers to drive, she refuses. He had loathed Randall. How could he possibly understand the emotion she's now investing in her losses? She doesn't understand it either. They sit in stiff silence while she tidies herself.

She pulls the car back onto the road and continues the trip south, led by Arm to the highway. Eventually she clears her throat and hoarsely confesses. "I met someone else. Here in Swannboro." She doesn't want to tell her brother that she'd fallen for a priest. "But it wasn't right." She pauses. "Not for him. I guess, not for either of us." To her surprise, he confesses that he had gone through a similar experience, with a man who turned out to be heterosexual. "And in the process, I broke a woman's heart," he says. "Something I have never done before." Rose wants to tell him that he's mistaken, to recite the names of his other victims.

Traffic thickens as they approach the shore towns and the heat in the car cooks the worn vinyl seats. Arm strains to roll down the back window on his side. "Take the next exit," he says wearily. "We'll drive the scenic route to Somerbury."

"What's in Somerbury?" she asks. "Besides suburbs and used car lots?"

"Taft's grave," says Arm. "I thought you knew." No, she did not know. She had thought he'd been buried in Swannboro. "But I never found the headstone," she explains.

"I met his sister," Arm says. "She and her husband buried Taft in their plot. I guess there were no other takers."

Rose is annoyed with herself for never digging deeply enough to unearth the names of Taft's relatives. Drew had taken the place of Taft in her preoccupations, changing the pattern in her quilt, but repeating the pattern of her life.

She's curious about Taft's sister. "What's her name?" she asks.

"Mrs. Streeter. A strange old bird. Lots of makeup, big hair, tiny feet. The bossy type. And honest as the day is long. We talked in her parlor over coffee. She blames a newspaper reporter for Taft's death, and I suppose there's some logic in that."

"A news reporter?" Rose laughs and touches her face, relieved to have a diversion.

"She had a theory that he was jealous of Taft because of a woman. So he released Taft's name before the drug trial. Silly, really. Anyway, a news reporter didn't actually kill Taft. The dragon lady did that."

"Who?" Rose nearly misses the exit, but swerves the car in time down a long ramp that leads to a river road.

"Some other time, remind me, and I'll tell you about it." Arm folds his arms and stares ahead. They're closer to the river now, which appears intermittently, a liquid ribbon woven through the heavy fabric of the woodland. The land slopes downward to the river on Rose's side, where sedate homes and a few large estates have private water views, while on Arm's side the land tilts upward to an overgrown forest that is cleaved here and there by dark, clandestine roads leading to castles, Rose imagines. Eventually they come to an area crowded with antiques stores, many of them no longer in business. Their ghosts compete with mortal commerce, gas stations and fast food, ugly each in its own way.

They turn on a road that delivers them to a bridge that resembles the bones of a wing. The bridge pavement hums as they cross, and so does Rose. It takes them across the river, the same one that had once flooded Swannboro's quarry. Rose looks to her left at a transitory view of dimpled quicksilver with luxuriant banks. Here, the river feeds a cultural center, a refurbished opera house, regally posed in a village of restored homes and storefronts in ice cream colors. As children, Rose and Arm had been treated to a performance of *Man of La Mancha* in the opera house by their parents. Arm had been lukewarm about it, but Rose had sung the songs for weeks, draping herself in an old shawl and pretending to be Dulcinea del Toboso, the woman Don Quixote had loved. Stomping and pirouetting, she would bellow in a voice too big for her claret mezzo over her mother's easy listening radio station. "Rose!" her mother would shout. "Simmer down!" But Rose had persisted, convinced that these were her songs.

"Don Quixote is dead," she says now, and Arm looks at her. "No," he says. "Actually, I met him not too long ago."

"Well, anyway," says Rose. "Don Juan is dead." As she speeds up, Arm puts his foot down on a phantom brake.

For a few miles, neither says a word, enjoying a stretch of their home state that has held onto its pastoral and domestic charms. They continue along the two-lane bracelet of asphalt past farmhouses, vegetable stands, stone and picket fences, symmetrical gardens, shag carpets of meadow grass and corn, the ragdoll faces of sunflowers. Past Salem, it ends in a gritty jumble of billboards, liquor stores, a racetrack and adjacent motels, then a luxury mall.

They talk about Eve. Rose had told her about Randall and she had taken it stoically at first. Rose had found Eve in her room later, facedown on the bed. Attempting to console her, Rose had stroked her back, but Eve had hurled herself around and slapped her mother on the face. Then she had whimpered and apologized and wept. And Rose had held her in silence, knowing that one wrong word could push her off the narrow, high ledge they stood upon.

"She's a tough little girl," says Arm. "She'll get through it. She has you."

"I sometimes wonder if she believes that."

"It can't hurt to remind her. I don't mean with words."

Rose tries to ignore the tiny jab by driving above the speed limit, then penitently slowing down. A few miles later, they enter a cemetery remarkable for its flatness and heirloom trees, prime real estate for the deceased, a village of mausoleums surrounded by common headstones. Arm suggests that they pull over beneath a catalpa, its mutant-looking pods and heart-shaped leaves still lush in the heat. They get out of the car, stretch, taking refuge in the shade.

Arm suggests that they make a toast. He had brought iced water in a jug, and from the glove compartment he removes a battered red thermos cup with a broken handle and hands it to Rose, who examines it closely. It has been chewed around the edges, a child's cracked school cup that her brother must have carried around for decades. It seems an unlikely relic to hang onto. Arm had hated school and all of its paraphernalia.

They trudge over crunchy grass toward a section of the cemetery that looks modern, but the epitaphs are from the early twentieth century. Thirty minutes of searching take them further back in time. "Are you sure this is the right cemetery?" asks Rose. The sky's mood changes as the sun enters a cowl of cloud, but the heat persists. Sweat trickles down Rose's neck and beneath her bra, and her feet begin to cramp. She pulls her hair up and rolls it into an untidy bun. When Arm launches off in a new direction, Rose limps after him.

But they can't find the headstone. The merciless heat drives them across a lumpy, dead stretch of grass to the pool of shade beneath a copper beech. "I need water," Rose says. Arm says they may as well toast to Taft right where they are. He pours water from the jug into his leaky thermos cup, holding it out to Rose. "You must say something before you drink."

Rose holds the cup up and closes her eyes. "To Taft," she says. "Whoever you were. Don Juan. Don Quixote. May you find God's peace." She drinks down the whole cup and holds it out to Arm. "Your turn."

Arm pours. "I'll second that," he says, lifting his cup. They finish off half the jug before turning to leave. But as they pass out of the beech's shade, Rose says, "Wait." She steps back into glare, then onto a little island created by a grouping of conifers near a large granite headstone with a roseate edge. "Over here." She motions to Arm.

Incised into the stone is the surname "Streeter" with no inscription. They stare down at the given names of three lives.

"Beulah," murmurs Arm. "Mrs. Streeter's name is Beulah." They find the stones beneath, edged by parched grass, which mark the graves of Anthony Streeter and Taft Said. In the strong sun, a marble urn gleams at the base of the main stone, containing nothing but a spider's web. Rose rinses the urn out with water from the jug and looks around for pinecones to put inside, filling the urn with her coarse, fragrant finds.

"In all my life, I've known only one other person named Beulah," says Rose on their way to the car. Coincidence, she thinks, is a dead man's way of pointing.

Driving back, they play recorded music. Arm surrenders his collection to Rose, who chooses Dvorak, Symphony No. 9 in E minor.

The *New World* spins beneath her thumb.

Looking for familiar signs and landmarks, they try to retrace their route, but keep losing the thread in the lush encircling hills around the river. They argue about exits and turns, one remembering, the other not sure.

Nothing looks the same going backward as it did going forward. So they agree, finally, to go home a different way.

The caravan is crammed with liquor, wine and beer boxes, free empties, left outside a warehouse nearby. Beggars can't be choosers. Taffeta had taken as many as she could carry, but she doesn't like the look of them. They remind her of her mother, who had drunk every sort of drink the boxes once contained, except beer. Beer was for the men.

Most of the boxes are packed and all are labeled. She has a master list. Between the occupied surfaces in the caravan, she had left a corridor for walking and getting to the sink, to her bed and to and from the bathroom. The table has been freed for bills and other business. Against one wall, she'd stacked boxes to build a solid cardboard tower. Henrietta is up there now, licking a paw then rubbing her face in long, rowing strokes. . Slinky, looking down from the precipice, opens his clean, pink mouth and yawns. The cats had found secret places to hide while she packed, but have since come out the other side, content with tops and banks and corners. Taffeta slits a Coors box open to remove a soap dish, some utensils, books and socks, another bent old pan, a roll of scotch tape, the picture of her grandma. The rest can remain packed until she requires their contents.

The new kittens are sleeping in a seltzer water box on a folded blanket. Their needling cries woke Taffeta up early, and she had forgotten her breakfast, so she slaps some butter on a roll at half past eleven. "Lord, bless this bread to my body," she says, eating over the sink, staring out the window at the dry grass with the dry earth showing through it. At least there are some tough-looking zinnias left. The Quonset is packed, but she'd left enough tools out for the time being. It needs a good bath. Tomorrow, she'll spray it down and sponge off the dead beetles and the late August grit. Should-a done it this morning, but too late now. The uncle will be here at half past noon.

Eve had told her all about him. A sorry man who doesn't like himself. She had known plenty of those, but this uncle is also good-looking like her daddy. Plays the violin like her daddy, too, the kind of music you have to dress up to listen to. The uncle is a dresser, a man who notices things. It wouldn't hurt to make a good impression. She dresses with care, in a fresh white shirt beneath dungarees she took off the line yesterday. Her hair needs work. She brushes it until it flies with static, then slicks it back with a wet comb and weaves it into a pigtail. Her face she can do nothing about, but she brushes her teeth vigorously with Pepsodent and water from a bottle. She spits out the toothpaste and swishes water in her mouth and thinks what a burden a body can be, the teeth in her mouth, the hairs on her head, the invisible, conspiring organs, but never any wings. Sledge is hunched in a chair watching her as if she were his next meal. "You got any complaints?" she asks.

Eve turns thirteen today, an evil age, but a kitten is a good gift for a time of chaos. She had been the same at that age, needing more than what there was around her, the dead, permanent odor of carnival food, the Devil jabbering away all day long on her mother's TV. She had needed her grandma, just as Eve needs her now.

She had found the kittens a week ago near the same warehouse with the discarded boxes. Two were barely breathing and she had been forced to put them out of their misery. The others went home in an empty Dewars box. Three of them, scrawny and flea-bit, but whole. For days, Pindrop has been trying to nurse them.

Taffeta had named the runt Swann. More than likely it was a boy, with a drowned, wild look like Sledge. The names of the other two, a tiger-stripe and a white one with a gray cap, well, that would be up to somebody else. The girl's mother had said Eve could keep only one, but that Taffeta could bring the two of them along and let Eve pick, because it was only fair. The mother is a pretender, pretending to be tough. Taffeta is counting on her caving in once she sees both kittens knit up together. Their big, groggy heads are tucked beneath Pindrop who washes them incessantly because she can't offer milk. "Got yourself some kittens after all," Taffeta says.

Taffeta looks at her master list for the box of her mother's plates, with the pattern of golden wheat blowing in the wind. She had packed them yesterday, but now she is changing her mind. She lugs a couple of boxes near the table and finds the Jim Beam. Such plates do not belong in an old whiskey box. No one is coming to dinner, but she decides to break her own rule about unpacking, slipping plates out of their wrappings and stacking them inside her cabinet with doilies in between. It's only in order to see them again and for something to do besides cleaning. The plates still have a luster; Taffeta hardly breathes while she handles them. If she were to break one, it would hurt her heart. A housefly lands on her hand and she brushes it away, gently shutting the cabinet door.

Then it's buzzing around, colliding with the ceiling, hiding and springing out in manic arcs. She lunges at it a few times before Slinky corners and pounces on it, then, before Taffeta can do a thing, the cat laps it up and swallows it whole.

She's never seen so many flies, as big as thumbnails, the result of her next-door neighbor, the janitor at the school. He hasn't made an appearance since that day she and Eve saw him messing with underage girls. She'd called the police about that, but it was her word against his, they said. Now he's disappeared and her word won't count again until he doesn't show up at work. Meantime, she has his flies to swat. Yesterday, she found a specimen nearly two inches long loitering on her stove. She had killed it, and ever since has been cleaning.

Taffeta scrubs the stovetop. It couldn't hurt. The uncle is a judger, she knows, as well as a dresser. He would notice stains and fly-spots. Taffeta whistles between her teeth as she scrubs, then rinses and wipes her hands on a dishtowel. Yesterday, she had cleaned with ammonia, which had served more purposes than one, but today it's just suds.

On the dinette table is the letter. It isn't the first letter, but this one had arrived in the hands of the town. Two men, a smiling one with a fake mat of hair and an unsmiling one who smelled like mothballs. She could see their shiny black car, could hear it purring because they never even bothered to turn off the ignition. Obviously not here for a social call. She'd seen the smiler's face in the local papers before and hadn't cared for it. Photogenic people, she has found, are smilers in front of you and killers behind your back. That other one, she wasn't sure what he was. An undertaker, maybe. They didn't like the smell of ammonia, that much she could tell. They had gagged out their message, delivered their letter, turned their tails and gone off in their hearse. The sheriff would be the next one on her doorstep.

Taffeta squints at the letter. Yesterday, she'd torn it up, then regretted it and saved the torn pieces. Like the others, it's from the Swannboro town council informing her of its right of eminent domain over her land for the purpose of "eliminating blight." They're giving her their final offer of just compensation, which is six thousand dollars. Accept the offer now or forever hold your peace, the letter is saying.

A fair deal is what they had called her land before. Blight is what they are calling it now. Taffeta takes the scotch tape from the Coors box and mends the letter. She hasn't decided what to do about it, but she'd better make her mind up quick. A letter like that can tear you up, can tear up your heart between one thing and another, all packed up one minute and setting the table the next. If she stays, will they raid her caravan, destroy her Quonset, poison her cats, dig the holes they'll need for their plans? Cheap government housing. She'd like to see them try. On the other hand, what good will it do to fight them? She doesn't have the money. She can only pray about it, hope for an answer, live out of boxes until it comes. And pray that it comes soon.

"Fret not because the wicked prosper," she says to Sledge. "At least they won't be stealing *you*."

Broom in hand, she goes outside and sweeps the earth around her caravan and in between her signs. Then she steps back into the caravan and tugs on her hat and her jacket with the fringe. The uncle will be here in a quarter of an hour.

Sledge is polishing his whiskers along the edge of the kitten box. He polishes and preens until one of his paws is suddenly inside the box, but not to do harm. Taffeta grasps and holds him belly up, then seats him on her lap and rubs his sorrowful head. "Sorry, old puss," she says softly. He arches his neck, allowing himself to be mollycoddled.

Last night, she had aired out a fishy-smelling angling basket and bunched a towel inside. Now she sneaks the two girl kittens out from under Pindrop and gently places them on the towel. They cling together, tails quivering, eyes shut to the world.

She really ought to let them sleep, but instead she steals them from their warm bed. She lifts them up to feel the pulse of their sweet lives, they are so soft, so warm, so light.

Acknowledgments

I'm very grateful for the town libraries in my area, which made it possible to study local history and become acquainted with facts formerly unknown to me.

I'm especially indebted to my family: my father's introduction to classical music, opera and the repertoire of the American musical stage; my mother's reminiscences, which gave me the idea for this novel; my sister's constant encouragement; my daughter's blind faith.

For a number of years I lived in the South, where I came to find another home. I have returned there many times in my thoughts and through the writing of this book. I'm grateful for both experiences.

A very special acknowledgment is owed to Prof. Steven Horst, who encouraged me to persist and whose careful reading led to a better novel. *Thank you.*

~D.W.

Doretta Wildes received her master's degree in English from Brown University. She is the author of a previous novel, *Rinse Cycle,* and a collection, *Peril & Other Stories.* She lives in Middletown, Connecticut.

24521677R00202

Made in the USA
Columbia, SC
25 August 2018